THE MOTHER
OF
ALL THINGS

THE
MOTHER
OF
ALL THINGS

Alexis Landau

PANTHEON BOOKS · NEW YORK

Library of Congress Cataloging-in-Publication Data
Name: Landau, Alexis, author.
Title: The mother of all things : a novel / Alexis Landau.
Description: First Edition. New York : Pantheon Books, 2024
Identifiers: LCCN 2023011391 (print). LCCN 2023011392 (ebook).
ISBN 9780593700792 (hardcover). ISBN 9780593700808 (ebook)
Subjects: LCSH: Women—Fiction. | Motherhood—Fiction. |
Self-realization in women—Fiction. | LCGFT: Novels.
Classification: LCC PS3612.A547495 M68 2024 (print) |
LCC PS3612.A547495 (ebook) | DDC 813/.6—dc23/eng/20230313
LC record available at https://lccn.loc.gov/2023011391
LC ebook record available at https://lccn.loc.gov/2023011392

www.pantheonbooks.com

Jacket images: Venus Callipygian (detail) 1st c., Roman.
Mondadori Portfolio/Getty Images: (arch) nuchao/Getty Images;
(rose) Nenov/Getty Images
Jacket design by Arsh Raziuddin

Printed in the United States of America
First Edition
2 4 6 8 9 7 5 3 1

For my parents and my children

All has been consecrated
The creatures in the forest know this,
the earth does, the seas do, the clouds know
as does the heart full of love.
Strange a priest would rob us of this
knowledge
and then empower himself
with the ability
to make holy what
already was.

—SAINT CATHERINE OF SIENA

If we keep talking about it in an idyllic way, as in many hand-
books on motherhood, we will continue to feel alone and guilty
when we come up against the frustrating aspects of being a
mother. The task of a woman writer today is not to stop at the
pleasures of the pregnant body, of birth, of bringing up children, but to delve truthfully into the darkest depth.

—ELENA FERRANTE, Frantumaglia

THE MOTHER
OF
ALL THINGS

PROLOGUE

Sofia, Bulgaria, Vitosha Mountains, August 2019

Ava glanced up into the trees and caught sight of a figure crouched in the branches. Shrouded by the overcast night sky, his bulky form and large uncouth hands betrayed him.

"There!" Ava shouted, rising from Professor Nikitas's warm maternal lap. "He's at the top of that fir tree!"

The women moved with speed and force, breaking loose like startled crows, through the woods and over the gushing streams they leapt from jagged rock to jagged rock, they flew toward him and climbed a great boulder that towered opposite the man's perch and showered him with stones and sharp branches broken off from the trees while others hurled their thyrsus staffs at him.

The man shuddered just above their reach, the tree branch buckling beneath his weight.

Breathlessly, they splintered more branches from pines and, with these wooden rods, attempted to lever up the tree by prying the roots loose.

Nikitas cried, "Women! Make a circle around the trunk and grip it with your hands."

A multitude of hands sprang from the darkness and shook the trunk with startling force. Blood sprouted from Ava's palms as she gripped the fir, shaking and tearing at it, panting and sweating. Torches crackled and encircled the tree, and the faces of the others blurred before her until the women became one woman filled with an ancient rage, spilling over into now.

1

The unraveling started on their way into the desert, the freeway congested, shimmering with heat, Sam and Margot whining in the back seat of the car, a chorus of accusatory complaints, while Kasper rolled calls about hiring a DP. Given the first-time director, the Russian financiers wanted someone older and more established, someone like Bill Adler, but Kasper argued heatedly into the phone that Bill didn't understand the youthful, crazy aesthetic of the film.

Ava stared out at the passing wind turbines and sand dunes, trying to feel something, even anger, but only stark waves of nothingness washed over her, as empty and hollow as the barren landscape flitting by, as she numbly listened to Kasper argue with Olga Tregulova, the Russian oligarch who controlled the film's financing. Olga had started out in the early 2000s selling used clothing from Germany out of her Moscow apartment, but she'd grown it into the biggest online clothing brand in Russia, called Polka Dots, before branching out into the media sector. Sergei, her husband, managed their film fund under her watchful eye.

Ava was also vaguely aware of an argument developing between Margot and Sam about Sam shaping his hand into a gun and pointing it at her.

"I didn't," Sam protested, his voice climbing into a high-pitched falsetto that betrayed his insincerity. "I was pointing it at you to say I love you, that the love is overflowing from me to you."

"Liar," Margot shot back.

"Guys," Ava whispered harshly, twisting around in her seat, glaring at them. "Papa's on a call. Quiet."

Sam pointed his finger gun at the back of Kasper's head. Margot suppressed a laugh. He imitated a hail of bullets shooting from his finger and then blew smoke off the imaginary gun barrel.

The dog, Coco, made whining noises from the last row, pawing at the kids' headrests, trying to climb over. Margot twisted around to hug Coco, wrapping her arms around her brown furry neck. "It's okay, Coco. Don't worry."

The camping trip to Joshua Tree was meant to celebrate Sam's tenth birthday, a promise made months ago, but that was before *Escape from Babylon,* before Kasper's life vanished into an idea, as though he'd joined an obscure cult in the service of producing an indie action movie dripping in 1980s nostalgia mingled with the world of late antiquity. It was about a down-on-his-luck guy who has just lost his job working at a Blockbuster. While living in his mom's basement, he grows addicted to the time-traveling world of a video game that becomes real. On his hero's journey within the video game, a series of obstacles are presented to him, in which he must overcome various villains to save a Macedonian princess (who looks a lot like his high-school sweetheart) from marrying a tyrannical Roman emperor with cannibalistic tendencies (think Nero). At one point, he mistakenly travels too far back in time and encounters woolly mammoths, Thor, and velociraptors before Alexander the Great makes a guest appearance and course-corrects time. Along the way, he meets his greatest rival, a Chinese kung fu master, who eventually becomes his best friend, a relationship complicated by the homoerotic tension simmering between them. In one of the main action sequences, the kung fu master's head gets blown off by a teenage werewolf, but in the next scene his head is back on and everything returns to normal. Kasper explained that in the *Escape from Babylon* universe, the absence of all logic made complete sense.

It was all happening so quickly she didn't have time to feel upset or to protest the fact that he was leaving in two days to begin preproduction in Sofia. It seemed like a bad joke, to imagine her husband moving to Bulgaria for six months, but it was happening.

And she knew how hard Kasper had worked to produce his first movie, after years of toiling away in the mail room to become a second assistant and then finally the first assistant, fetching coffee and pastries for meetings he wasn't allowed into, reading scripts and giving notes, searching for the next big idea that might launch his career. One of his old bosses once threw a stapler at his head. Another one of his bosses used to call him in the middle of the night, demanding that Kasper pick up his Viagra from the twenty-four-hour pharmacy. Plus, he was a young foreigner in the United States (he was the son of Montenegrins who had immigrated to Sweden in the sixties); he had moved to the States for college on a student visa, and then had relied upon his employers for work visas, his status unsteady and temporary. Until he got a green card after marrying Ava. When he joined a Swedish film company to head up U.S. production a few years ago, his boss, a highly attractive tri-athlete, was humane and understanding. He meditated and wanted Kasper to start meditating, offering to buy Kasper a personal man-tra, which Kasper declined. He asked Kasper about his kids, about the rest of his life, and treated him like a person. Kasper didn't have night sweats or anxiety attacks anymore and he believed that producing this movie confirmed he no longer languished in Holly-wood's purgatory of creative executives and eternal development deals, that his livelihood no longer depended upon the tyrannical whims of the Hollywood bosses who had checkered his past, that he was finally creating something he believed in.

And so of course Ava supported him, urged him even to "go for it," suppressing the knowledge that, in exchange, she would have to sacrifice a lot, that his achievement would mean the diminish-ment of her own work and ambitions. But she had shoved down that internal chatter, believing this was what a good wife did. And she wanted to be seen as heroic and self-sacrificing, thinking she would get some kind of metaphorical gold medal for enduring the marathon of single motherhood for the next six months. And didn't she want him to succeed? To follow his dreams? Wasn't that what marriage meant?

Today was Friday.

Kasper was leaving Sunday afternoon, two days from now. In a mad rush to keep his promise to Sam, they were still going camping, despite the looming separation that awaited, weighing on them.

He had offered out of guilt, given he was about to leave, that in Joshua Tree she should take some time for herself. To grade papers, or write, or go on a hike. Whatever she needed, he would cover for her and look after the kids. But he was stuck on endless work calls and she sensed the freedom of those promised hours draining away, his offer faulty, ill-conceived but well-intentioned. The image of her solitary shadow flickering before her on a dirt path leading into prehistoric boulders, passing gnarled cacti blooming magenta orbs, faded. She could put her foot down. Fight for that promised time. But this would cause another argument and she didn't have the energy. She wanted him to leave on good terms, with their marriage seemingly intact.

They sped by all the familiar landmarks: Harvest Health, which sold dried strawberries, licorice, and nuts in bulk. The sprawling outlets with designer discounted merchandise where they had once purchased a red Le Creuset Dutch oven for half price. The billboards for medical marijuana, casinos, and bail bonds.

Ava twisted around again and glanced back at Margot, who had started coughing. A dry persistent cough. It was a tic that developed when she felt anxious. It happened in class before tests and during scary movies. Last year, Margot's sixth-grade teacher had suggested they buy homeopathic cough drops even though Ava had explained patiently that it was a tic, not a cough, brought on by anxiety. The teacher kept talking about a wonderful little organic pharmacy in Santa Monica. "You should really check it out," she had said brightly.

It's neurological, Ava wanted to scream but instead she nodded, bit her lip.

But the way Kasper had delivered the news that he was leaving would cause anyone anxiety as it was a stretch of time that appeared never-ending, the longest they'd gone without him. Half a year. Only yesterday he booked his flight to Bulgaria. The financing had just come through and the production would start scouting locations in Sofia and assembling the crew on Tuesday. For weeks, Kasper had doubted the movie would come together, often reassuring Ava that he wasn't going anywhere, listing all the obstacles that stood in his way of the film achieving that coveted "green light," a light he'd given up on until it instantly blinked "go."

Kasper ping-ponged between elation and spiraling fear from the news. Elated by this rare chance to make an independent movie outside the studio system, and then simultaneously filled with terror that he might fail, the production vulnerable to so many pitfalls: the big-name actors might not sign their agreements, locations could fall through, the distributors might pull out, they could run over budget, exceed shooting days, the gossamer-thin structure he'd so painstakingly built collapsing in an hour.

Ava knew how high the stakes were, and how much higher Kasper made them with his own expectations, adrenaline coursing through him this morning as he packed and strategized, talking too fast about what to expect. She had been sitting on their bed, watching him shove clothing into his suitcase and she made a mental note to remind him of his toiletry bag. "It has to be all hands on deck," he announced to the sound of the zipper zipping around the suitcase, sealing up his life.

He might be able to come home after a month for a visit. But he didn't know yet. Production might pay for the plane tickets, or not. If not, it would be tough to come home. But maybe he could, for a few days. At first, he would stay in a hotel, then try to find an apartment rental. Somewhere central. Clean and functional. "It's a necessary sacrifice, relocating," he said, wedging a pair of running shoes beneath folded dress shirts, the question looping through her mind: *A sacrifice for whom?*

But what could she say? Don't go? The financial rewards were undeniable, especially when compared to her salary as an adjunct art history professor at a small college. But did making more money make his work more important?

The answer seemed to be yes.

Then she chastised herself: she should be grateful that his job afforded them certain freedoms, even if it resulted in her work meaning less or meaning nothing at all. He was only trying to work his absolute hardest to provide for their family. He shouldn't be punished for working hard, for making a living, for trying to succeed. She should be happy. Overjoyed even. Like some of the mothers from the kids' school who exhorted the pleasures of staying home, emphasizing how blessed they were that they *could* stay home, that they didn't have to work, that they were fully focused on their children without being tugged in a million different directions, their voices honey-dipped, sweet and unassuming, breathlessly cheerful.

So she told herself to feel appreciative of her situation, swallowing down any resentment toward patriarchy, toward Kasper, toward the way she had been backed up into the motherhood corner while the value of her work in the world slipped through her fingers, her book projects thwarted by a lack of time and quiet space to think, her advancement within the art history department flagging as the competing responsibilities of motherhood always won out. But her angry disappointment over the imbalance between them most likely contributed to existing power structures and insidiously, invisibly reinforced the status quo in which other women were much less free and fortunate than she was, much less economically stable, much less concerned with their own personal striving and ability to excel in the workplace. Women who were only trying to survive, to get by. Ava felt a gnawing self-hatred for focusing on her own goals, riddled as she was with careerism, for wanting as much freedom as Kasper took for granted, when she should feel ashamed for wanting more time and space to work than she already had. Such ballooning resentment toward Kasper felt unearned, dirty, oppressive; she knew it was disgusting even to hint that this might be hard for her, or to suggest that second-wave feminism hadn't fully succeeded, because it had failed other women far more. Failed the whole country, given who was currently president.

Which was why, in part, she said nothing of this, and nothing about how his time away, in a distant country, would surely take a toll on their family, on their marriage. It was akin to saying, *Go but don't go.* Or: *Go but make sure you feel guilty about it.* Sending mixed messages, putting him in a double bind, their relationship swirling into bitter arguments and squandered opportunities: all the things they'd once promised not to do to each other.

He paced the room, rambling on about failing, about how much was at stake, about all the money the financiers were putting up, his boss banking on him to bring it home, while she tried to invoke the stoic strength of military wives whose husbands were always leaving, even though this wasn't a war. Or the 1960s astronauts' wives with their beehive hairdos and many children gathered around the

TV set to watch daddy rocket to the moon. Those wives had sacrificed for king and country, for science and the space race, but for an action movie?

He stopped pacing and stared through the dusty screen at the distant blue hills of the neighboring canyon. "I have to tell the kids."

"That would be a good idea." He failed to detect the cool irony in her voice.

Kasper had sat down on the unmade bed and called for them. Margot and Sam instantly appeared in the doorway, probably listening the whole time. He motioned for them to come closer, explaining that he would be gone for six months, because of the movie. Finally it was happening, even though for weeks he had told them there were too many hurdles, that he wasn't going anywhere.

"But in three months you guys will come visit me for the summer. We'll be together again. Don't worry. Time will fly."

They stared at him.

"I'm going to miss you all so much." He tried to smile, his voice catching. Ava watched him, a coldness encroaching on her heart. At least he could have prepared the kids better instead of saying it would never happen. Explained, coaxed, promised better. Out of the corner of her eye she noticed, in his flurry of packing, that he had left a pair of underwear on the floor, next to the hamper, having missed it entirely.

Head in his hands, Kasper cried.

The kids stood there in a daze, unsure if they too should cry or comfort him. Unable to watch this spectacle of fatherly incompetence any longer she stormed into the adjoining bathroom, noticing his unpacked toiletries still standing on the counter, and that he had misfolded a towel. Instead of the towel being spread over the rack, so it could dry properly, it was bunched up haphazardly, retaining moisture, the opposite of dry. Overhearing Margot say, "It's okay, Papa. We love you and we understand," Ava tore the damp towel off the rack and hurled it onto the blue hexagon-tiled floor. It lay there, motionless.

Picking it up, she glared at the towel's unappealing grayish color—it had once been fluffy and white—while her pulse raced with the knowledge that her teaching semester was far from over, along with her unfinished book hanging in the balance. Already, she was behind on grading and behind on the book. Already, she gasped for air in the middle of a rough ocean, flailing, gulping down salt water. Drowning.

From the back seat, Margot let out an aggressive cough, louder and more forceful.

"Are you okay?" Ava asked, twisting around to look at her again, realizing that her daughter was wearing eyeliner, the dark pencil faintly winging upward from the outer corner of her eyes. But where had she gotten the liner? Ava didn't have any, but then it dawned on her—Margot had used one of her dark coloring pencils as a substitute and Ava had to bite her tongue to keep from saying anything. It would only spark a heated argument; trapped as they were inside the car, it would be better to bring it up later.

Margot cast a hooded glance her way, then whispered hoarsely, "I'm fine," before coughing again. She had become more volatile since she turned thirteen last week.

Sam pretended not to notice Margot's insistent coughing.

Kasper briefly muted his phone and gave Margot an encouraging smile. "Only one more hour until we're there," he said, reaching back to pat her knee.

Staring at the eyeliner, Ava still fought the urge to mention it.

Margot demanded, "What?"

She tried to smile casually. "Nothing."

"Then why are you giving me that look."

Ava turned back around. "I'm not giving you any kind of look."

Margot's therapist, a woman in her fifties with sandy blond hair and earrings in the shape of falling leaves, had informed Ava that her daughter's violent mood swings and explosive outbursts were mostly brought on by the hormones. "This developmental stage is very disorienting," she had said slowly. "I suppose you could call it the weaponization of hormones." Ava knew that the therapist had a daughter in college and she yearned to ask her how she'd made it through adolescence's dark tunnel, but of course, therapists don't discuss their personal lives. Ava had clarified what was happening at home, hoping the therapist would give her more advice. "Doors slam on a regular basis. She throws hairbrushes at the wall and becomes furious at inanimate objects. For example, when her shoelaces are all knotted up, and she can't wedge her foot into the shoe, it's the shoe's fault. When I try to help, Margot screams, 'Let me do it!'"

Ava leaned back into the cushiony chair, realizing how different Margot was from herself at that age, bottling and burying her distress, striving to please everyone so they'd see how diligent and good she was. Instead of throwing things, she starved herself, watching the blood seep through her satin pointe shoes during dress rehearsals for *Giselle,* or for *Coppélia,* a ballet about a beautiful doll who magically springs to life at night. Instead of screaming and slamming doors, Ava soundlessly closed her bedroom door and cried into her pillow. Instead of ripping pages out of her math textbook in a fit of fury, Ava studied harder and longer.

Instead of saying no, she always said yes.

After a few moments of silence, Sam and Margot started fighting again. About the armrest in the middle of their row. Sam claimed Margot was taking up more than her share of the armrest and he elbowed her out of the way. Margot yelled, "He hurt me!"

Sam whined, "You're hogging up all the space. You're a hog!"

Kasper slammed his fist into the steering wheel, muting his phone, and said this car ride was death by a thousand cuts, the way they were arguing, he couldn't focus on calls, trapped in the car like this. Ava considered how much safer it would be if she took over the wheel, but driving his car was one of the few things that gave him uncomplicated pleasure. And so, she swallowed down her suggestions about safety and driving, something she had become accustomed to doing, knowing that voicing her opinion in these already heated situations would only spark more tension between them.

On the way to the campsite, they stopped to see Erin's new house in the desert. She was spending the weekend there on her own, arranging lamps, putting down rugs, hanging up artwork. Erin and her husband, Nolan, had just bought the house a few months ago as a desert refuge, a place for reflection and seclusion, a place to get away from it all. Ava envied her solitude, the way she surrounded herself with all this blank space, the endless sky and furry Joshua trees her sole companions. There was even a little room in the back of the house dedicated to meditation with a low altar decorated with crystals and candles and dried flowers, a woven rug to sit on, incense to light, along with a deck of tarot cards.

Erin waved from the front door, expecting them.

The kids tumbled out of the car, their tennis shoes crunching over the gravel driveway, leaving Kasper in the driver's seat. His car door swung open, but he was still on the phone.

Inside, Erin glanced at Kasper through the wide rectangular window and asked if everything was all right? Her feathery eyebrows drew together in concern. Ava remembered the Erin of eight years ago, on Margot and Josie's first day of kindergarten. As part of orientation, the teacher made the adults form a circle on the playground and toss a beach ball to one another. When someone caught the ball, they had to say what their favorite thing to do was when they weren't with their children, before passing it on to the next person. The responses were predictable: reading, working out, yoga, going to the movies.

But when Erin caught the ball, she said, "I can't remember what I used to like."

Everyone laughed politely, but Ava's laugh was the loudest, the most in agreement with Erin's sentiment, and Erin smiled at her from across the circle. She wore a rose-colored jumpsuit and high platform sandals that Ava had found attractively daring, and after orientation, they both agreed it was ridiculous to make parents perform these theatrics of likability when they were all filled with nerves about their kids starting school, watching their little bodies filter into the brightly decorated classroom, the new backpacks enormous on their tiny frames. Erin had leaned in close, her relaxed curls brushing Ava's cheek. "Did you notice that I'm the oldest mom here?" she had whispered, incredulous.

"Honestly, not at all. You look terrific."

She let out a sharp laugh. "I'm fifty, too ancient to be playing games about what my life used to be like."

At the moment, Erin wore loose gray sweatpants and Uggs, a slash of red on her lips, the russet freckles sprinkling her cheekbones more pronounced from the desert sun. "For color," she said, gesturing to her lipstick. "Even if no one sees me out here, I see me, you know?"

Kasper now paced the circular driveway, gesturing while he yelled into the phone.

The kids played in the backyard, content with the rusted swing set the former owners had left behind.

"He seems really stressed out," Erin added, her eyes worried.

"It's about hiring a DP," Ava said, and then, seeing Erin's confusion, she clarified. "Cinematographer. Anyway, he's frantic about this movie, worried it won't come together. I've never seen him like this."

Erin made a pot of coffee and they drank it hot and black in the front room, staring at Kasper, who was still pacing back and forth on the gravel.

"It all feels intense, with him leaving in two days and cramming in this trip beforehand," Erin said in a small voice. "I mean, it's so unlike Kasper to not come inside and at least say hello." She paused, pursing her lips. "He's always been so friendly and talkative, you know? He can really talk to women. All the times he listened to me complain about Nolan, walking me off the ledge, asking the right questions . . . he's such a good guy. A nice guy."

It was true. He was a good guy, one of the best. Under normal circumstances, he was sensitive and kind; he never criticized her subpar cooking, he spent hours building intricate Lego cities with Sam and delighted in taking Margot shopping for school clothes. He sang in the morning when he made coffee, and he was a fantastic dancer. He liked to play pranks on them, cavort and chase the kids around the house, cradle the dog as if she were a baby; in sillier moods, he'd wrap a gingham dish towel around the dog's face as though the dog had transformed into his strict Montenegrin grandmother, Almina, making them laugh. On some nights, he lit candles in their bedroom, brought her a thimble of whiskey, and while the flickering shadows danced across the walls, they talked about the day and the days to come.

Holding the sturdy ceramic mug, its heat seeping into her palms, Ava asked Erin how things were with Nolan, trying to redirect the conversation away from Kasper, away from her own spreading sense of guilt.

Erin sighed, glancing through the sliding glass door at the rusted swing set, the withered sage bushes, the shallow hole where she hoped a firepit would go. In her palm, she balanced a long thin amethyst crystal, roughly cut. "We're taking a break right now. It's a huge relief not to be around all his depressive shit. But it's also lonely. I want a divorce, maybe?" She stared up at Ava with her large brown eyes. "But then we'd have to sell this house, which we literally just bought to save our marriage." She shook her head, letting out a regretful laugh. "I love this house. I don't want to sell it but I can't afford to keep it on my own. What do you think?"

"How long have you been out here?"

"A few days. I said I needed to arrange some things, but that was just an excuse." She shook her head. "He's taking care of Josie this weekend. When I think about leaving Nolan, the real reason I haven't yet is Josie. I couldn't bear being away from her with joint custody and all that."

"What do the spirit cards say?" Ava asked, knowing that Erin relied heavily on her spirit animal oracle cards.

"Parrot Spirit. Watch your words." Erin shrugged. "A warning against harmful self-talk. And also a warning about how we talk to others. I guess I've said some hurtful things to Nolan about how I really feel. How I'm not attracted to him anymore. How he's suffocating me with his depression." She sighed. "I sat before my altar today. I meditated and held my crystals. I asked the universe to help guide me, but nothing came up. I only feel more agitated and confused. About everything."

"Is he still on his meds?"

"The meds aren't helping, even though he's been taking them for two years. He doesn't even have the energy to make an appointment with his psychiatrist to deal with it. Meanwhile the meds are making him gain weight."

They stared into their coffee. "I think it's good that you're out here to clear your mind so you can get some perspective, you know?"

Erin nodded, her eyes glistening with tears.

Kasper finally came inside, fresh off the call, and collapsed onto Erin's leather couch. Lying against the soft tasseled pillows, he explained the whole dilemma about the DP in an engaging, funny way that endeared him to Erin, painting himself as the creative savior fighting for the good of the movie. Erin predictably took pity on him, swept up in his tale of woe, asking all the questions Ava had grown tired of asking: Why do the financiers want Bill Adler so much? What's so great about him? Was there anything else Kasper could do? What did the other producers think?

After a suspended pause, Erin's eyes widened. "I'm so sorry, Kasper. This sounds really difficult." Then she offered him some fresh coffee, which he happily accepted, sighing, hanging his head, basking in her female concern, his bare tan feet burrowing into the fluffy sheepskin rug.

Before they hit the road, Kasper went to the bathroom. In this short interval, Erin leaned over the coffee table and whispered loudly to Ava, "I mean, I get what you're saying. He was literally talking on the phone in the driveway for forty minutes, at least."

"And the entire car ride here, he was on the phone," Ava added.

Erin gave her a pleading stare. "I would be annoyed too, especially because this is your last family moment together before he leaves for a long time. But Kasper's just so nice, you know? I weirdly feel bad for him. He's really struggling. It's like I can't feel angry at him." Seeing Ava's expression darken, Erin added, "And you're angry, as you should be—it's all so sudden. And you didn't sign up for this, but you know, neither did he?" She sighed. "I'm sorry. This seems so hard. Like there's no right answer."

．　　．　　．

After checking into the campsite, they found a raucous Western-themed bar with long wooden tables for dinner, the floor sprinkled with sawdust, but Kasper disappeared to take another work call.

Ava sat there eating tortilla chips and drinking warm beer in the dim reddish lighting while the kids put their heads down on the sticky tabletop, complaining that they didn't like barbeque, the only thing on the menu.

She ordered them both a baked potato and lemonade.

When the food came, they each stared at their potato in a bowl with resentful dazed eyes, wondering where Papa was.

"I have no idea," Ava snapped.

"But we didn't even eat dinner together," Margot said, scanning the crowded restaurant full of men dressed in plaid shirts and cowboy hats, swaggering around in their tight jeans.

Ava wanted to band together with the kids, funneling their shared anger into a singular sharp point, but Kasper was in crisis mode. An understanding wife would manage the situation with grace and calm, thinking nothing of herself. But his work crisis could stretch out indefinitely, into months of martyrdom. Years even.

Signaling for the bill, she gulped down the rest of her beer and said as evenly as possible, "Let's get out of here."

That night in the tent she was marooned between Sam and Margot, their warm bodies pressed up against hers, their hot breath sweeping over her skin along with Coco's occasional snorts and muffled dog dreams, her fur smelling of dirt and sage.

Margot emitted that same dry cough every few minutes, rousing Ava from a light doze. She put a hand on Margot's chest and told her to breathe.

"I am breathing!" Margot hissed.

"Picture your abdomen filling up with air, like a balloon—" She stopped, realizing how annoying it was when someone else told you to breathe.

In the corner of the tent, Kasper crouched in front of his computer, typing away furiously, the bluish glowing screen illuminating his concentrated face, while darkness obscured the rest of his body, as if his head floated in space.

Margot rolled her eyes and turned over onto her side, her shoulders tense, her foot jabbing Ava's calf. She huffed into her pillow, "I can't sleep. My stomach hurts."

"Do you want some water?"

"I don't know. What if it's cramps? What if I'm getting my period? What if it hurts?"

Kasper's aggressive typing rushed into the semidarkness. She glanced over at him, confirming that he was worlds away, entirely captivated by the screen.

"It won't hurt that much," Ava reassured her. But then she remembered something her mother had told her about her grandmother Rose, who had called it "the sickness." When Ava's mother was a little girl, Rose was sequestered in her darkened bedroom for days on end, as if some malignant force had overtaken her body. Recently, Margot's dark thick pubic hair startled Ava every time she saw it. And her breasts looked more like breasts, as pointy as cones, her thighs fuller, her stomach rounder, the first stirrings of acne sprinkling her forehead.

Her physical transformation, which seemed too sudden, disturbed Ava, as though she were losing Margot before it was time. Ava had noticed grown men noticing Margot, her stomach turning at the thought of what these men were thinking. Last week, Ava trailed Margot as they passed through a crowded restaurant. The hostess was leading them to their table, and Ava saw two men in their late forties glance up from their plates, following Margot's lithe shapely figure with hungry eyes. A nervous jolt passed through her when Margot insisted on going to the restroom herself, disappearing from view while Ava anxiously remained at the table, her neck craning, trying to track Margot, fearing that some man, any man, would shove her into the restroom and trap her behind a locked door, that this would then become the defining trauma of their lives: the mother who looked away a second too long, the vulnerable daughter who wasn't protected.

Ava patted Margot's shoulder. "Don't worry." She felt the faint outline of Margot's training bra digging into her shoulder beneath her loose T-shirt and imagined that it was tight around Margot's chest, indenting a ribbon of red above her rib cage. Ava suggested she remove it. "You'll feel better without it on all night."

Reluctantly, Margot took off the bra. Ava watched her, an unwanted memory flickering before her: the thin red patent leather belt Ava had loved as a child. She must have been around four years old. Never taking it off, she wore it underneath her clothes, tight around her middle. Every few days she tightened it another notch. She wore it to sleep, not telling anyone about the red belt, as if by loosening or removing it, the whole world would unravel, as fearsome as Pandora's box of chaos spilling into the universe. Finally her stomach hurt so much her parents took her to the doctor. Lying down on the examination table, she still remembered the shock on the doctor's face when he raised her shirt and saw the tight red belt. Her parents had no idea.

How had they no idea? Ava wondered as Margot settled back into the pillow. She noticed everything about her children: when their nails grew too long, the gathering tangles in Margot's hair that demanded nightly brushing, a new tooth struggling to burst through. *Noticing is loving,* she thought, the memory of the red belt plummeting into her, leaving a faint outline of pain.

Kasper cleared his throat, the sound jarring her out of the belief that he might be a ghost, a visitation in the far dark corner, an apparition of a father. When she closed her eyes, even her eyelids felt tense. He kept whispering he was almost done, but minutes and then hours passed. The incessant tapping of his fingertips hitting the keys filtered into the tent, her heart hardening with each tap. Was this what it meant to be a wife? A mother? To pretend to sleep while roiling with a rage so white and hot it blurred the contours of her body?

The truth was, he was already gone. He had been for a long time. This disparity between them always had run beneath things, ebbing and flowing since the children were born. But she enabled the illusion, for herself and for him, that they shared the burden equally. That they were equal. But bit by bit, as the years passed Ava did more and more: she cooked all the meals and cleaned the house, checked all the homework and packed the school lunches and scheduled the doctor's appointments, birthday parties, and extracurricular activities all while teaching her sections and researching her book. She was always the first to hear about a low test score, a beloved sweatshirt lost at school, trouble with friends or trouble with math, the initial jolts of anxiety seeping into her before she figured out how to fix it. By the time Kasper got wind of what was happening, she'd settled the issue, absorbing the shock and worry for him.

Even though she had fostered this situation, it continued to baffle her. He'd played a magic trick on her, a sleight of hand, with his progressive attitude and leftist views, with his liberal arts degree and his high-powered Swedish sisters who had bicycled their young children to daycare and had picked them up at the end of their workday. All these signals had deceived her into believing they stood on equal footing, that he would companion her through the thorny valley of parenting. That they would be partners. But it wasn't equal, and she realized it never had been, crushed as she was with the conviction that her children's emotional and physical well-being, their happiness and ability to succeed, rested entirely on her shoulders. If she stepped away, even for a second, there would be no one left to catch them. A pain spread through her chest, rapidly encroaching on her heart, the muscle clenching when she thought about it for too long.

A magic trick. Yes. That's what this is, Ava thought bitterly, and then *poof!* Kasper would vanish. How would she talk to someone who's no longer here? How could she address the intricate dynamics of their faltering marriage from thousands of miles away?

You can't.

She finally dropped into sleep, thinking about Claire, a friend from grad school, who now had three children under the age of six and lived in New Mexico. She wondered what Claire would do in this situation, but this wouldn't happen to her in the first place because Claire had recently devised a new system, a kind of game with her husband that involved spreadsheets and flash cards to divvy up the emotional and physical labor of running a household. After first making a list of everything she did, which was 98 percent of all domestic and emotional work, including giving birth to their children, she raged over all the time and energy she had forfeited, giving it away for free. Such as the breast milk she had diligently pumped, which was worth its weight in gold. She felt angry at herself and angry at her husband and angry at the patriarchy that upheld gendered childcare and domestic duties as female. Claire described the list as running five notebook pages long, single-spaced and creased from multiple foldings, the penciled words smudged, faint and hard to read in places. She finally gave him the list in couples therapy, and since implementing the new system things were better, Claire said. He now packed and unpacked the diaper bag before and after family outings and scheduled the kids' dental appointments six months in advance.

But she still wanted to kill him.

Ava had attempted to make her own list, which was amusing and deeply defeating, as the entries veered from the utterly banal to the essential core of what it meant to parent: *Check homework every night. Cook healthy meals for kids—get creative with veggies! Arrange playdates. Hike in nature with whole family! Tooth care. Schedule annual pediatrician appointments. Sort through kids art. Store kids art. Make sure everyone flosses and wears sunscreen. Research and avoid endocrine disrupting products. Stay attuned to children's emotional signals and cues. Keep marriage intact.*

Sunday morning was windy and sunny, the sky filled with wispy clouds. They went on a hike behind the campsite. Because there was no reception in the foothills, Kasper couldn't check his phone. He pointed out cottontails scurrying in the brush, and with Sam and Margot bounding alongside them, admiring the cute bunnies, things almost seemed okay, as if he wasn't leaving for Bulgaria this afternoon.

As if nothing were about to change.

Coco raced after the kids, barking with glee.

Margot picked up the pace, running faster.

Sam lagged behind and fell in step with Ava, growing nervous that they'd lose Margot.

"We won't lose her. Look at this wide-open field. There's nowhere to go."

A little hill rose up before them, Margot disappearing over it.

Sam shook his head. "I'm worried." He reminded her of an old man who'd seen too many things go wrong to trust the reassurances of others.

The hill evened out and there was no Margot, the land flat and sprawling in every direction.

Sam started to fret.

A tumbleweed rolled by, swept along by a gentle wind.

Walking behind them, Kasper told Ava there was nothing to worry about, she'd just run ahead, like she always did. His phone rang and he quickly answered, turning to face the mountains, hunched over and cupping the phone to his ear to block out the wind.

"Are you sure—" Ava began, her question upended by the sight of a shimmering two-way highway in the distance, sixteen-wheelers speeding in both directions.

Swallowing a scream, Ava started to run.

Kasper was still on the phone, oblivious, his back to the highway.

Sam clenched Ava's arm, running with her, talking faster and faster.

When they reached the edge of the highway, Ava gestured wildly to Margot to stay where she was. Margot stood on the other side of the road holding Coco by the collar. In her jean shorts, her long dark hair whipping in the wind, she glimmered, mirage-like, vulnerable and crushable compared to the rushing cars passing in front of her as fast as bullets.

Ava yelled, "Don't move. I'm coming. Don't move!"

By this time, Kasper was running toward them. Sam froze, not knowing what to do. Ava told him to stay put and wait for Papa.

In a startling blur, Ava sprinted across the highway, her breath trapped in her chest. She heard Sam cry out Margot's name in the wind but she couldn't look back; she had to reach Margot, and when she finally made it across, she yanked Margot back from the oncoming cars and enormous trucks that could flatten her in an instant.

Once the road fell silent and empty, Ava walked Margot and Coco back across. Kasper and Sam stood in the brush, Sam's forehead pressed into Kasper's stomach, Kasper rubbing his small tense back.

For a fleeting second, Ava wanted to blame Kasper—why had he turned away at that crucial moment? How had it happened that he was on the phone, dealing with the DP, when his daughter was a breath away from death? Wasn't this evidence enough that something was deeply wrong here? But then she felt Margot's sweaty hand in hers, and her nervous watchful eyes searched for Ava's, filled with shame and fear that she had made a terrible mistake, and Ava knew that blaming Kasper, or herself, wouldn't make things right.

Everyone cried and hugged, offering all sorts of apologies. Kasper's phone slipped from his hand into the sandy dirt, and he didn't pick it up right away. Ava restrained herself from kicking it onto the highway so the cars could crush it.

Margot wrapped her arms around Ava and said she didn't see the road at first. She kept running, as if an engine inside her wouldn't stop. "I just wanted to run," she said simply, her cheek pressed into Ava's collarbone.

Kasper and Ava exchanged a fearful glance, knowing they wouldn't always be there to intervene, that at some future point the cars, or the boys, or the drugs would be coming too fast and too soon.

They rode home in complete silence, all of them still stunned, too unsettled to turn on the radio or talk. Kasper put his phone in the glove compartment, snapping it shut.

After an hour, Ava twisted around in her seat to find both kids asleep, Sam snoring lightly, Margot's head pressed up against the window, her hair falling over her face like a dark curtain.

Then Ava turned back around and stared at the long road ahead, filled with the sinking knowledge that the trip was a microcosm of their marriage, full of fighting and near-death experiences, that even when they tried to find joy in the bunnies, or in the way the sunlight hit the mountains tinging them gold, a malevolent force ran beneath it all, readying to shatter everything to bits.

. . .

They were still dusty from the desert, backpacks in the entryway, hiking shoes kicked off while Kasper prepared for his flight in a frantic rush. The dread before the workweek gathered in the pit of her stomach, anticipating teaching her class, picturing the students' bored nonplussed expressions on Monday morning as they twirled the ends of their hair or chewed on their pencil erasers while furtively checking their phones, scrolling through glossy Instagram accounts.

They were out of milk and toilet paper.

Sam had a mysterious rash on his stomach, probably an allergic reaction from some desert plant, and she made a mental note to call the pediatrician tomorrow. Margot's retainer had disappeared over the weekend, most likely chewed up beyond recognition by Coco.

They stood in front of the house, his suitcase on the sidewalk, the Uber seconds away. His eyes swam with apology while shining with optimism. This was his chance to prove himself to her, to Hollywood, to his benevolent Swedish boss.

He cupped her face in his warm soft hands and she then wrapped her arms around him. "It's going to be okay. Right?" he murmured into her hair.

The kids watched from the doorway.

"Of course," she managed, a knot in her throat. Eyes burning, she glanced down at the pavement, a thin line of ants marching toward oblivion.

She hugged him tightly, memorizing the feeling of his solid body against hers, his warmth and sturdiness, his shallow breath on her neck, his light brown eyes asking for absolution, silently thanking her for understanding, while also dreading what would happen if she didn't always understand.

The black shiny Uber whisked him away. The activity of his packing and showering and the thudding vibrations of his metallic suitcase when he dragged it down the wooden staircase left the moments after his departure unsettlingly still.

She stood with the kids in the entryway, the front door open. The sun shone brilliantly, the late afternoon sky cloudless, piercingly blue. She heard a hollow tinny vibration from some indescribable part of herself, a sound that made her wince from its desertion. Putting her arms around the children, she drew them close, whispering, *It's okay, it will be all right.*

For a moment they hugged her too, their intermingled breath suspended, and she sensed how much they willed their father home, imagining him walking through the front door five minutes from now, joking that he wasn't actually moving to Bulgaria for six months. What a ridiculous idea! Who would do that? They waited for his imaginary return within those silent seconds, until they broke away from her, running in opposite directions: Sam up the stairs to fix his Lego Batman plane, and Margot shooting through the open screen door and into the backyard, where she collapsed next to the dog, who nuzzled Margot, licking her braided ponytail in commiseration.

Ava remained frozen in the entryway, asking herself how he could so easily dismiss their life, seamlessly slipping out of it, while she couldn't leave, not even for a day, believing that if she left, the entire house would topple and everything inside would break, as in so many madcap comedies when Mom leaves for some urgent matter (never for work) and Dad's in charge, it all goes to shit with ruined laundry and pizza for breakfast but the kids are finally deliriously happy. The movie is funny and endearing; everyone laughs their heads off.

2

O n the plane, wedged between Margot and Sam, Ava was exhausted after a fresh fight over who got the window seat despite previous negotiations. It was decided that Margot would switch with Sam halfway through and move to the aisle seat.

With this settled, Ava savored the momentary lull as Margot and Sam were now hooked up to their devices on either side of her, their technology entirely absorbing. She drank some tomato juice, trying to crank back her seat, wishing she'd asked for wine instead. The fasten seat belt warning lit up, and the plane dipped. She gripped Sam's and Margot's forearms but they didn't notice, laser focused on their screens. Ava flinched at the sudden descent, an uncontrolled swing into darkness. The captain announced there'd be more air pockets up ahead so please remain seated until further notice.

The significance of this trip felt freighted, heavy as their many suitcases as she reflected on the last three months without Kasper. In the bluish dawn, she'd made coffee before the kids woke up, running her fingertip over the chipped rim of her favorite mug. The front door's muffled sigh when it closed behind her. The tangle of lemon and eucalyptus trees surrounding the house, the gutters filled with dead leaves, the line of ants that kept reappearing between the kitchen sink and the wall. Arguing with Margot over crop tops with skimpy spaghetti straps, an unacceptable flash of torso, too-short shorts. The fact that Margot had decided to shave without asking Ava, running the pink plastic razor up and down her legs, leaving the bathtub coated in hair. When Margot dried off, tiny bloody cuts peppered her legs. But sometimes she still played with dolls, the bathtub perpetually full of stranded damp Barbies; some were headless, some still clothed, the dye of their bright garments staining the white porcelain. Most were naked, all smiling up at her. She recalled the stabbing pain when accidentally stepping on a few of Sam's scattered Lego pieces, her sole dotting blood. And in an effort to maintain order, Ava developed an obsession with the label maker, the sight of those block letters imprinted on rectangular strips comforting: *Sam's retainer box, Margot's homework folder, cereal, pancake mix, arts and crafts.* A small glass of whiskey on her bedside table while she tensed at the sirens careening through Topanga Canyon, with its one road in and out, before checking the wildfire evacuation app. A stack of library books on women in ancient Greece, Greco-Roman religious practices. Her own unfinished book. The endless stream of student papers to grade, recommendations to write. Faculty meetings yawning into the afternoon while she calculated whether she'd make it in time to pick up Margot and Sam from Beyond the Bell at school. Late and sweating, while a mirage of metallic cars inched along the congested freeway as she gripped the steering wheel.

All the missed FaceTime calls from Kasper. When they did speak, a blurry pixelated apparition of a husband spoke to her, but the sentences were often time delayed and Sofia, that strange Eastern European city, loomed in the background. Given that he was ten hours ahead, his calls were often early in the morning or very late at night, causing Ava to wonder if she had spoken to Kasper or if she just imagined it. Sometimes she forgot large chunks of their conversation, or if they had even spoken at all. His life in Bulgaria, with the crew and all the intricate problems he constantly had to solve, was entirely divorced from the life they had shared in Los Angeles, and she started to experience the sinking feeling that he wasn't real.

That maybe he had even died and now Kasper's ghost visited her via FaceTime, reassuring her and the children that he was in Bulgaria, nothing to panic about, nothing to mourn. Soon they would reunite.

Or maybe she wanted to kill him for leaving and that's why it was easier to imagine him dead. Because if he was alive, she would have to contend with the rage of having been left.

She would have to kill him.

This dark fantasy pitched through her mind when the plane took another sharp dip. She glanced around at the other passengers, scouring their faces for fear. A woman frowned at her computer screen while the man next to her played *Candy Crush* on his phone. The plane tilted severely to the right, the windows filling with an aerial view of mountain ranges, glittering lakes, landlocked states. She clutched Margot's arm.

"Are you scared?" Margot asked, eyeing her with suspicion.

"Am I scared?" Ava repeated, unsure if she'd heard her right.

"No, I said, 'Is my *mascara* bleeding?'"

"Oh. It looks fine," Ava said, noticing her thickly coated lashes, the faint smudging beneath her eyes. A few months ago, Ava had given in and bought Margot some makeup. But it still jarred Ava to see how expertly Margot applied all the products, making Margot's disapproval of Ava even more exaggerated as she rolled her eyes whenever Ava asked her an "uncool" question: "How was your day?" or "What would you like for dinner?"

To distract herself from thoughts of crashing and Margot's moodiness, Ava scrolled through the movie options, lingering for a moment on one about a couple who loses their four-year-old son. The masochistic urge to see Nicole Kidman's unmoving botoxed face press the kid's tattered stuffed animal to her chest, her eyes glazed over with icy grief, proved almost irresistible. But then she skipped over it, knowing that she couldn't watch movies about dead or lost children. She would never be able to, no matter how many years had passed.

She finally settled on a documentary about the making of Barbie called *Tiny Shoulders,* thinking it might be something Margot would like. There were various interviews with the chief marketing and sales people about how to make Barbie more diverse, more accessible, more career driven, more body positive. They had started a "You Can Be Anything" campaign, showcasing Barbie as a paleontologist, a vet, a professor. They also displayed a plus-sized Barbie that Margot had received a few years ago for her birthday from Kasper's well-meaning, body-positive older sister. Unwrapping it, Margot had wondered why that Barbie was so fat compared to the others.

She drifted into sleep thinking about that plus-sized blue-haired Barbie, and if she was a bad feminist for buying Margot all those Barbies in the first place, even though Margot had loved to play with them; all the plastic shoes and bodies and synthetic hair would only end up in landfills, like every other plastic toy they had once played with and then discarded. Barbie was still better than TikTok and all the other digital platforms preying on young girls' malleable and increasingly fragile identities, wasn't it? Overlaying such self-lacerating thoughts were images of Barbie being manufactured in a Chinese factory, the heads traveling down a conveyer belt before the scene cut to a woman in a white lab coat painstakingly bent over a blank oval face, painting an upturned smile onto it.

In the humid, bustling Fiumicino Rome Airport, where their next flight connected to Sofia, a long line snaked around the gate. Sam dropped his heavy backpack at his feet and sat on it, his head in his hands. Margot swung her bag back and forth, lightly hitting Ava's thigh each time.

In front of her, Ava noticed a gray-haired Italian man wearing ironed slacks and a crisp linen shirt, his gold-rimmed glasses resting on the bridge of his nose as he watched a video on his phone. The volume was on low but she heard gagging sounds. She inched closer and glanced over his shoulder. On the screen, a naked woman was bound to a chair with duct tape covering her mouth and a thick black cloth tied over her eyes. Her head flopped to one side as a man in dark clothing beat her with a leather strap. He then punched her in the stomach repeatedly, each punch swift and tight before she moaned into her neck.

"Jesus," Ava said under her breath and stepped away, clenching Margot's hand in hers. "What is it?" Sam asked loudly.

The man furtively glanced around and then slid the phone into his back pocket.

She stared at the outline of the phone in his gabardine slacks while so many words rushed into her mind: *It's disgusting that you watch this, there are children nearby, you like to see a woman tortured?* She wanted to scream. Scream about this, and scream that she lived in a country where the president boasted of his predatory power to grab women's genitalia, and how he could easily shoot a person on Fifth Avenue without losing any votes. She felt foolish and embarrassed now, thinking back to the euphoria of the Women's March two years ago, her son on her shoulders, her daughter's hand in hers. Euphoria wasn't enough. Pink pussyhats, white pantsuits, and "The Future Is Female" T-shirts weren't enough. Today, she'd read that he'd held a massive rally in Florida announcing his 2020 reelection campaign, the angry white male hordes inciting him with their burning love, anointing him as cult leader in chief. It mystified Ava how people could love so much hate. It mystified her even more that a good portion of the country embraced such leathery patriarchy with open arms. The regression felt dangerous, like a punishment for the hope and promise of the preceding years when things didn't seem so violent and turbulent, but now she realized this startling hatred had been there all along, just waiting for the pendulum to swing back so it could be freely unleashed, without shame, without hesitation.

Over the loudspeakers, the attendant announced boarding and the line shuffled forward. The man moved ahead and Ava tracked his dense gray hair. She wondered if it had been thrilling for him that she'd seen it. And he knew she now couldn't unsee it as he disappeared into the plane. When she passed through business class to get to their row behind the heavy parted curtain, she caught sight of him nestled into his voluminous beige leather seat reading the paper, a masquerade of respectability.

Only an hour remained until they landed in Sofia, and she braced for seeing Kasper again after so many months apart; her teeth were dirty, her skin coated by plane air and sebum, her eyes watering from dryness. Then again, he might not even be at the airport. He had mentioned that a production meeting could run over and she prepared for the kids' disappointment, willing herself not to let it mingle with her own. Craning her neck, she stared down at the scattered anonymous lights of some unidentified city below.

Margot pressed her nose into the tiny oval window, her warm

breath leaving marks on the plexiglass. Sam played *Minecraft* on his iPad, explaining that the villagers were pillaging while he released hot lava all over the town as part of the offensive. Every time more lava flowed, it made a tires-crunching-over-leaves sound that Ava found oddly soothing, as it helped fight off the dread balling in her stomach. What if they were unhappy in Bulgaria? What if this was all a big mistake? Kasper had warned them of the long shooting days, which would then turn into even longer night shoots, of how unavailable he'd be, that this wasn't a vacation. The marriage could implode under the film's demanding schedule, under the pressure she put on herself to produce a draft to justify the summer sabbatical, their desirous ambitions clashing in a cacophonic explosion.

And if the Bulgarian summer camp didn't work out she'd be stuck with the kids all day with no time to write. But then she revisited the phone conversation she'd had with Isabel, the wife of Marc, the second unit director. Maybe it was her Brazilian accent, but her voice carried a warm current, massaging Ava's anxieties. And even though she'd never met Isabel, just listening to her over the phone made Ava relax as Isabel talked about how her son Luca had loved Cosmos Kids when he attended last year while Marc was working on another movie at the same studio. The camp assigned activities for the children based on their astrological sign, and Luca was Pisces, so water play and swimming really suited him. "And when he was at camp, I had all day to devote to my online courses," she had said. "Bulgaria is a magical place, you will see," she added, lifting Ava's spirits.

Perhaps trying to fix their marriage wasn't a good idea right now, given what her therapist, Richard, had told her in their last session before this trip. He had explained that Kasper would be too tangled up in the film to hear her. It was the equivalent of trying to talk to a warrior about emotional reciprocity as said warrior hurled himself into battle, spear drawn, helmet clamped over his face, thousands of horses thundering at his back. Instead, Richard advised her to wait for when Kasper returned in September, after the film wrapped, to confront these issues, and then yeah, gloves off, radical honesty, let it rip, but this kind of waiting made her feel like a coiled viper, seething with future plans of attack. She wasn't sure it was the best strategy, shelving her distress until the right moment presented itself before she struck. But she wasn't sure about anything anymore.

Sinking into the airplane seat, she missed Richard and she missed the feeling of stepping into his office every Friday morning, a calm settling over her, like lying beneath a weighted blanket. She pictured herself sitting on the beige suede couch among the ochre-toned pillows with the red tassels that she sometimes wound around her fingers. He had numerous books in his bookcase, including *The Great Mother*, which she had read. She faintly remembered something about how a good mother provides food and emotional sustenance, but she could also become a devouring, castrating mother, evoking retributive hostility in the child.

Was she one of the good nurturing mothers?

Or good enough?

Richard's own book stood on the shelf as well. *Porn: The Forsaken Goddess*. The cover featured the ancient goddess Ishtar cupping a breast in each hand, her hips two swollen hills, her waist whittled into a triangular point, the background full of swirling psychedelic streaks of magenta and tangerine. The book argued that porn was the ultimate taboo in the consulting room because patients never mentioned it, creating a significant absence in the relationship between the patient and therapist.

Ava believed this was true; she couldn't imagine talking to Richard about watching porn. How the images paraded in her mind long afterward. How the women's pierced nipples looked both appealing and painful, as if miniature steel dumbbells intersected them. How it was always the man penetrating the woman, the woman an inert, docile recipient of his desire, emitting little breathless sighs of feigned pleasure. How she felt a hot shame watching a woman being handled as a passive, highly sexualized instrument of male pleasure and she perpetuated the continuation of this archaic script by watching and liking it. What this said about her could only be bad. Maybe she was secretly a woman who hated women. A woman so culturally conditioned that she found mainstream porn hot. A woman with no sexual imagination, who only wanted to watch the oldest stupidest sexual fantasy that wasn't about sex at all but about power. A woman who was no different, perhaps, from that Italian man watching torture porn on his phone.

Well, she didn't have time to watch porn anyway. Part of her wanted to admit to Richard that she watched it incessantly, and that by aligning with his research she would become his best, most prized patient. His favorite. She often imagined Richard discussing her case with his cohorts, explaining how interesting and unique she was, how developed, how she far surpassed his other patients in the art of self-reflection. She also knew the purpose of therapy was not to dazzle the therapist with her brilliance or to make Richard love her, even as she couldn't stop herself from wanting to become his star pupil. The point of therapy, she had been told, was to grow comfortable with discomfort, with the notion that the therapist might not particularly like her and that she might find fault with him as well, and that they should freely verbalize such feelings in the safety of the consulting room. To have fights even, where patient and therapist could confront their shadowy ugly parts, which seemed impossible and embarrassing to Ava.

She stared out the oval window, at the unending pitch-dark, wondering if there would be a way to talk to Richard over the phone in Bulgaria. Her eleven a.m. time slot on Fridays translated to nine p.m. in Bulgaria, which seemed unworkable given all the variables of dinner and bedtime. Maybe she wouldn't need to talk to him as much as before. Maybe this summer would thaw some of her bitterness. Maybe she would view Kasper in a different light instead of focusing on all the freedom and boundless ambition she imagined he enjoyed without her. And she should be grateful for the magical arrival of the summer sabbatical, allowing her to travel here and work on her book. And grateful that production covered the cost of their travel as well as the apartment Kasper had rented for them.

And as far as she could tell, he hadn't yet fallen for one of those young nubile Bulgarian extras strutting around set, whispering Eastern promises. Right?

The captain announced that they were preparing for landing, the seat belt sign lighting up, coinciding with Sam whispering that he needed to pee.

The flight attendants strapped themselves into their jump seats. The plane plummeted downward.

"I really have to go."

"You can't," Ava said, pointing to the lit sign.

"I can't hold it," Sam said, squinting.

"You have to."

Sam shook his head and they both watched his gray sweatpants darken.

3

Sofia, June 2019

They landed at ten o'clock at night, the thick moist air hitting their faces as they stepped outside the tiny airport. Kasper waited in the rain-soaked parking lot, staring abstractedly into the murky night. Running across the glistening concrete, the kids flung themselves into his arms, breathless and delighted. Ava pushed the cart overloaded with their luggage toward him even though it kept swerving because of a broken front wheel. She felt real unadulterated joy at the sight of him, despite everything. He was here, tired but happy to see them. He pulled her into his chest. She inhaled his familiar scent, crushing her face into his shirt, closing her eyes, allowing herself to sink into the moment, however fragile and temporary it was. The kids started yelling excitedly because the cart skidded away, threatening to crash into another cart. She lurched toward it but Kasper wouldn't let her go, his strong arms holding her in place. "Who cares about the stupid cart? You're here!"

She laughed into his chest. "But the luggage . . ."

He kissed her with deep intent, as if to communicate all the waiting and longing they'd endured these past months while she confessed that her teeth were dirty, her face unwashed, but he shook his head, said he didn't care, and kissed her again.

Nikolay, the production van driver, waited for them, leaning against the door. Wearing a white tank top and acid-washed jeans, he extended his arms, as if he expected Ava to rush in for a bear hug. Kasper high-fived him and Nikolay slapped Kasper on the back, bellowing out, "So happy the family is here now!"

Kasper laughed, agreeing that yes, he was more than happy. He was overjoyed.

Nikolay yanked open the van's sliding door and the kids scrambled inside, claiming the back row. He reiterated how sad and lonely Kasper had been without her. "He miss you very much."

"Good," Ava said, and they all laughed.

In the van, they peered out at the city, trying to make sense of it, but from the highway they only saw looming apartment buildings lit up yellow inside, interspersed with large patches of dark foliage that, Kasper explained, were sprawling green parks. He promised the kids they'd love these parks, and Nikolay added that in summer, there were carousels and go-carts. "Lots of fun. Kids love it!"

The kids nodded, falling under Nikolay's bombastic spell. And they kept looking at Kasper, watching him talk to Nikolay and Ava, as if just being in his presence felt magical, like a fairy tale.

Ava also sensed the newness of Kasper, the novelty of sitting in a car with him, her hand in his, feeling the dryness of his palm, its smoothness and heat. The van flitted past monuments of soldiers and former communist leaders illuminated by bright white lights.

Nikolay flicked a cigarette butt out the window, the radio playing Bulgarian techno, and talked about how close they were to Greece, only a six-hour drive. "I drive you all to Greece for weekend trip! What do you say?"

"Sure," Kasper said, winking at Ava, a wink that meant they wouldn't actually travel with Nikolay to Greece.

"Are we close to the apartment?" Ava asked, trying to get her bearings.

"In a few minutes," Kasper said, squeezing her hand. "We'll turn off the highway and drive into the city center. Right now we're still in the outskirts."

She motioned to the large dark mountains in the distance. "And over there?"

"The Vitosha Mountains. The lot and the production offices are in the foothills of those mountains, in a suburb called Boyana. I'll show you all around tomorrow."

"Boyana very nice neighborhood," Nikolay interjected. "Fancy place."

Ava nodded, staring at the mountains scattered with points of light.

When they arrived at the apartment it was almost midnight. Humming under his breath, Nikolay unloaded all the suitcases while Kasper opened the heavy steel door, the key sticking in the lock for a moment before it gave way. Ava looked up at the communist block building, made of crumbling white stucco with bars on the windows, a TV flickering from one of the apartments. An old woman in a housedress and sandals glanced down from a nearby balcony and gave her a toothless grin. The street was quiet and dark save for a few feral cats scampering alongside the buildings, their tails tensely lowered. An impressive nineteenth-century domed building rose up half a block away, maybe an opera house or a theater. She wanted to ask Nikolay about it, but he was sliding the van door shut, and Kasper was already in the entryway, dragging one of her massive suitcases up the cracked cement stairs. Ava heaved two other duffel bags, catching her breath on each landing. The kids asked why there wasn't an elevator.

She shook her head, too tired to answer.

The apartment had high ceilings, wooden floors, and white walls. Large bay windows looked out to the decrepit high-rises across the street. They dropped the suitcases in the middle of the empty living room. The kids were hungry but there wasn't any food.

Kasper ran out to buy something to eat, leaving her to investigate this strange place that smelled faintly of cigarettes, bleach. And cats.

She immediately disliked the apartment, but tried to reason with herself that it wasn't so bad while searching for towels and soap so they could shower. She didn't know if it was safe to drink from the tap, but noting a pack of bottled water next to the sink, she decided against it. Margot and Sam flung themselves onto the gray suede couch in front of the TV. Ava walked gingerly over to the large glass windows, staring at the dark apartment windows across the way.

Then she checked the bedrooms: each room housed one bed with a bath mat beside it, apparently in place of a rug. She didn't know where to unpack the clothing and toiletries, as there were no countertops or cupboards or closets, and realized the apartment might have formerly been an office.

Sam clutched his stomach and moaned that he was so hungry he could die. She reminded him that they'd eaten on the plane, he wasn't starving, not even close, but he was extremely attached to the performance of his hunger.

Margot turned on the TV and started watching *Charlie's Angels* dubbed in Bulgarian. Ava unzipped one of the suitcases, filled to the brim with ACE bandages, Margot's nasal spray, lavender oil, Tylenol, Pepto Bismol, tampons, Miralax. It was the medical supplies suitcase, not the one with their clothes and toiletries. She closed it and sat on top of its hard shell, putting her head in her hands, too tired to rifle through another bag in search of clean underwear and toothbrushes.

On TV, the sound of explosions intensified in volume, ringing in her ears.

Sam suddenly sat up on the couch. "Don't they have Uber Eats here?"

A knock on the door startled them.

Ava opened it to the sight of Kasper holding a six-pack of Bulgarian beer in one hand, a loaf of bread and Nutella in the other. "Sorry. This was all I could find at this hour."

After gorging on Nutella smeared onto the soft white bread, the kids fell asleep on top of their bedspreads, still in their dirty clothes from the plane. Even though they were far too old for this, Ava tugged off their shoes and deftly changed them into clean pajamas before switching off the light.

They made love beneath the scratchy sheets. She had to get used to his body again, to being touched and held, so accustomed to her solitary nights when she had her thoughts to herself, her body cordoned off, belonging solely to her. Did she look different? Feel different? She relearned the weight of his body, the smoothness of his back punctuated by a splash of raised moles, the density of his breath on her neck, his fingers roving through her hair.

Afterward, the stark moonlight streaming through the dirty windows, they tried to catch up on the last three months. He told her that today he'd had an argument with Sergei about the visual-effects supervisor, who, during location scouting, incessantly played *Angry Birds* on his phone and, in production meetings, sat cross-legged in the middle of the conference table while smoking a pipe. Kasper had been fighting to fire him for weeks, but Sergei, or rather his wife, Olga, had final approval over the visual effects. "For a film with two thousand VFX shots, it's a real problem."

With her head on his chest, listening to his steady heartbeat, she told him that the kids would start camp next week once they got settled and she hoped to write during the day. Hoped there would be enough time.

"Yes," he mumbled, his solid palm resting on her back. He said he would try to have dinner with them most nights, but he couldn't promise, every day being so unexpected and chaotic, and Ava whispered, "I know, I know."

"How's the book going?" he asked.

She described how it was challenging given its hybrid nature; narrative nonfiction and at the same time, a monograph of one woman's life in ancient Athens, in 415 BC.

He nodded sleepily and she went on to say it was like filling in the blanks of history's silences of what an ordinary woman's life might have been like if she was literate and could write, if her experiences were considered worth recording, if she considered them worth recording. "I'm trying to inhabit an ancient consciousness to reclaim what the other half of the population experienced because we only know what men thought of themselves and what they thought of women, but not what women thought of women. In a way, the present could reanimate the past, reframe it—"

His snore, uneven and loud, interrupted her.

She listened to the rumble of streetcars, the ding of bicycles whizzing past, cars careening around corners, a bus screeching to a halt, the mechanized sigh of its doors opening and closing. In the distance, techno music throbbed.

And then finally, the quiet of night descended, a blanket of calm over the city.

4

I rise before dawn, in the purplish half-light. Birds stir in the courtyard treetops. The dog begins pacing down below, impatient for food. In other rooms, women and girls sigh, tossing and turning, my daughter among them, the one I will lose the soonest, as we soberly count the moons until her wedding, trying to coax and convince her that her future husband, a second cousin and a hoplite, has much to offer, but she roars with fury whenever I utter his name. I remind her that soon, she will no longer belong to her father's house and when I lit the household altar and put her doll next to the burning incense as a small offering for now, reciting a prayer to Artemis, the protector of virgins and forests, the benefactress of marriage, Eirene grew even angrier, and I feared her contaminating rage, afraid of how the gods would react, afraid she might be punished for such insolence with an uneasy childbirth, or worse.

I think back to my daughter as a young girl, only a few years ago, acting the part of the "little bear" swathed in saffron robes, frolicking around Artemis's sanctuary with the other little bear-girls, all of them untamed, untethered, reveling in their ritual wildness as they performed the arkteia, the slow solemn dance akin to the heavy steps of a bear, the double flute's sweet melody accompanying them. We women watched, having undergone the same ritual ourselves so many years past, and there we were, but as mothers, hoping to appease Artemis once again, vying for her protection, desiring that she guide our daughters through the narrowing isthmus of girlhood into the open sea of maturation.

About to rise from bed, to perform my laving before draining the chamber pot and rousing the slaves down below to light the hearths, gently I place a hand on Xanthe's ankle, touching her cool milky skin, feeling the blood pulse beneath it. She is my closest companion, my secret sister, and enslaved. My husband purchased Xanthe from her father ten years ago in Thrace during a military campaign. In moments of melancholy, the sulfuric sting of the Black Sea fills her nostrils, and when her eyes swim with water, I know she feels the crush of her mother's last embrace, the woman's misshapen coral beads denting her cheek, the saltiness of their intermingled tears. I hold her and together we mourn her lost sisters and brothers, the towering pine trees and lush forests she used to roam, the river full of stones that caught the light.

He brought Xanthe home with a handful of others from Caria, Macedon, and as far as Tanais at the mouth of the Don. We greeted the new slaves, tossed dried figs and nuts at the bedraggled procession as they shuffled into the courtyard. Like a wedding, I thought, taking in her shorn hair, her eyes the color of the changeable sea, one moment gray, one moment green, as her darting glance, swimming with fear, found mine. She was still a girl, having barely tasted the pains of womanhood, her gait unsteady, her limbs long and slender.

At that point, I was unaware of her talents in practical alchemy that she later revealed, once we trusted each other. She knows how to make silver golden by using Cyprian cadmia. Yellow the whitish stone with the bile of a calf, terebinth resin, castor oil, and egg yolk, which creates a golden sheen once combined and painted on the stone and then, gold.

Magic, I breathed.

No, she replied teasingly. "Nature conquering nature. Not so magical."

She has many other talents, hidden to most, such as concocting herbal remedies for potential ailments. Blood of a hare's fetus for fertile semen. Nine pellets of a hare's dung for durable, firm breasts. She knows the correct plants to attract magical beings or repel them with the use of hallucinogenic herbs and soporific substances, and she remembers the right proportions and combinations by consulting the two papyrus scrolls she managed to smuggle into her strophion, instructions handed down from her mother and, I assume, her mother's mother. She also interprets the stars and planets, their position in relation to a person's birth, which makes me tremble at the thought of what she knows of my fate, and my children's fate.

But that first morning when Xanthe arrived, bewildered in the courtyard, she reminded me of me, of the raw rushing terror I felt upon entering my husband's house for the first time, still warm from my nurse's embrace, still imbued with her scent (beetroot, milled flour, sweat), not knowing what kind of man awaited me.

But now I know. I know how little he sees me and how little he matters given his long absences that stretch over months and into years. And yet, in the dark I recognize his face with the touch of my fingertips: weather-beaten and cracked with age, a constellation of jagged crevices. I know his barrel chest coated with gray unruly hair and his muscular thighs crosshatched with scars, marking where he has cheated death. I know how he used to burrow into me, the sharp jolts of pain mixed with release quickly upended by the satisfied grunt of his sated pleasure while I still grasped for more, my desirous nature roaming through the thick withholding dark. I know he enjoys the varied pleasures of Athenian prostitutes, one in particular whom I often glimpse strolling the Agora, her purple robes trailing in the dust, her hooded eyes avoiding mine. She has borne him a son whom he loves, inexplicably, more than all the children I have ever given him.

None of this pierces as deep as it once did, as I approach the autumn of my years and he has left again, for the Sicilian invasion, armed with a fleet of one hundred triremes and five thousand hoplites. In my bones, I doubt his return. This is what the priestesses whisper through the burning incense: the hubris of men, with their chests as puffed up as pigeons, their grand ideas about future riches driving them onward, although this time, the generals, in their greedy haste, failed to make the correct sacrifices to the gods. And the ocean is rough. The city-state Segesta, the one they plan to capture in the south, may not be as wealthy as once believed, and perhaps Sparta is laying a trap. I think of his impending battles, his death even, as a momentary prick of salt on my tongue: brief bitterness and then I swallow it down. I have grown strong healthy children and I have the comfort of other women, our lives interwoven, creating a tapestry of care; friends and sisters, daughters and grandmothers, aunts, and even, despite inherent rivalries, mothers-in-law.

We laugh into the night, bursting with careless joy from the unexpected relief of absent husbands and dead ones, or relief from the ones who regard us as disparagingly as threadbare rugs, as pieces of cast-off driftwood. We need few words to describe our invisibility as we've all watched our husbands leave for the next campaign, or leave for the heat of another body, a younger, more supple one. When we exchange glances over a kindling fire, we don't have to explain the pain of losing our daughters to marriage and our sons to battle, our houses emptying of children as the years pass while we reapproach our long-buried girlhoods, our forgotten freedoms. We communicate this in one thrumming heartbeat, the stars shawling us, the forest breathing through our hair, harboring the sensation that every woman extends backward into her mother and forward into her children, our lives stretching over generations reverberating with this one perfect truth: we make the world and we can destroy it too.

5

Ava awoke to the sound of Kasper preparing coffee in the kitchen. Harsh daylight streamed through the windows in the living room, illuminating dust bunnies on the hardwood floor. She walked into a rectangle of sunlight, realizing there were no curtains. Anyone from the neighboring buildings could see her standing here in her underwear, but then she stared at the opposite windows and saw an older man in a bathrobe making tea, and in the next window a grandmother traipsed around her apartment naked from the waist up, her large, pendulous breasts cascading down her stomach while she smoked a cigarette.

For a brief moment, they made eye contact.

"You're leaving already?" she asked, trying to mask her nervousness.

Kasper handed her a cup of coffee and then poured another one for himself, explaining that the van was due to pick him up in ten minutes, he should have been at the production office already, but he wanted to make sure he explained everything to her before he left. On the dining room table were keys to the apartment and Nikolay's number if she needed the van for anything. "Your cell phone works here now—I set it up this morning on an international plan." She would come to the lot with the kids for lunch. Nikolay would drive them. "But let them rest, catch up on sleep." He kissed her quickly. She caught the fresh taste of his minty toothpaste, and then he was gone.

Staring at the metal front door, she lingered in the aftermath of his presence, as if she could still touch and talk with him, look at his face. Walking over to the galley kitchen, she opened the miniature fridge, finding a bushel of green grapes, six strawberry yogurts, and more bottled water. Snapping off a grape, she popped it into her mouth, grateful that Kasper must have gone out earlier to buy some essentials while she was sleeping.

Sitting down at the table, she studied the map, trying to figure out where they were in relation to the city center. The opera house was two streets away, surrounded by a large green park, as well as various churches and squares. She circled the National History Museum and wondered how long it would take to walk there. The museum had on loan the Locrian pinakes, a series of terra-cotta plaques from the fifth century BC unearthed near the sanctuary of Eleusis in Greece. The plaques narrate the myth of Demeter, the mother goddess of agriculture and grain and her virgin daughter Persephone: the first shows a girl embracing her mother while an older woman stands behind them holding up a marriage peplos. The second plaque portrays Hades's abduction of Persephone on his chariot descending into the underworld. The next scene displays Demeter weeping into the mirthless rock, mourning the loss of her daughter, and the fourth tablet shows the reunification of mother and daughter, similar to the first plaque, but it takes place after her loss of virginity; she's returning to her mother as a wife and mother herself, no longer the innocent young girl picking flowers. Ava thought about how separation begets reunification and reunification begets separation, recalling how when Margot slams her door in a rage, minutes later she emerges remorseful, flinging her arms around Ava before inevitably pushing her away again.

The museum also held an Athenian drinking cup from the same period showing a wild maenad, a female follower of Dionysus, the god of wine and madness. On the cup, she's gripped by manic possession as she dances barefoot, holding a spear (thyrsus) in one hand, in the other dangling a panther cub by its hind legs. Her hair is loose and spinning as she swirls, dancing ecstatically in honor of the god. Ava had read about how in ancient Greece, bands of women abandoned their homes and hearths, their shuttles and looms, and fled to the mountains, leaving everything behind including husbands and children. In the wild, under the influence of the god's frenzy, women unleashed every buried desire as they danced in the holy darkness.

The freedom to leave behind all domestic responsibilities, to step out of her identity as a wife and mother and head for the hills sounded delicious to Ava. She imagined drums, wine, secrecy, the unleashing of repressed impulses all justified as part of the god's ritual worship.

Dog-earing the guidebook map, she wanted to understand the layers of this city: Thracian, Greek, Roman, Byzantine, Ottoman, breathing beneath blocks of USSR era mass housing and the glass-paneled offices, neoclassical nineteenth-century concert halls, and 1950s Soviet modernism. Leafing through the pages, she felt an affinity with this ancient city steeped in stories and myths, battles and bloodshed, and unfinished business.

A delicate nut-colored bird tapped against the window and startled her. Luckily the window was closed. Whenever a bird flew into the house she panicked, feeling a deep need to keep the outside out. On its wing bend, she caught sight of a light blue panel and recalled the blue jays, harbingers of good luck, flitting from branch to branch at home in Topanga. She hoped the bird, perched on the balcony now, with its blue wing, meant good luck for Kasper's movie, for her book project, and for their marriage after all these months apart. From an early age, she had been superstitious, interpreting signs and symbols as predictors of the future, similar to the way seers in ancient Greece used birds, the livers of sacrificed animals, and other methods of divination to foretell the fate of an invading army, a marriage, the trajectory of an emperor's reign. Five years ago, on the first day of teaching her introductory seminar on Greco-Roman art, she was walking to class and passed a dead crow on the quad nestled in the dewy grass, its black feathers sticking up at an odd angle, and a quiet dread rumbled through her, bringing with it the sense that the semester would fail. The premonition turned into truth. Her students were dispassionate, while a select few dominated the class, causing rancor and jealousy among the others, who felt ignored. The students complained about this dynamic as well as their low grades in the teacher evaluations, the anonymous comments scathing.

She watched the bird hop along the balcony railing and wondered if it was a Eurasian jay, mostly found in wooded forests. But then why was it here, in the middle of the city? Good luck, she decided. After all, Kasper had managed to be there last night at the airport, brimming with optimism at their arrival. Maybe things would fall into place now that they were together. Maybe the marriage would improve without having to say too much about the lonely, resentful months without him, and the years before that too.

Sam wandered into the living room in his underwear, his bare chest perfectly tan, his bleary eyes blinking into the bright sunlight. She gestured for him to come look at the bird, but it had flitted away. He plopped down on her lap, his head lolling into her chest, and together they flipped through the guidebook. With her index finger, she traced various cathedrals and museums.

He wondered where Kasper was.

Taking a sip of lukewarm coffee, she reminded Sam that he was working, they shouldn't think of this as a family vacation. At night, when he was done with the day, she hoped they would meet up for dinner. And today they'd visit the studio. While explaining this, she imagined exploring the city with the kids, modeling adaptability and the capacity for adventure even if the street names were in Cyrillic and she didn't speak the language.

She flipped to the back of the guidebook and sounded out a few basic phrases that made Sam laugh: Dobar den! (Добър ден!/Doh-bur dehn!) Blagodarya! (Благодаря!/Blah-goh-da-rya!) Dovijdane! (Довиждане!/Doh-veezh-dah-nay!), but the large glass windows next to the table distracted her with its dazzling fractured light. The windows slanted open at the top, filtering in traffic sounds and congested air, but she realized they also swung open from the side, and because the windowsill was only a few feet from the floor, she pictured how easily Margot and Sam might tip out the window, hurtling six stories down onto the hot glittering pavement.

In the next room, she heard Margot opening and closing drawers, sighing with frustration.

Ava closed her eyes, pressing her face into Sam's rumpled hair, saying that they would also check out the summer camp today. It was right next to the studio, close to where Kasper worked.

"But I want to stay with you," he protested, clinging to her.

"You'll get bored going to museums all day."

"I won't."

"You will. You'll see."

Margot stormed into the living room wearing these fuzzy angora pajama shorts that Ava disliked and a padded bra. In one hand, she held her iPad and Ava vaguely wondered how long she had been on that thing. Her hair was loose and wild, spilling over her shoulders. She put her hands on her hips and stared accusingly at them. "Where's Papa?"

"He left for work," Ava said, her mouth dry, bracing herself for an argument.

"What?" she said, throwing up her hands. "He didn't even say goodbye? Does he care about me, even?"

"Of course he cares," Ava said without enough conviction.

"Yeah, right," Sam added with a sharpened sarcasm that made Ava's chest hurt.

"Listen," Ava said, gently pushing Sam off her lap. "Remember what I said about how he has to work while we're here? That this isn't a vacation?"

"This is summer break," Margot roared. "Why do you keep saying it's not?"

"I didn't say that," Ava said, her voice rising. When she was Margot's age, she never dared take this tone with her parents, or with anyone, too busy striving for some elusive gold medal. Why didn't Margot care about being good? Even a little bit? Why was anger always a breath away for her, so readily accessible?

Adrenaline rushed into Ava's limbs. She felt a fight coming.

Sensing trouble, Sam stalked off to the bedroom to change.

"On our first morning here, the first thing he does is leave? Again?" Margot loosely held the iPad in her hand and Ava imagined that it might get thrown somewhere. Maybe at her head. Maybe at the wall. Or at the window, crashing through the glass. She could never be sure.

Trying to keep her voice level, Ava started to explain that they would see him today for lunch; he was excited to show them around the set.

Margot interrupted, "I don't care about his stupid movie!" and then in one swift motion, she hurled the iPad at the steel door.

It left a small dent.

They both stared at the door.

A somatic weariness infused Ava, jet lag seeping into her bones. She sighed, head in her hands. "Feel better now?"

Margot swung around to face her, cocking out one hip defiantly. How much of her rage was performance? How much of it was real? Could Margot tell the difference between the two? Could Ava?

A naughty giddiness stirred in Margot's eyes, and Ava, sensing the absurdity of the situation, burst into uncontrolled laughter, followed by Margot's hiccupping laugh. They bent over, holding their stomachs, eyes watering.

Sam hollered from the other room, "What's so funny?"

6

T hirteen years ago, when they came home from the hospital with
Margot, it had stunned Ava to discover that her body and her
life had been irrevocably altered while Kasper's routine and physical appearance remained relatively the same. It was a secret no one
had told her, and she was shocked to witness him still enjoying many
pleasures of their pre-baby life: driving to work with the top down,
the warm wind sifting through his hair, taking showers and exercis-
ing, grabbing a drink with a friend after work, moving through the
world without being perpetually tethered to an entirely new human
with her own specific set of needs and wants.

On their fifth morning home from the hospital, Ava cradled Margot in her arms, this new pink body swaddled in muslin, the baby's
cheek pressed to her chest, a sheen of sweat gathering between
their skin, the morning sun pale through the bedroom windows.
She gently rocked Margot back and forth in the recliner, her breasts
aching, an ice pack wedged inside her underwear to lessen the pain
of the third-degree tears in her perineum. The stitches would dissolve all on their own, the doctor had announced triumphantly, as
if she should celebrate this feat of modern medicine. The breast
pump stood next to her on the desk so that she could pump after
nursing to start saving up milk to freeze for when she went back
to work, but the machine intimidated her with its valves and tubes
and flanges.

She was trying to reach a magazine on the desk without moving
too much when Kasper announced that he was leaving for work.
He said it simply, without regret or hesitation, fully dressed, his
messenger bag slung across his chest, the soapy scent of his freshly

showered body and woodsy aftershave permeating the room. They had only just arrived home a few days ago. He couldn't leave yet.

She wasn't ready.

Not at all.

Hold on, she thought, *I'm a mother now. I should be able to do this without any help. On my own, naturally.* But it jarred her, how he could leave this little life in her arms, utterly dependent upon Ava for survival. Seeing the expression on her face, he gently explained that a week had passed and it was time for him to return to the office.

"I just thought you'd stay home a little longer," she managed, a hard knot gathering in her throat, her head swimming with past conversations they'd had about his taking time off after the birth, something about one week bookended by two weekends, or was it five days bridged by a long weekend?

"I wish I could," he whispered and she couldn't speak when he gave her a quick peck on the cheek.

Ava listened for the front door to close and seconds later, it did.

Her life as a mother truly began in that moment: she alone would keep this child alive, and the difficulty that lay ahead was reserved solely and purposefully for her.

This, she realized, was motherhood.

During those endless first days at home, flashes of 1950s advertisements for washing machines and refrigerators skittered through her mind: women in full skirts and tightly cinched waists smiling brightly at their linoleum floors and clean countertops, some even finding their own reflections in the polished veneer. Ava scoffed at the idea that this stifling and regressive version of motherhood reflected her circumstances in any way, but after she fed and changed Margot and put her down in the bassinet, praying Margot would sleep for at least thirty minutes, she glanced around at the unmade bed, the diaper bin filled to the brim, emitting that sickening slightly sweet smell of infant excrement mixed with urine, and realized that the rest of the day stretched before her into an endless series of menial tasks that, by their nature, would never reach full completion, as such tasks required repetition, constant replenishment, hour after hour. She would probably change Margot's diaper ten more times within the next six hours, snap and unsnap the one-sie, check her phone for missed calls or text messages from Kasper, breastfeed, pump, change Margot, put her down for a nap, check her phone again.

This circular loop of activity ensured Margot's well-being, while it tore holes through Ava's former self. Would she ever read again? Write? Think clearly and critically about an abstract idea without it being overshadowed by a pressing desire for organic baby wipes instead of the regular ones they'd bought, or by the question of whether co-sleeping definitely caused SIDS?

Without the will to resist this overwhelming minutiae, she witnessed her world tapering down to the purely physical, immediate, material: she needed more balm for her nipples so they wouldn't crack, the swaddling blanket kept unraveling, the sound machine failed to replicate a human heartbeat, which only added to Margot's fussiness, and she was dehydrated from nursing every two hours, her throat perpetually parched with thirst.

It also hurt to take a shit.

They went on long walks. They fell asleep together on the half-made bed, the late afternoon light streaming through the large windows. Ava recalled that strong unadulterated sunlight prevented jaundice, so she kept Margot in just a diaper at home, delighted to see the squares of sun shining down on Margot's bare chubby thighs.

After she fed Margot, Margot fell asleep again, her tiny mouth poised on Ava's nipple, her breathing steady and calm, and Ava, petrified to move lest she waken her, had to remain still, half wondering when she would return to work, or if she would return at all, given that the idea seemed so unfathomable in this moment as she sat here, barefoot, exhausted, with unbrushed teeth and greasy hair, imprisoned by the hope that Margot would stay asleep for more than thirty minutes at a time.

She feared fading into the oblivion of motherhood, as she saw some of her friends take this path, friends who now appeared unrecognizable to Ava in their billowy smocks and stretched-out leggings, their faces scrubbed clean of makeup, their breasts leaking milk at certain times of the day even three years after birth because they'd kept breastfeeding.

But she was lucky to stay home with Margot. Kasper was missing out on these golden hours when time stretched and suspended, their breath coalescing into one breath, submerging them in a kind of amniotic serenity, the past and future obliterated by the overwhelming now. She was lucky to have this time, and lucky that work waited on the other side of these months, Kasper suggesting that she take more time if needed, she shouldn't rush back to her degree.

But she wanted to return. She knew this, even while suffering from sleep deprivation and flooded with anxiety over the tiniest of things, such as how to cut a baby's fingernails.

Margot had been born a few months before the end of a spring semester and Ava still had one year left to finish her PhD, the dissertation hanging in the balance in terms of who would sit on her committee, and she feared the quality of her work would suffer under these new conditions. At the moment, she didn't have much interest in the transition from the eighth-century geometric patterning on Greek vessels, decorative but without a story, to the use of figurative detail in the seventh century. When she thought about her argument, her brain clouded into murky boredom, and even the spark that had ignited her in the first place—that in the seventh century, for the first time, artists used bodies to show encounters with the gods—left her dull and depressed, depleted by the thought of all those meticulous notes she had taken in preparation to write.

And even though it felt true, she bristled at the term "mommy brain" that described a pregnant woman's absent-mindedness, an explanation for why women misplaced keys, or left the car trunk wide open, or walked into a room only to forget what they were searching for. A term roiling with misogyny. Ava saw that it extended beyond pregnancy into an undetermined number of years after birth. A term used by women and men alike, in a cheerful, well-meaning tone that suggested it was all in good fun, a woman's cognitive impairment.

But it wasn't all lethargy and forgetfulness. She was on high alert, noting every shift in Margot's mood so that she could learn about her, help her, love her. What made her fall asleep easily? What caused her to cry torturously in the middle of the night? Was the organic unscented extra-sensitive detergent causing her to break out in a rash, or was it something else?

The constant attention and care rendered to Margot made the rest of her life dissolve into vagueness and abstraction. It wasn't mommy brain. It was a brain so sharp and attentive to the survival of this little life that nothing else mattered. Forget about car keys and watering houseplants. Forget birthdays and thank-you notes. Forget everything. Especially forget an unfinished dissertation about geometric vases from the seventh century BC.

Even if she forced herself to sit in a locked room and write, she couldn't. Out of sight but never out of mind, consumed with all things Margot: pediatrician appointments, head circumferences, percentiles for weight and height. Feeding schedules, nap time, bath time, bedtime, tummy time.

The way Ava let Margot gobble up her undivided attention while knowing that she should apply herself to her studies reminded her of when she was an undergraduate, when all of her energy and focus were directed toward an older boyfriend she was involved with at the time. Someone she gave up too much for. Someone who, in return, gave up nothing. Such heightened feelings combined with the inability to think of anything else was not unlike now, with Margot. If Margot grew hysterical during bath time, Ava frantically hid her own distress while trying to soothe her. If Margot felt sleepy, Ava also nodded off. If Margot was happy, Ava's heart lifted with exhilaration. *Happy baby, happy mother*. Or maybe it was the other way around: *Happy mother, happy baby*, an insidious phrase implying that if she was unhappy in any way, Margot would pick up on the vibration of her emotions and mirror them. One way or another, a mother was faulted, blamed, and judged if there was anything remotely wrong with her baby.

Ava remembered meeting Erin at the Getty Villa, both of them encumbered with newborns while they blinked with exhaustion into the bright daylight that cascaded over the herb gardens and fruit trees and stone fountains emitting the soothing sound of water moving.

Sitting down on a nearby bench, both of their babies miraculously asleep in the canvas carriers strapped to their chests, Erin offered a piece of Zen wisdom she had just read, about how children were only guests in their houses. From the moment they're born, they needed to prepare themselves to let them go, that this was the true work of parenting. Growing them up so they could leave and forge their own path. "It's like holding a baby bird. Too tight and you crush her. Not close enough and she flies away too soon, unprotected. Hold her with the knowledge of future flight."

Ava thought about this as she soaked up the many listless afternoons singing to Margot, pacing the bedroom and rocking Margot in her arms while staring out at the palm trees swaying in the breeze against a flat blue sky, the feeling of oneness still coursing between them, as if they were still connected by blood and fluid, multiplying cells and placental tissue. It seemed impossible that Margot would grow up and separate from her, leading a life that didn't necessarily include Ava. She might even shun everything Ava had taught her. Incomprehensible, Ava mused, as the empty, delicious hours rolled by and Margot nodded off in the stroller after a long walk. Ava sat on the front porch, gently nudging the stroller back and forth (Margot needed constant movement to stay asleep), and observed the sky change from brilliant blue to deep indigo, the darkening color signaling that soon, Kasper would be home.

Every day when he relieved her around six o'clock felt like a miniature celebration: finally she could shower, change from one pair of sweatpants to another, and maybe even read a book for a few snatched moments. Staring at the printed words blurring together in the failing light, she overheard Kasper energetically change Margot's diaper, announcing every step of the process, making up a funny song about wipes and diaper cream as he went, feeling heroic about fulfilling his paternal duties with overwhelming enthusiasm while Ava realized that so many new mothers, including herself, became submerged in the undertow, lost sight of themselves, of who they once were and who they wanted to be.

As the weeks with Margot turned into months, she resented Kasper. Resented his freedom, his carefree glibness as he strode through the front door whistling, surprised to hear that it had been a rough day absent of naps and full of gas, or an inordinate amount of spit-up. The word "colic" hovered on the tip of Ava's tongue like a curse.

When she handed off Margot, who had been crying for the last four hours, Ava realized Kasper didn't give a fleeting thought to the questions plaguing her because he didn't have to. As a man, he was naturally released from such deliberations, murmuring into Ava's ear that whatever she decided was surely the right thing.

But at night, she lay awake thinking hard: Stay at home, but for how long? Was there an ideal age at which one could leave an infant in the care of someone else, i.e., not the baby's mother, without irrevocably scarring the child? Who would care for Margot in her absence and how would she find such a person? Was daycare safer because there were more eyes watching, or was a babysitter preferable, showering Margot with individual attention? Could Ava trust anyone beside herself? Could she trust herself? And if she could trust someone else, it would most likely cost a fortune, eclipsing her small student stipend. And once back in grad school, at what capacity could she work? How many undergrad courses would she be able to teach while also writing her dissertation?

She remembered going to her gynecologist for the three-month postpartum checkup. Her gynecologist, an older woman who had two grown daughters of her own, listened with concern as Ava explained her anxieties about returning to her studies and leaving Margot with a sitter, but at the same time, she admitted that she was unhappy staying home. Home was stifling and physically demanding, and she felt her mind wasting away, turning to mush, having gone unused for so many months. "I don't know if I'll ever write again. Or teach," she said, her voice breaking as she stared down at the gray linoleum floor, at the doctor's sensible flats.

Dr. Singh held up one stern finger in front of Ava and drew an imaginary circle around it with her other hand. "You are the center of your household. If you are unhappy, everyone is unhappy. You need to do what is best for you and all will fall into place. You'll see."

After this, she knew she had to return to work, Dr. Singh's firm finger floating in and out of her field of vision. The country of mothers, entry into which seemed to include forfeiting one's former identity, *not with a bang but a whimper*, was not for her. She started interviewing babysitters and wearing jeans again, the hard denim proof that the edges of herself hadn't entirely dissolved.

She found an older woman who smelled of starch and talked too much and Margot wailed the minute the woman picked her up, but eventually she calmed down. And eventually, Ava got into her car with still-wet hair, determined to drive to the university, determined to leave behind those yawning days of closeness, with all of its intensity and boredom, just for a few hours. She repeated under her breath: *The baby is a guest in your house, a guest in your house,* while gripping the steering wheel, unable at first to actually drive away, unable to move, so overcome with guilt and longing for her daughter, overcome by the separation that was occurring now, and by all the future separations they would endure to become themselves.

She drove away that day, and the day after, and the day after that until the pain dulled and grew routine, until it became part of her. The sight of Margot calm, clean, and well-fed greeted Ava upon her return in the late afternoon, and she held her daughter again, inhaled her milky, soapy scent, her heart contracting, knowing no greater relief than this.

7

Two hours later, they ventured out into the city, squinting from the glare of the noonday sun striking the sidewalk. Unsure which way to walk, Ava held Margot's and Sam's hands tightly, sweat gathering between their palms until Margot pulled away from her. Car exhaust and hot tar stung their nostrils, and tenting her nose with her T-shirt, Margot complained that it smelled like burning leaves and gasoline.

"Let's try to find the park nearby," Ava suggested, herding them along the crowded sidewalk, passing wizened old women in thick black dresses with dark scarves covering their heads, their backs bent over so far they could barely walk, as if they were perpetually bending down to retrieve a fallen coin. The kids stared. They'd never seen anyone so ancient and decrepit; these grandmothers seemed sprung from fairy tales full of Baba Yagas and Strega Nonas, with spines curved into question marks, leftovers from another century.

A woman and her band of children ran up and down the street, yelling, their tanned skin and pale eyes flashing before her, their bare feet coated in dust. A heavyset man in a suit yelled at the woman before she disappeared with her children down a narrow side street. He wiped the back of his neck with a handkerchief and kept walking, his newspaper rolled into a tight baton.

Ava strove to interpret the types of faces that brushed past them: the bald heavyset guys who smoked cigarettes and looked like mechanics or bricklayers, their expressions gruff and unpleasant, and slender men in ill-fitting suits and pointy leather loafers who worked at banks and offices, the old men with watering eyes who'd witnessed the Red Army invade, the women who walked with swaying hips, in tight jeans and low-cut tank tops, their dark hair pulled tightly into high ponytails, and the mothers in faded housedresses pushing strollers, their eyes ringed with shadows, while their children cried, pointing up at the changeable sky.

All the faces were closed off, turned inward, unsmiling. When she asked for directions, a woman gave her a disenchanted shrug and motioned dismissively down the street. Stray dogs slept under cars, all matted fur and ribs. Dumpsters overflowed with sweltering refuse on every corner, strewn with plastic bottles, soda cans, old shoes, half-eaten sandwiches, melting crayons. Babies screamed from open apartment windows, motorcycles whizzed by, beeping loudly. Flies hovered over crates of fresh fruit on the sidewalk, the purple figs soft, the tomatoes red and plump, still on the vine. A delivery truck backed into reverse, cascading over the curb while pedestrians made their way around it. Careening past, an ambulance's high-pitched siren cut through the dense noise before blending back into the traffic sounds.

One old man sat against the crumbling wall of a Greek Orthodox church, reading a waterlogged paperback, a toothpick poised between his lips. Wild roses sprang over broken fences behind which a litter of kittens curled up together, cushioned in a basket in the middle of someone's overgrown backyard, strewn with weeds and loose bricks. Margot stopped in front of the fence, reaching over it to pet the kittens, but Ava pulled her hand back, saying she shouldn't touch stray animals. Margot began to defend the kittens, while Ava motioned to the park ahead, a wide swath of green, promising shade and respite. They quickened their pace, overwhelmed by the heat and the trash, the rubble in the middle of the sidewalk, broken concrete parking blocks, an uncovered manhole, dark and fetid, into which anyone could fall.

At the park, people picnicked on the wide grassy fields. Old men played chess under the trees. Boys skateboarded up and down the walkways lined with thick hedges, water spouting from ornate stone fountains, the basins filled with one-cent stotinkas catching the sunlight.

They found a playground and Margot and Sam bounded onto the tire swing, happily swinging on it even though it was meant for younger children. Ava sat down on a bench next to a plump old woman who watched two toddlers, her swollen stocking feet resting on top of her sandals. She scolded the children when one of them stumbled, or when the other one tried to eat pebbles. The toddlers stopped, wide-eyed, before continuing on with whatever they were doing.

Margot and Sam shrieked with pleasure, hanging from the swing, as if they might fall off at any moment, and that was part of the thrill. On the opposite bench, a woman hunched over her phone, frowning at the screen. A middle-aged man wearing a heavy gold chain pushed his daughter on a nearby swing, staring dispassionately into the middle distance. The playground, filled with loud children and distracted adults, appeared just the same as Los Angeles playgrounds with their too-bright sunshine and hot synthetic turf the color of rust. The swoosh of swings, childish screams and idle chatter between mothers reminded her that things were not so different here: children still demanded attention and entertainment, mothers still worried about sunburns and germs, while a dad grudgingly pushed a kid in a stroller around the playground's perimeter. Sitting here, she imagined the flitting thoughts of the other surrounding parents. They most likely were preoccupied, as she was, with their unfinished work, what to prepare for dinner, their faltering marriages. At least Margot and Sam were enjoying this; it made her happy to see them inhabit their younger selves, the foreign environment somehow freeing them to reclaim something they had once loved.

After eating lime ice pops from a nearby stall, Ava called Nikolay to pick them up in front of the National Theater, the nearest discernible landmark. It was after twelve and they were meeting Kasper for lunch at the studio. The kids were excited to see the set for the kung fu academy, the props and the fake guns, the re-creation of downtown Miami, the fancy sports cars and the make-believe nightclub.

While they were waiting for Nikolay, the kids watched stage actors take a break in front of the theater's neoclassical façade. The actors lounged on the steps and smoked in their wigs, their faces whitened with powder, exaggerated rouge applied to their cheek-bones. A few wore torn jeans with seventeenth-century billowing blouses for the dress rehearsal. The women smiled at Margot and Sam, cooling themselves with silk fans. Margot scrutinized the large black mole painted in a perfect circle at the end of a woman's arched eyebrow. She took a long drag of her cigarette and gave Margot a sly smile, her dark eyes bright with the secret that she was a normal person taking a cigarette break before she became Louis XIV's mistress again.

The white production van pulled up to the curb and Nikolay jumped out and yanked open the sliding door, motioning them inside.

Ava sat with the kids in the first row.

He flashed a smile in the rearview mirror, his yellowish teeth small and numerous. *Carnivorous,* she thought.

"Going to studio?"

Ava leaned forward. "Yes, to the production office."

"Of course!" His brow furrowed as he started the van. Ava noted the multiple tattoos of American car brands along his forearms. Buick. Chrysler. Ford. Chevrolet. The American flag was stamped on his right shoulder. The American eagle on the other. All the tattoos had faded into a bluish-green color. He wore the same white tank top and baggy jeans, his hair pulled back into a scrawny ponytail.

He noticed her noticing his tattoos. "I love America." His eyes flitted to the rearview mirror and then back on the road again. "It's my dream, to go to California. My brother, he escaped this place. He lives in Munich now. But I cannot leave my parents. Someone has to stay here with them."

Nikolay drove fast through the city center, cutting off cars, running red lights, but that's how everyone drove here, he explained after he nearly ran over an elderly woman pushing a steel-mesh cart. "A life is not worth so much," he added. "If you have money and by an accident run someone over, no big deal. Everyone bribes." He rubbed his thumb into his first two fingers, gunning it through another red light.

Sam gripped her arm, his eyes widening. A quiet alarm passed over Margot's face. Ava whispered that everything was fine. They stared out at the jumbled architecture, the embroidered blouses for sale on the corner, the foreign language bookshop with thrillers in the window.

Nikolay shook his head. "But if I ever got chance, I would go to California. In a second."

She imagined his mother sitting in her dim kitchen wearing a floral housedress and heavy black shoes awaiting Nikolay's weekly visit. She sat and waited and lamented his lateness. Her Nikolay. Her joy and light, especially because the other son was gone.

They were on the highway now, heading toward the mountains. The van went even faster, flying over the asphalt. Nikolay lit a cigarette, his face contemplative. "In California, is it really like how it is in the movies? The beach, palm trees, beautiful girls?"

She thought it would be unnecessarily cruel to discount his fantasy. Maybe he lived for it. Maybe it was his dream to make it to L.A. Who was she to dismiss it?

"Yes," Ava said. "It's exactly like that."

He slapped the steering wheel. "I knew it."

Hot polluted air blew in through the open windows, along with the roar from other cars with no mufflers.

"It's getting worse and worse here in Sofia, because of the immigrants. That's why I want to leave." He jutted out his pointy chin. "They come here, don't speak language, criticize me for loving America—once they saw I have American flag pinned to my living room wall. They yell at me for it. And I'm like, fuck you guys. I was born here. I do how I want. Go back to your shithole country."

Ava cleared her throat, swallowing down the cresting nausea induced by his rant, along with his body odor, which suddenly smelled stronger than before: a mixture of tobacco and fried meat.

She turned her head, catching Sam's surprise at how much Nikolay was swearing. She felt dirty and sweaty, her thighs sticking to the faux leather seat. Margot leaned her forehead against the window and said her stomach hurt.

Nikolay added with gusto, "It's good he's building wall! Very smart man, keeping criminals out of America!"

Ava stared at the concrete apartment blocks facing the freeway, all the same beige color, with little square windows. Some of the windows were shattered. Some had cardboard in place of glass.

He turned up the volume on the radio. Another pop song came on, reminiscent of the Spice Girls, or maybe it *was* the Spice Girls.

"It must be better now in Bulgaria, after communism." She could always talk about the past. It was safer, more solid. Sort of.

They sped by median strips overgrown with trees. The Vitosha Mountains rose up before them, verdant and rolling. "It was terrible, terrible time under Zhivkov." Nikolay sighed, turning off the highway and onto the street that presumably led to the studio.

Out of the city, they passed wineshops and expensive terraced restaurants, well-kept red-tiled houses and looming architectural mansions composed of glass and steel. Roses lined the paved sidewalks along which the occasional woman pushed a stroller. But on the side of the road she spotted a few goats munching on tree leaves. An elderly man with a staff herded them along, smacking their backsides.

The goats refused to move.

Nikolay accelerated around a hairpin turn and she inhaled sharply. He lamented how under Zhivkov there only used to be one brand of cereal, one brand of underwear, one brand of toilet paper. "Can you believe? Only one kind of toilet paper, and you still had to wait in line all day for it. It was gray and thin and tore all the time."

They drove past an empty lot where another modern house would soon stand. Nikolay mentioned that Dimitar Iliev was building it, with two swimming pools and a roof deck that overlooked the city.

"Oh," Ava said.

"Do you know Dimitar Iliev? He's most famous Bulgarian soccer player." He swept a hand across the dashboard. "All these houses, all these swimming pools not possible before. Now the rich live up here, away from city. Close to the clouds."

They pulled up to the studio gate, where a man inside a glassed-in guard box nodded to Nikolay and then the high black gates automatically parted and he waved them through. There was a prominent sign next to the guard box that pictured a gun and a knife, a red circle around these items with a line slashed through it. They drove past a large run-down Soviet-era office building with a patchy lawn in front of it, encircled by a low hedge. The studio had been state run until the early nineties, and Ava could still sense the ghost of authoritarianism in the gridlike structure of the buildings, all painted that fading tsarist yellow.

Turning right, Nikolay said that everyone in Bulgaria was nostalgic for a ruler who could fix things. "A strongman."

"Don't they remember what it was like before, under a dictator?" Ava asked, noticing two lethargic German shepherds strolling alongside the road.

Sam shouted, "I love German shepherds!"

Nikolay locked eyes with Sam in the rearview mirror. "Don't pet, okay?" Then he lit another cigarette and parked in front of the production office.

They walked down a long drafty hallway, looking for Kasper's office. Near the entrance a tall pale skinny guy in nylon gym shorts ate Skittles out of a paper bowl. A few people speaking Bulgarian hung out around a coffee machine set up on a makeshift table. Marc, the second unit director, bounded around the corner, and when he saw her, he broke into a relaxed smile. "Hey, Ava! Isabel will be so happy that you guys have arrived! I'll let her know."

"Great," Ava said. She had met Marc a few times in L.A. over the years and found him ruggedly attractive with his graying beard and plaid flannel shirts. Ava wanted to ask him where Kasper was, but Marc looked harried and sweaty, frowning down at his phone. He apologized, explaining that he was late for a tech recce with the stunt coordinator but he'd catch her later, waving as he jogged out the door.

At the end of the hall, a tan energetic man wearing a hiking backpack and a red bandana around his forehead waved to Ava as if he knew her. She waved back and then poked her head into the production coordinator office and found two women sitting behind desks staring at large computer screens.

The kids trailed the tan guy, who motioned for them to follow him. "Your dad's office is just around the corner," he said kindly. "He's finishing up a meeting. Want some jelly beans?"

Following the kids, Ava bumped into another guy wearing khaki shorts and an *Escape from Babylon* T-shirt, a shadow of a mustache lining his upper lip. He introduced himself as the director's personal assistant, adding that his name was Cal. He hovered in front of her, as if the conversation should continue, and just then Ava heard Kasper's warm voice echoing down the hallway, the clap of his hands high-fiving the kids. Cal said he was here with his wife, and their baby, who was nine months old. "We moved here from Chicago, for the movie."

Ava asked how it was going for his wife. He shrugged and said the baby was suffering from jet lag, up all night and sleeping during the day. But he added that at least they lived next to the new Paradise Center, which was air-conditioned. Back home, his wife was a pastor, the kind who administered last rites to hospice patients, and the dissonance of this detail made Ava's brain hurt. She pictured his wife, a furloughed pastor, ascending the escalator in the mall, trying to maneuver the stroller while the baby fussed, and Ava wondered if this woman was angry to leave one of the most meaningful jobs, guiding a person from life into death, so that her husband could run around and fetch the director protein shakes and stock his trailer with Red Vines and beef jerky.

"Hey!" The tan athletic guy ran past them and said he was going to check on Jason in the trailer. Make sure he'd approved the most recent storyboards. He reached out to give her a high five, their palms awkwardly hitting. He smiled, his white teeth flashing against his tan skin. "I'm Lars," he said in a lilting northern European accent that always sounded charmingly innocent to Ava.

Cal snorted when Lars bounded out of sight. "He's Jason's *second assistant.*"

Ava found Kasper sitting in his office at a conference table across from a heavyset man in a maroon velour tracksuit with a double string of wooden mala beads around his neck.

The kids played tic-tac-toe on the whiteboard against the far wall.

The man gave his head a little shake, his wavy gray shoulder-length hair moving with him, and then he smiled sweetly and said his name was Yuri Shapiro. He had an Israeli accent, and Ava remembered that he owned the movie studio. Kasper pushed his rolling chair back a few feet and grinned at Yuri. "He's the man."

Yuri performed a little seated bow, his palms pressed together. Kasper had said something about Yuri organizing an annual yoga festival on the Black Sea. She had already researched yoga studios in Sofia, surprised to find that there were at least twenty in the city center. She asked him which yoga studio he liked best.

Yuri's gray-green eyes glinted with interest. "Yoga Vibes is good. So is Mandala. Teachers are all good there, but you know, you are your own best teacher." He gave her a cryptic little smile.

"Lunch?" Kasper said, standing up from the table. Yuri fist-bumped Kasper and wandered out of the office, speaking in Bulgarian to someone in the hallway. The kids wanted to explore, pulling Kasper along.

Ava followed, but a corkboard filled with a collage of images, inspiration for the movie's aesthetic, caught her eye and she paused before it: red Corvettes flipped over freeway off-ramps. The rolling soft dunes of the Saharan desert. A procession of horses outfitted in Roman imperial armor in the middle of a parking lot at night. Rain-streaked streets. In the upper corner of the board there was a little square photograph of one of the main stars, Timothy Lim, who played the kung fu master, his smooth, perfectly sculpted bare chest visible beneath an open leather jacket. He held the gun close, mimicking the pose of so many action heroes before him, his sharp angular jaw locked in a permanent flex. He had been in numerous action movies, and *People* magazine had named him sexiest man of the year, twice. Examining his chiseled features and striking eyes, Ava agreed.

They walked to lunch, passing different sets that Kasper explained were always here, used by various crews and production teams. The kids ran onto New York Street, sitting inside a yellow Checker cab. Margot stood in front of a replica of a department store, the windows filled with half-dressed mannequins. There was even an operational traffic light and a subway entrance.

Kasper called for the kids, and they came running toward him, laughing, filled with disbelief at this place, as if they'd stumbled upon a hidden fantasy land. Out of breath, their cheeks mottled red, they asked so many questions, their sentences overlapping, running together.

He took their hands in his and said, "Okay, Sam. So you want to know where the action vehicles are? And, Margot, I'll show you the costume department after lunch, okay?"

Walking behind them, Ava sensed how much he enjoyed showing off this make-believe world, as if all this effort, and all these people laboring to make it real, justified his absence, or at least explained it.

They passed through a replica of Beijing's Forbidden City and an ancient Roman amphitheater. The next lot was St. Paul's Cathedral and London high streets, after which they stumbled into one of the sets made for *Escape from Babylon,* the kung fu training academy. Sam and Margot stood before the façade of a neoclassical building with thick columns wrapped in red silk banners with Chinese characters streaming down them. Giant statues of past kung fu masters flanked the building. Sam threw up his arms and shouted, "This is so cool!"

Running up the steps, they tried to open the double doors, but Kasper laughed and said nothing was behind those doors. It was only a façade.

At lunch, Ava sat with Kasper and Rafe, the first assistant director, in the courtyard of the commissary. Rafe had a boyish face and a charming English accent, occasionally flashing a roguish smile in Ava's direction. Forty and single, Rafe admitted that he was addicted to Bulgarian Tinder.

Kasper went to get some water, disappearing into the commissary.

Rafe turned his bright gaze onto Ava and asked how long they'd been married.

"Sixteen years."

He looked delighted by the sturdy round number, and then he remarked that Kasper would be a splendid man to grow old with. They both laughed, but while she laughed Ava wondered if this was an underhanded slight of some sort, implying that, at this point, Kasper wasn't a good husband.

Rafe furiously salted his food. He shook his head and said that he wished he could find "the one." Taking a savage bite of meat, he asked, "I mean, how did you know with Kasper?" His question carried sarcasm mingled with genuine interest.

"Love at first sight." This was the truth, even though it sounded entirely untrue, a cliché, a pat beginning to a fairy-tale story.

"Come on. How did you really meet?"

He tilted back in his chair, balancing on its hind legs, the position arrogant and casual, reminding her of how her cockier male students sometimes did this when she called on them in class as they stretched and yawned, nonchalantly leaning back into their chairs.

No. She wouldn't allow him into this deep font of memory, the place where their marriage began, the electric span of seconds when she sensed the potential vibrating between her and Kasper, that they might become something together. Make a home with children in it, promising their futures to each other, promising to never walk away.

They were both helping a mutual friend move from one shoebox apartment to a similar one across town. Ava stood on the yellowing front lawn holding a desk lamp and noticed Kasper's bright orange sneakers, the floppy brown hair falling in his eyes that he repeatedly brushed away, his good-natured helpfulness, handling the armoire and the mirrors with care, knowing just how to place fragile items into a U-Haul without a scratch. When they finished packing, he jumped into the kidney-shaped pool from the roof in his underwear, unabashed that his briefs were white cotton and transparent. Ava chalked this up to his Scandinavian upbringing, where everyone seemed to roam around naked on rocky islands, like in a Bergman film. After swimming, he spread out a towel in the sun and asked Ava to sit next to him. She was reading the Arts section of the newspaper and he admitted to not having seen any of the movies she liked, mainly foreign language ones, and she teased him about this, given that he was a foreigner himself. While they talked about movies, which was the reason why he had moved here from Sweden, she recalled a trip to Stockholm with her mother when she was twenty. She had spotted many attractive young men handling produce with the utmost care with babies strapped to their chests. The men were stylish and tall, dressed in dark wool, snugly comfortable with their progressive masculinity, and Ava made a mental note to remember that these men would make good partners. Seeing them pedal by on their bicycles with fresh flowers in the front basket, she imagined them as even-keeled and supportive, happy to share the burden of housework and parenting, happy to hold a screaming baby in their arms in the checkout line, shushing the child calmly as any mother would.

In the sun by the pool Kasper mentioned two older sisters and that he had grown up among women, and Ava assumed, brushing against his warm muscular shoulder, that he wouldn't be like the ill-tempered Italian she had dated in college, the one who once ate her entire dinner off her plate and often implied, because he went to Harvard, that he was infinitely smarter than she was.

After the pool, Kasper suggested they drive to the beach even though the sun was setting. In the car the air was heavy and dense with anticipation. They drove into the deep orange sunset, his hand on her thigh, her palm on the back of his neck. She felt as if a soft blanket had fallen over her, stopping her breath, the desire for him thick in the back of her throat. He pulled over to the side of the road and announced, "I'm going to marry you."

"Yeah, I know," she said.

Rafe leaned forward, crossing one leg over the other. "Really? Seriously? Love at first sight? Simple as that?"

Ava shrugged, still wading in that pond, the initial flush of love cascading over her. Even now. Even here.

"My problem is that within the first two minutes of meeting a woman, I always think she could be *the one*. But then, after those hundred and twenty seconds I realize she's not and then I have to decide whether or not to fuck her."

The words "have" and "fuck" and "her" coming out of his mouth stung, and she started to say that maybe it wasn't up to him: that was his problem, thinking he could choose and then dispose of women so easily. Just then, Kasper returned with a Coke and a few chocolate bars, explaining that he was exhausted, he needed some sugar to get through the rest of the day.

Kasper and Rafe talked about the upcoming shot list, which involved a complicated action sequence, worrying over the stunt-man's sprained ankle. Sitting across from Rafe in the shaded heat, Ava was incensed by his male arrogance, the way he flaunted it, causing her to feel complicit in his performance, angering her even more.

The men ate with heated intensity, shoveling the stuffed peppers and slices of tasteless bread into their mouths. She watched them eat, no longer hungry, the wilted pita bread and hard falafel balls attracting flies that she kept shooing away. Before the food came, the kids had run off to explore the grounds. Their pizzas sat there, pooling oil, losing heat.

Ava glanced around at the scattered tables and dusty courtyard, wondering which building the kids had disappeared into, and then she noticed that everyone here was white and male, all of them infused with the throbbing pressure to make this movie, the rest of their lives erased until further notice. There were no women, aside from a few local Bulgarian women in the makeup and costume department, a reminder that Hollywood was still predominately an old-boys' club, despite the outraged articles and think pieces she'd read about changing it. And even though many of the men here, Ava knew, were fathers, they didn't appear to miss their children, shoveling food into their mouths, glancing down at their phones, readying for the next setup, letting calls from home go direct to voice mail. And after having witnessed Kasper's sudden departure she now understood how easy it was for men to leave, how this kind of work tore at the fabric of a marriage with its far-flung locations and demanding schedule. Kasper had convinced himself the movie was the most important thing, as if he could shelve his family: easy to bring out when he needed them, easy to stow away when he didn't.

But would she still want him after this was all over? Especially now, after realizing that she could raise Sam and Margot on her own, that she had been doing this for a long time anyway?

In the middle of explaining to Rafe that the production designer had come in on budget, Kasper caught her eye and smiled with slight embarrassment as if her silent presence jogged the memory that he still had a wife. His expression reminded Ava of when she used to walk in on Sam playing with his action figures. He smashed the figures together before throwing them up in the air, adding explosive sound effects, and then suddenly he grew aware of Ava standing in the doorway, oddly torn between his reality and the one that existed outside himself.

8

After lunch, the men cleared out of the courtyard. Ava watched Kasper and Rafe walk away, their necks bent in concentration, staring down at their phones. On the table they'd left a half-eaten chocolate bar that was starting to melt and two empty espresso cups.

She found Margot and Sam standing over a jagged concrete hole inside the main building. Every few minutes a kitten's head would pop out, whining for food. An argument arose about feeding the kittens. Ava pointed out that there was already a pail of milk here, they didn't need to give the kittens anything more, plus it might make the kittens sick. She added that the mother cat might reject the kittens if they had been touched by humans. Ava doubted the veracity of this statement, but it convinced Margot to leave the kittens alone. They walked back to the production office, where Nikolay waited with the van. Passing the metal workshop, Sam paused, watching some Bulgarian men in face shields weld weapons, heat and light sparking off scabbards.

An affable voice called out her name. "Ava! Welcome." Bill, the DP, walked toward her, introducing himself even though she already knew who he was. She knew he had a young French wife half his age, and that they lived in a fourteenth-century Bordeaux farmhouse. Kasper had fought hard to get another DP, but Olga had insisted on Bill. For weeks, Bill had been a source of great strife for Kasper, but he seemed so friendly she felt sympathetic toward him.

He ruffled Sam's hair, her son looking up at him with suspicion. Bill said that his wife, also an academic, had just arrived and he hoped she and Ava could have coffee. Ava found him charming and debonair in his pressed jeans and linen shirt. While he was talking about his subpar hotel room—the coffee was weak and none of the staff spoke English—she felt sorry for him because he was old, close to seventy-five, and desperate to hold on to his career, to still matter, while the younger producers, Kasper included, were all too eager to toss him out.

In the van, the same hot polluted air blew through the vents.

Ava fastened her seat belt, turning around to check that the kids had done the same.

"Do you know where the camp is?" she asked Nikolay. "It's called Cosmos Kids."

Margot and Sam stared at her, hot and tired, their seat belts still undone.

"Of course I know!" Nikolay said. He barreled out of the studio gates, nodding to the guard. "It's up hill, five minutes from studio, am I right? Forty-eight Georgi Georgiev-Gets Street?"

Ava nodded, motioning for them to fasten their seat belts. They sighed and kicked the back of her seat, annoyed to visit the camp, already dead set against it, probably because she was so insistent on it.

She turned back around when she heard their seat belts click. On the short ride there, the roads were bumpy and uneven, half-finished, ending in broken cobblestones or sand. Piles of bricks stood in pillars in front of houses under construction. Lush undergrowth sprouted over low stone walls, and sometimes Ava glimpsed a villa behind a wrought-iron gate, all the surrounding wildness flattened into a perfect green lawn. Nikolay pointed out that most of the big houses belonged to Russians. He hummed along to the radio playing a techno version of Bulgarian folk music while scrolling through a dating app.

He swiped right every time.

From the outside, the camp looked like a regular house on a narrow leafy street: white stucco with a red-tiled roof and concrete steps leading up to a wooden door. From an open window on the second story they heard a teacher making an announcement in Bulgarian, chairs scraping against linoleum, someone sharply clapping twice.

Ava pressed the buzzer, her chest swelling with hope that this would work out. That once the kids were in camp during the day, she could fully dedicate herself to the book.

Margot and Sam stood behind her, arms crossed over their chests, their expressions darkening.

A guitar strummed from the backyard. A child screamed before someone hushed him.

The door opened and a large matronly woman with short patchy hair and a floral apron greeted them, her wide pale face pinched and sweaty. She explained in broken English that she was preparing snack, a honey cake. "But children in kitchen need help. Can you wait in hallway for director, please?"

Ava nodded, taking in the cubbyholes with kids' tennis shoes stashed inside, backpacks and water bottles and loose paper. Crayon drawings of houses and stick figures, flowers and grass were taped to the walls. The front room had wooden blocks, storybooks, and some toy trucks spread out on a circular orange carpet for the younger kids. The air was heavy with baked goods and an unidentified spice of some kind: cumin, or coriander.

Sam muttered that this place was babyish.

Margot agreed.

Ava told them that Marc's son, Luca, went here for camp and loved it. "You'll see, it will be okay. There are lots of field trips."

Just then the camp director emerged from her office and greeted them warmly in perfect English. Ava sensed the kids stiffen behind her. She also tried to hide her alarm.

The woman's left eye hung entirely loose from the socket, bulging and distended as if it might jump out on its own accord at any given moment. It was hard to focus on anything else. Ava couldn't look away now because then her shocked discomfort would be obvious.

She introduced herself, explaining that she had emailed her a few weeks ago about placing the kids here for summer camp, could they could look around? Her mind raced with various scenarios: maybe a horse kicked her in the eye, maybe it was a tumor, a birth defect, a side effect of Graves' disease, which apparently made eyeballs bulge . . .

"Yes, of course. I was expecting you. My name is Bilyana, but you can call me Yana."

"Great," Ava said, motioning for the kids to follow Yana.

Reluctantly, Margot and Sam trailed behind them while Ava half listened to her talk about the lunch menu. All the ingredients were organic, they grew herbs in the garden, and every Tuesday they went hiking in the nearby mountains, and they went swimming on Thursdays at the pool in the city center. Upstairs the kids did art projects and some basic woodwork.

Ava gave Sam an encouraging smile, because he loved to make things out of wood and cardboard, but he flashed her an insolent stare.

Standing in the main room, Yana explained that while the average age was eight, two eleven-year-old girls attended, and a boy Sam's age, along with a few other boys who were almost nine. "So there are enough older children here for them to play with," Yana added, opening the double doors into the backyard.

When Sam and Margot saw the wooden play structure with a rope swing and a climbing wall they bounded into the yard, running past some kids jumping rope. The yard merged with a grassy knoll, where the older kids were playing some kind of spy game that involved hide-and-seek and toy guns made out of bright orange plastic. This piqued Sam's interest, and he loitered at the bottom of the hill, eyeing the kids. Margot swung on the rope swing, sizing up the two older girls. Yana pointed out that Luca, Marc's son, was up there on the hill too. The kid looked half-wild, with long tangled hair and no shoes. He sashayed around the other kids, cutting a wide circle, demanding that they chase him.

Ava said, "At least Margot and Sam will know another kid who speaks English so they don't feel out of place."

Yana laughed gently. "Oh, don't worry. All the children here speak English. Everyone learns it in school."

"Sorry. Of course. It's only Americans who don't know any other languages."

Yana's gentle laugh lingered in the air. She had since put on glasses, which greatly reduced the noticeability of her bulging eye, but Ava worried she had done this because she had noticed Ava noticing. She motioned to the playground swirling with kids playing freeze tag. "It seems really nice here. Thanks so much for showing us around."

Margot and Sam looked at the kids up on the hill. Aloof and suspicious, they crossed their arms over their chests.

Yana put a hand on Ava's shoulder. "When would you like them to start?"

"Next Monday?" Ava said, fending off a regretful pang. They didn't look happy here, and she already anticipated all the arguments they'd have every morning on the way to camp, and the litany of complaints they'd shower her with once she picked them up in the afternoon. But she needed time to work, to think, to write.

In the van, Nikolay was in a contemplative mood, smoking a hand-rolled cigarette and listening to Britney Spears.

The kids grumbled that they didn't like the camp. They kept talking about Yana's bulging eyeball, wondering how it got that way and if it could happen to them.

Ava pointed out that the other kids seemed nice, trying to steer the conversation away from the eyeball, adding that Isabel and Marc's son, Luca, liked the camp.

Sam stared forlornly at the passing greenery. "Luca is weird. He was pretending to be a wolf and wanted all the other kids to be his wolf cubs."

Margot crossed her arms over her chest and said she was too old for the camp.

They passed by the studio gates and the kids shouted in unison, "That's where Papa works!"

"Yay, Papa!" Nikolay cheered, shaking a fist in the air. Then he glanced at Ava in the rearview mirror. "Do you want me to stop at studio?"

"Oh, no thanks. He's busy."

The kids were crestfallen and complained that they barely saw him.

"What do you mean? We just had lunch with him," Ava retorted.

"And now you're forcing us to go to that stupid camp," Sam said tearfully.

"We'll be trapped there all summer. We won't see Papa at all," Margot added.

"You'll see him at night for dinner. Remember?"

They stared back at her, unconvinced.

9

O ut of guilt, Ava had decided to give the kids a week off with her before starting camp, and in those first days, they explored the city, dipped in rich Byzantine history, remnants of the ancient world simmering beneath its surface. At the same time, Sofia doggedly strove to be modern, with various advertisements for sleek day spas, executive rental suites, and "wellness" gyms. One looming billboard touted a lifestyle membership service called Quintessentially with a picture of a young, attractive couple drinking champagne on a leather couch, a pug in the foreground positioned on a sheepskin rug, staring dolefully out at the viewer. They passed a dimly lit cheese shop that looked as if it had been there for centuries, only to glance up at a towering glass office building reflecting in its mirrored paneling an onion-domed basilica. As they walked by the office building, its automated doors swooshed open, and for a moment an air-conditioned chill enveloped them.

They tried banitsa for breakfast, egg and cheese tucked into crenellated layers of phyllo dough. And for lunch, sarmi (stuffed cabbage) along with tarator (cold cucumber soup with dill). In the afternoons, they sought out the best ice cream, sampling different shops. She showed them churches and museums and the Sofia synagogue, a beautiful Moorish revival Sephardic temple with a Venetian façade. They rested in the pews, and while staring up at the enormous brass chandelier, she willed them to absorb all the beauty: the colorful glass mosaics decorating the columns, the inside of the cupola painted a celestial blue dotted with silver stars, as if the dome captured heaven.

The streets were hot and humid, and sometimes they walked

too far and couldn't find the way back to the apartment. Someone always had to go to the bathroom at an inopportune time or became extremely thirsty. Busy intersections blared with horns and traffic. They once stood in front of a roundabout for ten minutes, unsure how to safely cross over to the other side. It was hard to tell which cabs were okay to flag down and which ones were not: The shiny black ones with advertisements for facial hair removal? Or the pale yellow Soviet-era Ladas with rusted fenders and seat belts that didn't work?

They got lost in an enormous park that spanned city blocks, searching for a fabled playground with ziplines and a rock-climbing wall that Kasper had described over the phone. In the end they only found some plastic monkey bars and a metal slide hot to the touch. They sat down on a green bench in the shade and watched some Bulgarian children play happily on the bars and burning slide, their mothers laughing while gently pushing prams back and forth. Ava observed the mothers, wondering what their lives were like, wondering if they felt as lost and confused as she did.

She dragged the kids from one church to another, explaining about Jesus, the saints, the Virgin Mary, impressing upon them the architectural terms "nave" and "altar" and "flying buttresses," and the meaning of the cross. Seizing this as an educational opportunity, she tried to teach them about the gravity and history of these churches and symbols, which meant so much to so many people for thousands of years. She wanted them to understand the artistic manifestations of faith and why it was beautiful even if you weren't a believer. She gestured to the votive candles flickering before a hand-painted icon of Saint Ivan Rilski in the narthex of Alexander Nevsky Cathedral.

Sam and Margot gazed around the dim, mysterious interior, taking in the domed ceilings, the elaborate hanging candelabras haloed with innumerable lights.

Slipping a few coins into the donation box, Ava told them that they could each light a candle and make a wish, it was a form of prayer.

They didn't know what praying meant.

"Praying is kind of like," she paused, "magical solutions to real problems?"

"Like when you really want something to happen even though you know it won't?" Margot asked.

"Or praying we don't have to go to that camp with the lady whose eye is falling out?" Sam chimed in.

"Yeah," Ava said hesitantly. "Kind of."

Standing now in the main basilica, she drew them over to the altar with a larger-than-life gilt carving of Jesus hanging from the cross. "That's Jesus, remember? He's the main character in this story."

They looked unimpressed.

She continued, "He's the most important guy, and the rest," she gestured to the mosaicked saints, "are supporting characters." They nodded, understanding the analogy, having heard these terms before from Kasper. She hesitated to add that women had been entirely shoved to the sidelines, even more so than the men, supporting the supporting characters.

Painted on the wall behind Christ was Mary bent over in grief, emitting a spray of oblong-shaped tears. She was cloaked in pale blue, and a gold flat halo encircled her veiled head. Beneath the painting in elaborate cursive it read: *Mater Dolorosa.*

The Grieving Mother.

She felt a sharp, sudden pang, an echo of grief's sting from many years ago, when she had also lost a son. Her first child. A stillbirth. He might be floating in the cosmos somewhere, among clusters of galaxies.

Or not.

She closed her eyes, blinking away the memory of the cemetery with its crematorium, the perfect rows of gravestones lining the bright green lawn, and the little box they gave her with her son in it. Reduced to ashes, as light as air.

Sam announced, "He's naked."

Margot giggled. "Except for that tiny loincloth."

"Look at the blood dripping from his hands and feet. It's gross."

"It's not real," Ava said, swallowing down a swell of grief. "It's supposed to show his suffering."

Sam and Margot argued that he was already super dead, so how could he still suffer? She told them to keep their voices down while drawing their attention to other surrounding details, to the atmosphere that inspired faith: the smell of incense and ash, the cool, dark wooden pews, the sense of safety and containment radiating from these sacred spaces.

But a faithful atmosphere was wholly different from actually having faith, which was why Margot and Sam didn't know about any of this, having inherited the same nothingness from her, not fully understanding who Jesus was, baffled by the bearded men wading past them in their heavy black robes with ropes for belts and stiff cylindrical hats, the word "priest" an empty noun.

The only thing she had taught them over the years, that they read regularly together at night before bed, were the Greek myths. When Ava was small, her own mother had read D'Aulaires' *Book of Greek Myths* to her, the vivid images seared into Ava's mind: Gaea's star-filled eyes, her verdant body heaving with trees and mountains, rivers and oceans, staring up at Uranus, enthralled by the heavens, the first coupling that began the first beginning, generating the first stirrings of life on earth.

The gods, with their frivolities and petty jealousies, their feuds and favored mortals felt more real and alive to Ava than the virgin birth, Mary's pure immaculate motherhood, the punishing regard for all things bodily, material, sexual, female. And certainly, the Greek gods were more favorable than the Old Testament God, irreproachable and vindictive, singular and male and full of fury for the way humans kept messing up his plans.

In terms of a religious upbringing, she had only experienced the anemic coldness of a synagogue with her father, staring at the bimah, the velvet-wrapped Torah hidden from view, the artifice of how she and her father had sat there a few times a year, during the High Holy Days, filled with nothing but boredom and hunger, wondering when the service would end so they could go home and eat. The male rabbi intoned complete devotion and forgiveness to Adonai, "our Lord," which meant God, but saying God's name was a profanity as He was too sacred, too immaterial to mingle with anything human, especially female. Historically, Judaism forbade women to read or touch the Torah, given their inherent impurity, and even the sound of female voices could distract men from higher spiritual pursuits because a woman's voice carried a dangerous quality to it, sinful and seductive. This history enraged Ava, and shamed her too, as the Hebrews, her people, were the first to create the concept of monotheism in the form of a singular male godhead, while in turn, they repudiated the body's natural desires and rhythms, deeming humans, primarily women, brimming with sinful sexuality, the opposite of divine. Linking the feminine with the divine, as people had done for centuries, became a justification for death by stoning.

But the question had been circling in her mind for years: How did the patriarchal godhead manage to hog all the idolization and worship, when something divinely female and multiple had preexisted for thousands of years? It was also true that in Greco-Roman religion people worshipped both gods and goddesses, but the gods held more power than the goddesses, the system still skewed toward patriarchy.

Thousands of years earlier, there had been Maya, mother of all forms and names, Isis and Cybele, Ishtar and Kali, the faint echo of the invisible Shekinah in Judaism, Amaterasu the celestial Japanese goddess of the sun and the heavens, the Nigerian goddess Oshun of Yoruba cosmology, and Lilith, the first woman, who came before Eve, who refused to have sex and lie beneath Adam in the Garden of Eden.

Where were they now?

These powerful goddesses had been muzzled and banished, pushed underground to make way for the grandiose entrance of Yahweh and Jesus, Mohammed and Gautama Buddha, all of whom demanded undivided love and devotion, just as men did.

And any woman who exhibited the spark of the divine in her, who had a special faculty for healing or prophetic divination, was deemed a witch. Each century eliminated them by burning or drowning, beheading or stoning, or simply shoving them to the margins of society.

Why would she believe this Judeo-Christian story that wasn't written in her favor?

Why would any woman?

And why would she pass it down to Margot and Sam?

Once outside the church on the stone steps, Margot insisted on seeing a picture of Jesus, hunting inside Ava's cavernous purse for the iPhone to search Google images.

It felt blasphemous to google Jesus right here, while people radiating humble faith skirted past them, entering through the heavy wooden church doors. Ava pulled the kids down the steps, searching for some shade, but they'd have to cross two roundabouts to get to a park.

Waiting for the light to change, Sam and Margot bickered about who got to hold the phone when a man with a long tangled beard and Birkenstocks strolled by, walking a dog on a raggedy rope. His skin was tan and weathered from the sun, his golden hair long and flowing.

"He could be Jesus," Sam said.

They all watched the man's lithe figure bound across the busy intersection.

Finally the light changed and she clenched their hands in hers, readying to cross, thinking about her grad school friend Claire, who grew up evangelical with the certainty that Jesus would protect her no matter what, and if not, it was because her faith faltered. She had spoken in tongues and fainted in church, falling into the arms of fellow congregants, into that warm humming web of safety and containment. Even though Claire had since left the church and had married a Marxist with whom she shared three children, she still carried that innate sense of protection within her.

It sounded so simple and right, to move through the world with that secret knowledge, but such faith felt utterly foreign to Ava.

Instead, Ava treaded on unstable ground, vigilant for what fate might deal out. Some days she grew acutely aware of death's proximity after passing a bad accident on the freeway. Or after reading about another school shooting, she grasped at the certainty that such a thing wouldn't happen to her children, when of course it might. There were no guarantees, nothing to pacify the unbearable pain of swimming within these doubts.

Sometimes she half believed that, because she had lost her first son, she wouldn't lose her other children, as if someone kept a tally. But time's march proved inescapable. In an abstract sense, she was always losing them: they pulled away from her with each ticking minute. This morning, her phone magically delivered an image of Sam at ten months old, one of those "on this day" photos. The proximity of that moment rushed into her, and for a brief, exhilarating span of seconds she felt his small body attempting to twist out of her embrace, the pilling cotton of his onesie, the intoxicating scent of his powdery skin, his delighted shrieks. Her eyes watered, admiring his soft face flooded with bright curiosity, whereas now, barely an echo of this child could be found, his face narrower, his body gathering up hard edges, his tone often sharp, verging on sarcasm to see how it would land, to see what she would say.

10

O ur bodies, as the earth, are tilled to bring forth new life, new bodies. We recognize the quickening within us followed soon after by heavy breasts and swollen feet, sickness at dawn and wakefulness at night, the first odd kicks and then, some moons later, a head or foot momentarily pressing into the womb's wall before receding, the skin of our taut stretched bellies rippling and undulating in anticipation of the child's arrival.

Together, surrounded by sisters, mothers, friends, and the midwife, we labor in the bedroom. Pessaries are often needed to induce the birth. At the crucial moment of crowning, a ritual cry of joy surrounds us, an exultant ololuge, a vibrating crash of sound. Afterward, mother and child submerge in a ritual bath in which the defilement of birth is washed away. Once the child is swaddled, dry, and safe, one of us hangs an olive branch on the house door if it is a boy, or a tuft of wool if it is a girl, to indicate a productive future of weaving and looming.

Sometimes, to scoop out the remains afterward, the baby is placed on two water-filled goatskins before the cord is cut. The goatskins are pierced, and as the child sinks slowly toward the ground, the afterbirth is gently pulled out by the cord.

We inhale the downy fuzz of a newborn's head brushing our lips, the first gasps of his breath taken outside of us, greedily gulping down the world, and then he is laid, a warm bloody mess, onto our chests. We watch his eyes flutter open for the first time, his milky gaze finding ours, the first face he will see, the face of creation, the one he will never be able to forget.

There is beauty and levity and bursts of joy in a shared gaze, in an afternoon under the trees, in the way you try to catch the shifting prisms of sunlight and shadow, in the way the moon shines down upon you as you sleep. Your wobbly walk turns into a run, but you always come back.

We also know how quickly new life can slide into death, as easily as a coin toss. We have extracted children from the bodies of their dead mothers. And we have aided mothers to expel a dead fetus from her womb by shaking her violently. Four of us seize the woman by the legs and arms and give her at least ten firm shakes. We take the robes of mothers who have perished in childbirth and offer them to Artemis. And when a birth goes well, we shower Asclepius, the god of medicine, and his daughter, Hygieia, the goddess of health, with gifts and libations, for we all know life's pleasures are worthless in health's absence. We have buried infants wrapped in the embrace of their mothers. When both die, it's the deepest sorrow.

And even if we survive childbirth, we must brace ourselves if our child is chosen for exposure. Daughters are taken over sons, even if it's the first birth. Even if she's healthy in all other ways, she must prove her worth under a frigid night sky or a merciless sun while we wail, the wind carrying our lamentations loud enough, we hope, for the gods to take notice.

The deed itself is a terrible one, carried out by a midwife or a slave, as they place the baby in a deserted spot, possibly near a rubbish heap, shrine, or crossroads where there's a chance someone will discover her. We hold our breath, praying that another woman finds the child, a woman who yearns for one but cannot have one, due to illness or sterility. We remember Creusa of Athens, eternally haunted by memories of her child, born out of rape. She swaddled him and gently laid him down on the ground. He stretched out his arms to her but she forced herself to walk away without a backward glance.

11

On Friday, Ava took Margot and Sam to what had become, over the past week, their favorite church square. The Church of Sveti Sedmochislenitsi had a garden and a fenced-in playground, and across the street there was Gelateria Savini, which sold the best gelato in the city, according to Sam and Margot.

They'd eaten an early dinner, the summer night filled with a soft twilight, a merciful break from the day's heat. Ava relaxed on a nearby patch of grass and watched them from a distance without having to actively watch them. This allowed her to read and think for a moment. In this parenthesis of calm, she sank into the thick humid air and surveyed the other kids playing parallel to Margot and Sam, the bored mothers sitting nearby, the errant father pacing the playground, the grandmothers in headscarves casting curious glances her way. Little kids cried when they fell off the swings or the horse rocker, flooding her with warm relief that they weren't her kids, whom she'd have to run to and console.

With a thick research book open on her lap, she absently stared at the trees swaying in the wind, allowing her mind to empty. Leaning back on her elbows, the grass cooling and moist, she noticed an elegant older woman with short gray hair standing in the middle of the square talking on the phone. Her shoulders were hunched over in an effort to better hear the voice on the other end of the line. Something about the way the woman's head was cocked and the intensity of her stance made Ava's pulse race—could this be her old professor, Lydia Nikitas, here in Sofia?

Ava remembered the first time she took one of her classes, sitting in the round, Nikitas at the center. In the semidarkness, Nikitas stood at the lectern, clicking through slides of ancient vase paintings. The first slide was of a red-figure kylix from 480 BC depicting the death of Pentheus surrounded by maenads who were in the process of tearing him apart, limb for limb, as Dionysus, the god of wine and ecstasy, danced in the background. The scene referred to the ending of Euripides's play *The Bacchae:* Pentheus is killed for spying on secret religious rituals in the woods, and when the women discover him hiding in the trees, they tear him apart, screaming with rapture.

What would she say to Nikitas after all these years? Would she even remember Ava, or act as if she didn't, given how things had ended between them more than two decades ago? The woman wore an iridescent trench coat, reminding Ava that sometimes Nikitas could be rebelliously fanciful, arriving at the lectern with a colorful scarf draped around her neck, or a series of Bakelite bangles cascading down her wrists in an attempt to appear festive.

Ava watched the woman in the early evening glow. She shifted her weight from one hip to the other, her face still obscured by the swoop of dense gray hair.

Getting up from the grass, Ava moved closer, trying to see if this really was Professor Nikitas, but it seemed impossible without the woman noticing her loitering around in the nearly empty square. Light drained from the sky, the last gasps of day before night fully eclipsed it. Ava took stock of the playground, noting Sam and Margot flitting from swings to slide to seesaw, before refocusing her attention on the woman, who had since walked farther away, toward the far end of the square. She stopped every few seconds because the phone conversation was so engaging, as though she were solving a difficult equation, holding all the numbers in her head.

Her kids out of sight, Ava felt a slight stab of worry. The woman spoke Bulgarian into her cell phone in a brisk, authoritative way that sounded familiar. Ava almost called out, *Professor Nikitas,* but then the woman slipped her phone into her purse and walked off, disappearing into traffic.

Making her way back toward the playground, she tried to calm down and convince herself it couldn't have been Nikitas. And even if it was, why did she feel so electrified by the possibility of it? She sat down on a bench, relieved to see that Sam and Margot were playing tag with a few Bulgarian kids while an oceanic wave of nostalgia for her twenty-two-year-old self overcame her. The Ava who had wanted to please Nikitas so that she could become her most beloved student. As the only tenured female professor in the art history department, Nikitas had radiated a magnetic power, infamous for her demanding and oftentimes harsh pedagogical style, but her academic rigor incited students to win her praise, which she dispensed in strategic nuggets of affection. Sophomore year Ava had succeeded in becoming her research assistant, spending long afternoons at Nikitas's rambling Victorian house off campus, typing up stacks of indecipherable notes, drinking cup after cup of milky Earl Grey.

Nikitas had been writing a book on the Goddess culture based on surviving artifacts and myths dating back thousands of years, spanning from ancient Crete to Celtic Ireland. Goddess worship, she argued, was universal, manifesting as an egalitarian matrilineal society, and later destroyed by the invading Indo-European peoples from the distant north and east, tribes known as "battle-axe" cultures. The invaders arrived in waves, the last and most devastating wave between 3000 and 2800 BC, and these infiltrating groups, she concluded, were destroyers, not creators, of culture, as they worshipped the power to annihilate and dominate, evidenced by their burial mounds, which held the remains of chieftains and their horse-drawn chariots, spears, iron blades, swords with scabbard mounts, and bronze helmets engraved with male deities offering protection to the warrior in battle. In addition to their possessions, wives, children, and slaves were buried alongside them. Thus began, Nikitas wrote, the male dominator culture, which reduced women to property and, in turn, fragmented and diminished the ancient Goddess religion. Reading the concluding sentence—*As these ancient rites eroded, so did women's rights*—Ava felt her blood quicken with recognition, as though this explained everything.

On weekends, Nikitas went into Manhattan, where she owned a flat downtown and rumors circulated that she was in a relationship with Francesca Rossi, a classics professor, who was beautiful and

Italian. Ava used to fantasize about bumping into Nikitas and Rossi on an anonymous city block, the wind gusting around them, blowing open their coats. But this never happened.

When her senior year arrived, Ava had to choose a thesis topic. Nikitas urged her to focus on the denigration and fragmentation of the Great Goddess, showing how She was then incorporated into patriarchal religious systems, splintering into subservient consorts to the gods. In Greco-Roman religion, the original Great Goddess could be found as a trinity: Persephone, Demeter, and Hecate. Maiden, mother, crone, reflecting the waxing and waning moon, the cyclical nature of the seasons.

But Professor Arnott, head of the department, counseled Ava against it. She still felt his hand on the small of her back guiding her into his office, while he muttered about the scant evidence of matriarchal religions, let alone this idea of a central "Great Goddess." The most she would find on the topic, he explained, sitting down in a low leather chair before gesturing that she should sit too, in the folding chair opposite his desk, were fertility statues such as the famous *Venus of Willendorf*, which was likely an aphrodisiac made by men for men. She pictured the crude figurine with those engorged breasts and swollen belly, blank face and braided cap, and no arms or feet, hence no movement or authority. Merely totemic and primitive, she was transportable and disposable. The way men wanted women to be.

He emphasized that it was foolhardy to proclaim masculine or feminine dominance in prehistory, before the Greek gods and Homeric epics. "It remains an open question and not one that I recommend you delving into as your senior thesis." And then he suggested, as a kind of consolation, in his lilting singsong Scottish accent, that in later religions, the mother was worshipped in the figure of the Virgin Mary and the female saints, but that didn't change the fact that the culture was still misogynistic. He excitedly opened up a nearby book and showed Mary enthroned on the west-facing façade of Chartres Cathedral with the baby Jesus on her lap, from the twelfth century. "She's almost a goddess," he said, his breath smelling of stale coffee and the half-eaten Danish on his desk, "but Mary doesn't quite make it. Indeed, she holds the future, the transcendent being sitting right there on her lap, and yet she's the source, not the savior."

Ava still recalled Dr. Arnott's plump finger pressing into the book, the tip turning white from the pressure he exerted on the photograph of Mary enthroned in stone.

She took the safe route, writing about flattened, virginal, haloed, bloodless Mary as a representation of the divine feminine, instead of the vital, sexual, and sometimes violent Great Goddess that Nikitas had wanted her to write about, the one that she was afraid to research for lack of finding enough sources. Nikitas stepped away from overseeing Ava's thesis, but she was still on the review committee.

Despite the snub, it seemed as though Nikitas had backed off, allowing Arnott to take the helm, and Ava completed what she believed was a satisfactory thesis until the morning of the defense arrived at the end of May, just before graduation week. Arnott, Nikitas, two younger faculty members, and Ava sat around a cherrywood conference table, and after Ava presented her main argument, while they leafed through individual printed copies of her thesis, Nikitas started in.

At first, she had niggling concerns about the use of parentheticals instead of footnotes, and the misquoting of a particular source, which Arnott explained was a minor error, nothing to ponder too heavily. But his manner was dismissive, almost hostile as he reached for another soggy Danish from the box in the center of the table. As he bit greedily into the pastry, something pushed Nikitas over the edge of civility. Her countenance shifted from mild irritation to a darkening rage, and it seemed as though she grew taller, her girth widening, until she finally stood up and paced the room, ranting about other holes in the argument and that it contributed nothing to the field of Mariology. Ava felt her cheeks burn with shame, sweat peppering her white dress shirt worn especially for this occasion. She tried to focus on the mild breeze drifting in through the open stained-glass windows while students lazed on the quad, someone playing bongo drums, the smell of weed wafting through the spring air, but she could barely breathe, her neck hot and itchy, her hands placed uselessly on her lap, their inertness only accentuating her helpless position as Nikitas motioned with disgust to a copy of the thesis on the table before reaching the full summit of her fury—and in that moment, Nikitas appeared as monstrous and intoxicated with her own rage as the many-armed Kali-Ma, the Hindu goddess with her necklace of skulls and a bloody tongue hanging from her mouth.

Now, in the middle of the square, a group of boys jumped on and off their skateboards, the sharp clattering of the wheels against the concrete invading her reverie, causing her to tense up. She heard violence in their movements, even though the boys were just boys: young, frustrated, on the cusp of sex. She wondered if they knew how hostile it sounded and that's why they did it.

On that long-ago spring morning, everyone sat frozen around the conference table, stunned into silence as Nikitas stormed out of the room, slamming the door behind her. Ava could barely take her eyes off the scuffed surface of the table, as though looking at something so mundane and physical, imbued with the objective truth of its existence, could rescue her from the intensity of her shame, but then Dr. Arnott's calm, melodious voice reassured her that Nikitas had a temper, they all knew that, and he was so sorry she had been the target of her fury when he was really the one she wanted to eviscerate.

In the aftermath of the committee meeting, Nikitas withdrew her recommendation for Ava's application to Yale's art history graduate program, and Ava didn't get in without it. She graduated in the rain without honors and then moved to the city, taking an entry-level job at an academic press that published art history books. It took many years, filled with odd jobs and false starts, before she applied to graduate school in California and tried to resume the career that she had once envisioned for herself. But Nikitas's rejection lingered, morphing into Ava's belief that she was an academic failure for aligning with Arnott, the middle-aged white male professor who, by his scholarship and bumbling, overly sincere existence, unwittingly upheld the status quo. She also harbored guilt over dropping out of academia for such a long stretch, for becoming more of a wife and a mother than a scholar. Attempting to regain her footing, she taught, researched, and started various book drafts while also caring for her children, her husband, their household, and yet, she became convinced that she was actually failing at all these things.

12

Sofia, June 2019

S he watched some Bulgarian kids yell and signal to one another, playing an intricate game, the rules of which eluded Ava, but that involved taking a certain number of steps forward, and then freezing, the children little statues, resolute and serious, until one of the boys yanked a girl over to a nearby tree and pretended to tie her to it. The girl had lost because of some violation, and now she was bound to the tree by an imaginary rope while the other children continued to step forward and freeze. Step forward. Freeze. The children believed in the rope so much that Ava also saw it: its frayed thickness the color of putty. The girl, with her graceful neck and long silky ponytail, blended into the tree's slender branches, recalling Bernini's sculpture *Apollo and Daphne*, Daphne filled with so much terror her feet took root, her hands turning into blooming foliage, her naked body rapidly transforming into a tree, her terrified open mouth indicating that anything was better than enduring the climax of Apollo's hot pursuit.

Ava walked over to stand sentry at the playground's entrance. Pretty soon she'd give her kids the five-minute warning that it was time to leave; Kasper was supposed to meet them here and then they'd walk home. She read somewhere that raising children mainly consisted of dispensing these five-minute warnings.

Sam raced toward her and Ava thought about how the kids alternated between needing her and pushing her away, that motherhood required this constant dance of rejection and reunification. A few months ago, Sam had stopped holding her hand. They would walk to school holding hands but when the school's brick steeple came into view, Sam's palm stiffened in hers and she'd find her own hand hanging there uselessly, empty and unwanted. Then he would run ahead, disappearing into the throng of kids flooding the entrance, the only consolation a backward glance in her direction when she called out, somewhat feebly, "See you later . . . I love you." She brushed the hair out of Sam's eyes, his forehead clammy and warm against her fingertips as he rambled on about how in some places the snow was so soft a person could sink into it and then get buried beneath layers of heavy snow and die. "I learned about it on *Minecraft* Survival."

"Hmmm," Ava said, blocking out what he was saying while still trying to appear interested, because it was about video games, something she found incredibly boring.

"And on *Minecraft* Survival you need to gather natural resources like fuel and coal and make furnaces in caves to keep the zombies out—the zombies are called creepers. A creeper's head explodes if you get too close to it."

She widened her eyes. "Wow."

"It's okay—you don't have to act interested when you're not interested," Sam said.

Kasper texted that he was here, but finishing up a call. She scanned the area, catching sight of him on a bench on the other side of the square. She didn't want the kids to see him, to realize he was both here and not here.

A few minutes later, Kasper walked toward them and her heart lifted. He had left early in the morning, just before seven, in a mad rush for an emergency meeting with the production team because the financiers hated the newly built sets; they were complaining that the kung fu academy was still too small. With the first day of shooting approaching, the tension mounted.

As he came toward her, she realized he was still on the phone. It was just harder to tell because of those white earbuds embedded in each ear. He muted the phone for a minute and gave her a quick kiss on the lips. His breath smelled of coffee and exhaustion.

"Hi," she mouthed.

Sam started to talk, but Kasper sharply gestured that he was almost done and turned away, moving a few feet ahead, his shoulders hunched up around his ears. The group of teenage boys slamming their skateboards against the flagstones caused him to walk farther away.

Sam flitted back to the playground and Ava sat down on the bench, unable to read in the failing light. Glancing over at the square again, she noticed that Margot wasn't there. She hadn't been watching for the last five minutes, busy with Sam. Standing up, her heart creeping into her throat, she scanned the whole area before feeling a body knock into hers, arms encircling her waist, squeezing tightly.

"Were you scared?" Margot asked.

Ava steadied herself against the bench. "I was wondering where you went. One minute you were there and then . . ."

"I wanted to surprise you."

Ava sat back down. "Okay."

Margot leaned against the bench. "I'm really thirsty. Can we get some water?"

"It's late, Margot. We're about to walk home. You can have water at home."

She sat down next to Ava, staring intently at her. "I got my period." All around them, kids ran and yelled. The skateboards struck the flagstones. A dog barked, lunging at someone's backpack. Sam slid down the slide again.

Ava took a deep breath. "Okay." She paused. "Are you okay? When did you notice it?"

Margot broke into a smile. "Just kidding."

"Just kidding?"

"Yeah. I didn't really get my period. I was just thinking about it."

When they walked home, Kasper was no longer on the phone. He made a big show of turning it off and sliding it into his front jean pocket, grinning in that guilty way that infuriated Ava, inviting her to reward him for this small fatherly act. She could also see he was exhausted from prepping, from all the interminable budgetary meetings with the financiers. Walking alongside him, she tried to suppress a flare of anger over the late nights and endless phone calls; he had warned her it would be this way. Any show of resentment was unjustified. Still, it was hard to ignore the burning in her chest, a bright, blazing spark.

The night air felt lighter and thinner, a relief from the drenching afternoon heat. Kasper walked ahead of her with the kids, the three of them holding hands, and Ava noticed how they basked in his renewed curiosity about their day, their faces upturned, their eager eyes drinking in his attention, vying for it.

Nearing the apartment, she recognized certain landmarks: the casino on the corner with its billboard of gold coins raining down into someone's cupped palms and the little bakery next to it, with its flaky phyllo dough rolls filled with soft cheese, and then the coffee shop up ahead with a sign that advertised "American coffee" along with the pithy line "Life is too short for bad coffee!"

"How was camp?" Kasper asked.

They groaned, rolling their eyes. "We hate it."

"That's not true," Ava protested, coming up behind them. "We were only there for about fifteen minutes on Wednesday. You can't hate something in such a short time."

Kasper passed a hand through his hair. "I thought they started already."

"They start next week. On Monday. Remember?"

She swallowed down the urge to chastise him for not even knowing the simple location of his children, for having the luxury of remaining entirely unaware and oblivious to the daily machinations of their lives.

It was a luxury a mother could never afford, but one that was automatically granted to fathers. Her mother-in-law, Greta, once recounted that Kasper's father had traveled continually for work, leaving her to raise their three children. Her eldest daughter was bullied at school, which was concerning, but because her husband was gone all the time, she dealt with it on her own, telephoning the principal and arranging a meeting with the other parents. Eventually, the situation improved, and by the time her husband returned, he wondered, with mild interest, how Klara was faring with those girls who teased her. Greta snapped, explaining the issue had been resolved weeks ago, but here he was sailing back into their lives, the winds low, the waters calm, unaware of how much effort and distress had gone into smoothing out not just this problem but the various dramas and situations that would keep occurring. On top of this, when he came back, Greta hosted elaborate dinner parties for his clients, playing the charismatic wife who was happy to have a seat at the table, entertaining the businessmen with her ribald jokes and witty banter. Ava still recalled when Greta had rehashed this, agitation lacing her voice as she drank a glass of red wine on the white linen couch, as if barely a day had gone by between those past ordeals and the current moment. Her hazel eyes lit up, simmering with age-old anger, but it was too late now. She had already spent her life in the service of feeding someone else's potential, clearing the path and lighting the way for him.

An hour later, Ava lay next to Kasper in the half-dark bedroom.

He searched for her hand under the covers. "How was your day?"

They lay on their backs, staring at the undulating shadows playing across the ceiling, and she was tempted to tell him about the Professor Nikitas sighting in the square tonight, but decided against it. It didn't seem important anymore, and it probably wasn't even her. Instead, she recited a string of insignificant events: her mother had called, the kids had ice cream after dinner, and the concept of a spatula didn't seem to exist in Bulgaria.

Turning toward him in the darkened room, she asked what he was thinking, only to find him asleep, his mouth open, his slender hands folded over his chest in perfect symmetry as if he lay inside a coffin.

She thought about waking him up, half out of spite, half out of the desire to make a point that he conveniently fell into a deep sleep the moment she began talking, but instead returned to memories of Nikitas, to moments she hadn't thought about in decades: the Take Back the Night marches led by young women, each cupping a single lit candle in their hands, illuminating the dark campus. Nikitas's trademark button fastened to her blazer commanding, "Don't Suck: Bite," which Ava used to stare at during lecture. The fact that in the early eighties Nikitas had founded a separatist female community called Womyn Land in northern Michigan, and then Ava faintly recalled that Nikitas's first book, *The Right to Reject Sex,* had argued that pornography promoted a culture of rape and toxic masculinity, and that sex with men, even voluntary sex, even marital sex, was actually women colluding in their own oppression. That women didn't know what they really wanted because they were always being told what they wanted. Nikitas had marched with Adrienne Rich and Audre Lorde, with Barbara Smith and Gloria Steinem, fighting for parity in the workplace and a redefinition of rape as a crime of power and violence as opposed to one involving lust or passion. She had fought for women's rights during a time when collective female rage and grief still seemed to matter, when it was still worth fighting for.

But Ava had grown up in the eighties and had seen the wild popularity of *Fatal Attraction* and *Basic Instinct,* the screen dominated by these psychopathic murderesses coupled with the fearsome claim that if you were a woman over forty it was easier to get killed by a terrorist than find a husband. In high school, she had energetically attended a women's studies class, led by Joan Siegal, an old-timey feminist who was the president of the local Los Angeles chapter of NOW, but sitting there, Ava feared she didn't look like a serious enough feminist to Joan because she wore lipstick and denim miniskirts and desperately wanted boys to notice her. She purposefully dressed down on the days she had that class, stuffing her lipstick into her front jean pocket, untucking her flannel button-down shirt, trying not to care about her appearance even though she did. They discussed *The Beauty Myth,* but it didn't seem like a myth to her. Everyone wanted to be beautiful.

By the time Ava arrived at Columbia in the mid-nineties, there was a patina of unsexiness and embarrassment around calling oneself a feminist as all things roared with sex: thongs and Brazilian waxing, feathery-winged Victoria's Secret models parading down runways, and a starved Kate Moss positioned in various degrees of undress dolefully staring down at the world from towering billboards. There were Viagra commercials and Girls Gone Wild, Madonna in a pointy black leather bustier, and a sixteen-year-old Britney Spears in a school uniform singing "Baby One More Time." On *Sex and the City,* a vibrator shaped as an endearing purple bunny became famous, prompting one of Ava's college boyfriends to get her the same vibrator in an attempt at experimentation, but it was too large and clunky and it ended up making Ava feel inadequate, as though not bursting into multiple spontaneous orgasms were a personal failing. While she clumsily tried to be "bold" and sexually assertive, this new liberated sexuality that everyone praised made her feel as if she was just participating in her own exploitation. At the same time, she wanted to be desired and have the power to shape her own desires, to feel attractive and sexual without the shame of wanting this.

In some ways, she was still confused about what she wanted, or what she thought she wanted. And she felt conflicted about what feminism meant now, with all the rigid opinions about what feminism wasn't without knowing who, or what, it was for. It was clear to her that women were experiencing a palpable political backlash, a maximum regression of sorts, but hadn't the world always hated women? And now, the women's movement monitored its own boundaries for trespassers, for pretenders, for oppressors while fiercely debating who was entitled to call themselves a feminist or not, the internal strife ouroboric, fixated on purity, causing Ava to assume her usual apologetic crouch because she probably didn't deserve to call herself a feminist. She learned that the agenda had been colonized by white women since its inception, rendering her very existence offensive, problematic.

She still wondered, from time to time, if there was even a group to join. How would they organize and around what principles? Was it possible to do this without offending anyone? Without contributing to the preexisting power structures? But hadn't women claiming their own space, their own power, always caused controversy? On occasion, Ava felt nostalgic for the 1970s feminism that her mother had lived through, with the consciousness-raising groups, the winning of reproductive rights, the performative bra burning fueled by the conviction that they were finally toppling centuries of patriarchy.

Or even just a few years ago, feminism suddenly seemed glamorous and fun for the first time, paraded around as the zeitgeist, with Beyoncé sampling Chimamanda Ngozi Adichie's viral TED Talk "We

Should All Be Feminists," while the cultural moment shouted "lean in," because if you could do everything, you could have everything, and this combination of self-actualization and glittering female ambition felt stylish and cool.

Until it went out of style.

Recently, she had been reading *Bad Feminist* by Roxane Gay, enjoying it greatly, feeling a certain kinship with Gay's ideas. Reading it, Ava likened being a "bad feminist" to being a "bad Jew," the category inescapable. She couldn't distance herself from it, the "bad" classification brimmed with so many conflicting meanings and definitions that sometimes it felt like nothing, and other times it seemed laughable compared to the "real thing," whatever being a real Jew or a real feminist meant. The book had been lying on the credenza in the entryway when a friend, a mom she knew but was not very close with, saw it there while dropping off her son at Ava's house. Because of her perverse need to always explain herself, Ava held up the book and half joked, "I'm a bad feminist. What kind are you?"

The woman blinked a few times and said, "Who cares?"

All this, while Ava and her friends could no longer utter the words "emotional labor" or "wellness" without cringing, without irony, without exhaustion, and without laughing at their own stupidity and whining, as if a man doing some extra dishes once in a blue moon, or buying one of those coffee mugs with "Not Today Patriarchy" printed on it in bold lettering (along with a "Consent Is Sexy" T-shirt) could remedy anything. The entire project of feminism seemed used up into nothingness, a rubble heap of thwarted objectives as compensation for domestic labor, universal childcare, and real control over their own bodies rapidly faded as attainable realities.

Faded more every day.

Watching the country unravel, its cracks widening into chasms, she and her friends found themselves awash on the shores of middle age with the arresting appearance of jowls and deepening frown lines and bodies battered by childbirth, bodies that no amount of wellness tonics, cupping, or bee venom therapy could fix. But at least, they said to one another, they had not become like their mothers, who had either not worked, or worked too much, stayed in bad marriages for too long, or, in Ava's case, didn't stay at all. Her mother was currently on her fifth marriage, pursuing the institution with inexhaustible resolve while hating the actual men she married, something Ava was determined not to do.

Despite the small act of not following in her mother's footsteps, things were tunneling toward worseness, toward disaster. Ava felt it in her bones. Individually and collectively, she felt it. What kind of country was she living in now, as they all looked on in complacent horror? And what kind of woman was she, following her husband to Bulgaria, hoping he'd return to her without knowing if she wanted to return to him? What types of lessons was she inadvertently teaching Margot about marriage, about motherhood? And Sam? And how would a woman such as Nikitas view her now?

Unable to sleep, Ava got up to write. She'd written the first few chapters, unsure where the book would take her, but this past week, she'd been immersed in organizing the apartment. They had moved a few days ago to the first floor because the windows in the old apartment were not up to code and Ava had kept imagining Sam and Margot tipping over the low windowsills, falling to their deaths six stories below. And the new apartment had a tiled terrace that opened into a lush garden with an occasional cat prowling through the undergrowth. The kids had left milk out for the cat, predicting that in the morning, the milk would be gone. They had fallen asleep talking about the cat, discussing its possible likes and dislikes, wondering if it had a home. While lying at the foot of Sam's bed trying to come up with a name for the cat, Ava felt jealous of the time she'd spent unpacking, folding laundry, procuring pots and pans for the kitchen, attempting to rejigger the toaster. She resented the wasted hours she could have spent writing, reminding her of what it was like back home, her mind compressed with household duties, piecemeal dinners, missed dental appointments, and the particular evilness of plastic straws while beneath these swimming anxieties she debated her worthiness as a mother, as a scholar, and when, approximately, the natural world would end.

But here, she wouldn't sink into the usual guilt and self-flagellation. She wouldn't second-guess every decision or admonish herself for taking time to write. Yesterday, in the middle of the flat afternoon, she let the kids gorge themselves on a Bulgarian sitcom so she could read, and after dinner she hooked them up to their iPads and, as they transformed into glassy-eyed drones, she started to write about an ancient Greek woman's life. She wrote about the tedious minutiae, the never-ending wheel of domestic labor, her only relief within the cool dawn, or late at night while everyone slept when she could finally inhabit herself.

13

Athens, 415 BC

A woman's work is silent and continuous as we refill the animal skins with grain, care for slaves and children who have fallen ill, transform raw material into what can be consumed or worn as adornment. We protect the house and the possessions within it, all of our work generated by what a husband provides, whose labors would be useless without us to manage his procurements.

We hear of errant wives who fail to tend to their households as though pouring water through a sieve, and at such gossip my husband shakes his head, his eyes temporarily gleaming with gratitude for my dutifulness. I stare down at my callused fingertips, at the tiny cracks in my palms, at the bulging blue veins running beneath the top of my aged hands. My lower back throbs as if on fire, my knees ache and crack, my neck is sometimes so stiff I cannot turn my head for days, but this is the cost of his praise, which he dispenses as sparingly as a handful of drachmas.

Sometimes I think the cost is too great to be this kind of woman with no reward. "Where is our great reward?" Xanthe and I sometimes crow with sarcasm, proposing a laurel wreath of filigreed gold, a diadem inlaid with topaz, or a golden band to encircle our sagging arm flesh. And then we dissolve into hysterical laughter because there is no reward.

Xanthe and I, we stand side by side behind our looms while we weave, exchanging knowing glances as we observe the other women working along with us in the drafty downstairs room next to the kitchen. Dust from the earthen floor coats our bare feet. Beads of sweat gather at the nape of our necks, even with the half-open windows allowing in a tepid breeze. First we scour the wool, ridding it of burrs and dung and the dense smell of earth before gently combing it through with a brush to separate the fibers. Then we dye the wool in a large vat and wait for it to dry. In the afternoon, we gather up the clean tufts of creamy white, to prepare it for the drop spindle. Xanthe prefers to stand, the gathered wool cascading over her knuckles like a small cloud as she spins, elongating the separated piece down to her thighs, the weighted wooden disk encircling the spindle creating a suspended tension that pulls and lengthens the piece from the woolen tuft up above. Once it's spun, we thread it onto the loom.

Eirene fails at this part every time. Every time, her spindle drops and clatters to the ground, or she pulls the strand from the fleece too aggressively and the thin winnowing line breaks off from the gathered woolen mass. When I try to show her again, she yells at me before storming up the stairs, where I hear her tearing off the blankets and pounding her fists on the limestone walls, which she has already dented many times. Her frustration festers with each passing day in the weaving of a chlanis, the special robe all new brides must present to their husbands the morning after the wedding night. But little progress has been made and I fight the urge to help her, to weave it myself, knowing that my overzealousness might thwart this upcoming marriage in some unforeseen way. "You mustn't meddle so much," Xanthe whispers into my ear, and I know she's right.

I find Eirene with sheepskin blankets strewn around her, and already I'm annoyed that I will have to restore them to the bed, but then my heart softens at the sight of her, head in her hands, crying. Her large feet splayed out on the paving stones, her lustrous hair falling over her arms, a curtain of black beneath which she hides. "I hate it," she whispers harshly. "How will I weave in a strange house when I can't even do it correctly now? And under the watchful gaze of his mother, no less? What will it be like?" Her left eyelid twitches, a portentous tic that comes and goes, one can never know the reason, but I think it means her marriage will be arduous, that she will not take well to it.

"It will be for you what it was for me," I tell her, trying to smile, but it's more of a grimace.

Leaving her, I return to Xanthe and the others. Sometimes we weave in silence and sometimes we break into song to pass the time. Especially when the shadows deepen across the courtyard, the day's end approaching, we sing. It's not exactly singing, but lamentations in the form of song. We lament our ancestors, singing their myths and stories so we do not forget. We sing to the gods and goddesses, seeking their favor, reminding them of our love. We sing of our frustrations and losses, of our grief and rage for all that we have endured, and we endure it together, our voices blending and rising, filling the rooms with a vibrating melancholy that draws Eirene back down the stairs to stand beside me where she resumes her work at the loom.

Over the past moons, Eirene has sprouted breasts and pubic hair, and I show her how to singe off the hair with a quick flame and how to wrap her breasts in a strophion to keep them in place. I show her how to use the discarded woolen scraps, leftovers from the loom, when her monthly bleeding begins and how to clean herself. And she has started wearing an amulet charm of herbs and roots that Xanthe compounded for her. Around her neck, pressed against her skin, it alleviates the erratic pains when the bleeding comes. Often, she retreats to a darkened room, a compress dipped in rose water and lavender oil placed on her forehead, a woolen bundle between her legs.

I peek in on her, fearing "the illness of maidens," as the doctor calls it, an illness that seizes a girl during this vulnerable time. The womb might wander throughout her body, causing torpor, hysteria, headaches, pallor, dizziness, vomiting, and the sense of being suffocated, followed by suicide in some unfortunate cases. Everyone knows this is a time of trepidation for mother and daughter alike, when suicide increases tenfold some say. It happened to a neighboring family, whose daughter fashioned her new girdle into a noose and used it to strangle herself. Her sister found her hanging from a roof beam, such a bloodless silent death. It was particularly upsetting because she was ripe for marriage, having recently started to bleed. Some say she did it to avoid her upcoming marriage while others say she knew she was infertile and to avoid this shame she took her life. Xanthe thinks she was possessed by Artemis, the virgin goddess, who tends toward vengeance when a girl abandons virginity for the marriage bed. Perhaps the girl's family did not honor the goddess properly with sufficient offerings. But I believe she feared defloration, and in a panic, thought death preferable.

I still hear the funereal cries of grief that emanated from their house early that spring morning when they found her, and my heart clenches, fearing for Eirene. Fearing I might not watch over her closely enough and then it will be too late. Fearing the gods have already made up their minds, her fate spun. Fearing that I will fail to ferry her across this threshold, losing her along the way. Fearing that she will emulate this girl's suicide, finding such an early death attractive in its final defiant refusal.

Despite this circling dread, I still fastened the new girdle around Eirene's waist, the same girdle her husband will look forward to removing on their wedding night. Demonstrating how to tighten it, my fingers clumsily run along the braided fabric and I feel the sting of my own diminishing fecundity while Eirene's increases. Some months I bleed only a faint line, or nothing at all. And with every new day, my beauty fades, but out of habit, I still carry a skaidon to ward off the sun and I apply little circles of rouge made from mulberries and seaweed to my puckered cheeks, my lips slick with beeswax. My thick dark eyebrows have thinned, and so in moments of vanity, I adhere dyed goat hair coated in resin to my brows to thicken them up. No one sees me beneath the veil when I venture out with Xanthe to purchase salt and dye, but I still want to feel beautiful, recalling the days when men and women used to notice me, their gazes as strident as arrows, and then I chastise myself for such empty vanity.

Undressing, I observe my body, altered from years of childbirth and domestic labor. I touch my thickened thighs and crinkled abdomen, my breasts deflated of air, hanging down my chest as if I were smuggling a pair of dead eels into the house. I startle at this new woman, a woman I barely recognize as myself. This withered crone. And then I remember that Eirene and I are both preparing to relinquish parts of ourselves for new parts, changing in ways we cannot yet fully understand.

14

At first light, the shapeless Monday greeted her, the morning heat gathering in the curtains. She sat up in bed, her T-shirt sticking to her chest.

Kasper stood in front of the mirror attached to the back of the bedroom door, buttoning up a linen shirt. He turned away from the mirror but not without first giving his reflection an appraising glance. Sliding into his dark blue jeans, he asked, "What are you going to do today?"

The emptiness that stretched before her appeared absurd, especially when he asked what it entailed, because it entailed nothing.

Today the kids started camp and the freedom she would soon have startled her.

When she visualized her life back home, she pictured herself moving so fast all she saw was light, motion, spinning freneticism: yanking out damp laundry before dumping it into the dryer, emptying the dishwasher only to reload it, fiendishly wiping down countertops, always finding smudged jam under the lip of sandstone or, inexplicably, a loose rusty nail on the floor that could kill the dog if the dog chose to swallow it. The endless stacks of papers to grade, her inbox crammed with emails from anxious students, notifications of skipped faculty meetings, book chapters to write.

Erin had once said that all she did every day was keep everyone in the family alive, even the dog, whose teeth needed daily brushing, otherwise he would develop another costly gum infection. She said this starkly, her face blanching, as if deterioration breathed close, but in a way, all these little devotional acts mothers performed, from preparing food to making sure the clothing was clean and the sheets changed and the spiderwebs wiped from the ceiling corners did keep everyone alive, in a cumulative sense. But taken individually, every detail appeared so small and insignificant that one could easily dismiss it. If she just stopped and did nothing here, perhaps Kasper would notice that the great tremor of activity had ceased and the reality of an empty fridge, hungry children, dirty teeth, and unmade beds would come crashing down on him.

She might experiment with neglect. What if she didn't make breakfast? What if she didn't neatly line up their sneakers in the hallway every day? What if she didn't clean this apartment, ever?

Lacing her fingers together, she stretched her arms overhead.

The kids stirred in the next room.

"I don't know what I'm going to do today." She paused, watching him bend down to tie his impossibly white sneakers. "You're taking them to camp this morning, remember?"

"I know."

"Do you know where to go?" She said this with an internal cringe, already knowing he had no idea.

"Of course," he said, straightening up before striding into the kitchen for coffee.

She listened to him pour.

"Actually," he called out, "can you text me the address?"

She rolled her eyes.

He reappeared in the doorway, holding two cups of coffee. "It's not very good. The coffee, I mean." He smiled, feigning helplessness. Or learned helplessness.

She could never tell.

At least he would drive the kids to camp on the way to the set every morning, agreeing to this one small task, and Ava would pick them up by three o'clock.

The rest of the day and into the late evening Kasper would be unreachable, especially today, on the first day of shooting. Kasper moved around the apartment gathering up his laptop and notebook, his keys and wallet, while trying to appear calm and unbothered, but she knew him well enough to detect the strain in his voice, a certain staticky energy pulsing through his body that he masked with an overly casual demeanor. He had to keep the production on schedule, praying that the weather held and there wouldn't be a thunderstorm in the afternoon, derailing the outdoor scenes.

Knowing this, Ava would resist calling him with any questions, even though she couldn't figure out how the washing machine worked; the instructions were in Bulgarian and Russian. Last night when she'd tried to run it, bubbles and soapsuds flooded the laundry room and poured into the apartment hallway. She didn't know where to purchase bathing caps for the kids (the camp director was adamant that they wear them during swimming lessons) and she wondered if the grayish inch of water that accumulated after every shower would ever drain.

After the front door closed, the place finally empty of Kasper and the kids, the quiet hum of the apartment, which she had never heard before, cushioned her in luxurious calm. The day stretched before her; she could do anything with it. The palpability of such idle freedom was thrilling, similar to the first moments of unwrapping a new can of Play-Doh, the dough retaining the perfect mold of the can, the color intense and fresh. She could stay in the apartment and unpack the rest of their things, or finally start writing in earnest. She could venture out to the old Greco-Roman temple, ruins now, in the city center, try a yoga class, or anonymously enjoy a shopska salad in a restaurant.

Or she could lie down on the hardwood floor and stare at all the space-themed photographs on the walls, many of them featuring Sandra Bullock in a fetal position floating in the Milky Way, stills taken from a movie in which she plays a beautiful astronaut, suggesting that this apartment was routinely rented out to film people.

Instead Ava scrolled through *The New York Times* while lying on the floor, reading the Health and Wellness section first as she always did. For some reason, learning about ways to avoid a knee injury as a marathon runner or that lavender oil had the same effect as Xanax comforted her. Intrigued by the headline "Can These Period Crusaders Convert You?" she clicked on an article about the founders of the Period Company, which pictured two women around her age sporting an enviable radiant dewiness to their skin. One of them was a famous Hollywood stylist, looking both angelic and savvy in a pink button-down shirt and jeans. The other one had bushy untamed hair and wore a black velvet jumpsuit. The women talked about the profound power of bleeding and the sensation of sitting in one's own blood. The underwear was also sustainable and waste-free. They emphasized the emotionality of when bleeding starts and that you don't have a tampon or a pad, it's just amazing Mother Nature! The message was that you should not hide your period away, that you should stop thinking of menstrual blood as contaminating or sinful, but celebrate it!

To Ava, it seemed unlikely that these women, however ambitious and forward-thinking, could erase millennia of fear and disgust around menstrual blood, which was prevalent in every major religion, from Judaism to Shintoism. Aristotle claimed that a woman could cloud over a mirror if she gazed into it while menstruating, and given menstrual blood's potency, a woman could disturb and distort the air around her, forming a force field of rage harmful to men. Considered unclean and polluting in many cultures, bleeding women were exiled into seclusion for the duration of their menses, relegated to a special hut or dark corner of the house. It seemed as though these women in the newspaper were trying to emphasize the curative and fertilizing properties of menstrual blood. It hadn't always been disgust and revulsion. In Greco-Roman times people used it as a love potion with mixed results. The Norse goddess Freyja was celebrated for bleeding red gold into the sea, and many tribal societies rejoiced at a girl's first period with ritualistic initiations, such as the Kinaalda, a rite for the Navajo girl that reenacted the first flow of the "Changing Woman," their goddess of seasons and life cycles. But for the most part, menstruation had become hated, feared, and denigrated, a gift turned into a curse, like so many aspects of the female experience.

Even knowing all this, Ava couldn't imagine Margot wanting to sit in her own blood, and she couldn't imagine herself suggesting such a thing to her daughter, despite these new companies touting its mystical, organic, and celebratory qualities. Rather, Ava would teach her to leave no trace, to keep it all tidy and sanitized because no one ever wished to confront the evidence of all that life and death, intermingled.

She then imagined Margot getting her period at the exact moment when her own eggs withered into uselessness, which wasn't far off. She wondered if there could be such a precise intersection of menarche with menopause, like two astrological charts perfectly overlapping.

In the bathroom mirror she surveyed her face and neck. Static lines ran across her forehead, reminiscent of her father's deep grooves there. One could fit a nut into them. The lines were only deepening. Her mother had pointed this out a few months ago, advising that Ava get Botox, and her suggestion didn't seem so offensive anymore. Turning her head to the side, she noted an increasing bulge gathering under her chin, as though she were storing seeds in there for the winter. "Submental fat" was the medical term for this protuberance. She thrust her chin forward and back, watching how it stretched out tautly but when she tucked her chin in, the skin puckered back into its folds, as versatile as an accordion. She thought about the salvation a turtleneck might provide, and a sudden deep kinship with Diane Keaton overcame her. Then she wondered if it was possible to wear a turtleneck in the summer, a sleeveless one, but of course that would showcase her flabby triceps, or "bat wings," as they were referred to on the internet. Somewhere, Nora Ephron was laughing as Ava considered all these non-options, trying to fend off the mixture of repulsion and bewilderment that often invaded her sense of self. She wished she were less vain, that she could just stop trying to "age gracefully" with all these useless retinol creams, collagen supplements, and morning jogs. Most of all, she wished she hated herself less for something no one could control.

Opening the sliding glass door to the patio, she stood barefoot on the hot tiles and watched the trees sway imperceptibly in the wind. The black fluffy cat eyed her from the garden down below. Beyond that, a tangle of dark shrubbery and overgrown trees, and then a chain link fence shrouded in ivy stood at the far end of the property. She barely heard the congested boulevard from here. Looking up, multiple crumbling balconies stacked one on top of another. Faded laundry hung from lines. A dog's tail stuck out between balcony bars. An old woman swept her patio with the TV on in the background. Ava wondered if anyone saw her, standing here in her underwear and oversized T-shirt, sipping cold coffee, and holding her phone. The sun beat down on her scalp, the soles of her feet burning.

She went inside and plopped down on the gray suede couch and stared at the black TV screen, aware of the waning morning, and that this precious time without obligations would dwindle away if she didn't make good use of it. Thoughts of her book swam into her mind, nagging her with the sense that she was trying to write about too many aspects of a woman's life. How to capture a whole life? With hardly any evidence of how Athenian women perceived their own experience while they were weaving, spinning, washing, birthing, and nursing, Ava would have to imagine it. Women's work, she concluded, was invisible and continuous, and so essential and life-giving that without it civilization would have died out a long time ago.

15

S he decided that the National History Museum would provide some necessary shape to this first shapeless day without Margot and Sam. And with luck it would offer some inspiration for her writing. Getting dressed, she reminded herself that the day belonged only to her, and suddenly she felt rich with time.

On the way there, the cabdriver played the thumping techno that pervaded Sofia, the constant pulsing bass vibrating throughout the city. She stared at the streets, trying to orient herself, wondering if he was taking her closer to the museum or farther away, the cab swerving through roundabouts and racing down narrow alleyways, nearly grazing brick walls crowded with graffiti: swastikas, the hammer and sickle, a skeleton smoking a cigar, "Death to Putin," and red roses blooming from a gun barrel. They passed Sveti Sedmochislenitsi Church, which she'd read was originally a Greek temple dedicated to Asclepius, the god of medicine and healing. It was later converted into a mosque, known as the Black Mosque before it became a church at the beginning of the twentieth century, as most things were once one thing and then another in this country. Ava thought about how the Thracians and then the Greeks settled here only to be invaded by the Persians before falling under Nikolayc rule. Next, the Ottoman Empire took over for five hundred years before the Russians swept in to "liberate" the country, only to control it with tsars and puppet princes before the avalanche of the twentieth century shook up its identity once again.

On the museum steps, a tired, dusty family sat while the mother distributed moon-shaped slices of apple. The children nibbled on the white flesh before depositing the skin into their mother's open palm. Standing behind a line of Japanese tourists for the ticket office, Ava watched a tired museum guard on his break check his phone as he tapped the ash off his cigarette into a nearby hedge, and a schoolteacher direct a group of rowdy kids in yellow T-shirts to form a line. Ava sensed the people's ingrained malleability after enduring centuries of invasions and waves of opposing political and religious ideologies. *To survive here, you have to become a chameleon*, she thought.

After a confusing exchange with the woman behind the counter, which involved showing her driver's license and explaining that she didn't want to rent an audio set, Ava wandered into the main hall, filled with Greek and Roman sculptures and tombstones. She paused before a golden burial mask from the fifth century BC, the male face wide and flat, with large oval eyes and thin geometric eyebrows. Passing through the interlocking rooms and clusters of tourists gathered around a collection of Greek red Attic vases from the Archaic period, she found the Locrian pinakes, and after spending some time examining them up close, having already peered over them in art history books, another odd-looking red clay tablet caught her eye. The Astra Tablet, found buried beneath the Telesterion at the sanctuary of Eleusis, about ten miles outside of Athens. The plaque, as stated, had been dedicated by Astra herself, her name written along the bottom border. Ava stepped closer, taking in the scene. The typed information card indicated that this tablet was the only known representation of the Eleusinian mystery rites. In the frame, a grouping of initiates bearing torches danced into the tableau, and at the bottom, a seated goddess held a sheaf of wheat. Ava guessed she was Persephone, given that she inhabited the bottom area of the tablet, the underworld. But the focus of the tablet was a woman who first paid homage to Persephone. In the above parallel register, the same woman stood before Demeter, and then the same woman could be found in the triangular pediment wearing a crown of myrtle, in celebration of having completed the mysteries, ascending from darkness to light, from the underworld to the upper world.

Ava stood here for a while, losing track of herself, her mind dissolving into the low chattering din, the echoing footfall, and even the tour guide's high nasal voice failed to distract her from this weightless moment. Unable to remember the last time she spent an afternoon in a museum on her own, this solitary time felt sacred, silky; she wanted to mete it out, and remain here entirely undisturbed, with no one demanding water, the bathroom, or a snack.

Stepping away from the Astra Tablet, she nearly bumped into an older man in a straw fedora and slim-cut jeans who had been standing behind her. He flashed her an apologetic grin and loudly stated that he was American, on the Smithsonian tour.

"Which tour are you on?" he asked her.

Annoyed by the intrusion, she tersely said she was here for work, trying to end the conversation as quickly as possible, but he talked about the great food he had enjoyed and his expensive hotel, the Grand Millennium. "Would you like to meet me there for a drink later?"

Staring at him, she intuited the wreckage of his life: failed marriages, estranged sons, an enlarged prostate, a big mortgage. Gout. A similar type of man had tried to pick her up many times before, with that same shaggy graying hair, eyes glinting with prurient interest, a slight swagger to his walk, convinced he was still as virile and powerful at seventy as he had been at twenty. Suppressing the impulse to laugh, she realized only old men flirted with her now, gambling that a forty-something woman would appreciate them, given her own advanced age and lessening value, as opposed to the much younger women they really wanted.

Before leaving, Ava stopped into the museum café for a quick coffee. Exposed brick walls were decorated with photographic stills of Bronze Age artifacts: spears, plates, daggers, a golden cuff meant to adorn a woman's wrist. A glimmer of iridescence caught her eye: it was the same trench coat, the same woman with the dense gray hair, now stepping up to the counter to order a coffee. Ava strained to see her face, and then in a flickering moment, the gray-haired woman turned her head, and that familiar beak-like nose and ice-blue eyes, the decisive way she indicated a particular pastry behind the glass case sent a piercing nervousness through Ava's chest.

It was Professor Nikitas.

Ava watched her pay and carry her coffee and pastry to an empty table next to a recessed window. She started to rehearse what to say, how she'd introduce herself and remind Professor Nikitas of who she was, bracing for the awkward blank expression that would surely pass over her face.

After paying for an espresso and biscotti, Ava sat down at a diagonal table and held her breath, stalling. Maybe she shouldn't say anything. It was arrogant to assume that Nikitas would remember her. So many students had passed through her classroom and sat in her office. At this point she must have served on at least fifty thesis committees. And Ava's thesis wasn't so unique that it warranted remembrance twenty years later.

Ava stared down at the silverware, the animated chatter of some Spanish tourists overlaying her thoughts.

"Ava Zaretsky?"

Ava looked up, startled by Professor Nikitas's glacial blue eyes. Nikitas motioned for her to come sit, patting the tabletop.

Smiling now that Ava sat in front of her, Nikitas fiddled with the black glasses hanging from a chain around her neck and peered again into Ava's eyes, as if they were long-lost comrades. Her sharply defined features appeared even more chiseled with age, her skin dry and tan, with numerous wrinkles lining her face, which only made her eyes bluer, intense and challenging. But she sported the same short haircut and appealing androgynous style, dressed in slacks and a navy shirt, with little adornment save for the heavy brass bracelet in the shape of a snake that she occasionally twisted around her wrist.

"Ava Zaretsky," she announced theatrically. "What are you doing in Sofia, of all places?"

After Ava explained that her husband was making a film here, Bulgaria was a cheap place to shoot, Professor Nikitas nodded, her gaze still focused, unwavering.

"It's surprising to see you here too." Ava decided against adding that she'd seen Nikitas in the church square a few nights ago, sensing that she wouldn't have wanted to be spotted like that, caught unawares.

Nikitas took a small sip of coffee before placing it down on the saucer. She explained that Sofia University had graciously invited her to lecture as a visiting fellow at the National Archaeological Institute, which was connected to this museum. She taught in the Department of Thracian Archeology, "alongside Dr. Milena Tonkova," she added with a flourish, and Ava nodded, as if she knew who Dr. Tonkova was, making a mental note to find out. "I quite like Sofia. It's a city of contrasts . . . At first I thought the people were quite closed off, but after living here over the past year I'm beginning to find my footing."

"Do you think you'll stay in Sofia?"

She smiled wistfully. "Perhaps."

"I didn't think you'd remember me, especially so out of context." Ava gestured to the brick walls and Spanish tourists studying a museum map.

"Of course I do." Nikitas reached over and took Ava's hand. Nikitas's hand felt dry and papery, coursing with heat.

"I'm sorry," Ava blurted out. "About what happened with Professor Arnott, my main line of argument was unsatisfactory to you, I know that now, but . . ."

Nikitas squeezed her hand. "I was angry at him and took it out on you. Unfairly."

"It was a long time ago," Ava managed, her voice small and nervous. "But thank you for saying that, Professor."

"Call me Lydia, for god's sake."

Heat rushed to her cheeks; she'd shown too much reverence.

Professor Nikitas continued, "I was too hard on you. And you were so young." She let the last part of her sentence hang there uncomfortably, as they both knew Ava's youth was not the real reason why her argument had caved in on itself. She had been afraid to choose something without the backing of academia behind it, without male backing, scurrying into what seemed a safe and easy corner of research at the time, instead of focusing on what she really cared about.

Nikitas lowered her voice. "I assume you heard I left Columbia."

Ava shook her head.

She sighed. "Oh, it barely matters anymore. It was entirely fabricated, in case you're wondering. Naturally, everyone's wondering. It's a he said, she said kind of thing. Impossible to prove. You know how it is."

How is it? Ava wondered, guessing there had been the kind of academic scandal so common these days, with Nikitas falling on the wrong side of it.

The café began to empty out. The afternoon light shifted, deepening into amber, the hour approaching when Ava had to fetch the kids from camp, but she pushed that internal twinge away. Time with Nikitas rippled with a charged energy; she didn't want to leave. Not yet.

Ava leaned over the lip of the table. "What are you working on now?"

Nikitas smiled mysteriously. "Something new. I'm getting a sense of it, conducting field research." Her long tan fingers briefly drummed the table. "It's startling how the past animates the present, how these ancient rituals still carry so much psychic weight, even if we forgot them, even if we don't practice them anymore, the magic is in our bones, you know?"

A shiver passed through Ava, uncertain what Nikitas meant. The mystical Orphic religions that predated Christianity? Gnosticism? Isis and Horus? Wicca?

Ava glanced down at her watch as discreetly as possible, not wanting to appear rude. It was already past three o'clock. Way past. Almost four. She was supposed to pick the kids up at three.

Her throat closed up, heat rushing into her face. The camp stayed open for another hour, but how long would it take Nikolay to drive here, pick her up, and then drive up to the camp? At least another hour, she calculated, panic engulfing her.

What must Margot and Sam be thinking? That she had forgotten them? Abandoned them on their first day at camp? Was she a terrible mother?

She was a terrible mother.

Nikitas ordered another espresso from the waiter and then announced, "Now. Tell me about your work. I assume, not wrongly I hope, that you haven't given it all up?"

Her phone vibrated inside her purse and she grabbed it. Three missed calls from Kasper along with a text: *Where are you? Are you okay? Camp called and they have the kids. Call me!*

Nikitas reached for her hand across the table. "Has something gone wrong?"

Ava shook her head, gulping down air. "I lost track of time. I have to go. I'm really sorry."

Blindly, she ran out of the café and into the crowded museum. Pushing her way through tour groups, she found the exit and scanned the street for cabs, any cab with a green light. A long line of taxis stood in front of the museum, but when she approached the first guy, muscular and stubbled, he nodded, and she momentarily forgot that nodding meant "no" before he mumbled something in Bulgarian, motioning farther down the line. The next guy was smoking a cigar and reading the newspaper and ignored her when she asked if he was free. Finally, she convinced a driver dropping someone off at the museum to take her; he reluctantly agreed, but it seemed they were all oddly unwilling to drive. Maybe because she needed to go to Boyana, and maybe it would take too long in afternoon traffic, but the fare would be higher. She didn't understand, but it didn't matter what she understood or not. She just had to get there.

The cabdriver sped down the highway. His bald head gleamed and he argued with someone on the phone, growing angrier and angrier, while smoking a cigarillo. She had to keep tapping him on the shoulder, showing him Google Maps, but the route kept changing. He swore every time it rerouted. Soon they were racing through the back roads of Boyana; she recognized the streets but didn't know where to turn. They dead-ended into a crumbling stone wall, and he jerked into reverse, the flimsy Lada hurtling backward. Saliva accumulated under her tongue, her glands secreting an odd metallic taste.

He shook his head and answered the phone again, shouting into it. On the meter, the fare climbed up to one hundred lev, which could be fifty dollars, she wasn't sure. She gripped the overhead strap, but it was flimsy and strained from so many other past grips. A goat lazily strolled into view and the driver swerved to the right, nearly hitting it. Her stomach jumped and then she fleetingly glimpsed the street where the camp was. She could even see the building's terra-cotta tiled roof.

"Stop!" she shouted.

He lurched to a halt.

"I'll get out here." She handed him 250 lev. The meter read 200, but she'd added a generous tip for traveling so far.

He spat out the window and demanded 300 lev.

A rising tide of anger engulfed her. She got out of the cab and slammed the door. "No, I'm not paying more than that."

"Fucking American bitch," he shouted, followed by a cascade of Bulgarian curses.

As she ran toward the camp, the angry crunch of tires against gravel resonated behind her.

Sweating and breathless, she pressed the buzzer.

The door swung open. A large foreboding woman wearing a denim apron filled the entryway. All the other children had already been picked up, and a pervasive gloom hung over the empty rooms, the wooden blocks neatly stacked up in wicker baskets, the wind-swept playground eerily quiet. She only heard utensils rattling in the kitchen, someone rinsing off plates in the sink. Just as Ava began to explain that she was here for Margot and Sam, they burst through the doorway, flinging their arms around her.

"Mama," they cried in unison. "You're here!"

"We thought you forgot us. Or that something bad happened to you," Margot said, eyeing Ava suspiciously.

Ava hugged them close, guilt piling into her throat like wet sand. "I'm so sorry. I lost track of time, and then the taxi driver got lost, and Google Maps wasn't working . . . I would never forget you."

The woman in the doorway shook her head and disappeared around the corner.

Margot nuzzled her face into Ava's chest and Ava patted down her poufy mane.

Sam leveled his gaze at her, a strange stoic expression clouding his eyes. "You forgot us. On our first day. Just admit it."

"I forgot the time, not you," she said, quickly texting Kasper that she was with the kids, everything was fine. Then she texted Nikolay, asking if he could pick them up and take them home. Nikolay texted back a thumbs-up emoji.

"What were you even doing?" Sam persisted, sensing her reckless distraction, knowing that her attention had momentarily shifted to someone other than himself and he was right. She had forgotten them in the thrall of Nikitas. Forfeiting her usually vigilant time tracking, she had surrendered, weightlessly suspended in conversation, and had willingly succumbed to being late.

The woman returned with their backpacks and started bemoaning the fact that Ava's children didn't eat anything all day.

Ava realized this woman must be the cook.

The cook gazed up at the sky as if beseeching God and continued: "I tell them: Eat, eat, it's not good for you to starve all day, but they don't take any food, not even water, not even bread with Nutella, they wouldn't eat, they wouldn't drink. Nothing, nothing."

"I'm so sorry," Ava said. "Back home they barely eat their lunch at school. They would rather play. It's just the way they are."

"And then," the cook continued bitterly, "your children laugh at food. They say it is disgusting, and now other children also start saying same thing. Then no one eat, not even other kids who always ate before this happened."

"Oh," Ava said, "I didn't realize. I'm really sorry."

The cook regarded her with a mixture of resentment and pity.

While they had been talking, Margot and Sam started fighting over who could hug Ava the longest while the cook motioned for them to carry their own backpacks. "Help Mama, she needs help. She can't do everything for you."

Ava took the backpacks while she felt the children tightening their grips around her, shoving and pushing each other out of the way, regressing, it seemed, to their inner toddler selves.

The cook hurried into the kitchen and came back ferrying freshly baked honey cake. She held out two warm slices on a paper towel. "Please, take. Maybe they will eat something now."

Ava nodded, touched by her warm gesture. "Thank you . . . thank you so much. And again, I'm sorry about what they did. I will talk to them about it."

The cook shrugged dispassionately. "They don't like the food I make. I don't know what they like."

"It's okay. They don't have to eat anything. Don't give them anything."

The cook stared at her, as if Ava had instructed her to beat them.

16

Inside the van, Ava sat in the front seat and offered Sam and Margot the honey cake, but they shook their heads in vigorous refusal. She ate it instead, and tasted cinnamon along with an abundance of baking soda. Still, it was good and settled her stomach.

Nikolay had just gotten off the phone with his girlfriend. Apparently, she was angry that he didn't want to spend the weekend with her.

"But I need my fucking freedom!" he told Ava. "Seeing the same face in the morning, and the same face when I get home at night—that life, it's not for me. I like to make woman happy and when she is no longer happy, then I say bye-bye." He waved playfully, as if saying goodbye to a baby.

The kids sat silently behind them, pretending not to listen.

"And you know," Nikolay said, his shiny aviator sunglasses reflecting the passing trees, the high-rise apartment buildings, "it's not just men who should be allowed to have affair. Women too, married women. I don't think they are sluts, or anything like that. They like sex, just as much as man. Why do we say they don't? What kind of bullshit is that?" He cupped Ava's bare shoulder and she sharply shrugged off his hand. Nonchalantly, he stretched his arm behind her headrest and let out a labored sigh.

The seat belt pressed tightly across her chest. Sweat gathered under her arms and trickled down her sides. Ava twisted around to glance at Sam and Margot. They stared back at her innocently.

Without warning, Sam silently farted, the ghastly putrid smell intruding into the air, so noxious that it took shape, gaining density and volume.

Margot yanked her tank top over her nose and coughed aggressively.

Nikolay rolled down all the windows and waved his hand around. "Oh, that's bad. Really bad. Hey, Sammy boy, you okay?" He grinned into the rearview mirror.

Ava spun around in the seat and hissed, "Sam! Please! Contain yourself!"

Sam shrugged and said the camp food made him do it.

"You didn't eat a thing there," she whispered. "And you can't just let it out—it's disgusting!"

He nodded, but a small self-satisfied smile spread over his face.

She asked Nikolay to please turn on the air-conditioning. "He has indigestion," Ava explained. "Sorry."

"I think fresh air would help!" He waved his hands around, indicating a refreshing breeze despite the stagnant humid heat that filtered into the car from the freeway combined with the moist fumes that still lingered in the air from Sam's fart.

Ava sank back into her seat, exhausted.

Sam announced, "I wish we could go to Jumbo."

"What's Jumbo?"

Margot rolled her eyes. "It's this huge superstore that has all these toys and things. Luca said he goes every week with his mom."

Nikolay grinned at the kids in the rearview mirror. "You want Jumbo? I take you to Jumbo. It's on way!"

Ava cut in, "I'm sure Nikolay needs to get back to the production office; he has other people to pick up today . . ." The prospect of Jumbo filled her with a vague dread, but she felt guilty about her lateness, how inexplicable it was in their eyes.

Nikolay stated, "I'm here for you guys! Whatever you need!"

Sam shot Margot a conspiratorial smile and they chanted, "Jumbo! Jumbo! Let's go to Jumbo . . . pleeeeease?"

As the name implied, Jumbo was a massive superstore with multiple descending levels filled with every kind of toy as well as other household items. All the toys were on the ground floor, crammed together on shelves under fluorescent lights, speakers blasting the same Bulgarian techno music she heard all over the city. Sam ran in the direction of the Lego section and Margot disappeared into aisles of Barbies. It wasn't even Barbie, but a knockoff version called Betty. Ava stood between the Lego section and the Betty section, unsure which kid to track.

"Margot? Sam?" she called out shakily among the other shoppers, feeling light-headed in this airless low-ceilinged store filled with disposable products, as if she'd just stepped into the internet, accosted by an incredible amount of choice.

Sam came running up with an enormous Lego set, and while he begged for it, she dragged him into the Betty section.

"It's only twenty dollars," he pleaded.

"But that's in lev," she told him, trying to calculate how many dollars it was. Fifty? Half of that? "Margot?" she yelled. The techno bass pounded through the black speakers overhead. All the Bettys behind their plastic wrapping stared back at her with dead smiles.

Sam joined in: "Margot?" She heard the bubbling panic in his voice, knowing that one of the main jobs of being a parent was to contain her own panic, no matter how worrisome things got. But Sam was panicking, sensing her panic, because Margot had vanished.

Swiftly turning the corner, they found Betty palaces and convertibles and an underwater sea castle stacked up in a pyramid with other Betty products. But no Margot.

"Margot!" Ava screamed.

Sam sharply tugged on her hand. "What if she's lost? What if someone took her?"

"We'll find her."

Sam was on the verge of tears. "How will we find her? Look at this place!"

"She's here, somewhere," Ava said, fighting off a dark doom. Her hands started to shake as she recalled all the other times Margot had disappeared.

They ran back toward the entrance, wildly scanning the sections where she might be: pink flip-flops and bikinis hung from hooks, mermaid towels, swim caps, costume jewelry jumbled together with beach umbrellas, rain boots, and decorative paper fans. She almost asked one of the employees if they'd seen a girl with dark hair, but the employee, a goth teen with a septum piercing that looked infected, morosely trudged by with headphones on, pushing a shopping cart filled with returned merchandise.

They ran back to the Betty section, screaming Margot's name. The place spun, all the bright plastic merging into one tangled mass.

Sam motioned that he was going to check the bathing suit section again. "Margot might be there. She likes bikinis."

Her windpipe tightened and narrowed while she imagined the story she would tell about losing Margot in Jumbo: It was the last time she ever saw her daughter. The Bulgarian police thought it was likely a kidnapping, Mafia ran the city after all, and Sofia was riddled with criminal activity, full of dark underworlds. Jangled by the sight of tweezers being sold by the twenty pack, along with foam toe separators, Ava changed the story: The Russian Mafia had held Margot ransom for five days, but then a competing gang stole her, selling her on the street to the highest bidder, whose identity was still unknown.

"Mom!" Margot stared up at her, her hands on her hips, her dark eyes challenging. "I've been here the whole time."

"Where?" Ava cried. "You disappeared. We couldn't find you!"

Margot sucked in her cheeks. "I was just picking out some fake nails. Can I get them? Please?"

Sam ran up to them, out of breath. "You found her!"

"You don't have to make such a big deal out of it," Margot snapped.

"Not such a big deal? I thought I lost you!" Fear surged through her again. She tried to breathe, to not lose it in this low-ceilinged megastore, the fluorescent lights making her hot, sweat gathering in the nape of her neck, beading along her upper lip. "You can't wander off anymore, we've talked about this. And especially not in a foreign country. I have to *protect* you!" Something ruptured inside her when she screamed "protect," like an earthquake thrusting a fault line. She gestured wildly, as if propelling her arms around would make Margot understand better, but in the process she accidentally knocked over a pyramid of Rubik's Cubes.

The crash of the merchandise scattering across the floor refocused her, and she took in Sam's and Margot's shocked faces. They were shaken by such a public display of emotion. She weakly extended her arms as they rushed to her. Holding her children close, breathing in the smell of their hair, their summery sunblock scent, Ava explained, attempting to sound calm and normal, that it was very dangerous to run off, she could lose them so easily in this country, they didn't even speak the language.

Anything could happen.

Margot pursed her lips, nodding. She looked up at Ava, her chin pressing into Ava's collarbone, and Ava searched Margot's unblinking eyes, hoping to convey that some unidentified male violence could happen if she didn't stay close, if she wandered too far. Too far for Ava to get there in time.

Sam hissed to Margot, "You always do this, freaking her out."

Margot punched his arm. "Shut up."

Sam started to cry.

Two middle-aged women in pastel pantsuits passed by, glancing at them. They carried armfuls of beach toys: miniature shovels, pails, rakes, sieves. A toddler ran after them in a diaper and no shirt, screeching indecipherably.

Ava scanned the area for the checkout line, but then saw a sign with a red arrow pointing down to the next level. Trapped, they would have to descend multiple levels to get out, where elevators would ferry them back up to the exit, but not before wading through rugs and Teflon pans, high chairs and suitcases. She faintly remembered seeing swim caps at one point, and knowing the kids needed them for camp she almost went back to grab them but a sudden leaden exhaustion erased all desire to do so. The kids complained that they had headaches and wanted to leave too, but Ava said, while they rode each escalator down, that this was the only way out.

Getting into the van, the kids were forlorn, as if they had been expelled from Eden, clutching their purchases to their chests. She sat with them, not wanting to sit next to Nikolay.

The drive back was muted and subdued. Ava sank into the seat, remorseful over losing her temper, replaying the scene, trying to identify the trigger point that had set her off. She felt guilty about arriving so late at the camp with only herself to blame. And the initial panic of Margot's disappearance, reverberating with other times she'd wandered off, set her on edge. Or had Nikolay's libidinousness primed her for rage?

No, Ava realized, it was none of these things.

It was Nikitas.

Sensing everyone's dyspeptic mood, even Nikolay remained quiet for the rest of the ride. Through the window, a storm gathered, the tenebrous sky readying to unleash a late afternoon downpour. And then Ava remembered that tonight was a dinner with the key members of the production to celebrate the first day of shooting.

17

W hen they got back to the apartment, Ava immediately googled "Lydia Nikitas + Columbia." From the next room, the kids argued about what to watch on TV. Headlines from 2018 popped up about a sexual harassment case in which one of Nikitas's students accused her of inappropriate commentary and touching. A hand on his knee. A hug held too long. Ava kept reading the article despite the rising crescendo of yelling. The accusation divided academia: old-time feminists, such as Judith Butler, supported Nikitas, saying this was another example of the predictable ways in which men have always undermined and invalidated powerful women who challenged the patriarchy. The younger feminists were on his side, pointing to the vicious pattern of victim blaming and noting that harassment happens to both men and women in subordinate roles. "It's about power and dominance, not necessarily gender, and we believe that Professor Nikitas abused her power in this case," they stated.

Sam yelled that Margot had stolen the remote, holding it hostage. "It's not fair," he hollered, waiting for Ava to swoop in to the rescue.

Ava stared at the photograph of the accuser. He had ruffled brown hair and wore a navy button-down shirt, olive-green khakis, and a nice watch. With one arm crossed over his chest, he stood in the middle of a cobblestoned street somewhere in Europe, looking like a disgruntled J.Crew model.

Toward the end of the article, they quoted Professor Nikitas: "Mr. Oberman's problem isn't with me. It's with his own writing, which is incoherent and lacks argumentative force. His frustration simply stems from not being smart enough." The article closed by stating that after much deliberation, the university had decided to suspend Professor Nikitas for the upcoming academic term.

Hungry for more, she typed in "Nikitas + Sofia University" and found a few images of her standing at a lectern, delivering a lecture in a low-ceilinged auditorium with mustard-colored walls. Then she typed in "Nikitas + Sofia address" and a bunch of links popped up in Bulgarian, a few leading to internet cafés and one advertising a Greek-themed restaurant. She also did a search for Dr. Tonkova, the woman whom Nikitas had mentioned, and found that she was head of Greco-Roman Antiquities at Sofia University. In the thumbnail photograph, she wore a white silk blouse, her black hair cut into a severe bob, but otherwise, the photo was nondescript, her CV in Bulgarian.

When she checked on the kids, they were contentedly watching *Moana* dubbed in Bulgarian. They didn't react when she told them to get ready for dinner.

Kasper drove along the slick black road wending through lush forest on the way to the restaurant, which was nestled in the foothills of the Vitosha Mountains.

After a few silent minutes, he asked what had gone wrong today.

Ava stared out at the passing greenery. "I was at the museum and lost track of time. Then the cabdriver couldn't find the camp. It was a mess." She had already decided against mentioning Nikitas, sensing he would disapprove somehow.

"We were the last kids there," Sam said from the back seat.

"It was only us with the mean cook," Margot added, her hair gathered over one shoulder while she tried to brush it out.

Ava twisted around. "She's not mean. She just wants you to eat normally and stop rudely complaining about the food." She stared at all the tangles in Margot's hair.

"What?"

"Will you let me do it?"

Margot yanked the brush downward but it got stuck in the tangles. "No."

Turning back around, Ava noticed a plastic bag at her feet, finding two swim caps inside. Kasper offhandedly said that the PA had found those for the kids' swimming lessons at camp.

"Oh, thanks," Ava said, feeling a wave of gratitude that he had remembered this, which she had mentioned a few days ago. She took one out of the bag, thinking it looked too small and already anticipating the kids complaining that it was squeezing their brains when a sudden memory invaded of Professor Nikitas standing before her in the college locker room, tearing off her black swimming cap, her thick gray hair cascading around her delicate ears. Ava had swum laps in the gym pool and was in the middle of changing when Nikitas approached her, fully nude, having come from the shower, her pale skin flushed from the hot water. Ava had pulled the towel tighter around her, trying not to glance down at Nikitas's untamed gray pubic hair, so poufy and unkempt it demanded attention. The wet pubic hair triangulated into a fine point, from which water dribbled onto the tiled floor.

"Eva, right?"

She had nodded, not bothering to correct her, and wondered when Nikitas would grab a towel. If she would grab a towel. Instead, Nikitas casually put one foot up on the low wooden bench, her inner thigh opening like a door. "Your comment in class the other day was quite insightful. You should speak up more." She searched Ava's face. "Why don't you?"

"Oh," Ava said, turning away to scramble through her canvas bag for underwear and shorts, "I get nervous speaking in front of people."

Her warm hand encircled Ava's forearm. "You shouldn't."

Kasper squeezed her thigh, jolting Ava out of her reverie.

The engine was off, his car door open. "Ready?"

Ava nodded, still seeing Nikitas's tall naked body before her, the distinct smell of chlorine, the reverberating moist wetness of the locker room filled with other women's voices.

Getting out of the car, she told Margot her hair was a mess. "You can't walk in there like that."

"I don't care."

Unable to resist, Ava said, "Let me brush it," gathering up Margot's hair in one hand, holding the brush in the other.

Yanking her head away, Margot screamed, "It's my hair! Don't touch it!"

Ava let go, giving up. When Ava was little, her babysitter used to brush the knots out of her hair in front of the bathroom mirror while Ava held back tears from the painful tugging, not saying anything, too afraid that she might upset the woman. Watching Margot storm off toward the restaurant, Ava marveled at how unwilling Margot was to submit. To anything.

The sudden rainfall had left the forest shining with greenness, radiating moisture. Along the perimeter of the restaurant, a mill passed water through a gurgling stream, and as they approached the log cabin, the smell of roasting meat on a spit, burning coal, and chimney smoke wafted in the air. Kasper reassured her that it was a special place to experience a traditional Bulgarian meal.

They were seated outside at a long table under a wooden pergola, tendriled vines and thick ivy hanging down from it. Low flames danced from a large flat circle filled with coal that encompassed nearly the whole courtyard on the far side of the outdoor area.

Isabel walked toward Ava with outstretched arms. "So glad we finally meet in person."

"Yes," Ava said, embracing her. Isabel smelled of the forest: of sage and bark and mint. She exuded an easy warmth, her shoulder-length hair still damp from a recent shower, her reassuring eyes a mineral green. She wore a fringed cream poncho and large hoop earrings, and multiple rings graced her fingers. Ava felt as though she already knew her from their one phone conversation, and a fluid ease passed between them as they talked about the camp, Cosmos Kids. Isabel mentioned that their apartment was two seconds away from the studio. "It has a pool, so come over anytime after camp and bring the kids swimming," she said, handing Ava a glass of rakia. They paused, casting a glance at the kids, who had their own table nearby. Already Sam was showing Luca his action figures and Margot was bent over her pad of paper, furiously sketching.

Kasper settled down at the table's far end with Marc, Rafe, and the director, Jason, along with his girlfriend, who was playing the

Macedonian princess in the movie. Bill and his wife, Sophie, sat on Ava and Isabel's end.

Numerous plates of meat on kabobs and fresh feta crumbling in blocks passed by, ferried by waiters wearing red fezzes and crimson embroidered vests with tall black boots, bringing to mind anti-Semitic Cossacks from the nineteenth century, but different, Ava told herself. In the center of a nearby table, packed with Korean tourists, a pig rotated on a spit garlanded by flowers.

More chilled bottles of rakia, the national drink, plates of shopska salad, marinated olives, and stuffed peppers appeared, covering the table. Ava downed another shot, its strong sweet apricot flavor burning her throat, lubricating herself for a long night of potentially awkward conversations.

Sam and Luca started bickering at the next table, and Isabel and Ava rose at the same time, Isabel's eyes dancing with amused annoyance at the situation, and Ava smiled back, delighting in the sound of her Brazilian accent, which made the words softer and more forgiving as she reasoned with Luca to behave, to be "elegant" was how she put it, her voice akin to a melodious river. After the boys settled back down, Isabel freely complained about all the time she spent with Luca given Marc's insane hours. She admitted to leaving him at camp for as long as possible, joking about picking him up after three o'clock most days, often the last kid there, a sad sight on that orange carpet surrounded by those worn-out blocks.

Ava told her about how she had bumped into her old professor and entirely forgot to pick up Margot and Sam, on their first day of camp no less. "I felt so guilty."

Isabel laughed. "Don't be so hard on yourself. They're totally fine, you see?"

Ava loved Isabel's nonchalance, so refreshing, an invitation to not care so much, satisfied with the conditions she set for herself. It reminded her of something her therapist, Richard, had said about American mothers feeling the constant pressure, always worried about not being good enough—a judgment that's perpetuated by the culture, by other mothers, and most of all by themselves. Richard had pointed this out during their sessions, as if boring his finger into a complicated knot, attempting to pry loose the different strands of self-attack, how it caused her unnecessary grief, how she should interrogate it when she felt judgment casting its rich dark shadow.

Isabel finished off her rakia and explained that in Brazil, nannies raised children, not mothers. She shrugged. "I barely saw my parents growing up. That's the way things are there. But in the U.S., it's like you have to be your kid's best friend, play Lego with them every day, go to the park, worry about every little thing. It's exhausting."

Ava agreed and said her parents did what suited them best. They'd had none of this manic obsession with parenting techniques that were supposed to create well-adjusted, happy kids when kids seemed unhappier than ever these days.

"Exactly. My mother traveled, saw friends, went out to parties at night. It wasn't like it is now," Isabel said.

Kasper gestured for them to return to the adult table. They were ordering main courses. Already buzzed from two glasses of rakia, Ava and Isabel made their way back while Isabel explained that she was trained in alchemy, describing how she ground up crystals and herbs according to a person's astrological sign, and that she had been giving Luca and Marc various tinctures to improve their health.

"How did you learn about it?" Ava tried to imagine ingesting hard rock.

Isabel smiled. "My grandmother was an herbalist." She passed a hand through her hair. "It's in the family."

Ava pictured Isabel's grandmother on a hillside, gathering herbs into a suede satchel dangling from her wrist. Maybe she ground the herbs with a mortar and pestle. Maybe she sprinkled them into a simmering cauldron. Maybe she was a witch in the truest sense of the word: a medicine woman and healer who compounded natural remedies from the earth.

As if reading her mind, Isabel said, "My grandmother, even though she was brought up Catholic, practiced Candomblé. She always said if a person didn't come to see her due to love, they came due to pain. The rituals induced physical and spiritual healing, sometimes by entering into trance states, spiritual possession, things like this." She paused. "Like Santeria and Voudoun, Candomblé also has a pantheon of deities, which then over time merged into the Catholic saints." She shook her head, laughing gently. "Catholicism tried to crush these native religions, but so many Brazilians still believe, visiting healers even though they are devout Catholics." She paused, her light green eyes communicating secrets. "Some say it's black magic or devil worship, but it's nothing like that."

They sat back down at the table. The men were deeply involved in a discussion about an action sequence, agreeing that the storyboards for that scene needed more specificity. The director, in his black baseball hat and hoodie, nodded to himself, making a secret calculation in his head. He scrutinized the stuffed peppers on his plate, having scooped out all the rice because he was on the keto diet. The way they talked about the movie, with such urgency and precision, blurred out the surroundings as if no one else was here.

Only Bill joined the women in conversation, throwing a jaunty arm around his wife, Sophie. He dug into the block of feta and asked what Ava wrote about and she tried to provide a brief summary of her book but all the details came out garbled, indecipherable to her own ear even as Bill nodded along. He sipped his red wine and commented that Ava reminded him of his ex-wife: intellectual, type-A, Jewish. While Ava wondered how he had guessed all these things about her, he told her that he had four sons and his ex died of pancreatic cancer ten years ago, but then Sophie nudged him in the ribs and complained that she had abandoned her dissertation to marry him. This summer, she announced, she was determined to finish it. She told Ava it was about the relationship between music and intergenerational trauma, focusing on the composer Béla Bartók and singer Margit Bokor.

While she explained the thesis in vague, meandering terms, something about the war's effect on their later symphonic pieces, Ava remembered Kasper's explanation that Bill had dated Sophie's mother in Paris in the 1960s, and now, he was married to Sophie, an arrangement so baldly incestuous that Bill often reveled in it by holding up his phone when Sophie FaceTimed him, announcing in a clear, proud voice to anyone who would look, "That's my daughter calling. Ha ha ha, just kidding. She's my wife."

Sophie gave Bill an indulgent smile, smacking his hand when he reached for more feta, and loudly whispered to Ava that he expected her to make three meals a day at their house in the French country-side, but it was very tiring. The minute she was done clearing one meal, the next one demanded preparation. She felt like rebelling.

He kissed her wetly on the cheek. "The lady doth protest too much."

"It must be impossible to get any work done, cooking all the time," Ava said, growing irritated by Sophie's moist brown eyes and girlish teasing, her being saddled with this domineering husband who was a silly nuisance, like a cumbersome child who needed constant tending, as opposed to a grown man who could make his own lunch. It was both expected and odd that he had married such a young woman, forty years his junior, to masquerade as his mother, but, Ava guessed, only young women without children had the energy for this, to play the part of daughter, wife, and mother rolled into one.

As if reading her mind, Sophie said they were trying to get preg-nant, but a few months ago she had suffered a miscarriage. "We were seven weeks."

"I'm sorry to hear that," Ava said, bristling at the use of "we" when describing pregnancy. And if they managed to have a child, she imagined Bill growing cantankerous, demanding even more of Sophie's time and affection. He would undoubtedly become jealous of the baby, especially if it was male, mirroring the Greek god Cronus, who had devoured his own children in a fit of black rage.

Everyone was quite drunk at this point, the surrounding foliage and undergrowth smudging into something menacing and off-kilter, the thick forest appearing darker, more tangled.

Ava thought she heard coyotes screeching, the disconcerting sound echoing down from the mountains. "What's that?"

"Hyenas," Isabel joked. "Or monkeys. I don't know." Her chunky knit poncho fell off one shoulder, exposing a pale blue lotus tattoo.

"Gray wolves populate this area," Bill said with authority. "I wouldn't go up there alone, especially not at dawn or dusk."

But to Ava the howls sounded closer to human cries—higher pitched, hysterical.

The kids played tag, bumping into nearby tables, almost tipping over wineglasses, and watching them whirl around made Ava nervous, especially because of the large flaming firepit. And Margot, her wild hair flying behind her as thick as a cape, ran so close to the flames.

"She's beautiful," Isabel said, her gaze trailing Margot.

"A beautiful handful." Ava glided over the question: How to harness such turbulent force? She didn't want this wild free part of Margot to erode and contort into a more docile version of femininity. But Ava also thought Margot must learn how to accept no for an answer, intuiting when to push and when to yield, that it was a dance of biding one's time and speaking one's mind—a dance, she thought, that men never bothered to learn because they didn't have to.

Isabel finished off her rakia and switched to red wine. "I'll do Margot's chart sometime. It would be interesting to see what her rising sign is."

"Okay," Ava said, fearing what disturbance the stars might spell out and wondering if Isabel would have the heart to tell her. Ava half believed in astrology, tarot, the synchronicity of signs, shamans, energy fields, all of it falling under the umbrella of magical thinking, which she was prone to because it felt alluringly mysterious, as though a stream of invisible truths ran beneath the hard material world.

Finally, the main courses arrived. The kids were manic, playing freeze tag in the parking lot, where they weren't allowed. Isabel and Ava traded off who ran after them. Sometimes on the way back from the parking lot, she paused in front of the Bulgarian waitstaff performing their traditional dances on a makeshift stage in the main room. The long table of Korean tourists had been replaced with Italians who clapped and whistled along.

When Ava returned, a sense of unease had settled over the table. The men glanced around, discomfited by the surrounding forest and the waiters carrying blazing torches into the courtyard. From the kids' table, Ava heard Margot's familiar dry cough. The tic was kicking up again. *She's tired,* Ava thought. *It's been a long night.*

The clashing cymbals and rumbling drums signaled for everyone to gather around the firepit, which now, Ava saw, was no longer flaming but filled with smoldering hot coals. The kids were excited by the mystery of it all, sitting down in the front. Ava and Isabel stood behind them. Tourists and other diners from the restaurant spilled outside to watch.

Margot twisted around, her eyes fearful. "What's happening?"

Kasper smiled and stroked her cheek. "Don't worry. Just some kind of performance."

Margot's eyes lingered on his face, unconvinced. Turning around, she coughed repeatedly into her palm. Ava squeezed her shoulder, but she jerked away.

Four older Bulgarian men in traditional garb pranced around the outer rim of the circle, their pants rolled up, their feet bare, warming up while the Bulgarians in the audience called out encouragements. The drumbeat quickened, growing more frenetic and lively. Sam and Luca giggled, while Margot sat deathly still, her arms tightly crossed over her chest.

First one man ran over the hot coals, swiftly, almost imperceptibly, and back again. Everyone clapped and hooted, and he took a deep bow, smiling broadly, and then repeated the feat. After a few minutes, the other three men joined him, darting across the coals back and forth until Ava realized they were making the shape of the cross: halfway up, and then across, the music hypnotic, their expressions stoic, as if they had transcended physical pain, while their movements were agitated and reactive, sharp with ritualized intensity. They started dancing toward the middle of the circle and then out again while beckoning to the crowd in a seductive manner. The Bulgarians cheered and laughed. The men kept beckoning, as if they wanted a lock of hair, an extracted tooth, a talisman of some sort.

Ava realized they wanted the children.

The men comically gestured, asking if they could pick up Sam, Luca, and Margot, the children fulfilling some innate ancient need. An expectant surge rippled through the crowd, filling Ava with the sense that she must say yes, allowing these older costumed men their request.

And it seemed, even with the comic atmosphere, the cheering people, the men joyfully exposing their unscathed soles, that it would inspire divine wrath if she refused, evidencing a deeply rooted ungenerosity, an aberration that would not go unpunished. She knew that fire walking descended from a pagan purification ritual passed down from the Thracians. The ritual was a bid for protection against lurking evils, and if one made it over the fire unharmed, it was a sign that the gods would protect you for another year.

This "manifest suffering," such as treading over burning coals, was supposed to unearth and exhume past trauma, or menima, the original "ancient cause of wrath." The phrase threaded through her mind. What caused such ancient wrath? Something essential and life-giving must have been taken away, and now they were forever making up for it, trying to retrieve it.

The men swiftly picked up Luca and Sam, the boys immediately tensing in the arms of strangers, their bodies as rigid as wooden planks, reminding Ava of unmoving icons. Prancing over the burning coals, they held up the boys as if they were hard-earned prizes. The crowd erupted into applause.

Then one of the men motioned that he could take Margot too, but she shook her head in refusal.

By this time Luca and Sam had been returned to their seats, laughing nervously, unsure whether or not they had liked it.

Ava put a hand on Margot's shoulder and gestured that no, Margot would stay here with her.

The man nodded, backing away. The fire performance was over.

Ava held Margot's damp hand in hers as they made their way to the table. Kasper was tallying up the check while Isabel smoked a joint somewhere off in the woods. Sophie leaned her head against Bill's chest, yawning into his shirt while he smoked a cigarette from his pack of Gauloises, announcing in a lordly tone that the wine here was shit; he couldn't wait to return to his farmhouse in Bordeaux where they harvested their own grapes.

Margot slid onto Ava's lap as she repeatedly cleared her throat, and Ava knew that Margot had sensed the dark history writhing beneath this watered-down ancient ritual: girls were often sacrificed to the gods, their burnt remains smoldering in a roaring bonfire. Agamemnon offered up his daughter Iphigenia for fair winds. Andromeda's father had chained his daughter to sea cliffs to appease Poseidon. And every year in ancient Athens, countless female infants were left exposed to the wilderness in hopes of erasing the future burden of their dowry, whereas a healthy male baby never had to prove his worth.

The ride home seemed to last forever as they sped down the winding hilly road toward the city center. The kids fell asleep, their heads lolling back and forth, their mouths slightly open, emitting warm sweet breath. It was almost midnight, and Ava's head pounded from all the rakia and wine, her stomach sloshing from the marinated meat skewers that had kept appearing on the table.

Isabel vaped from a discreet stainless-steel pen, aiming it out the window, explaining it was odorless, the kids couldn't smell it.

They're asleep anyway, Ava thought. *And it's Bulgaria.*

Cutting through the silence, Isabel said that she was also interested in intergenerational trauma, picking up on the conversation with Sophie that had taken place hours ago, before the dancing and the fire walking.

Kasper drove calmly, lost to his own thoughts. Marc nodded off in the front.

She said that one of the functions of Candomblé was to root out the origin of a person's trauma after coaxing them into a trance state. The ancestors or the gods might appear and speak through them. She coughed from the vape pen and then passed it to Ava. "It's mellow," Isabel whispered, the streetlights momentarily illuminating her face, her dark pupils enlarged.

She showed Ava a picture of a Candomblé ceremony on her phone.

Ava stared down at an image of many Afro-Brazilian women dressed in bright white dresses and skirts, headdresses gracing their heads and strings of colorful beads swinging from their necks as they danced. From their eyes fluttering closed and slack mouths, Ava could tell they were in the grip of a trance, having moved beyond the material world. The next image showed a woman lying face-down on the ground, her skirt fanned out as other people danced in a circle around her. Her elbows rose upward, her bare feet hovering above the floor. The caption read: "A worshipper lies on the floor during a Candomblé ceremony honoring goddesses Lemanja and Oxum in Itaboraí, Brazil."

Ava took a puff of the vape pen, and then another, drowsily wondering what her family history would reveal once she slipped into the grip of such a trance, what kind of trauma prowled in the margins of her story. Handing the pen back to Isabel, she twisted around to catch Margot observing them, probably wondering why Ava had been sucking on a pen, and why they still weren't at the apartment yet. They had passed the same Soviet monuments and Eastern Orthodox churches.

Ava thought about how Margot had recently asked to be called Rose from now on, not knowing this was her great-grandmother's name. There was a reason why Ava had named her Margot—it was free from any negative family associations, as ornamental as a pearl, which was what the name meant. She didn't want Margot to inherit anything from Rose, not even a name, fearing that mental illness, trauma, and bad tendencies bled across generations, or skipped over them, laying claim to the wrong person at the wrong time. A kind of doomed psychic inheritance. She wondered, glancing over at Isabel, who was now humming a Brazilian song under her breath, her eyes fluttering closed, if she should have let Margot be carried over the burning coals, as though the ritual might have somehow protected her from the ghosts of the past.

From all those bad mothers.

18

Athens, 415 BC

S ometimes I glimpse my mother from afar, and catch my breath
at her chiton, dyed a deep purple, fashioned to reveal the
curves of her body, her dark hair flowing freely and uncovered
down her back, brazen in the sunlight. She strolls on the arm of
a general or philosopher, headed with him to the symposia or to
nightly revels brimming with wine and men where she entertains
them with witty remarks, and later, her dulcet voice recites the
Homeric hymns, bringing sentimental tears to their eyes, remembering a time they have never seen. Men still applaud her beauty,
vying for her attention, which she bestows, as fickle as Aphrodite,
shining her light on one man and then another.

Watching Eirene approach womanhood, I harbor the fear that
she mirrors my mother in how she looks and comports herself,
with her fair skin and dark hair rushing down her back. As my
mother does, Eirene seeks attention wherever she goes, capturing
lustful male gazes, and I witness the sheer pleasure flushing her
cheeks when she notices men noticing her, even at this young age,
whereas I have always crept about unnoticed by most, not beautiful
enough to inflame desire. A kind of safety, yes, but also I wonder
what it would feel like, to be beautiful and admired, to be wanted.
Even a taste of it would be thrilling; instead I hear the careful
language people use to describe me: slight and olive hued, with
dark eyes, wide flat feet and rounded shoulders, a splash of moles
across my torso. Unremarkable but passable. Marriageable, at
least. But Eirene's beauty is something else; it must be tamed and
molded, otherwise she could fall victim to it, as unprotected as my
mother, a woman without a home, untethered to anything real.

But to what degree can we shape our children? Are they as porous as limestone or does a point exist after which their characters fully solidify while we waste our breath trying to mold them into someone more pleasing? Xanthe says they are who they are, already formed in the womb, and it doesn't matter how much you sing and nurse them, teach, punish, or praise them. The fates decide their path, weaving, spinning, and cutting the threads of their lives no matter what we do.

My mother left when I was seven years old because a daimon, an evil spirit, ruptured the marriage, a vague reason often meaning a pair's temperaments are misaligned, promising strife rather than domestic peace. Or perhaps Hera, the protectress of marriages, punished my mother because she was jealous of her great beauty, which was rumored to have rivaled that of the goddess and thus ran the risk of capturing Zeus's forever-wandering eye.

But I've been told my mother came with a large dowry (twenty talents at marriage, and ten talents at the birth of a son) and my father slept with the slave boys and brought prostitutes home. They were foreign women captured from eastern colonies, the kind found in any common Athenian brothel. He treated them as queens in my mother's house, showering them with pendants and cuffed golden bracelets inlaid with gemstones. He sometimes locked himself and a prostitute in their conjugal bedroom for days on end, and my mother was expected to deliver wine, nuts, and fruit for their sustenance, to further fuel their boisterous lovemaking that we could hear through the walls. My mother left the house one morning as dawn broke, the purple-tinged sky yawning open. She yelled at the silent streets that she would rather be paid for sex than endure such humiliation without payment, that hetairai boasted far more freedom than she could claim, than any wife could. My father didn't want to lose her handsome dowry and he ran after her, flinging his arms around her middle, but she had hidden within the folds of her himation a bronze-handled dagger, filched from his personal quarters, that she then sank into the flesh of his forearm. He screamed like a frenzied pig, growing faint at the sight of his own blood, his womanly shrieks rousing sleeping slaves and slumbering dogs, while the women, who always rise the earliest, watched from their windows in quiet approval.

This is how I know the story of my mother.

For a time there was no woman in the house, until my father married a distant cousin, a woman who was charmless and tight-lipped, with a deep-lined face, sorrow etched into her brow. She had lost her first husband and all of her sons on the battlefield and she hated her daughters because they refused to receive her in their households for fear of catching her misfortune, as though she were contaminated by the gods' displeasure.

But she was reliable and economical, skilled at overseeing the slaves and housing the stores of wine and grain. Nothing ever went unnoticed or to waste and she often worked at the loom in the gloomy ground floor room for hours on end without complaint—content, it seemed, to be of use. My father, finally tempered by old age, no longer brought home foreign women, and she, in turn, always offered him a gentle look and a silent tongue. Once, I even unearthed a lead tablet buried beneath our fig tree inscribed with an incantation to increase my father's love for her by summoning the Eurasian woodpecker, a common love spell. If my father was sufficiently enchanted, the appearance of the bird by her window would confirm the spell's completion. I tried not to laugh when I read the tablet: "Wryneck, wryneck, draw him to me. See how I still burn for him; I must win his favor so that he loves only me and not that terrible woman, the one who has made a ruin of his heart." And then I felt guilty in my laughter, realizing how desperately she strove for his affections, fearing he did not really love her but only found her useful.

When it came to me, her eyes narrowed into fine hard points as you can only imagine how often she saw the whisper of my mother stirring in my face, in the way I moved and spoke, as though I were a ghostly emissary from the past offering nothing but disgrace.

19

After the dinner in the woods, she dreamed she was seven years old again when her mother inexplicably left the house on a cool April morning thickened with the marine layer. For work, her father had said gruffly, watching her pull out of the driveway, but it was for another man.

Two days later, Ava found her mother's cat stretched across the driveway headed for the bushes. The cat had wanted to hide itself away to die, but she didn't make it across in time, expiring on the warm concrete. Ava drew a goodbye picture for the cat, bulky crayoned rainbows and a sun, the still-alive cat prancing among flowers. Gently, she placed the picture on top of the dead cat before her father lowered the coffin, a cardboard box, into a pit he'd dug in the backyard.

Her mother returned a few weeks later to get the rest of her things before moving into a condo on the beach, and her father started dating Chava, an Orthodox Jewish woman. Chava's hair was the color of a raven, her long tapered nails painted dark red, and she had a laugh that sounded like crackling fire. Ava could still hear Chava's deep voice, raspy from cigarettes, could still smell the strong musk perfume Chava sprayed behind her ears and feel the weight of those golden bangles that Chava allowed Ava to try on sometimes. A certain night crystallized in Ava's mind: Chava led her upstairs to the bedroom and on the bed, there was a white box with a big red bow on it. She told Ava to open it, and inside, nestled in tissue paper, lay a black velvet dress with a burgundy sash for Ava to wear to synagogue. When Ava asked what synagogue was, Chava laughed uproariously and said to Ava's father, "Does this poor girl even know she's Jewish?"

And so she taught Ava how to be Jewish. Together, they walked five miles every Saturday morning to the synagogue, Ava sweating in her new velvet dress, but she was determined to prove her worth to Chava, to not complain that her feet ached in the too-tight patent-leather Mary Janes, and to not ask why, during the service, a white curtain separated the men from the women and why the women wore these heavy wigs when Chava didn't. At home, Ava could not have her usual glass of milk with meat at the dinner table and the kitchen suddenly became kosher, with separate new white plates reserved for meat and another set, blue rimmed, for dairy. The utensils were boiled and separated and Chava started talking about installing a second sink. Beginning on Friday at sundown, Chava could not touch a light switch or turn on the TV. Instead, she went to her mother's brick Queen Anne–style house in Boyle Heights, bringing Ava along. Chava also had a beautiful teenage niece who was tan, slept on a waterbed, played varsity volleyball, and whose boyfriend drove a convertible, all of which made the niece supremely cool to Ava. They sat at a long wooden table covered by an embroidered tablecloth for Shabbat dinner and, while Chava and her mother conversed in Yiddish and the niece held hands with her gentile boyfriend under the table, Ava wondered if Chava would adopt her, if she could just blend into Chava's family.

As suddenly as Chava had appeared in Ava's life, two years later she was gone, after a bad fight with Ava's father. They had been arguing a lot lately because Chava refused to back down over certain Jewish rules, such as the fact that Ava's father insisted on running on the treadmill every Friday night after sundown to release tension from the workweek. Chava found this unacceptable. There was also the time when her father had taken Ava to see the Kirov Ballet, which Chava vehemently opposed because Russia hated the Jews, now, then, and forever. At a dinner party, Chava derided one of Ava's father's friends for driving a BMW because it was a German-made car. She threw up her hands, tipping over a nearby wineglass. A little bit of red wine seeped into the tablecloth. The friend stood up from the table and shouted on his way out, "He used to drive a fucking Porsche," gesturing to Ava's father.

Violent yelling and tearful ultimatums vibrated behind closed doors. Ava put her ear to the bedroom door, her stomach in knots, trying to decipher if Chava would stay or go. She wanted her to stay.

For a few years, Chava sent Ava birthday cards from Tel Aviv, where she had moved. In her large loopy script, she wrote about how much she missed Ava and loved her, and how sad she felt, not seeing Ava anymore. After her father met a new woman, the cards stopped.

Ava ping-ponged between two homes: one week at her dad's, one week her mom's. Back and forth in the car every Sunday afternoon, the handoff day. At her father's, she couldn't wait for the week to end and often fell asleep hoping that Chava would wake her once morning came and she would drink in her beautiful face again: the bright red lipstick and black eyeliner, the sunlight splintering through the wooden shutters illuminating her dark hair in a golden glow. When she awoke, Ava was often confused about where she was before checking the wallpaper. Floral print meant she was at her father's house, blank white walls her mother's.

At her mother's, a new man invariably appeared for the night, for the week, for a stretch of months until her mother grew tired of him, and he would vanish. In the morning, Ava often found a strange man sitting in her seat at the breakfast table, disoriented by the sight of this new person inhabiting the breakfast nook, wearing an old bathrobe with his hairy chest exposed, or smoking a cigarette while reading the paper. A man who might ruffle her hair or ask her what subject she liked best in school while she stared at her toast, a lump in her throat. A man who was a waiter or an orthodontist or a music archivist. One of the men, a psychiatrist, had been a medic in the Israeli army and insisted on racing her up the tangled steep hill in the backyard, beating her to prove his physical prowess. The orthodontist gave her packets of strawberry-flavored floss and mini tubes of toothpaste. The music archivist, often surrounded by a heady cloud of marijuana smoke, told her what music to listen to: the Velvet Underground, the Doors, Van Morrison, the Stones. The waiter cooked them elaborate meals that her mother said were fattening, pushing the plate away.

Eventually, her mother hated all these men, raging and screaming and throwing them out one by one. In the aftermath of every breakup, she consoled herself with the mournful folk ballads of Joni Mitchell and Lucinda Williams but she couldn't stop stepping into the ring of fire. Her favorite songs were "House of the Rising Sun" and "Summertime," songs with melancholic lyrics that she sang into the half dark while Ava drifted into sleep.

Ava liked the men and felt bad for them when they had to leave. She understood that they had loved her mother, but somehow it was never enough for Cynthia. As parting gifts, they left Slinkys, My Little Ponies, invisible-ink pens. Toys to remember them by. Toys that seemed to say: *We had a good run, kid. Take care and so long.*

Cynthia often took Ava out to dinner on school nights because she hated to cook, said it was a waste of her time. At the restaurants, men always sent over drinks. Champagne cocktails, cosmos, dirty martinis with a toothpick spearing a line of green olives. On the accompanying napkins they scrawled their telephone numbers with a catchy line. *Hey beautiful, I'm your man. Where have you been all my life? Come with me to Ensenada next weekend.*

Cynthia loved it. Sitting next to her, Ava watched her mother light up while a pit grew in her own stomach. Why didn't the men care that she was having dinner with her mom; didn't they know not to intrude with their suggestive offerings and leering smiles? And worse, why did her mother encourage their advances, flirting back, accepting all those drinks? Ava watched her mother illuminate a room while she trudged in her shadow, feeling matronly and dowdy, angry that she felt older than her own mother, that she had always been the one to remind her when it was time to go home, to know when the party was over.

Now a mother herself, Ava was in awe of Cynthia's unabashed pursuit of love and admiration at all costs, how she shrugged off guilt as easily as shrugging off a featherlight shawl, offering her standard unapologetic refrain when Ava said it had been hard to meet all the different boyfriends and husbands, and hard to cope with the number of times her mother returned home late, smelling of dark laughter, to which Cynthia crisply replied, "I'm sorry you feel that way."

But her mother enjoyed having a travel companion, especially when people started mistaking them for sisters; she carted Ava along to Madrid or Rome or Athens and taught her about art, dragging her from one museum to the next, and this was how all those paintings and images seeped into her consciousness from an early age. The Dutch masters. Goya's *Third of May* and El Greco's elongated suffering saints, ashen and gaunt. Rembrandt, her mother's favorite, because of the way he worked with light. Hieronymus Bosch's *Garden of Earthly Delights*, the depictions of heaven and hell populating her dreams for years. They roamed the marble halls of the Prado, the Uffizi Gallery, Rijksmuseum, the Villa Borghese. And the Met, with its ancient Greco-Roman section full of twisting marble statues, sarcophagi, pediments, and friezes. The alluringly nude Aphrodite was her mother's favorite: the goddess of erotic love and beauty, the most sought-after and admired. Her arms were lost, her nose chipped off, but originally, Ava learned, her arms had reached forward to shield her breasts and pubis in a gesture that both concealed and accentuated her sexuality. The other goddesses—veiled, pious, and matronly, such as Hestia, Hera, Demeter—didn't interest her mother.

Sometimes Ava thought about her mother's mother and she felt bad for what her mother had endured as a child and realized that, given the circumstances, her mother had come out okay. Things could have been much worse. Rose, Cynthia's mother, was a schizophrenic who could barely make a sandwich. She lay in bed all day with crippling migraines and the curtains drawn, heckled by her sister-in-law for being overweight. Her husband periodically beat her with a golf club, his folded-over belt, whatever was at hand. She moved timidly through her own house, a shell of a woman walking on eggshells. Rose's mother, Devora, had been sweet natured, but she died young of a brain hemorrhage. After this, a blank. No one knew anything about Devora's mother, only that she was born in some Russian shtetl terrorized by pogroms and then erased by World War II.

When Ava was little, Cynthia dragged her along to visit Rose in a nursing home in Encino, the hot dry valley air filling her nostrils even before they stepped out of the car. Once inside, the smell of cafeteria food mixed with urine, and the frail elderly patients, staring up at Ava from their wheelchairs lined along the hallway, made her dizzy. A swift blanket of dark invaded her field of vision, the linoleum floor tilting upward and dissolving beneath her feet. Looking down, she didn't recognize her own hands. Her mother sighed, "We haven't even seen her yet and you're already passing out."

Her mother carried her out of the place and only once they were in the parking lot did Ava regain her footing, her forehead damp, her heart still beating too fast. During the car ride home, Ava stared at her mother's hands, fixated by their ugliness: her knuckles were perpetually swollen, the nails yellowed and roughly oval, the thick bulbous blue veins running beneath her thin skin like malevolent rivers. Ava had the same hands.

Despite all this, Ava still hoped that Cynthia would mother her more, a yearning that heightened after Margot's birth. In a delusional postpartum haze, Ava had fantasized that her mother would rock Margot, change her diaper, or take her out on walks in the stroller to allow Ava to sleep for a few stolen hours, but instead her mother lounged on the couch and asked for a glass of champagne, chitchatting about the latest movie she'd seen or her new favorite restaurant while Margot cried, fussy and gassy, her spit-up peppering the floor and leaving thick yellowish smears on Ava's T-shirt.

When Ava once tried to hand Margot to her mother because she had to go to the bathroom and didn't want to place the baby down on the playmat, her mother stiffened, her arms instantly rigid, muttering that she was too nervous to hold the baby, she might drop her on the head.

Now that she was growing up, Ava could see how much Margot resembled Cynthia and not Ava; they shared the same pale skin and dark eyes, the same long black-brown hair. The same kind of piercing beauty. Cynthia taunted Ava about their resemblance, teasing, "Margot looks exactly like me. Everyone says so. She doesn't look like you at all." It used to anger Ava, because it was true, but now she resigned herself to being the bridge between her mother and her daughter. She saw how her mother's beauty and general disposition had jumped over Ava, as blithely as a stone skipping over water, and found its nesting place in Margot.

20

Sofia, July 2019

H er eyes fluttering open, Ava sensed that her mother was here, the scent of her gardenia perfume and Dove soap wafting in the air, her hand resting on Ava's forearm, but then it was Margot sitting on the side of the bed, staring at her.

She caressed Ava's face. "You look pretty when you're asleep."

Ava sat up, rubbed her eyes, her daughter's face coming into focus. "Thanks." She heard Kasper in the shower and glanced at the time. Seven thirty. He'd leave soon to take the kids to camp.

"Are you okay?"

"Yeah, just a lot of dreams."

"Me too."

"Did you have a bad dream?"

Margot hesitated. "No, it wasn't bad . . . it was just . . ."

"Just what?"

"I was having sex."

Ava was now fully awake. "Oh," she said, stifling any sign of alarm. "What happened? I mean, what do you mean by sex?"

Margot shrugged, her cheeks flushing. "I don't want to talk about it."

Ava cleared her throat. "Okay."

Margot smiled mysteriously, and just as Ava was about to ask a few more questions her phone buzzed with texts. She grabbed the phone off the nightstand, hoping it was Nikitas. A week had passed since their encounter, after which Ava had sent her an email that it was great seeing her, they should meet again soon. She'd sent the email to her Sofia University address with no idea of how often Nikitas checked it during the summer months. Maybe rarely. Maybe not at all.

Since that day in the museum, Ava had started reassessing her life choices through Nikitas's eyes, imagining that Nikitas would judge her for coming here to support Kasper, and for a movie that she would pass off as another hyperbolic adolescent male fantasy that only perpetuated the wrongness of things. *Why would you waste your precious time and energy uprooting everyone to Bulgaria when you have important things to write, ideas to explore? What do you have to show for yourself at forty-five? A marriage? Two kids?*

Anyone can do that.

Nikitas's imaginary scolding rang in her ears as she read the text chain, none of the messages from Nikitas: *Hey! Fourth of July cook-out at our place Thursday—will be a blast! Any food allergies?*

The texts had come in overnight from moms with whom she'd been vaguely friendly, but their faces were now a blur of smiles.

Ava wrote back: *We're in Bulgaria for the summer but thank you for thinking of us!*

A mother on the chain replied: *OMG! This whole time I thought you were in Bolivia. Ha ha ha.*

Checking her work email next, Ava saw that a former student had written her two weeks ago about a recommendation for an internship. She remembered that he was from San Diego, a surfer with sun-bleached hair and a studied casualness, but at the end of the semester he had demanded a higher grade, negotiating with her as if he were buying a car.

She deleted his email.

After Kasper left with the kids, she performed some small meaningless tasks that helped to dissolve some of her displeasure that Nikitas hadn't emailed her. She took out the trash, tossing the bulging plastic bags into the dumpsters in front of the apartment. She squeezed a few drops of peppermint oil that Isabel had given her into the insoles of Sam's and Margot's sneakers to freshen up the stultifying odor of bacteria and sweat that had been accumulating there because they refused to wear socks.

When she finished, a sense of mindless accomplishment washed over her and she felt less anxious about Nikitas and less shaken by the dreams of her mother. Resolved to work on her book this morning, she cleared off the dining room table. The kids had left their goggles tangled up next to her notes, and she noticed that Kasper had forgotten to pack their water bottles, which still stood next to the kitchen sink, unrinsed. She sighed, trying not to imagine them collapsing from heatstroke on a hike. Staring at the computer screen, she waited for inspiration, her thoughts diffuse, streaming in multiple directions. Leaning back into the chair, she chalked up her wandering mind to this foreign country and foreign city, rationalizing that she was still getting her bearings, when in truth, there was something missing.

Something like blood, hair, and bones.

Breath and sweat.

Something real, lived, and experienced.

At eleven, she took a yoga class at Yoga Vibes, seeing the same anorexic woman from last time on her mat next to the arched window, armed with a large canister of Greek mountain tea, which had healing properties, according to Isabel. After this, Ava had lunch on her own in a café and then went to a park and sat on the grass, reading *Middlemarch,* starting from the same place, forgetting what she had read the previous day, the type small and dense, the paper tissue thin. But she was determined to reach the end, where Dorothea feels that her creative efforts have split into multiple streams, between child-rearing and offering Casaubon eternal encouragement, while her own work has languished, but at the same time, she's resigned to this fate, to the unhistoric contributions of a hidden life.

Scrolling through some recent photos, she texted Erin a few that conveyed Sofia's gritty melancholic mood: a graffitied wall, the "blue unicorn" ice cream Margot and Sam loved, the dimly lit interior of an antique books shop with old issues of *The New Yorker* in Russian. The last photo she sent was of the steeple of the Seven Saints Church against a darkening sky.

Erin: *I love these pics. I miss you!*

Ava: *Me too. How are things with Nolan?*

Erin: *I'm sending you something I wrote last night. Hold on. Check your email.*

*We are angry. And tired. Worn to the bone. Our bodies aching
from carrying all those grocery bags and orgasms that were
promised but never came. Fed up! Of thinking ahead, of taking
the silent blame for that birthday card that was never sent to
your husband's sister or mother or aunt, cause why didn't he?
Why didn't he.*

*And when the anger and weariness suddenly head straight
into all that wisdom we've gestated through the years—the
strength, the silent confidence brewing, the insight to finally
know that we've had it. We feel every part of our aching bodies.
We feel a desire that was never matched, a burning anger that
was never released, because we all know only witches get angry
and when they do the world will burn.*

Ava texted: *Are you okay? Just reading your email.*

Erin: *We finally started couples therapy today. Nolan complained
that the older female therapist was on my side and that we ganged up
on him. Halfway through the session he walked out. Male fragility is
so fucking frustrating.*

She added a crying cat emoji and Ava hearted it.

That afternoon, Ava and Isabel hiked in the mountains, the city
a smoggy apparition from this height. Unspoiled paths shaded by
towering spruces and firs led upward at a vigorous incline alongside a mountain stream. Isabel knew these trails because she had
lived here a year ago when Marc worked on a different film at the
same studio. She was used to the itinerant lifestyle of packing and
unpacking, following Marc to the next gig, having already relocated
to Prague, Budapest, Atlanta, and New Orleans over the last two
years. In each new city, Isabel set up camp, unconcerned if Luca
missed half of second grade, bringing along his textbooks that they
never opened. Ava marveled at Isabel's laissez-faire attitude, wishing she was more like her, wishing that she worried less about Sam
and Margot and "let go more," as Isabel often suggested.

Worrying is a love language, Ava had read somewhere, but it was

also an exhausting one. To the kids, she was an annoying hall monitor, and to Kasper, an anxiety-ridden wife. But was it asking too
much, wanting Kasper to dip into some of her concerns? Or to at
least pretend to? Even if Sam forgot all of his multiplication tables
and Margot's mood swings worsened? Margot's temper flared at the
slightest provocation, information at which Isabel only smiled and
shrugged, saying it was all the fire in her sign: Aries, the ram. Ava
liked this explanation; she couldn't be blamed if it was up to the
stars, her children's personalities baked in by the time they were
born.

Entering a shaded patch, Isabel agreed. "They are who they are,
but so many parents walk around tearing their hair out, thinking
they can change the basic elements." She took a sip of water from
her canteen.

Ava caught her breath, the steep, unfamiliar terrain ferrying the
air out of her lungs.

Isabel moved ahead, a multicolored bandana wrapped around
her wrist. The trees breathed a deep emerald green; shards of sunlight filtered through the pine needles.

A few older hikers passed, stabbing the ground with hiking poles.
A group of Dutch tourists trailed behind them before disappearing
down another path, their jovial laughter echoing off the mountains.
And then silence returned.

When they arrived at a stream, Isabel bent down, refilling her
canteen, explaining that silver ran through the water, and in Roman
times, people traveled here from far-off provinces to drink its restor-
ative powers.

"Come," she said, smiling. "Give me your bottle."

Worry fluttered at edges of herself as she anticipated dysentery,
or worse. But she handed over her empty bottle, watching Isabel
fill it. While she bent down, Isabel's shirt rode up a bit, revealing a
tattoo that Ava hadn't seen before.

Taking a small sip, the water tasted brackish, slightly metallic,
but Ava gulped it down anyway. Gesturing toward the left side of
Isabel's lower back, Ava asked if the tattoo was a new one.

Isabel smiled. "It's my first, from when I was sixteen. A fairy."
She pulled up her shirt more so Ava could get a better look. Ava

made out a smudged greenish figure with blurry wings perched on a moon, her head turned in a backward glance, one eye closed in a wink.

"She used to be a sweet fairy." Isabel's voice stirred with laughter. "But now she's a witch."

They both started laughing, almost hysterically. They bent over for a minute to catch their breath, their palms balanced on their knees.

Two young women emerged through the trees, their taut tan stomachs glistening with sweat as they held up their phones to take selfies, instructing each other on the most flattering pose. They laughed, flicking their ponytails, examining the photos before taking new ones.

While Isabel tightened the laces on her hiking boots, Ava admired the young women's elastic bodies, unblemished by age or childbirth. Time mercilessly marked her body, her breasts deflated of their former puffiness, her stomach crinkly after the three pregnancies, especially noticeable when she attempted a plank. Balanced on her forearms the other day in yoga, she had witnessed her distended abdomen, the sight frightening, reminding her of hanging elephant skin, a part of her body she no longer recognized as her own.

Standing up, Isabel suggested they run the rest of the way down. They left the young women behind, gaining speed as the path tunneled downward, and for a moment Ava believed that she could outrun her increasing invisibility, her physical decline. Running through scrub and brush, careful not to catch her foot on a jutting tree root, an unwanted memory of her mother invaded in which she routinely plucked up the skin on the top of her hand and watched how long it took for it to snap back into place, explaining that the longer it took revealed how old a woman really was. Young supple skin immediately returned to its original smooth position, while she demonstrated that her thick veiny skin stood upright for a few seconds before slowly sinking back into place. As a child, Ava had been unnerved to watch this repeated over and over again at the dinner table, a contest between her mother and her mother's best friend as they competed to see whose skin stood up longer. Then they would pinch the top of Ava's hand in a hostile attempt to compare youth with age, health with degeneration.

A few days later, Isabel started a series of online classes that took up most of the day. One was a shaman certification class; she was also studying feng shui, explaining that for good luck the kitchen, which was the heart center of the house, needed to have the color red, plus copper pipes, and so on. Sometimes when Isabel talked about feng shui or her spirit journeys on ayahuasca, or the various crystals and minerals she compounded for Luca to ingest, Ava felt her mind flatten into blankness. It was too much information, a foreign language she didn't understand. And she feared that if she took it too seriously there would be no end to it, no boundary between what was real and not. Already, that boundary felt fragile enough here.

Without Isabel, Ava hiked the mountain on her own, her mind still swimming with details of her encounter with Nikitas: her bracelet in the shape of a snake, her animated interest, while Ava also sensed it was coated over with disapproval when Ava had told her she was an adjunct. She'd seen it: the irritation that clouded the professor's face when Ava sprang up from the table, rushing to get her kids. She had a gaping sense that they still had so much to talk about, but the conversation had been cut short, almost violently, by the intrusion of Ava's real life.

On the way up the mountain, she kept checking her email, hoping Nikitas had replied and knowing that it was stupid to look at a phone in nature, that the whole point of hiking was to not think about Nikitas, or about anything else. But already a week had passed and Ava feared her email hadn't gotten through, or that Nikitas didn't care enough to respond.

Sliding the phone into her back pocket, she glanced around at the wild forest, full of unfamiliar sounds, absent of Isabel's reassuring chatter. Overgrown trees created a tunnel of shade, shielding the sky from view, making her feel, as she waded deeper into the woods, that she was descending into unfamiliar territory, even though she knew she had walked this way before with Isabel.

Feeling a stab of anxiety, Ava told herself this was a quiet, secluded place, nothing bad would happen. She would find her way back.

But something about the shaded thick forest, the scarred tree trunks, and the dark fertile soil breathed blood, as if summary executions had taken place here, death marches, partisan raids.

Or ancient sacrifices of some kind.

Pre-Christian.

Pagan.

The path wound up the mountain and, rounding the corner, she glanced upward and thought she saw two black hounds darting through the underbrush, their forms sleek and fast. She froze, the air turning unpredictable, vibrating with her own fear. Squinting from the light splintering through the trees, she strained to see the dogs, to confirm that she had in fact seen them, but only an eerie stillness settled over her, accompanied by the sound of her own thudding heart. Slightly dizzy, she knelt down, tenting her fingers on the ground, deciding that she'd seen nothing.

After walking for another half hour, she felt better and thought about turning back when she came upon a cave built into the mountain. The ancient Greeks considered caves entrances into the underworld, linking the living with the dead.

At the mouth of the cave, a little shrine had been erected: a ceramic vase filled with a dried bundle of wheat, votive candles burned down to waxen stubs, and a lock of shorn hair, the strands smooth and shiny, reminding her of Margot's hair, that deep brown-black color. She reached out to touch the hair, the feeling of it against her fingertips electric, jolting her with a vague memory from some unidentified past, echoing a preparatory, ritualistic moment that marked the end of something, allowing for the beginning of something else.

Her eyes traveled upward, to the wooden icon of the Virgin Mary with the baby Jesus nailed above the cave's entrance. There she was again, Mater Dolorosa, this most famous mother of all, immortalized for losing her son, for the unendurable grief that followed even though he came back to life, even though he died to atone for humankind's sins. Ava wished she felt comfort in this image, but she imagined her own dead son hurtling through darkness, through unending night, through dark atomic matter. This icon of the Virgin

Mother frozen in eternal mourning offered no comfort and neither did all the other grieving mothers who preceded her: Hecuba hermetically sealed herself off from the world to weep over the loss of Polyxena. Niobe was still rumored to shed tears on Mount Sipylus over the killing of her twelve children. Clytemnestra's daughter Iphigenia was sacrificed by a father who didn't know how to be a father.

Such sorrow never forgets, Ava thought, steadying herself against the cave wall. Over time, it transmutes into guilt and memory. No amount of offerings or prayers mitigate it, and mothers sometimes kill in the wake of such blinding grief.

She ran her fingers over the fluffy wheat bristles before withdrawing her hand. As she crouched here in the dirt, it felt sacrilegious to linger here too long, but something about the rough-hewn icons, the agricultural symbols, the lock of hair, and the vertiginous dark emanating from the cave beckoned, echoing of the ancient Goddess. The one that Nikitas had wanted her to write about in college. The one she had forsaken.

21

We have all buried a child with our own hands. I am not especially cursed. It is easier to tuck my painful remembering into the surrounding chorus than bear it alone. Just as I'd rather recall past stories of mothers, deranged with grief, than dip back into my own suffering, which is not the whole of experience but a small tiny piece of glass embedded in a great sprawling mosaic.

But in unguarded moments, my own private grief rushes in, hurtling me back to when I was a new bride, heavy with my first child, merely fourteen years old. Too young, some say, to carry a child to full term. Toward the end of the eighth moon, I didn't feel him moving for three days and my womb felt dry, oddly shrunken, as if filled with nothing but light and air. I paced the house, placing my palms this way and that on my stomach. I lay down, willing him to move, hoping I would feel something if I remained still, but fearing my husband's gossiping sisters, I stood up again and pretended all was fine, taking my place at the loom again.

By the third night, I started to bleed, passing large clots. I stole into the woods, like a hunted animal, stalking the silent forest for a place to rest, my inner thighs slick with blood, a searing pain shooting through my back and lower abdomen. I squatted in front of a rock surrounded by the protection of trees and held on to it as if it were a mast, and after some agonizing hours of sweat mingled with guttural cries, my whole body shaking with effort, I pushed him out, a perfectly formed baby boy, so still and blue, his heart must have stopped days ago. He had matted dark hair, his pursed lips delicate, as if carved from marble. Instead of burying him in the forest, where the animals would dig him up, I wrapped him in a muslin cloth and carried him back for a proper burial, all the while burning with shame. I had failed so early in my marriage and everyone would talk of my misfortune, wondering in what other unforeseen ways I was cursed. And I had loved him, the boy I imagined him becoming, filled with anguish that I would never know him, save for this tiny stilled life cradled in my arms.

Nearly home, I saw the torches burning in the courtyard, the women waiting for me, my mother-in-law among them, and I almost pretended he was alive, as if I could fool them, or fool myself. But when I approached, the swooping women encircled me, spiriting away his small swaddled form, and the rituals began.

They washed, dressed, and anointed his body with oil. And then laid him out on the garlanded bier in the main room of the house. I knew what to do, as I had witnessed many times before, holding his head in my hands while the other women stood beside me with arms raised, tearing at their hair and striking their breasts. Some scratched at their cheeks, relishing the sting of blood. We rubbed ashes into our hair and smeared dirt over our faces. The hearth extinguished, we sang lamentations until dawn, our voices blending into one voice, the heavy dense sorrow vibrating through my sternum, blooming into my throat, and pouring into the room as the burning frankincense emitted sweet fumes.

Just before dawn, we walked to the cemetery on the city's edge. I gently placed him, wrapped in the finest of linen, into the simple stone sarcophagus to mark his grave. We lathered the carved stone with oil and garlanded it with flowers, so that from afar, the oil would glisten in the sun for all to see. Then we poured honey and wine into the earth for the dead to drink.

Afterward, we visited the temple of Artemis to make the necessary sacrifice that would begin to purify the pollution that death and birth bring upon a house. Even while we slit the piglet's throat and I dedicated my bloodied robes to the goddess, the choice parts of the pig burning up into thick plumes of smoke, I heard whispers. My mother-in-law reminded everyone of the day she had first glimpsed my long face at the betrothal ceremony when her beloved little dog died on the spot, a sign, she said, that I would

bring death upon her house. Others shushed her, saying we'd all
lost children, I was no different. My sister-in-law remembered
when they wrapped a cloak around me and burned incense beneath
my womb and the smoke rightly passed through and out of my
mouth, a sign, she added, that I could bear children. But then the
usual discussions about my womb ensued; was it too wide or too
small, or had I picked up a heavy weight, ate too much or too little,
drank excessive amounts or suffered from a fright? Rumors and
theories circulated throughout the house and ribboned through
my mind for days as I tried to determine what I had done wrong. I
feared someone would start a rumor that they'd spied me jumping
up and down, touching my bottom with my heels with every leap,
that this had caused his death, when in truth, I had followed every
precaution, resting and eating moderately, taking my daily walks
and working calmly at the loom with the others. And knowing that
the anger of Artemis, the virgin goddess and huntress, was always
a risk, I had visited her sanctuary many times before marriage and
during pregnancy, offering her sweet fruits, honey cakes, libations,
and when I could, small birds as sacrifices so that she would not
become a vengeful lion, striking me down, but a tamed yoked
goddess who would ensure safe passage during childbirth.

We all hope good things will flow from pious acts, but we also
know that nothing is guaranteed, as our fate sits in the lap of the
gods. We all hope that Artemis will come to our aid in our most
painful hour of labor and release us from suffering, but in my case,
she turned cruel and bloodthirsty, her quivering arrow shooting
into my womanly destiny, shattering it. Perhaps past injustices
done by my mother enraged Artemis, my mother who ruptured my
lineage with her strident defiance, infuriating the gods. And so I
keep paying for my mother's actions in the currency of grief.

After ten days, the purification process began. We swept the
house with seawater and I took a ritual bath, the bracingly cold
water pouring over my shorn head as I sat shivering in the terra-
cotta bathtub, scabbed knees pulled up to my chest, my pitiful thin
frame bruised from beating myself, my tears intermingling with
the cool freshness.

We relit the hearth and made votive offerings to Hygieia,

Artemis, Demeter, and Persephone, while I placed a lock of my shorn hair onto the household altar. Arms outstretched toward the rekindled hearth, I made a public plea for protection in childbirth, in front of all the women and gods to witness.

After I buried my son, I shared in Demeter's pain, she having lost her daughter Persephone to the underworld, as I felt the same ragged grief for many moons. But then I remembered how Persephone emerges from the underworld, their reunion sweet, blooming with new growth, new chances and days. And yet Demeter cannot keep her forever. Every winter Persephone descends into the underworld again and Demeter must await her daughter's return in the spring. I awaited another child, another chance, hoping and trying for a better outcome next time, while in dreams I yearn to embrace my lost son once more.

22

A few days later, Ava called the university, asking to be connected to Professor Nikitas, but the secretary transferred her to a fax machine. She hung up and called again, only to encounter the same aggressive sustained beep, and after that, Ava began to accept that she might not see Nikitas again. That their chance meeting was only meant to happen once, the singularity of it preserving its specialness somehow. And maybe it was for the best, given the strong emotions her sudden appearance had stirred in Ava, as if Nikitas held up a magnifying mirror to her life, forcing Ava to see the neglected patches, all the ways in which she was failing.

This afternoon, after Ava and Isabel picked up the kids from camp, Isabel invited them over to her apartment. It was oppressively hot, and her place was only minutes away from the studio, with a pool. When Ava walked inside, it was a shock. Drying on a sagging clothesline strung from one end of the small kitchen to the other were various herbs arranged by size and shape: ragweed, lavender, yarrow, nettle rhizome, ginger, garlic. Mortars and pestles were stacked up on the stove. While the boys ran to Luca's room to unpack a Lego set, Margot and Ava stood frozen in the kitchen, their fingers interlocked. It seemed as if the entire ecosystem of roots, leaves, herbs, and stems was now bottled into carafes filled with homemade tinctures. Written in Isabel's cramped scrawl, notes marked the most recently harvested batch of angelica, burdock, and mugwort. Ava scanned the spines of the books neatly piled on the counter: *The Practical Handbook of Plant Alchemy, The Illustrated Herbal,* and *Secrets and Virtues of Medicinal Plants.* Isabel also kept multiple mason jars, scattered around the kitchen and lining the windowsills, stuffed with oregano and parsley for cooking, along with various other herbs that she said were good for digestion and PMS, for sleep, anxiety, and depression. She talked about how so many essential oils were adulterated in the extraction process, but here in Bulgaria she knew where to find pure oils, especially rose oil.

Pausing, she spritzed some rose oil into Margot's hair from a nearby bottle.

"That smells nice," Margot murmured, mystified by all the labeled jars and dried herbs suspended in the air, as if she had stepped into an ancient apothecary.

"It's hydrating and helps with anxiety," Isabel said before handing Ava a little satchel filled with lavender and marjoram for improved sleep, instructing her to boil it first. Ava inhaled the earthy scent through the linen cloth and Isabel added, "I give a small amount to Luca at night."

"Where do you find all this?"

"From my garden." She gestured through the sliding glass door to a row of plant beds lined up on the balcony. "Same herbs I grow in Brazil. And I get the ones I can't grow here in specialty shops."

Out of the corner of her eye, Ava saw a handful of slippery jack bolete mushrooms resting near the stove. Isabel whispered, "Don't worry. I would never leave the dangerous kind out."

"What kind is that?"

Isabel's eyes danced mischievously. "The kind that give you the visions."

Ava pictured psychedelic colors melting into one another, flowers blooming open and closed, faces dissolving into pixels. She thought of the cover of Richard's book: fertility statues surrounded by swirling gusts of tangerine and magenta.

Margot wandered off to see what Luca and Sam were doing.

Isabel opened a bottle of chilled rosé, joking that she'd become an expert on the varieties of the Bulgarian grape.

Raising a glass, Isabel whispered, "To beatific visions."

They clinked glasses.

Ava took her first crisp sip. "To visions," she said under her breath.

·   ·   ·

By six o'clock, buzzed and loose-limbed, they dove into the pool with the kids, the cool chlorinated water a reprieve from the afternoon heat.

Her foot skimming the pool's chipped basin, she wondered if she had become a late afternoon drinker and if so, did it matter? Erin had once denounced the mommy drinking culture, in which moms enabled other moms to drink, as some kind of reward for being moms, giving themselves a free pass to pour vodka into sippy cups and sneak it into the playground, their kids running wild while they toasted one another in shared rebellion, breaking the rules and smiling into their secret drinks.

But, Ava thought, as Isabel opened another bottle after they returned from the pool, both of them still in their damp bathing suits, towels wrapped around their waists like bulky skirts, they were in Bulgaria. Maybe she could loosen her self-imposed rules. Maybe it was okay.

Isabel looked up at Ava when the cork popped, her bedroom eyes hazy, the green cloudier today. "I drink way too much here. And we smoke at night after Luca's asleep. Bulgaria, I say, so it doesn't matter. Anything goes here."

Ava nodded, watching Isabel refill their glasses.

Later on, while Margot was drawing with Isabel's colored pencils fanned out on the marble floor, and Sam and Luca were playing a Spider-Man video game on the enormous flat-screen TV in the adjoining room, Isabel did Margot's chart.

Ava sat across from her at the kitchen table and watched Isabel smooth her hands over a complicated printed-out graph, circular in shape like a wheel divided into pie slices, with various shadings, diagonal lines, and planetary signs. After asking for Margot's birth date, location, and time of birth, she spent some quiet minutes plugging this information into her laptop.

Ava stared at the condensation forming on her wineglass and drank more rosé, her head lightening to the sound of the video game's explosions and rapid gunfire.

Margot sighed angrily. She'd torn through the paper from erasing too hard. Ripping it from the pad, she started a fresh drawing, huffing under her breath.

"So," Isabel said, scanning the chart before glancing up at Ava. "I'll start with the positive aspects: decisive and willful, full of fire, a natural-born leader, fiercely independent . . ."

Margot looked up at them. "Are you talking about me?"

Ava's face flooded with heat. "Yes. But it's more about how the stars and planets reflect your personality."

Margot frowned. "Is it good or bad?"

Isabel laughed gently. "It's not like that. It's more like describing someone as having brown eyes or large feet . . . it's just part of who they are." Seeing that Margot had already gone through most of the drawing paper, Isabel suggested that she get another pad in the bedroom, inside the desk, top drawer on the right.

Margot reluctantly walked down the hallway, knowing they would continue talking about her.

Isabel took a generous sip of wine and brushed her long bangs away with the back of her hand, her voice dropping. "You know, it's a tough sign, so full of fire and force, stubborn and unbending. Aries, if gone unchecked, can be selfish and brash, impatient, and dangerously impulsive . . ." She paused, gauging Ava's reaction.

Ava tore off a piece of pita bread. These were all traits Ava battled with every day in varying degrees of intensity, depending on Margot's mood. She slumped down into the wooden chair and ate more bread. "Sounds exactly like her."

Isabel went on to explain rising signs and houses, ascendants and descendants, Jupiter's and Saturn's movements in relation to Margot's birth sign. "Fire, fire, fire," she reiterated. "It's going to be a hard path, but the mother sign is very strong here." She circled something in light pencil at the bottom of the chart, a sign that looked like a crab, for Cancer. "The mother grounds her, protects her but . . . she will resist your protection with every fiber of her being. It will be painful for you, her rebellion, but you must let her go."

Demeter in search of her lost daughter swam into Ava's mind. But maybe Persephone had to leave. Maybe she willingly went with Hades into the underworld, where she became queen of her own riches, descending into such depths to discover who she really was. Maybe Ava's job was to grow Margot up to become herself. Maybe that was the job of all mothers.

A guest in your house.

Isabel's finger pressed down on another indecipherable symbol. "And you see here? Margot's central orienting goddess is Lilith . . . meaning she's absolutely uncontainable. That's her identity, it's squaring her nodes, meaning that these opposing energies in her chart create this intense tension, which we hope will resolve over time, you know, like a knot becoming a braid, but she must first embody Lilith's wild feminine energy."

"Lilith?" Ava caught her breath, fear kicking between her legs. Lilith was Adam's first wife, thrown out of the Garden of Eden for refusing sex with Adam. When she refused again to return to Adam, God turned her into a demon goddess and killed all her children, after which she unleashed her fury onto the world. To feminists, she was a hero. To Christians, Lilith was a dark force of feminine sexuality, something to be repressed and killed off.

Ava stiffened, resisting the information, even though it felt true.

Isabel added softly, "The more you try to stop her, the more she'll fight against you. You just have to love her, embody that unconditional Cancer mother energy, and trust her, you know? If you ease up, she'll have less to rebel against." Isabel continued to explain that Ava was going to have to let Margot do crazy wild things, that she couldn't really stop her anyway, even if she tried. "It's because of her wound from a past life . . . she holds that memory of being thrown out of the Garden of Eden, of being told what to do and punished for holding her ground. The wound is real and alive. You both have this past life karma together, and you're meant to resolve it in this life." Isabel paused, her gaze floating over to the window, to the mountains rising up in the distance and the gathering storm clouds. "I'm picking up on the sense that you were her mother before, in another life, but you controlled her too much, your grip was too tight and then something happened. A painful rupture of some sort; she was ripped away from you, or you lost her in some irrevocable way."

Sam and Luca yelled at the screen over something that happened in the video game, causing Ava to flinch. She had been listening so deeply to Isabel that she forgot where she was in time and space.

Isabel took Ava's hand in hers and Ava felt her warmth, her care. "In this life, you can resolve that old wound." A shiver passed through her, knowing that Margot had always been angry, she had come into the world that way, while the cause of her fury remained unidentified, shrouded in psychic layers Ava had never parsed.

She felt her eyes watering, her throat closing up. "I don't want to mess up being her mother in this life by repeating past mistakes. But I feel like I'm messing up."

Isabel shook her head. "You're not. I mean, we all feel like that. Right?"

They laughed half-heartedly.

"The shitty mom complex," Ava added.

"Hey, can I quickly do your chart to see how it overlaps with Margot's?"

"Okay," Ava said, shoving her hands under her thighs, the pressurized weight comforting.

Isabel waited a moment after typing in Ava's information to see how their two charts overlapped. She leaned back into her chair and then forward again, as if she couldn't fully believe what she was seeing. "Oh, okay. This is wild. Her sun is right on your moon. Her sun is at twenty-nine degrees Pisces within one degree of your zero Aries moon. You were destined to be her mother . . . you're actually the perfect mother for her."

Ava let out a bark of a laugh. "Seriously?"

Isabel lowered her voice. "She was born into this deep sense of loss that you were already carrying. And that's you, the grieving mother, Ceres. It's huge in your chart."

A plunging sense of certainty overcame Ava; Ceres was the Roman name for Demeter, the grain goddess who lost her child, the only goddess in the pantheon who was acutely injured in this way, experiencing a type of sorrow unique to mortals and not meant for the gods.

"Margot's Lilith energy is channeling something through you . . . she's here to help you too. For some reason, she needed to come into this world and rebel against you, and you needed to be jolted by her rebellion."

She smiled faintly, clicking through the images on her computer, realigning the charts. "But you can begin a different relational frequency in this new age that's coming . . . Uranus is shifting and becoming the primary energy of our times. It's the planet of revolution and rebellion that dissolves existing power structures and systems. Margot won't have to rebel against patriarchy when patriarchy is already dissolving, right?"

In that moment, the kids appeared, announcing that they wanted to swim again. Sam and Luca stood by the door, towels draped over their angular frames. Margot complained that her bathing suit was still wet and she didn't want to wear it.

"You can borrow one of my bikinis," Isabel offered.

Margot's eyes sharpened with approval. "Bikini?"

"Yes, a bikini," Isabel said, her voice brimming with laughter as she gestured for Margot to follow her into the bedroom.

Margot emerged in a black string bikini, posing before the full-length mirror, her mouth pouty and puckered into a kiss, giving herself the peace sign with one hip cocked out at an exaggerated angle, something she must have seen on social media even though she didn't yet have a phone. "I love it," she said, more to her reflection than to Isabel.

Isabel gave Ava an apologetic shrug and Ava relented. "I mean, it looks great on her."

"*Ex-act-ly,*" Isabel said, gathering up more towels for the pool. "That's what I'm talking about."

The elevator plunged to the ground floor, the boisterous laughter of the kids a din beneath which Ava slipped, her mind swimming with this new information, picturing Margot being thrown out of the Garden of Eden and her resultant rage. Picturing herself as Demeter wrapped in a dark cloak, wandering the world for her lost daughter, also full of rage but a different kind, undergirded by deep loss. Ava perceived that this loss motivated the idea that if a mother could just keep her children far from harm then she would never have to suffer the pain of losing one of them again. But of course that wouldn't work; that suffocating hovering, that desire to shield them forever when they had to leave her and rebel. They should do this. But what mother doesn't desire that her child be protected from risk and injury, from the inevitable turning wheel of time? Every six months when she cleaned out their closets and held up their shrunken T-shirts or caught a random selection of photos flashing across the Apple TV of Sam at two, banging his fits on the high chair tray, or a newborn Margot who barely filled the bathroom sink as Ava washed her tiny body, she felt it, the ache of passing years and days.

The elevator doors swished open and the kids tumbled out, their flip-flops clacking against the granite floor, and she followed them, hit by the harsh truth that motherhood meant existing in a state of perpetual loss, beginning at each child's birth and trailing her like a lengthening shadow as Sam and Margot grew and changed. While she would inevitably fail to protect them from life's vicissitudes, she still yearned for some magical pact that after she was gone Margot and Sam would be okay.

Ava observed Margot running through the lawn, playing tag with the boys. She was fast, her long lean legs carrying her far, her thick wavy hair flaring out behind her. Laughing easily and freely, and despite her posturing in the bikini, she was still largely unaware of her beauty, of how men would start to see her, like the muscular middle-aged guy soaking in the bubbling Jacuzzi in a Speedo and aviator sunglasses, a gold chain glinting on his chest, which he absently stroked. Ava wasn't certain if he was watching Margot from behind his shielded mirrored gaze, but she sensed him following her quick flitting movements, keeping track of how close and how far she moved from him, as if he might, in an unsupervised moment, snatch her up and whisk her away to some dark underworld, just as Hades abducted Persephone without leaving a trace, except for a few shredded flower petals floating on the surface of a lake.

23

S he hates me. She loves me. She feels nothing for me. I watch
Eirene from the upstairs window, my heart contracting from
our recent fight. In her anger, she nearly smashed the tall terra-
cotta vase, a wedding gift from her future husband, that stands
on display in the vestibule. We have so little time left together.
What if she only recalls the heated intensity of our conflicts? The
rancorous yelling?

She circles the well in the courtyard, running her palm over its
lip, perhaps flooded with visions of throwing herself into it. Some
say, especially the doctor, that she is vulnerable to hysteria because
the mouth of her womb has not fully opened, so all the blood is
rushing to the heart and lungs, making her feverish and erratic.
Marry her as soon as possible, the doctor had said last time, with a
knowing gleam in his eye. He considered her one of the wild ones
who must be yoked by an early marriage. He assured me that her
hysterical womb would settle once it housed a child. Just when
I thought the doctor would leave, after I'd paid him a few extra
drachmas and made an offering at the kitchen hearth to Asclepius for good health, he sat down again on our bench in the shaded
portico, rearranging his tunic with the utmost care, and the sight
of his yellowed scraggly toenails threatened to dislodge my midday
meal. Just as I swallowed down the acidic sting of salt and cheese,
he gave me a hard look, as if I were to blame for Eirene's wandering
womb, a Hippocratic theory he greatly cherishes. He began to tell
me, as though I had never heard of this before, that the womb
is an animal within a woman that is deeply desirous of bearing
children. If this desire remains unsatisfied for too long, "as is

the case with your daughter," he reiterated, the womb becomes restless and starts to wander throughout the body. It may float up to the bladder, or to her brain, causing suffocation, sleepiness, or foaming at the mouth blocking the passages of breath. Last time, he had proclaimed that Eirene's womb was lodged in her liver and we must push it down with our hands and then tie a bandage around her ribs to stop the womb from rising up again like a bobbing cork. To appease him, Xanthe and I tied this bandage around Eirene's rib cage, despite her spitting protestations, but the moment he left the house we ripped it off, laughing uproariously, for we all know that these fits of hysteria, even her brief delusions, are manifestations of grief, a preparation for the impending departure that always arrives too swiftly for a girl, whereas my sons are rich with time before they must prove themselves on the battlefield.

Nonetheless, to confirm that her ill temper does not spring from some unknown biological source, but is baked into her character and thus unavoidable, Xanthe read the stars and the planets to determine their influence upon Eirene, starting at the time and place of her birth. She whispered that the soul journeys through the descending layers of heaven to be born, and as it passes through each successive sphere it acquires various attributes that are later manifested in one's destiny. Once I uttered Eirene's birth date, I feared what Xanthe would discover and waited in anguish, pacing the courtyard, thinking of nothing else.

A few hours later, Xanthe returned with vaguely recognizable symbols inked onto a piece of parchment and pointed to Mars (a circle with an arrow extending from it) and Venus (a circle balanced on a stem with a cross through the stem) as well as the moon, shown as a crescent, all seemingly scattered (to my ignorant eye) over Eirene's circular chart. When she interpreted the symbols I tried not to reveal my displeasure at Eirene's fate: She is ruled by Mars, a bold, heavenly sphere. And Venus, impulsive and passionate, which stirs lust in the hearts of men, and finally the moon, whose sphere influences the sowing and growing of bodies, and at least with this, I felt a wave of relief, knowing she would bear children.

Yet I felt anxious about the rest. Noticing my hesitancy, Xanthe drew me close, and, with uncharacteristic authority, compared a mortal life to that of a goat hitched to a cart. If the goat follows the path that the cart is taking, its life goes more or less smoothly, but if it arrogantly attempts to deviate from the path, it will be knocked down and dragged along painfully. Pausing, Xanthe stroked the top of my hand with her warm fingertips. "Best to be a good goat and surrender yourself to the path mapped out in the cosmic order."

24

After getting out of the pool, still dripping wet, Ava saw a missed call from Richard, her therapist, and realized that she'd skipped their phone session earlier. She slipped the phone into her purse and decided to forget about it. Already, she'd rescheduled twice, the ten-hour time difference hard to navigate.

For dinner they went to Leo's, an Italian restaurant close to the studio where Marc and Kasper would soon join them. They ordered eggplant dip, braised radicchio, and stuffed grape leaves, and a bottle of red wine, nibbling on the appetizers while the kids careened around the playground, screaming because a dog barked on the other side of the fence, its loud, rough yowling startling Ava every time.

Already tipsy, Isabel said bitterly, "Even after I move across the world to be with him, he still can't show up for dinner on time."

"It's the nature of this business, I guess," Ava said, a hollow dread spreading through her, as if Isabel were welcoming her into a club for abandoned wives, a club she had never wanted to join.

"He's never home. How am I supposed to get pregnant, then?"

"Do you want another child?"

"We tried IVF before he moved here, but that didn't work." Isabel laughed into her wine, holding a cigarette aloft. "Anyway, we're not trying anymore. That chapter is closed."

Some kids were poking a stick through the fence, teasing the dog.

The dog grew agitated, growling and yelping. Frowning, Isabel craned her neck to see what the matter was.

Ava leaned over the table. "How did you know that I lost a child before Margot? I mean, when you said that I was the grieving mother?"

Isabel's eyes glazed over, imbued with spirits. "It's all over your chart."

She felt that plunging sensation again, as if trapped in an elevator descending too fast.

"And you still think of him," Isabel added softly.

Ava took a generous sip of wine, fending off that familiar bitter pang in her chest. "All the time."

The bark grew sharper and more insistent and Ava sprang up from the table, walking over to the chain-link fence. She instructed the kids to stay away from the dog; it was unkind to taunt him with a stick, she said, and maybe he could bite them through the fence.

The other Bulgarian parents watched in mild amusement, sipping their wine. The women were dressed up for a night out, in high heels and silk dresses, their thick hair long and sleek. The husbands all looked the same: bulky, clean-shaven, in button-down shirts and heavy gold watches. Ava felt comically underdressed in her Birkenstocks and jeans, her hair still wet from the pool, her mascara smudged. She sensed the other women appraising her, wondering why she didn't put more effort into her appearance, wondering why she cared so much about a barking dog, not knowing the ache of loss beneath it.

Halfway through her telling them to leave the dog alone, the kids dispersed. She glanced back at Isabel, who was hugging Marc while he put down his backpack.

Her heart sank, seeing that Kasper wasn't with him.

At the table, Marc said that Kasper was still at the studio, stuck at a tech recce for the next day, mediating arguments between the DP and the production designer. "Man," he said, shaking his head, "I feel for him. He doesn't even have time to eat."

Marc and Isabel conferred over the menu, their voices lowering in the familiar way that couples revert to when discussing mundane things, her hand running through his silvery hair, his body relaxing into hers. Ava felt a pang, as if she were a widow, watching the two of them.

Another bottle of wine arrived and when they raised their glasses to toast, Ava tried to smile but a lump gathered in her throat, half aware of the kids flitting around the playground and then back to the table again, complaining, laughing, cajoling her into saying yes to more tokens for the toy vending machine, where they could win another Slinky, another mood ring, another useless piece of plastic they would forget about the moment they ripped open the clear capsule. Her mouth felt cottony from the wine.

Kasper arrived as they were paying the bill, the kids' half-eaten burgers still on their plates, the table a mess of spilled lemonade and splattered ketchup. Ava had ordered Kasper a steak with roasted potatoes to go, the plastic box steaming up from the inside.

When he walked into the restaurant, Isabel and Marc drunkenly cheered, the kids running up to Kasper as if he were some kind of celebrity. Ava watched the whole scene, her hands turning into fists under the table, trying to mask her resentment while also knowing she had agreed to this whole arrangement.

Why was she so angry?

The question sputtered in her brain like a skipping record during the cab ride home, suddenly remorseful about missing therapy, as she was alone with her churning thoughts. Kasper sat in the passenger seat hunched over the takeout container, stuffing rare meat into his mouth, explaining the twists and turns of his day, the brutal meetings with the financiers that went nowhere, the fact that they were running low on funds. "Hmmm," Ava said, wedged between the kids in the back seat, feigning concern. Olga promised to wire another two million by midnight on Friday; then again, she didn't always keep her promises, but what could he do? Shut down in the middle of production? Especially with Timothy Lim flying in tomorrow? He shook his head with incredulity.

The kids stared out the windows, their eyelids heavy.

Sam asked for water.

"We don't have any," Ava replied flatly.

"I'm thirsty."

"You can have a glass of water when we get home. We're almost there."

Kasper went on to criticize Bill: he moved too slowly and had no aesthetic of his own, but of course Olga praised him.

The cabdriver missed the exit, swearing under his breath. A calm female voice, speaking in Bulgarian, instructed him to take the next exit. Or at least that's what Ava thought the GPS was saying.

"And he disappeared during lunch. For two hours. Jason lost his shit."

She got the sense, listening to Kasper, that he had told many people of his travails and she was the last person to hear the saga of today, as if it were some kind of privilege, and she couldn't stop imagining herself as one of those little chrome trash cans, the kind you flip open with the ball of your foot, and in poured his grievances, his foot pressing down on the lever, never letting up.

Kasper passed a hand through his hair. His phone buzzed loudly in his pocket and he took the call. From what Ava gathered, it was about fixing the prosthetics for the teenage werewolves.

Inside the apartment, the chores she hadn't finished this morning confronted her: the wet laundry had not been taken out of the machine to hang dry on the metal rack. The children's toys were strewn across the living room rug with such abandon she thought she might start screaming: Barbies splayed this way and that, an ocean of their plastic accessories and shoes, Lego pieces shoved under the couch and into the far corners of the room. Kasper commented that the place was a mess, and she sharply accused him of assuming she should clean up after everyone.

"I'm not," he said defensively. "I'm just stating a fact."

The bedtime routine began. Just like at home, the kids tried every tactic to slow down the process. They danced maniacally in their underwear, pleading for a few more minutes of free time, finally allies in their fight against the clock, when the rest of the day they had continuously argued with each another, sometimes violently.

Kasper yelled at them to brush their teeth but the cacophony of background noise drowned out his demands. Standing up from the couch, dizzy from rising too quickly, Ava readied herself to intervene, but glancing down at her phone, she was startled when a text message from Professor Nikitas flashed on the screen. She read it hungrily, lingering on her word choice, her use of punctuation.

Hi Ava! I apologize for the late response, but I just read your email. In summer, I rarely check my university email otherwise I would have replied sooner. Yes, it was so nice running into you at the museum. Would you be available next Thursday night for dinner?

Her mind swirled. Could she go? Who would watch the kids? What would it be like? Should she accept right away or check with Kasper first?

The bedroom door slammed and Kasper pounded his fist against it. "Come out now. This is unacceptable!" Sam and Margot erupted into hysterics on the other side of the door.

Ava wrote back: *Sounds nice! I would love to come. What can I bring?*

Thursday night arrived like a secret pact even while she doubted she'd make it to Nikitas's house for dinner. Kasper might call with a change of plans. Nikitas could reschedule. One of the kids might fall ill. And she'd had some trouble arranging a sitter, but Isabel told her about this childcare service that specialized in Bulgarian college students who were fluent in English. Kasper couldn't make it home early enough; he was working until nine, prepping for tomorrow. The next payment for production had been miraculously wired on time and Timothy Lim had started shooting two days ago. Ava caught a glimpse of him walking from his trailer onto the set, his stride long and confident, his feathered mane resting on his shoulders; he'd grown it out for the part. Right before he disappeared into the soundstage, his blazing eyes roved the crowd before settling on Ava, and she felt as if she couldn't breathe for a few seconds. So that's what charisma was, true star quality: he could stop anyone's heart just by throwing them a half-finished glance.

The kids were excited that the babysitter ran a dog hotel in her spare time. She said stray dogs were a real problem in Sofia, as they probably noticed, so 10 percent of her babysitting proceeds went to homeless dogs. She herself owned four dogs, and while she showed them pictures on her phone, Ava rushed around the apartment searching for her hoop earrings, a clip to put up her hair, car keys to the rental that Kasper usually drove to the studio in the morning. This morning Nikolay had driven him, leaving the car with her. She felt unnecessarily nervous, and it bothered her that the anticipation of seeing Nikitas again was making her feverish and edgy. She heard herself overexplaining everything to the sitter, the sound of her own voice grating: the toothbrushes were next to the sink, pasta stood on the stove, they went to bed at nine.

When she closed the door behind her, she paused there for a few extra minutes to listen. The sitter explained in a tired voice, "Come on, guys, let's get ready." She said something else and the kids erupted into laughter. Relieved, Ava rushed down the stairs.

Ava drove slowly along the one-way leafy street, searching for the address, having already circled the block twice. She was running late, a chilled bottle of white wine in a fancy box resting on the passenger seat, her palms clammy. Finally finding the address, she glanced up at the pale-yellow art nouveau building, with arched doorways and wrought iron balconies, slender fenestrated windows framed in dark wood.

A deep resonant lyre strummed into the evening air, and she wondered if it was coming from Nikitas's apartment. All the windows blazed with golden light, and before pressing the buzzer, she smelled roasted garlic and simmering meat, realizing she was much hungrier than she thought, having skipped lunch.

Nikitas's voice barked through the intercom, startling her: "Ava?"

"Yes! It's me."

"Come up! Come up!"

The door buzzed open.

The apartment flickered with candlelight, filled with the aroma of paprika and slow-roasting meat, the sound of that entrancing lyre floating in from a nearby room. The whitewashed walls and hardwood floors, the freshly cut flowers in vases positioned in various alcoves, the small oil paintings of pastoral scenes, and the wood-beamed ceiling all made her feel at home, as if she could sink into these rooms and disappear for a while.

Nikitas rushed into the hallway, the color high in her cheeks, her pale eyes shining.

"I was just turning the meat. It's wonderful to see you." Her warm hands clasped Ava's face and Ava felt like a child, bathed in maternal praise. She wanted the feeling to last forever.

Nikitas took a step back, her long white linen robe fluttering over her linen pants and blouse. She wore a crimson velvet scarf, the color reminding Ava of a ripple of blood against all the white. Her hair was freshly washed, the comb's grooves running through the dense gray, and a light coating of makeup accentuated Nikitas's patrician features, enhancing her stateliness.

She gestured for Ava to follow her down the hallway. As they passed by a closed door, the sound of leaping, barking dogs pounded against it. Ava tensed when Nikitas shouted, "Mulchanie," and they immediately stopped. Nikitas explained that they were Tonkova's German shepherds, two old, kind-eyed dogs who became aroused whenever someone new visited the apartment. "They sound much fiercer than they really are," she assured Ava, but Ava felt unsettled by the thought of that door opening, the dogs bounding out.

Nikitas ushered her into the living room where Dr. Tonkova sat on a velvet ottoman near an open window, playing the lyre, her eyes closed and lips parted in quiet intensity. She also wore loose white linen but with a purple scarf, deep and regal, hanging limply from her neck.

The music was deceptively calming, lulling Ava into abstraction, when suddenly an atonal note reminded her of where she was. Nikitas touched her shoulder and whispered that Dr. Tonkova had performed at the National Palace of Culture and at Bulgaria Hall.

Ava perched on a nearby leather pouf and waited for her to finish playing, overcome by the sight of this woman so self-possessed, belonging only to herself. She was vaguely aware that Nikitas had left the room to finish preparing dinner. A Persian cat strutted across the rug, stretching itself out, its silvery fur and icy blue eyes reminiscent of Nikitas.

It took stock of Ava, its tail flicking.

Ava held out her hand, knuckles up. If Kasper wasn't allergic, she would love to have a cat.

The cat trotted over, massaging the side of its face against her knuckles. She kept still, allowing it to use her as a textured surface and noticed from its collar that its name was Agave. The cat purred with appreciation, and the deep raspy vibration emanating from its body combined with the lyre made Ava sleepy. On the low coffee table, a leather-bound copy of Euripides's *The Bacchae* was placed next to a small wooden bowl of dried rose petals. Passing her fingers through the petals, Ava's thoughts traveled back to that day in class when Nikitas had lectured on the maenads, describing with glee how the women, in the grip of madness, had torn Pentheus to pieces, fueled by an insatiable bloodlust that ended with his head on a spike. But Ava had always wondered what happened after. After his legs had been torn from his torso, his shoulder ripped from its socket, his flesh shredded to ribbons? Did the rage subside and die down? Did the women return to their homes and families, to all their wifely duties, without complaint? Perhaps the women were even more serene after such a euphoric outburst, their rage temporarily sated. But surely the violence had found its way into them, embedded, as tiny as a sliver of glass.

Her gaze traveled over to a photograph in an engraved silver frame, and she recognized the young girl in profile on a horse, leaping over a low jump. The picture had once stood in Nikitas's office.

When Tonkova finished, Ava complimented the beautiful music.

"Thank you," she said, setting the lyre down into its velvet-lined case. Her black eyes held the same intensity as her music, and her dark hair, a blunt bob streaked with a dense column of silver in the front, reminded Ava of Susan Sontag's iconic hairstyle.

She took out a cigarette and offered Ava one. Not having smoked since her twenties, Ava accepted it anyway; it felt liberating to do something she never did, to become someone else for a night.

"That photograph of the girl on the horse. Is that Nikitas when she was young?"

"Oh, no," Tonkova said, bringing over an amber ashtray. "That's her daughter, Alexandra. She's a poet." She said this in a perfectly ironed English accent.

"I didn't know she had a daughter."

"She has had many lives, that woman."

"And I noticed your British accent. Did you grow up there?"

Lighting their cigarettes, Tonkova explained that her father was British, in the foreign service. He met her mother right after the war. She had escaped the Eastern bloc by crossing over into Greece, a lightly guarded border, along with some other Bulgarians and East

Germans. They didn't want to be swallowed up by communism, already spreading into the country by 1944.

"They knew what was coming." She smiled, revealing large white teeth, unmarked by the red lipstick that perfectly coated her lips. "I was born in London, but they moved around so much, I grew up everywhere. Although I always return to Sofia. Something about this city, its gritty beauty, the way it looks both forward and back, caught between the past and the future, Janus faced, intrigues me."

Ava nodded, drinking up Tonkova's worldly, confident air. She stubbed out her cigarette in the ashtray, Tonkova's curious eyes on her. "And how long are you here for? Lydia mentioned something about a movie filming at Boyana Studios."

"Yes," Ava said, jarred by the sound of "Lydia," the name seductively dark, like crushed velvet. "My husband is producing a movie here. He's been in Sofia for almost four months, but we arrived about a month ago . . ." She paused. It felt as if they had been here for years.

"And you're working on the movie as well?"

"Oh, no. I'm just the producer's wife," she joked sarcastically, but from the look on Tonkova's face, she instantly regretted it. "The kids hadn't seen their father in so long, we decided to come over when school let out for the summer." She went on to explain that she taught at a university and was working on a book, but the sound of herself justifying her existence made her cringe. All the words ran together, paltry and weak, failing to mask the truth: she was here as an appendage to Kasper, to take care of the children and of him while she floundered, unable to wrap her head around the book. Given the scarce scholarship on her subject, Ava had resorted to some unsubstantiated claims about the experience of ancient Greek women. How it felt to live their lives. But this was conjecture. A shot in the dark. The kind of work that was routinely criticized for its sweeping assumptions. Knowing this, she felt uncertain about the project, unsure if she should continue with it. But the history was starting to seep into her blood, the research taking on a life of its own.

.   .   .

The dinner table, decorated with flickering votive candles and an embroidered tablecloth, presented a lavish spread of grilled minced meat, pickled vegetables, stuffed peppers, and shopska salad, along with moussaka that Nikitas said she had mastered to impress Tonkova.

Tonkova joked that no Bulgarian worth their salt would take a wife who didn't make good moussaka.

The red wine was strong and full-bodied, and Ava lost track of how often Tonkova refilled her glass, but she didn't mind. She also resisted checking her phone for missed calls from Kasper, or texts from the sitter; it was her first unfettered night in years and she didn't want anything to interfere with the feeling that she was a person in the world, independent of her family. Nikitas and Tonkova politely asked about her book. She said it was about a woman in fifth century BC Athens; each chapter would focus on a different aspect of her life. "The domestic sphere, civic life, marriage and childbirth, women's religious roles . . ." Her voice trailed off.

"Her life?" Tonkova asked, digging into a stuffed pepper.

"I've written the first few chapters about her domestic existence. I don't know if anyone will be interested in that." Ava stared down at her plate, her cheeks burning, unwilling to mention the fictional first-person lens. She wasn't a true academic. Not *really*. Not if she was making things up by attempting to inhabit another point of view, forgoing objectivity in favor of phenomenology.

Nikitas cleared her throat, gently setting down her fork. "It sounds quite ambitious. I imagine for a project of that scope, for an academic press to take it seriously, one would need multiple essays from various contributors."

Ava nodded, gulping down more wine.

"When is the delivery date?" Nikitas asked.

Ava mumbled August, but most likely September considering the slow progress, her head spinning from all the questions they fired off: What was the defining argument? How would she distinguish this study from others like it, such as Sarah Pomeroy's groundbreaking 1975 social history of ancient Greece, *Goddesses, Whores, Wives, and Slaves*? And most pointedly, why did she want to write about this?

The cat's tail lashed her shins. She felt her throat closing up, her stomach twisting into a Gordian knot. "I'm still drafting it," she blurted out. "I'm not really sure what it's about yet."

A look passed between Nikitas and Tonkova. One of pity. Or disappointment. She was still the floundering undergraduate Nikitas had taken under her wing. That spring morning crashed into now, Ava frozen at the conference table, the disapproval on Nikitas's face cutting, her arctic gaze conveying more than she ever could with words or margin notes: Ava wasn't a serious scholar. Not then. Not now.

Nikitas leaned over her plate, her voice lowering to a hush. "Surely you do know, Ava. Don't undermine yourself. You always did that."

For a moment she felt as if she might bolt from the table, or pee in her pants from her bursting bladder, but instead her voice filled the room, as though someone else spoke through her, for her. "When I started reading about women in the ancient world, I felt a connection to some of their struggles and their life stages, especially because I have a daughter on the verge of adolescence. Back then, women lost children to illness or disease all the time and accepted that they would lose their identity to marriage. They submitted to how unfree they were because their survival depended on obedience, on surrender. Marriage existed for the sake of producing a son to continue the male line of inheritance, and the ability to do this was the measure of a woman's worth." Ava cleared her throat. "I know today things are much better for us. Obviously. But look who's in the White House. Look at the Catholic Church, where women still can't be priests. Look at how the state still tries to control our bodies and threaten our reproductive freedom. Look at how the culture demands that we be maternal to our children, eternally sexy to our husbands, and the hardest worker in the room for the least compensation. We bend and splay into impossible positions to please others and then we feel guilty about feeling angry or unfulfilled. And then we're told guilt and anger is bad, it eats away at you, so instead we should practice *self-care*."

Nikitas laughed harshly. "As if breathwork and meditation rectifies millennia of patriarchy."

Tonkova leaned back from the table and lit a cigarette. "Self-care, wellness, whatever you call it, it's just spiritual materialism. Buy this adaptogenic supplement or this meditation app or this rose quartz water bottle and all that ancient rage will melt away in an instant."

"Exactly!" Adrenaline coursed through her limbs, her mind as sharp and quick as a blade, rife with crystallizing thoughts.

Nikitas cut in: "That's all well and good. Now tell me something I don't already know." Absorbing the sting of her comment, Ava nodded, ashamed of her enthusiasm. She had only described a problem, one of the oldest ones, instead of solving it.

Excusing herself for the bathroom, she felt slightly dizzy from all the wine, her throat parched from the cigarettes. Wandering down the hall, she lightly ran her fingertips along the whitewashed walls, then stopped before an alcove that housed various replicas of ancient objects: a pair of bronze cymbals, a terra-cotta pomegranate, a deep drinking cup, a coiled-up snake sculpted from wood. And a terra-cotta corn husk, or maybe it was a miniature penis. She wasn't sure. Lightly, she touched the clay penis and then the snake, the scales intricately carved.

When she returned, Nikitas and Tonkova had gained new energy, encouraging Ava to sit with them in the living room for some freshly cut figs and baklava. Dinner weighed heavily in her stomach, and she felt the urge to go home to Sam and Margot. Kasper had left an unintended recording of himself walking down the street, keys jangling with traffic in the background, suggesting he was on his way home, but she wasn't sure of this. The sitter didn't write back when Ava texted she would be late, increasing her general sense of anxiety. Reluctantly, she sipped some mastika because, as Tonkova explained, it helped calm the stomach, similar to Greek ouzo.

Suddenly the lights went out. Ava could only make out the smoldering tip of Tonkova's cigarette. Nikitas retrieved lit votives from the dinner table and brought them into the living room, her face more angular and dramatic as shadows danced across it.

They sat in the candlelight, Nikitas muttering that this happened at least once a week. Tonkova said she enjoyed the momentary lull; it forced her into stillness. Her eyes adjusting to the semidarkness,

Ava saw them clearly now. The cat, perched on the velvet arm of the couch, purred loudly as Nikitas stroked its back, her long elegant fingers hypnotizing.

Nikitas came over to sit next to Ava. The cat darted away, the little bell on its collar ringing sweetly. Her breath glided over Ava's ear, warm and dense, carrying the scent of garlic and wine. "Ava, I think you've found the true focus of your book. The question you ask about what to do with all this ancient rage and sorrow was answered by the Greco-Roman mystery religions. These secret rites gave women meaning and purpose, as well as religious power." Professor Nikitas clenched Ava's hand, her palm radiating dry heat. She continued speaking quickly and softly, as if someone might burst in and interrupt them. She told Ava that all magical power in the ancient religions resided with women, the first evidence of the Goddess dating as far back as 7500 BC. "But the men," she hissed, "the men murdered the women, keeping alive only the youngest girls, who were never taught what their mothers had known, while the men hoarded all the knowledge for themselves. In Laussel, in the south of France, numerous female figurines were recently discovered, lying broken, deliberately destroyed."

Ava's heart throbbed with remembrance for the unnamed and dismissed women who had spoken of this prehistory, who had tried to carry on the traditions of their grandmothers, who didn't survive because of it.

Nikitas's harsh whisper cut into her thoughts: "Finally, it's been acknowledged that many more Neolithic female figurines exist than male ones. Even Hesiod describes earlier generations of divinities as female. And these female-centered religions, such as the mysteries, were by women for women. This link carried through to early Christianity . . . Jesus's primary initiates and disciples were all women! The one thing the church is most terrified of is women having religious power, because that means we'll have power everywhere." Nikitas shook her head. "Christianity: the oldest-running boys' club in Western civilization."

Tonkova asked into the undulating shadows, "Is it likely, do you think, that after all Her years and millennia of changing forms and names that She is now able to let Her daughters know who they really are?" She placed a warm hand on Ava's shoulder. "This is what your book is about. Don't you see?"

The lights flickered back on with a brief sharp buzz and in her hands, Ava held a book, leathery and soft.

"Keep it," Nikitas whispered. "It's my favorite play. And the most exemplary."

She blinked into the bright lights. "Thank you," Ava said, pressing *The Bacchae* to her chest, wondering, *Exemplary of what?*

Standing in the foyer, Tonkova reached out to smooth down a few stray strands of Ava's hair, saying that it had been so nice to meet her. The sensation of Tonkova's tapered fingernails raking against her temples felt delicious, as if a viscous liquid rushed into her limbs and spread into her groin. It was the same sensation she had felt as a small child at one of her parents' parties when a friend of her mother's had found Ava in the vacant living room drinking the dregs of white wine from each half-finished glass. The woman had lightly scolded her, running her long dark nails through Ava's hair, telling her to go back upstairs to bed, she was too little to be up this late, making no mention of the wine.

Nikitas leaned into the doorframe. "We're going to Greece. Come with us."

"Greece?"

"Eleusis. It's the site of the ancient Greek sanctuary to Demeter and Persephone, ten miles outside of Athens, and probably the most sacred sanctuary of religious ritual in Panhellenic culture. What occurred there remains a mystery. Anyone who spoke of their experiences faced death by stoning or, at the very least, exile and ostracism."

Tonkova nodded. "Thousands of initiates took part in the mysteries every year, coming from all over the Mediterranean world. Based on *The Homeric Hymn to Demeter*, Eleusis is where Demeter wept on the mirthless rock in search of Persephone and where the goddess then founded the Eleusinian mystery rites. The place still radiates a religious intensity, a magic that I can't put into words."

"You've been there?" Ava asked, her mind racing to figure out how she could go with them to Greece and how she would explain it to Kasper. And what about the kids? She couldn't just leave them.

Nikitas nodded, her eyes glittering. "In three weeks, we're taking a group to Eleusis to partake in the ancient rites. Reenact them. Think of this as field research for your book. I want you to come."

"If you agree to participate in these rituals you cannot speak of them," Tonkova added.

"I understand," Ava whispered, her voice thick in her throat.

When she got home, the babysitter was lying on the couch watching a reality cooking show. She sat up and rubbed her eyes, reporting that the kids fell asleep around nine.

Ava asked if Kasper was here.

The sitter stared at Ava blankly, the TV flickering with manic chefs chopping up onions and bell peppers.

"My husband?" Ava clarified.

"Oh, I haven't seen him."

After the sitter left, Ava cracked open the kids' door to find Sam's head hanging off the foot of the bed and Margot crunched up on her side, her angular body lit up by the bracing white moonlight streaming through the window. The outline of Margot's outer hip jutting up and the inward swoop of her waistline, a perfect hourglass, was the shape of a young woman at rest. Her silhouette caused Ava to inhale sharply, unprepared to think of Margot in this way.

A few hours later, Ava lay on top of the cool sheets, listening for the front door to unlock and the familiar sound of Kasper's keys dropping into the ceramic bowl, followed by his exhausted sigh. Her arm was flung out onto Kasper's side of the bed, her palm upturned, as if urging him home, her thoughts murky and swimming: the cat's furry tail lashing her shins, the sacred objects laid out in the alcove that she shouldn't have touched, the feeling of Tonkova's long nails grazing her temples, Nikitas's pressuring gaze whenever their eyes met across the table, the acidic sting of the mastika still on her tongue. And all her ideas about motherhood and marriage, about patriarchy and religion that had been stalking through her mind for decades burst forth as fluorescently as comets cascading through a dark universe. She didn't want to lose the momentum and excitement she'd felt over dinner. She didn't want to second-guess, once morning came, that her book was really about the mystery religions. The language to write about this without having lived it had eluded her, but now the chance to inhabit this ancient experience dangled before her. How could she leave Sofia? She imagined they would be gone for at least two nights, given the nine-hour drive. But her heart sank; it didn't seem possible with Kasper on set all day and night shoots starting soon.

Enveloped by the bedroom's semidarkness, she stared at the leather-bound copy of *The Bacchae* resting on the windowsill, bathed in moonlight, and imagined herself at night in ancient Eleusis with Tonkova and Nikitas and the other women, surrounded by a chorus of cicadas and stones humming with primeval history, the stars their only witness.

25

S urrounded by the damp wetness, they hiked among the towering evergreens, the firs glistening from a recent storm, the
silvery stream rushing down the mountainside with renewed
force. Isabel talked about the upcoming new moon with a particular intensity that Ava hadn't noticed before as she described the
pulsing energy of new ideas and projects stirring within her. For
example, she wanted to create a website for her herbalism where
people could learn which herbs to take for various ailments with
a link to schedule consultations. And the herbal treatments would
be informed by their natal charts. "I've been meaning to do this for
such a long time, but I finally know *now* is the time. I don't want to
wait anymore. I can't wait."

Snapping off a twig that obstructed the path, Ava ventured, "I
was invited to go to Greece, to the sanctuary at Eleusis with my old
professor. She's leading a group of women there, a reenactment of
these ancient religious rites." She paused, drawing a breath. "Do
you want to come with me?"

Isabel stopped in the middle of the path, intrigued.

Ava continued, "I don't really know what happens during the
rituals. But it sounds like a spiritual experience."

"Yes. I want to come. You know I'm into that sort of thing." She
smiled and continued walking down the path before adding, "It
doesn't scare me."

"Okay," Ava said, coming up behind her. "We're meeting in the
forest on Friday evening to discuss the trip. But it's a secret. I mean,
don't tell Marc. Just say we're having dinner or something."

After the hike, they stopped for lunch at a café run by Yael, an

Israeli woman from Tel Aviv who made her own hummus and served a deliciously spicy shakshouka for breakfast. The brass wall chimes hanging from the door clanged behind them as they entered, while Isabel whispered that Yael had recently gotten out of a bad marriage, taking her two kids with her.

Sitting down, Isabel said, "So, tell me more about Nikitas."

Ava described the magical feeling she had at Nikitas's apartment a few nights ago: Tonkova playing the lyre, the odd carved objects on display in the alcove, the sense of tunneling back to her original interest in matriarchal religions, about how the Great Goddess then trickled down into the Greco-Roman rites, and then with the advent of Christianity any suggestion of the divine feminine had been eradicated, flattened, deleted from history. "It's what I wanted to write about twenty years ago, but a male professor convinced me otherwise," Ava said, stirring a teaspoon of brown sugar into her black coffee. "Anyway, she lives in Sofia with Dr. Tonkova now, but I can't tell whether or not they're romantically involved. Dr. Tonkova will be there too. I don't know anyone else who's coming."

Placing a meze plate on the table, Yael cut in, "They're romantically involved. Here. Eat. It's on the house."

The hummus glistened with oil and sesame, festooned with olives and grape leaves, with warm pita folded into an embroidered cloth waiting to be torn and dipped. Ava bit into a grape leaf, the acidic sting of capers and dill hitting her tongue.

Laughter stirred in Yael's eyes. "Dr. Tonkova has been leading these rituals for years." Her voice dropped. "I went to the Thesmophoria last fall."

"Thesmophoria?" Isabel echoed.

"It's an ancient agrarian festival in honor of Demeter, centering around fertility and the cycle of the seasons. Only for women."

"Are you going to Eleusis?" Ava asked.

"Yes." Her dark eyes gleamed with secrecy. "I hear it will be different because she's leading it with another woman this year, some American professor."

"Professor Nikitas," Ava said.

"How will it be different, do you think?" Isabel asked.

Yael shrugged, a small smile playing on her lips.

On Saturday, they lazed around the apartment. Headphones on, the kids were hooked up to their iPads, lying on their stomachs, their faces inches from the screen. Kasper was stuck on work calls. It was hot and humid outside, the muggy sun overbearing by midmorning. Even the curtains felt warm to the touch when Ava drew them together to filter out the relentless sun. She puttered around the apartment, tidying things only to give up halfway through. All she could think about was the trip to Eleusis, a sharp exhilaration radiating throughout her body, making her forget to wash the pillowcases and give the kids breakfast, to wring out their bathing suits from camp, which were still damp at the bottom of their backpacks.

Out on the balcony, Kasper fielded calls from Sergei's lawyers because one of his executives, Dimitri, had flown in to oversee production and allegedly harassed two young female assistants on the crew. He'd cornered one woman when she was coming out of the restroom and wouldn't let her pass, badgering her about why she didn't have a boyfriend. Sergei's lawyers were pressuring Kasper for the names of the accusers, but he refused to hand over the information.

"We have no choice but to have this investigated," Ava overheard Kasper say through the open sliding glass door. "And Dimitri isn't allowed anywhere near the lot. He can stay in his apartment or fly home."

Sitting down at the kitchen table she sipped some lemonade, the tart sweetness stinging her tongue.

Kasper strode into the kitchen still in his boxers and sat down opposite her, pulling out his earbuds and muttering that the movie was turning into a shit show.

Ava was about to say something encouraging when her phone pinged.

Kasper glanced down at his phone.

"It's for me," Ava said, reading Nikitas's text. *I'm in the neighborhood and have something for you. What's your address?*

"Who is it?"

Come by! I'm here. 193 Ravovski Street.

"Nikitas."

"Why is she bothering you on a Saturday?"

"It's not a bother." Ava slipped the phone into her back pocket. "She's dropping something off."

Kasper frowned at his phone. "Another email from Olga and Sergei, threatening to sue us for defamation." He took his coffee and went outside to make another call to the production lawyer.

In preparation for Nikitas, she threw their muddy tennis shoes into the coat closet, fluffed the couch pillows, moved the metal rack displaying all their drying underwear into the laundry room, and yanked the iPads from the kids' hands, telling Sam and Margot to change out of their pajamas. "It's almost noon!"

"But," Sam protested, "you said we could . . ."

"I don't care what I said," she snapped, shuttling them into their room to change.

Just then the intercom buzzed and she skipped down the few steps to the vestibule and opened the heavy steel door, the brash daylight streaming into the close darkness.

"Hi, Ava," Nikitas said, weighed down by groceries. She reached into a canvas bag and handed Ava something soft wrapped in brown paper twined with string. "You'll need this." She touched Ava's arm. "And I have that book for you too."

Ava held the door open with her foot. "Would you like to come up? I made fresh lemonade."

Nikitas swept past Ava, already climbing the stairs.

Ava ran up behind her. "I invited my friend Isabel to the meeting about the trip, and I hope she will also come to Greece. Is that okay?"

Nikitas stopped midway on the stairs, and turned to face Ava. "Do you trust her?"

"I do," Ava said. "She's an herbalist."

"An herbalist. Good," Nikitas said before pushing open the apartment door, which was already ajar.

In the kitchen, Nikitas gave her *Ancient Mystery Cults* by Walter Burkert, a seminal text for Ava's research, she explained as she placed down her grocery bags.

While Ava poured them lemonade, Nikitas added that Burkert, a German philosopher and scholar of religion, wrote the book thirty years ago. "We now have even more archaeological evidence to support his theories."

Ava gazed down at his author photo: he looked pretty tame, with gold-rimmed square glasses and gray hair neatly parted to the side, a tie paired with a tweed jacket. Ava guessed the jacket also sported brown suede elbow patches.

She heard Kasper arguing on the phone down below in the garden and wondered if Nikitas heard him too, but Nikitas acted as if they were the only two people here, as if she had erased his male presence. Her slate-blue eyes combed the kitchen; the fake succulent plants from IKEA on the windowsill, the view of the congested boulevard through the cheap diaphanous curtains, the countertop crowded with items that didn't belong in a kitchen: Margot's hairbrush, Sam's balled-up swimming trunks she hadn't bothered to wash, keys, wallets, sunscreen.

Suddenly she felt anxious, wondering what Nikitas thought of this place, of her existence, which appeared so ordinary and domestic, burdened with children and a husband, with damp beach towels and a cast iron skillet in need of scrubbing. She apologized, starting to tidy up a bit more, but Nikitas stopped her.

"I don't care," Nikitas said. "Come sit with me."

Ava sat down opposite Nikitas, forcing her hands to rest on the table.

Margot and Sam shuffled toward the kitchen, dressed.

They stared at Nikitas as if she were an exotic bird that had mistakenly found its way inside the apartment, a plumed peacock fanning out its jewel-like feathers in warning or seduction.

"Hello, children."

"Hello," Sam replied in a desultory tone.

Ava gestured for Margot to say hello too, but Margot was in a bad mood, restless and annoyed that they hadn't left the apartment yet, due to a vague promise about an afternoon in the park with Kasper, followed by ice cream.

Ava flashed her a pointed look, and with effort, Margot said, "I'm Margot."

"Your mother has told me a great deal about you."

Had she?

The kids both gave Ava a questioning stare and she explained that this was her former college professor, who was now teaching in Sofia.

"I've known your mother for a long time. Much longer than you have!" Nikitas joked, her eyes fixed on Margot. "I'm sure that's a strange thought, that your mother had a life before you came along."

Sam shrugged and wandered off into the living room, where his toy soldiers were arranged in various positions of battle.

Margot remained in the doorway, assessing Nikitas, trying to puzzle out why this older, ungrandmotherly woman was lodged in their kitchen, shawled in dove gray with hair to match, her straw hat encircled by dried flowers, along with those dusty sandals and yellowing toenails.

Not taking her eyes off Nikitas, Margot announced that she was hot and bored. "Can we go?" But Ava could tell that Nikitas interested Margot, otherwise she would already have flitted away.

Just then Kasper strolled into the kitchen to put his coffee cup in the sink, and the sight of Nikitas startled him, especially because he was still wearing his paisley boxers. "Oh, hello," he said in a strained voice, trying his best to sound friendly. "It's nice to finally meet you. I apologize," he gestured to his state of undress. "I didn't realize Ava had invited you over."

Nikitas gave him a cool passing glance. "No need to apologize," she said before turning her bright gaze back on Margot and Ava, asking Margot what *exactly* she wanted to do today, agreeing it was very hot, and maybe they could go swimming; there was a breathtaking waterfall up on Vitosha, a beautiful spot for a Saturday. "Perhaps we could all visit there one afternoon."

Margot's expression softened; she wanted to know more about the waterfall.

Nikitas gestured for her to come closer. "The water falls from a great crashing height over jagged rocks and at its base there are these little ponds you can dip your feet into. The mountain water is so bracingly cold, so wonderfully refreshing." Listening, Margot absently reached out to touch the flowers on Nikitas's hat, but then she stopped herself.

Nikitas laughed. "Oh, it's all right. Go ahead. It's just an old hat for the sun."

Kasper had since left the kitchen and was now storming around the apartment, pushing toys aside with his foot and loudly opening and closing drawers, hunting for his watch, which Ava thought she'd seen on the kitchen counter. She would normally have sprung up to help him, entrenching herself in his concerns, but she didn't really care about his lost watch and didn't have the energy to act as if she did.

"Mom, I'm starving," Margot announced. "You said we'd get lunch soon."

"Margot, can't you wait a few more minutes? Professor Nikitas is just finishing her lemonade."

"Ava," Nikitas said, her eyes brightening. "I have all these fresh groceries. Why don't we whip up some lunch here?"

"Oh, that's very kind, but I wouldn't want to . . . ," Ava started but then Nikitas flashed Margot a smile.

"What do you say, sweetheart? Want to help us cook?"

"Sure." Margot shrugged. "Sounds fun."

Nikitas turned on the oven and started making Bulgarian moussaka, a rush of strong herbs filling the kitchen, sweet paprika and earthy cumin. She instructed Margot to dice up the button mushrooms and told Ava to peel and chop the potatoes. Moving around the kitchen as if she lived here, Nikitas set a large pan dabbed with olive oil over the stove and when it sizzled with heat, she added the mushrooms, garlic, and onions, asking Ava for a casserole dish and a bouillon cube. Flustered that the apartment might not have these things, Ava found a casserole dish in the drawer under the oven and after scouring the pantry, she retrieved an old box of bouillon cubes. She handed them to Nikitas, who exclaimed, "Good girl," which made Ava flush with satisfaction.

Nikitas stirred the bouillon and tomato paste into the pan, telling Margot to sprinkle some nutmeg and white pepper in while she continued to mix it.

From the next room, Ava heard Kasper and Sam flop down on

the couch and then Kasper turned on a Marvel movie. Ava guessed it was *Black Panther,* the violent crashing sounds intensifying.

Leaving the kitchen for a minute, she told Kasper to turn it down, but he said all their cooking made it hard to hear the movie. Sam agreed with Kasper, both of them giving her an annoyed look. Just as she was about to start an argument, Nikitas called from the kitchen, "Ava, do you know where the oven mitts are? I'm about to put in the moussaka!"

Kasper gestured for her to come closer.

"What?" Ava whispered.

"What is she still doing here?"

"She's making lunch!"

"She's hijacking our entire day."

"Ava?" Nikitas trilled.

"I have to go," Ava said tensely.

Kasper shook his head and kept watching the movie.

When lunch was ready, Nikitas served it with ceremonial pomp while Kasper sat there with a dark look on his face, his jaw tensed. She gave him a small portion, much smaller than the rest, and Ava could tell that Kasper fought hard to maintain a polite façade.

Sam said it was too spicy, crinkling up his nose, but Margot loved it, and Nikitas remarked, "Well, now you know how to make it!"

Kasper methodically shoveled the food into his mouth; he only ate this way when he couldn't stand the company, and for a fleeting moment, Ava felt bad for him, having to unexpectedly endure Nikitas's presence.

His phone buzzed and he excused himself from the table, taking his plate with him.

When he was out of earshot, Nikitas whispered innocently, "Is he always this sullen?"

"He's just under a lot of stress with the movie."

"Hmmm. It sounds very important, making another one of those shoot-'em-ups." She let out a mirthless laugh.

After lunch, Nikitas made a fuss over saying goodbye to Margot, promising to take her to the waterfall, promising future times when they would meet. She bent down to Margot's eye level. "I stayed too long, didn't I?"

Margot looked disarmed by the question, detecting a bit of performance in it, but at the same time she enjoyed the attention, how Nikitas considered her feelings so wholeheartedly, in front of everyone. The kitchen was in disarray, as if a cyclone had blown through it, and when Ava started to clean up, trying to at least get one load stacked into the dishwasher, Nikitas took her aside and said, "Oh, let him clean up. It's the least he can do."

Ava heard Kasper on another call, barking into the phone about getting the production lawyers back on the line. Steering her toward the front door, Ava said, "Thanks so much for lunch. It was really delicious."

Nikitas cupped Ava's face with both hands. "Thank you, Ava. We'll cook something else next time. I have a lot of recipes up my sleeve!"

On their way to the park, Kasper was moody and petulant, grumbling that Nikitas had shown up unannounced and forestalled their family day together.

"You were on calls anyway," Ava said, that hot irritation flaring up again. "Either way, we would have been waiting around for you, as always."

"As always?"

Ava ignored his question, resisting the invitation to fight in front of the kids.

Sam and Margot walked ahead, spontaneously holding hands. They headed toward Borisova Garden, a large sprawling park with a Ferris wheel and a ride with swings that propelled outward at a dizzying circular pace. But the walk there was already tiring, wading through pedestrians and traffic, the air thick with pollen. A motorcyclist roared by, drowning out the last part of Kasper's protestations that he had only stayed on the phone because Nikitas was there. Otherwise, he argued, he would have hung up a long time ago.

"And then, just when I think she's about to leave, she starts making lunch!"

"We were all hungry. It was a nice spontaneous gesture."

"She totally ignored me."

"She asked you some questions."

Kasper shrugged. "Barely."

"So you weren't the center of attention for once. Is that the problem?"

"No, but it's weird that—"

Ava cut him off, her voice sharpening above the traffic. "Well, now you know what it's like."

He stopped in the middle of the sidewalk, facing her. "Like what?"

"To be ignored and invisible. To not matter." She kept on walking, clenching her hands into fists, quickening her step to catch up with the kids at the upcoming intersection.

He jogged next to her, sweat sprinkling his white T-shirt. "So that's how you feel? And it's my fault, right?"

They waited for the light to change.

Sam teased Margot about having just stepped in dog shit while Margot dragged her sneaker across the sidewalk, trying to get it off.

Ava pressed the button for the stoplight, knowing it didn't work, that it was only here to placate people.

She banged it with her fist repeatedly.

"You know that doesn't work."

"Yes, I know."

"Sam, stop!" Margot yelled, shoving him into the street, but Ava caught hold of him in time.

Kasper yelled, "Don't push your brother!"

The light changed and they crossed, Margot still dragging her foot along the pavement.

Kasper squinted into the bright sun. "She obviously hates men."

"Don't be so reductive."

The kids ran ahead, into the park with its shade and green. Kasper reached for Ava's hand and teased that Nikitas had sat there like a queen, lording over the kitchen, while he was her lowly servant interrupting their special tête-à-tête.

"It wasn't a tête-à-tête," Ava retorted, the phrase annoying her.

"Come on. You know what I mean."

Ava tried not to smile. "A tête-à-tête is a *private* meeting."

He cupped her shoulder, willing her to laugh, and then he started doing a little dance at the entrance of the park, like the way he used to dance in clubs when they were young, jerking his body to an imaginary techno beat. Bulgarian parents brushed past him, their expressions guarded as they rolled strollers onto the shaded pathways. Swept up by his own performance, he almost smacked a grandmother with his helicoptering arm. The woman scolded him, making a big show of her disapproval, while Kasper apologized in his pidgin Bulgarian.

His absurdity was endearing and at the same time, Ava didn't want to give him the relief of her laughter, which would signal that she had relented, that she forgave him for all past and present injustices. For the injury of having been left in so many ways and times, alone and embattled, while he slipped in and out of their lives with these colorful flamboyant gestures of reconciliation.

"You're embarrassing us!" the kids shouted, their voices ringing with admiration. They loved watching him act foolishly to win them over because they loved being won over.

Later that night, when Kasper was in the shower, Ava carefully unwrapped the package from Nikitas. A white linen blouse paired with matching pants tumbled out of the brown paper. Holding the clothing up to her body, she could tell it fit perfectly. She brought the linen to her face, inhaling the sweet fresh scent, reminiscent of wild strawberries, the fabric capturing summer in its fibers.

The faucet turned off and then the glass shower door squeaked open.

Quickly, she folded up the clothes and placed them in an empty bottom drawer no one ever used.

26

D emeter and Persephone have been appearing in our dreams, making themselves known to us because, as mother and daughter, we are about to embark on the same wrenching separation. And so we will travel to the sanctuary at Eleusis before Eirene's marriage, rejoicing and mourning the severing of the cord that binds us. Along with countless others, we will become initiated into the mysteries, and yet I don't know what to expect. Part of me fears it. And part of me longs for the day when we will set out, not long from now, along the Sacred Way leading to Eleusis. I yearn to make contact with the divine, to touch the hem of Demeter's sky-blue robe, and to weep into the mirthless rock along with her, releasing all that pent-up sorrow.

The chief priestess of Demeter, who leads initiates through these mysteries, lives at the edge of the forest in the thrall of ancient trees and stones. Xanthe and I have heard that she can draw down the moon, eclipse the sun, rush streams back to their fountainheads, and break the jaws of serpents with her incantations.

It is rumored that this priestess—her name is Lysimache—was once married but she lost her only daughter to drowning. I halt along the shaded forest path, unsure, for I notice that Eirene's left eye twitches again, auguring some danger. And then, through the spreading pine branches, I spot two eagles flying from on high. For a suspended moment they glide through the air side by side, peacefully, but my heart clenches when they begin to circle overhead, flapping their wings, screeching raucously. The larger one breaks off, soaring back toward Athens, away from this wildness. Our eyes lock and I catch death in its glance.

Instinctively, I take Eirene's arm, but she jerks away and walks ahead. Coming up behind me, Xanthe reassures me that, despite these signs, not to fear: we have performed all the preliminary purifications necessary to cast our eyes on Lysimache, who, although mortal, lives close to the divine.

I touch the lapis amulet hanging from a chain around my neck, hidden under my himation. Enjoying its smooth oblong shape, I remember my husband mocking those who believe in amulets and stones, that only rustics, old wives, and children take refuge in silly charms. I still hear his voice ringing in my ears, deriding me: "There she goes, oiling her skin with fragrant perfumes, feasting on hyacinth bulbs and whelks, imbibing Chian wine, and wearing crystals and precious stones and scraps of leather stitched with Ephesian incantations."

Still, before he left for battle, he made sure to wear his peridot ring carved with an image of Poseidon, the god of the seas, to protect against shipwreck, the vibrant green stone gleaming on his pinky finger.

As though reading my mind, Xanthe whispers, "It's a blessing he's away." I nod, swallowing down a tight knot in my throat, knowing she's right, but I feel small and afraid, ill-equipped for these next steps. My husband would be suspicious of the priestess, echoing my own thoughts: an understanding of the cosmic order might signal a sagacious and kind person close to the gods, but such secret knowledge could also suggest a certain proclivity to break moral rules whenever she pleases.

The forest deepens, offering rich shade, a relief from the unrelenting summer sun, and I glimpse Eirene up ahead, her white peplos bright against the brown-green underbrush. Just as she disappears from view, the path curves and I catch sight of her again, her forceful stride, her stubborn determination not to glance back at me, but nonetheless my heart settles, confirming she is right there, within reach.

After much waiting in Lysimache's enclosed courtyard under the shade of olive trees, she finally emerges from her quarters. The sweet strumming sound of a lyre floats over the stone walls as if announcing her entrance. Lysimache wears a billowing purple peplos, one milky blue eye unfocused and lolling, the other one as penetrating as a spear. Despite her wandering eye, as she approaches us, she sees right through me, through my hesitation and doubt, through my desire for guidance, deep into my fear of losing Eirene. She appears ageless; perhaps she massages olive oil into her skin to ease the creases, but her hair is the color of iron.

Lysimache pours a libation cup over a small fire kindling in the outdoor hearth, the flames curling to life, muttering a short incantation before settling down on the stone bench next to me. I motion to Eirene, and Lysimache's eyes light up at the sight of her. "An upcoming marriage, yes?"

I nod. "She rages against it with every particle of her being. As a young girl, I submitted to marriage. We all did. Why doesn't she understand what she must do?"

"She understands." Lysimache smiles thinly. "Perhaps you are jealous of her rage. Her ability to unleash it so freely when you never allowed yourself to approach its intoxicating heat."

Eirene and Lysimache exchange a look across the fire. I feel as though they are ganging up on me, taking sides, and my chest tightens. I am still her mother, and this woman, priestess or not, lost her daughter to a watery death. She cannot abscond with mine so easily.

I lean forward. "But such untrammeled fury is dangerous for a girl. She'll be hurled into the street with no home to return to, except her father's house. A disgrace."

Lysimache turns her bright, keen gaze on me. "Why are you so worried about disgrace?"

My cheeks burn. I have no answer.

Lysimache clucks her tongue. "At our age, we no longer need to trade submission for security. You should have outgrown this folly by now."

"B-b-but Eirene still needs security," I stammer, reeling from her insult, as though I were a little mouse scurrying into safe corners.

"Her rages," Lysimache inhales, "remind me of me, anguished by the intolerable loss of our real power centuries ago. Perhaps she doesn't consciously understand, though she senses the distant destruction of the Great Goddess rushing through her, the triple-headed trinity: maiden, mother, crone. Immortal and eternal, She is many and one, creator, sustainer, and destroyer of life. Just as the moon waxes and wanes. Just as the earth dies so that it may come alive again."

Xanthe adds, "In a jealous fit, Zeus swallowed up Metis, his first wife, for she was too wise; he feared her power."

"Despite their beloved sky god, shaking the earth and throwing his thunderbolt tantrums, men still fear us. Fear what our bodies can do. Fear what other realms we inhabit and the future we intuit. They fear we live closer to the divine and they are right." Lysimache bends down, her fingertips tracing a circle on the forest floor before she tosses more wine into the fire in honor of Demeter, and the new moon's arrival, and with it a fortuitous beginning to the Eleusinian mysteries she will lead a handful of days from now.

Then she looks at me again with a queer smile. "But we still feel Her in our bones, yes?"

"Yes," I mumble.

Lysimache smiles, her gaze traveling over to Eirene before she stands up and takes both of Eirene's hands in hers. For a second, a tight nugget of jealousy burrows into my breast before I shove away such pettiness.

I close my eyes for a moment, inhaling the moist fresh air, startled by the sensation of Lysimache's curative fingertips touching my face.

"I feel grief from many years ago. Raw and deep, it still lives within you."

A choked sob escapes me and I nod, my eyes stinging with fresh tears over that old wound.

27

Sofia, July 2019

Nikitas and Tonkova lit the way through the dense Vitosha forest with their crackling torches, singing songs in Greek that vibrated with purposeful sorrow, a sorrow that could bend into joy. Tonkova's two German shepherds ran alongside the group, their movements sleek and smooth, their ears flattened down. Ava held Isabel's hand, her senses sharpened, aware of every branch crunching underfoot, of the swaying pines and the lush undergrowth, of the fact that she had left the kids with a new babysitter whose doleful brown eyes somehow brought to mind a deer on the brink of slaughter.

She had called the babysitting service at the last minute, panicked that she would be unable to come when Kasper phoned about having dinner with Timothy Lim after wrapping, so he wouldn't be home in time. "And what are you doing? Seeing the witch again?" Since the day Nikitas had installed herself in their kitchen, he referred to her as "the witch"—an inside joke with the kids, which Ava did not find funny.

"It's only dinner," she said, making it sound harmless. "We're going to that Bulgarian restaurant, you know, the one in the forest."

Nikolay dropped her off at the base of the mountain in the restaurant parking lot. On the drive over, he was distracted, checking his phone, saying that he was supposed to meet a new woman tonight. "She's hot in photos. But who knows? I take a chance."

He pulled into the parking lot, his eyes glittering with interest when he noticed the women walking together toward the mountains.

"This is the place?"

"Yeah, the restaurant."

"Right," Nikolay said. "They have the best kebapche."

"What's that?"

"Bulgarian spiced meat on a mini kabob. Very good."

"Sounds great," Ava said, getting out of the van.

She stood in the parking lot and waved, making sure he drove away before she joined the others at the trailhead.

Clutching Isabel's hand, Ava was grateful that she'd come, and had gone to the trouble to arrange a sitter for Luca. And grateful that she wasn't alone, as she didn't know any of the other women except for Yael. She estimated they numbered around twenty and assumed most were university students from the look of them.

Just as they approached the clearing, a woman cried out that she'd seen someone.

Tonkova shouted in Bulgarian, "Who's there?"

The dogs froze, emitting a low growl.

They all stood still, the forest quivering with the sharp, quick movements of crickets, foxes, deer.

Out of the corner of her eye, Ava caught a figure passing through the trees. "There! I see him."

Barking wildly, the dogs bounded ahead, arrowing into the uncertain darkness.

Tonkova stormed down the procession, her robes flying behind her, and told everyone to keep moving, not to worry, she would sort it out.

Isabel glanced at Ava. "Did you really see someone?"

"Maybe just shapes in the forest at night," Ava said, watching Tonkova disappear into the thicket of bushes and trees.

After hiking up the trail for another half hour, they arrived at the cave with the offerings at its mouth: the pomegranate, the bundle of wheat, the mysterious lock of dark hair, and the Virgin Mary, her head bent in supplication, bound up in alienating grief. An electrical current coursed through Ava and she tensed with unidentified fear. Something about the cave, magnetic in its rich darkness, beckoned her in and down.

Isabel held her arm. "Are you okay?"

Ava took a breath. And then another one, holding it in before exhaling, counting to three. "I think so."

Isabel searched her face.

"I'm okay," Ava said.

Nikitas and Tonkova instructed them to form a circle around a pile of branches and stones that they kindled into a small fire. Tonkova reassured everyone that she'd scared off the man. He'd been heading the wrong way, trying to find his way back to the parking lot.

The altar, two stones pushed together, rose up between Nikitas and Tonkova. Standing in a tight circle with the other women, shadow and light danced across their faces, and Ava recognized the anorexic woman from yoga class. Yael stood next to her and flashed Ava a conspiratorial smile, her dark eyes ablaze with excitement. The circle pulsed with the forest and the night, and in these suspended moments she didn't worry if the kids were behaving with the sitter or when Kasper would get home.

Tonkova spoke first. "What you behold here tonight you must not divulge, as this vow of silence is an essential understanding among us. The word 'mystery,' from the Greek verb 'myein,' means to close the lips and the eyes. At Eleusis, we will travel from darkness into light, descend into the depths only to be reborn, reflecting the agrarian life cycle of death and rebirth with each passing season." She paused, the tendons in her neck tightening, her dark eyes catching the firelight.

Ava's feet hurt in her sneakers and she felt a chill; she was wearing only the linen blouse and pants. Inching closer to the fire, she held up her hands to the flames, plumes of smoke spiraling upward. Catching Isabel's eye, Ava realized this might not be all that new or strange to her friend, who had lived with an indigenous tribe deep in the Amazon before she met Marc. She said she came out of that time with markings on her face and visions of spirits after ingesting hallucinogens derived from herbs and powdered tree bark.

Nikitas's voice cut through the expectant air. "You know, it's quite interesting when the male takes over, he comes in proclaiming,

'This is the one and only God and anything before or after this idea is heresy.'" She clucked her tongue, as if scolding them. "But your heart knows. Your heart knows he isn't the Great Mother."

A smattering of laughter.

Ava felt Nikitas's eyes on her face as if she might call on her, as if this were a classroom.

"There's a misleading overlay in our tradition," Nikitas continued, gaining momentum, gesturing enthusiastically. "Within this overlay are clues back to the original Mother Goddess in areas as far apart in time and location as the earliest records of Sumer, India, Africa, Australia, China, Egypt, and classical Greece . . . The Great Goddess created the heavens and the earth, She has many forms and names. She can be found at twilight where the three roads meet as Hecate, or as Demeter, responsible for all that grows. Summoned by candlelight and prayer, She is the invisible Shekinah who blesses the Jewish home for the Sabbath meal, and She is Cerridwen the Celtic goddess. She is Amaterasu, the central sun goddess of the Shinto pantheon, upon whom the world depends to keep shining light. She is Saraswati, the Hindu goddess of wisdom. And over the past years, my research has revealed that Ashtoreth, the reviled 'pagan' male deity of the Old Testament, was actually female: Astarte, also known as the Great Goddess, the Near Eastern Queen of Heaven, and in other contexts as Inanna, Anat, Istar, Isis, Hathor, our many-named Divine Ancestress. As you can see, She was once everywhere and now She is nowhere."

Ava listened, transported back to her university days when Nikitas would hold court while Ava blissfully absorbed her lectures, marveling at the construction of her arguments, her metaphors and phrasing. She felt that same silky bliss now, so fully engaged that the rest of her uneasy flitting mind blurred into soft focus.

"For example, the ancient site of Hacilar, in present day Turkey, which was a Neolithic community in 5800 BC—the statuettes unearthed there all portray the Goddess represented in Her three aspects: a young girl, a mother giving birth, and an old woman. The male is subordinate, acting as either Her child or consort. This matriarchal religious structure created the mother right and the clan system in which land, inheritance, power, and prestige descended through the female line, from mother to daughter, rendering paternity irrelevant. Evidence of tribes in Africa portrays queens who each year selected a different lover before discarding him, sometimes fatally. And accounts from Nigeria indicate that the queen kept a paramour until he made her pregnant, at which time a group of women strangled him—he was no longer needed, his worldly duty accomplished."

They all laughed nervously.

"But after waves of northern invasions, Her altars were destroyed, Her image desecrated. As the invaders gained more territories over the next two thousand years, the male deity took over, becoming the dominant religious figure, as Her husband or even Her murderer. Over time, She was belittled, excised from history, forbidden, and ultimately forgotten."

Nikitas took a breath, and Ava felt her own breath expand, filling her diaphragm the way she had tried in yoga, but she had never breathed the way she breathed now, hidden chambers and cavities swelling and filling up. A warm wind sifted through her hair and she took in the spray of stars across the sky, an aching emptiness spreading over her chest for all that had been lost.

"We don't need to reinvent our history. We only need to remember," Ava said. She hadn't planned on saying anything, but the words involuntarily flew from her mouth. Nikitas nodded approvingly and everyone clapped, silently digesting the ideas. Glancing around at the other women, some young and unmarried, others older, weighed down with experience, as she was, Ava questioned whether they were following their real path or a prescribed one, if they had really wanted to become mothers and wives or had unwittingly fallen into it, bound to archaic formulations of what a woman should be, ideas created by men for women.

Ava recalled walking with her mother down a dusty trail in the Santa Monica Mountains surrounded by purpling wildflowers. Newly married to Kasper, she was unsure about having children or if she would be a good mother. But her mother convinced her having children was the most wonderful thing, that she would be missing out on the best part of life otherwise. Although the moment felt false, weightless. Having only mothered Ava half the time, she left out the part about motherhood being sometimes painful and grueling, beset with anxiety, guilt, inadequacy. But Ava didn't know this yet. She only saw their two elongated shadows cast upon the earth before them, as distorted as Giacometti sculptures, and she remembered thinking, despite a gnawing uncertainty, *I'll follow in my mother's footsteps, she's trying to pass her wisdom down to me and I should take it.* Now Ava realized that her mother was only passing down what her own mother might have relayed to her, and all the mothers before, and she wondered what kind of story she would pass down to Margot.

What kind of truth.

A wave of animated conversation engulfed her, easing that distant memory out of her mind. One of the younger women started playing a bamboo flute. She perched on a rock nearby, the notes rising and falling. Tonkova strummed her lyre, following along with the flute's melody. A woman wearing clogs and a blouse embroidered with crimson flowers poured wine into small tin cups, while her friend handed them out. Nikitas mingled, weaving through the scattered circle, kneeling down before a few of her students, talking and laughing with them.

Isabel gave Ava a cup of wine and one of the little round sesame cakes that Yael had prepared for tonight, whose shape resembled a vulva. Ava bit into it, and then sipped some wine, soaking the cake so that she didn't taste its bitter spices.

Tonkova approached, drawing Isabel aside, and Ava watched them recede into the darkness, creating an invisible circle around themselves. Tonkova looked pleased, asking Isabel questions, listening closely, her hand resting on Isabel's shoulder. Ava thought she heard Isabel say that certain edible flowers could heal intrauterine trauma and realized that Nikitas must have told Tonkova about Isabel's herbalism.

Ava recognized the woman from yoga crouched on her haunches, her gaunt face illuminated by the flames while Nikitas spoke to her intently about something that felt private by the way they leaned into each other, closing up the space between them.

Sitting down on the ground, she felt tipsy from the small amount of wine, her stomach grumbling; suddenly, Nikitas faced her, squatting, her fingertips tenting over the earth. "How are you? Feeling okay?"

Ava smiled. "It felt like we were back in the classroom."

Nikitas laughed, silver fillings flashing from the back of her mouth. "This is only the beginning, a gentle introduction, if you will." She shrugged, as if what had happened tonight didn't hold much significance. "We need to prepare for Eleusis. Beforehand, there is fasting, purification, a procession along the Sacred Way, which leads to the sanctuary where we will perform a reenactment of the mysteries."

"And then?"

"What do you mean?"

"I'm just trying to imagine it . . ."

"As we walk along the Sacred Way, we recite *The Hymn to Demeter*. Some scholars believe the hymn was part of a female oral tradition handed down from mother to daughter, capturing a distinctly female point of view." She broke into a smile. "Oh, here I am, getting too heady, overly academic. You'll see. It's something that must be experienced instead of intellectualized." She lightly tapped Ava's forehead, implying that Ava also put too much stock into thinking and not enough into feeling.

Tonkova and Isabel walked toward them, laughing over something. Isabel mentioned morning glory seeds and Tonkova replied, "Ergot too."

On the way down the mountain, Nikitas linked her arm through Ava's, asking about her family. Her questions sounded tentative, as if balancing on slippery stones. "Does Kasper know you're here tonight?"

"He thinks we're having dinner. I said I might be home late, like last time." When she explained this to Kasper, he had been hunched over his computer, barely glancing up from the screen, and a few minutes later he had asked, "What did you say?"

"And the children? Who's looking after them?"

"A sitter."

They kept walking down the hill, and she could tell from the decreasing incline that they were almost at the bottom, where the parking lot was. Then she thought about being inside Isabel's warm car, their hair smelling of pine, gossiping about the night.

"What do you think," Nikitas asked, "of bringing Margot to Eleusis?"

"Oh," Ava said, taken aback. "I'm not sure." A nervous sweat sprang up between her breasts. "I thought these rituals weren't meant for children."

Isabel and Tonkova walked in front of them, their heads bent over Isabel's open palm, examining some herbs that she had plucked from a nearby bush.

"Oh, she's not a child anymore. Don't you see that?"

"She's somewhere in between," Ava admitted.

Conversing in a mixture of Russian, Bulgarian, and English, the rest of the women trickled down the mountain. From the parking lot, open car doors emitted a dull beeping. Goodbyes resounded throughout the forest. Headlights blazed on, the white light too bright at first.

Seeing Ava's hesitation, Nikitas explained that in their reenactment of the Demeter-Persephone myth, it would be like a play. They would inhabit the roles of Demeter, Persephone, and Hecate—the grieving mother, the lost daughter, and the wise crone—in order to psychically experience the cyclical shifts in their lives.

Ava silently wondered how they would manifest these stages, and what would happen in actuality: Would the whole thing feel strange? Terrifying? Liberating? Or something else altogether that she couldn't even imagine?

Nikitas continued. "For centuries we've passed through these stages alone, without guidance, blind to our own power. Don't you see? Men fixed it this way, erasing these practices to keep us cowed and afraid, under the thumb of their patriarchal godheads. Shouldn't Margot know the real story before she starts to learn the wrong one?"

In the car on the way back, Isabel played Brazilian samba, saying that they always danced to this music in the streets during carnival. With all the windows down, the humid summer night filtered into the car.

Isabel passed her a joint.

Ava took a deep inhale and held her breath, letting the smoke fill her lungs. "Is this even legal here?"

"It's deeply illegal," Isabel shouted above the music, and they both started laughing. "I think it's like six years' jail time."

"Wow, okay. Good to know," Ava said, passing the joint back to her. "What did you think about tonight?"

Isabel lowered the volume. "The forest was magical, pulsing with this strong crazy energy. I didn't expect to feel so transported . . . you know, because it was only the first time?"

Ava nodded, thinking back to what Nikitas had said about men destroying these rituals, perhaps because the rites were powerful, vibrating outside of ordinary time.

They talked about driving to Greece and what they would tell Marc and Kasper. Ava said that Nikitas had mentioned renting a van together and Isabel joked that Nikolay could drive them.

Ava laughed. "He'd love to come along with all the women."

"Yeah," Isabel agreed, "he'd disguise himself as a woman to brag about the wild things he saw."

Ava stared out the window, the wind skimming over her forearms. "I don't know if I should bring Margot with me, if she's ready for it. Honestly, I don't know if I'm ready."

"Dr. Tonkova told me it's going to become much more intense. That we should be prepared." Taking one last hit, Isabel threw the rest of the shriveled joint out the window into the wooded darkness before turning onto the highway, the dark mountains rising up behind them.

"She asked me to compound ergot and morning glory seeds to mix into the wine for Greece."

"For visions?" Ava half joked.

"Glorious ones," Isabel said.

When Ava returned to the apartment she found the kitchen a mess: pasta stuck to the pot, crisp fusilli pieces trapped under the burner, splashes of sauce crusting the counter. The babysitter left a note: *Kids behave okay but a little wild* with a smiley face. She glared at the mess and restrained herself from cleaning it up, from doing what she always did so that Kasper wouldn't have to.

She checked on the kids, finding their toothbrushes suspiciously under the bed along with Sam's lost sneaker that had gone missing weeks ago. Pasta sauce flecked Sam's chin, and Ava's plum-colored lipstick caked Margot's lips.

Then she noticed that the window, which faced the street, had been left wide open, something she specifically told the sitter to close so they wouldn't be awakened later by garbage trucks and ambulances.

Deftly, she went over to shut it, knowing that the real reason she insisted on shut windows was that she didn't want anyone to steal her children, spiriting them away into the night, and she shuddered at the image of an empty bed.

"Mama?" Sam called out weakly just as she was about to leave the room.

She came over to him, peering into his round brown eyes. "Are you okay?"

"Where were you?"

"Out with some friends, remember?"

He nodded, mulling something over. "I had a bad dream."

Ava waited for him to continue.

He swallowed noisily. "Papa was Winter Soldier, Margot was Wonder Woman because she can survive anything she's so tough, you were Supergirl of course, and I was Spider-Man, because he's my favorite."

"Why was it a bad dream?"

He twisted her wedding ring around and around. "Because Winter Soldier was once Captain America's best friend but then he died and came back to life, but he was brainwashed by Hydra. I feel like Papa is Winter Soldier because he's been brainwashed by the movie; I don't know if he'll come back to us the same as he was before."

She hugged him tightly and whispered that Papa was coming back to them; he wasn't brainwashed, just distracted and worried about work, but he was still in there, the real Papa.

In their bedroom, Kasper slept in his clothes, snoring into the dented pillow with his eye mask on. She kicked off her tennis shoes, his deep undisturbed sleep infuriating. She wanted to shake him awake and make him feel all the fear and worry that had just coursed through her: the messy kitchen, the open window that appeared like an invitation to a kidnapper, Sam's stress over his chronic absence. Standing over him in the dark, she revisited past crimes of mariticide: Upon his return home from battle, Clytemnestra murdered Agamemnon in the bath, the water blooming red. And even a good wife like Deianeira mistakenly killed Heracles using a centaur's toxic blood, thinking it was a magic potion to ensure his fidelity, but it drove him to throw himself onto a funeral pyre. And then there were the women who traveled in packs: the Sirens, Furies, Harpies, maenads, their collective rage feared much more than the vengeance of one scorned woman.

But he would only be confused by her anger, blinking into the predawn light, wondering what all the fuss was about in that befuddled innocent way of his, his naked face marked by pillow creases.

Instead she went out onto the balcony and sat down in the string-backed chair, watching the sky lighten from murky gray to powdery lavender, the birds rustling in the trees, beginning their song. The fluffy black cat with its golden eyes and twigs stuck in its tangled mane emerged from the undergrowth in search of food only to stop in his tracks and stare at Ava, wondering why she was here.

28

A few hours later, she awoke to the sound of Kasper whistling in the shower. Cartoons floated in from the living room, where the kids ate cereal on the couch. She overheard Sam telling Margot that in medieval times, a knight could get stabbed while riding his horse, but the horse kept galloping even after the knight fell off.

Sometimes, from another room, she expected to hear Margot cough or sniff, the tic rearing up again, but since Isabel had given Ava a combination of herbs she compounded in a tincture for Margot, a mixture of lavender, rose water, and magnesium, the tics had disappeared. Ava added a few drops of it to Margot's chamomile tea every night, and even sipped a little herself. She wasn't sure the tincture worked, and maybe it was just a coincidence, but either way, it tasted good.

She scrolled through her Instagram feed, admiring Erin's new series of paintings entitled *Uterine Dreams:* nebulous floating orbs of verdant green and cerulean blue interspersed with searing flashes of deep fuchsia that Ava interpreted as the feminine aspect, brimming with heat, blood, life. She hearted all five paintings. Then there was a photograph of Erin's bare tan feet casually crossed on a small wooden table next to half-full bottle of Talisker scotch. The photo cut off at midcalf, but Ava could see that she was wearing these cool ochre wide-legged pants. She started to heart the photo just when Kasper strode into the bedroom with a towel wrapped around his waist, freshly shaven. Smiling brightly, he sat down on her side of the bed, the scent of his woodsy aftershave infusing the air. She flipped the phone facedown so she wouldn't keep staring at Erin's pants.

Kissing her on the forehead, he announced, "Let's go to the Black Sea this weekend. A little getaway. It's supposed to be beautiful there."

"But . . ." Ava said hesitantly. "Don't you have to be here, in case anything comes up?" She feared getting the kids excited over nothing. He might cancel the trip at the last minute. But the sight of him happy and relaxed, his full attention on her, tipped her into optimism.

He squeezed her shoulder. "Olga finally wired the funds at two a.m. this morning. So we're good, at least for another few weeks. Plus, I really need a break."

On the way to Sozopol, she felt the air shift, Kasper's shoulders slackening under her palm as she rubbed him there, the orange sun setting in the summer evening. She placed her straw hat on the dashboard, and when they stopped in the middle of a wheat field for Sam to pee, she took a picture of the hat against the yellow fields through the windshield, the sky dramatic with gathering storm clouds shot through with electric pink.

Driving through the countryside, they passed small rural villages: old men herded sheep along onion-domed Russian Orthodox churches, crumbling stone walls demarcating abandoned fields, houses with red-tiled roofs nestled in the foothills. All this empty space that no one wanted.

The kids fell asleep in the back seat with their headphones on, their screens flickering with images of some Christmas movie about Labrador puppies who would save the day. She gently removed their headphones and took in their innocent faces, how young they still were. Looking at them, she silently forgave all the eye rolling and bickering, the teasing and the meltdowns, the clogging of the toilet with too much toilet paper, the damp towels and twisted bathing suits left in a forgotten heap on the bathroom floor.

It didn't matter; they were hers and she loved them.

Even more so when they fell into contented sleep.

She put her hand on the back of Kasper's neck again. Touching his skin made her feel close to him. He'd turned off his phone and stashed it in the glove compartment. Sometimes, she still thought she heard its wind-chime ring, and he admitted to also hearing it, confessing that everything had been too much lately.

She asked, "What do you mean by *too much*?" She hoped he would talk about the distance between them and all the time away from the kids, from her, time they would never get back.

Night had fallen, the sky a murky indigo. Sea air filtered into the car; sulfurous salt mingled with fetid seaweed.

"Last night, one of the stunt guys who doubles for Lim got into a bad fight with the stunt coordinator. We had to let him go, but then he threatened to commit suicide in his hotel room. He's on a plane home now." Kasper shook his head. "Then this morning, Jason had an anxiety attack because Sergei showed up in the editing room demanding to see the assembly when Jason hasn't even seen it yet." He sighed. "And my back went out."

"What about that 'magical masseur' who comes to set?"

"Yeah, Viktor is great . . ." He trailed off, focusing on the road. "Did we miss the exit?"

"I don't know," Ava said, disappointed that he thought the problem was his back, and the host of ongoing issues with the movie, all externals that masked what ran beneath: she didn't know how much longer she could play along and pretend everything was okay, that they were okay.

But now, for the first time, she had dipped into something bigger than herself, bigger than their marriage. The promise of a shared ancient secret pounded through her: an insistent internal drumbeat, reassuring her that she wasn't alone.

Eleusis, with its visions and magic, awaited.

The next morning in the harsh fresh sunlight, the kids jumped into the cold hotel pool. She read Burkert's book while Kasper dozed next to her, his palm resting on her thigh. Taking out a pen, she underlined: *The word "mysteries" conveys the fascination of secrecy and the promise of thrilling revelations. Even those not well acquainted with the mysteries may associate them with the concept of orgies. This book contains no revelations of this kind; instead it aims at the methodical interpretation of scattered and often frustrating evidence about forms of religion that have long been extinct.* Burkert then explained how this idea of the mystery rites stood in stark contrast to the proclamation of the Christian apologist Clement of Alexandria, who denounced the mysteries as the work of demons, replete with murders and burials, and said that such deranged, ungodly rites must be annihilated.

Nikitas's severe blue eyes flitted before her, and she felt a surge of exhilaration flecked with anxiety, her pulse accelerating when she reread the phrase: *murders and burials.* But of course, that's what a man, a Christian in the second century, would say, demonizing the old Goddess-based religion to sway potential converts to Christianity.

Kasper turned toward her and smiled sleepily, motioning to the other people at the pool. He whispered into her ear, making fun of the muscled men with hairless oiled chests and their girlfriends in white sequined G-string bikinis, with their hard surgical breasts bursting beneath the little triangles of nylon. "Russians," Kasper mouthed, and Ava nodded, watching these couples take multiple photographs of themselves posing before the sea.

An American family sat to their right a few chaise lounges away. Their two teenage sons sank down into their chairs, ensconced in dark hoodies and sunglasses while watching YouTube videos on their iPhones. The woman barked at her husband, "Where the fuck is the first-aid kit?" Her tone startled Ava in its hostility, cutting through the pool din. She wagged her finger in his face, her lips coated in white sunscreen, her large unwieldy body wedged into the chaise. Her husband was thin and frail and he immediately obeyed her, deftly retrieving the first-aid kit from their straw beach bag before allowing her to apply the antibiotic ointment to his wound, a minuscule cut on his shoulder from what Ava could tell. The woman berated him, reminding him of his tendency to forget himself, to not take care, they'd gone over this many times. He nodded in mild agreement, contemplating the sea with a distant remorseful stare. She shook her head and said she was going for a swim. Her husband watched her stalk off before returning to his book.

Sam cannonballed into the pool, and cool drops of water sprinkled Ava's legs. Margot dove in after him. Enjoying the feeling of Kasper's warm soft hand encircling her thigh, she thought about how Aristotle suggested that in the final stage of the mysteries there should be no more learning (mathein) but only experiencing (pathein) coupled with a shift in one's state of mind (diatethnai). Was that what Nikitas meant when she said the rituals couldn't be understood in advance?

He inched closer to her. "How was dinner with the witch? You never told me about it."

"Oh," Ava said, attempting to sound casual, even though the night in the woods breathed hotly through her. "Isabel and Nikitas got on really well, especially because Nikitas is interested in herbalism." There. That sounded convincing.

"So now you're all cozy?"

Ava laughed but said nothing more, just as Athenian women knew enough to keep the mysteries a mystery. When men began to participate, they corrupted the rites into wild orgies, draining the rituals of religious meaning, infusing them with vulgarity. By the end of the fourth century AD the Roman emperor Theodosius, an ardent Christian, banned pagan worship and ordered the destruction of Demeter's temples and shrines throughout the Roman Empire.

Her sanctuaries were never rebuilt, rendering the mysteries extinct.

Eleusis was now only ruins.

Ten minutes later, the woman returned from the beach, standing, with hands on hips, over her husband, who had remained in his same spot by the pool. Still bristling with ire, she reiterated his carelessness, how she had to think of everything. He nodded, mumbling, "Of course, dear. Next time I won't forget." Perhaps she was exacting her revenge after decades of wifely submissiveness or lashing out after enduring his various affairs, Ava thought. Or maybe she had always been the aggressor, relentlessly torturing him for his mistakes. As they aged, Ava imagined the wife growing even more powerful and mighty while he faded away into her rich, domineering shadow.

Kasper took the kids down to the beach and she watched from the pool deck. They walked a long way into the sea, given the low tide. Once far enough out, Sam swam away from Kasper and dove under each gathering wave. Every time, his small backlit head emerged from the surf. But when he disappeared beneath the next cresting wave, a stab of anxiety throbbed through Ava—maybe he wouldn't pop back up again, and Kasper, busy coaxing Margot farther out, exclaiming that the water wasn't cold, might not notice until it was too late.

She held her breath, hugging her knees into her chest on the warm concrete surrounding the pool. For an extended number of seconds, she couldn't see Sam in the water.

Why didn't you come sooner?

Sprinting down to the beach, she almost slipped on the slick stairs, her heart crashing around in her chest. *Too late. Too late. Too late.*

By the time she reached the sand, the kids were out of the water comparing who was the better swimmer.

Kasper asked if she brought towels.

She marveled at their young bodies, alive and breathing, beaded with salt water.

He gestured for the kids to follow him back to the pool. "C'mon, guys. Towels are up there." He met her gaze. "You okay?"

"Yeah," she managed. "I just felt nervous, watching Sam dive under the waves like that."

Kasper broke into an easy smile. "It's good for him to test his limits."

She squinted into the sun, wondering if she trusted Kasper in the absence of her watchful eye, as if she were the only one who could save her children, given her innate motherly intuition. By this logic, if they died it would also be her fault. A terrorizing double bind.

Eastern European men stood, hands on hips, in the surf, in their skimpy Speedos, with broad hirsute chests, laughing heartily at their children, who sat on the hard flat sand, crying each time the foamy tide flooded their sandcastles. A flock of sandpipers pecked at an empty stretch of beach in the distance.

Just because Kasper didn't worry as much as she did, was that a reason to believe he'd let their children drown?

Ava lingered on the beach a little longer, her feet sinking into the warm sand, overhearing from the pool up above the kids argue over who got which towel, and how quickly this argument aggravated

Kasper because he was rusty, unused to the constant stream of bickering, which had essentially become background noise to her.

"Guys," he yelled. "It doesn't matter!"

She reveled in his aggravation, wanting him to suffer what she had endured all these months. Even if it was only for a few days.

Her phone pinged with a text from Isabel that included a photo of Nikitas and Isabel in Isabel's kitchen before an array of dried herbs laid out on the table next to the mortar and pestles.

Preparation, Isabel wrote.

Ava texted back a glass of red wine and an herb emoji, trite electronic symbols that immediately embarrassed her. She deleted the text chain, not wanting Kasper to see it.

Before walking back up to the pool, she inhaled the sea air, recalling that the Thracians had first named this sea the Black Sea because of its inhospitable nature, along with the hostile foreign tribes that had settled along the coastline. In winter, great storms raged here. But the sea appeared docile now, the little waves falling over themselves.

That afternoon, they walked around historic Sozopol crammed with primitive wooden houses and narrow cobblestoned streets that led up to a promontory where the Turkish coast glinted across the way. As they climbed the hilly streets, the overcast sky broke apart, and the kids complained about the sudden heat.

Kasper shook his head and shot Ava an exasperated look. Having him here to exchange a glance with, to create a unified front against the kids, made her realize how much she had missed him.

He reached for her hand, their fingers intertwining.

The kids scrambled up ahead, drawn to all the little stalls selling cheap trinkets: evil eyes, beaded necklaces and silver bracelets, wooden figurines of cats and serpents. Tearing off their sweatshirts, Margot and Sam wanted ice cream and key chains, their high-pitched voices coalescing into a whining chorus.

"When's lunch?" Sam asked.

"I'm starving." Margot crossed her arms over her chest, immovable in the middle of the street. Like a river, the oncoming tourists in their Tevas and nylon fanny packs parted around Margot before merging back into a steady moving throng.

Kasper caught her eye and Ava recognized his dilemma: *Should I give in? Or is it still too early for lunch?*

"Okay," Ava said, smiling. "Let's eat."

"Great," Kasper said, pulling out his phone to look up Yelp reviews of Sozopol restaurants.

The place had a sea view, braids of garlic dangling from the wood-beamed ceiling, while a bearded man played an accordion, traveling from table to table holding out his felt fedora for tips.

She felt calm next to Kasper, the kids sitting on the other side of the table, the Balkan music with its hints of melancholy in the background. Using the thin white paper overlaying the tablecloth, Kasper sketched Margot, her chin in her hand, her eyes dreamy. Her drew her lustrous hair and cleft chin, the perfect bow of her lip. For Sam, he drew a cartoon of the Flash speeding through space. He sketched with concentration until the food came, the kids holding their breath, watching him. Margot got upset when a little drop of water splashed the edge of her portrait. Sam tore off his Flash drawing and carefully folded it up into precise squares and put it in his pocket, patting it down.

They dug into grilled shrimp and octopus, marinated red peppers and salty fried calamari. For the first time, she felt relaxed, sitting here, Kasper making funny jokes and the kids laughing, forgetting that his presence was only temporary.

After lunch they followed the signs to Cape Stolets, where a fortress from late antiquity overlooked the sea; it was a popular tourist attraction and many people walked that way, a cacophony of languages crowding the air. Margot and Sam were in better moods, wielding large ice cream cones that threatened to topple, rivulets of strawberry streaming down their wrists.

The path narrowed. A sign pointed to the promontory where the famous fortress stood, and then another sign pointed in the opposite direction, toward a peninsula that jutted out from the mainland, to the shrine of Persephone and Demeter.

Ava stopped.

"Which way?" Kasper asked, coming up behind her.

"I didn't know they had this shrine here. It's what I'm writing about. I mean, this is so weird."

Kasper examined the sign. "It's recently been excavated: 2018, it says."

The other tourists passed by like cattle, heading in the other direction.

They walked down the steep cobblestoned path to the sea. The ruins of the shrine, in the shape of a horseshoe, overlooked waves breaking against black rocks, as if it could get swept away during the next powerful storm, forgotten again. A small museum stood nearby.

The kids ran around the ruins, their shouts echoing off the water.

Kasper strolled the shrine's inner circle, glancing around dispassionately while Ava ran her hand along the hot stones, sensing the meaning once imbued here as worshippers knelt down in the dust, offering up a goat or a pig for sacrifice, praying for fertile wives, enough grain to get through another winter. Praying that life would prevail.

What would I sacrifice? she wondered, staring out at the windy sea roiling with whitecaps. *Or have I already sacrificed too much?*

Ava coaxed Margot inside the museum, wanting to show her this rare archaeological evidence. Cool and dimly lit, patchouli incense wafting in the air, burning from a cone-shaped vase in the far corner. The two small rooms each contained a long glass case displaying artifacts uncovered from the recent excavation.

Kasper and Sam cavorted around outside. Through the small open doorway, she heard shrieks of delight that always accompanied a game of hide-and-seek.

Something about the interior, its dimness and smoky scent, the low ceiling and earthen floor, trapped her breath in her throat, as if by breathing she might violate this ancient space that touched the future. Margot clenched her hand, as if she sensed it too: the past rushing into the present, the mother-daughter myth circulating through them, like blood.

The case featured little votive offerings described as gifts to the goddesses. As they read the placard, condensation formed on the glass surface from their breath.

Traces of the hewing into the wall are still visible, in which the entire space was filled with gifts. Various statuettes of baked clay and terra-cotta were unearthed, indicating that this location was an active shrine to Demeter and Persephone. The heads of the statuettes are all female depictions. The one with the younger face is Persephone, while Demeter is older and sterner with a more rotund, aged face.

The votive gifts showed a reverence for Demeter's wrath. Thinking about her power, Ava realized hers was the most feminist of the ancient myths, because Demeter overpowered Zeus, withholding the most precious thing from the world—life—to get her daughter back from Hades. She made men suffer and taught them a lesson about the limits of female sacrifice and empathy, refusing to cede until she got what she wanted. As the Greeks understood, and feminism had long pointed out, by rejecting motherhood women could bring the world to its knees.

Margot took her hand. "Mom. Are you okay?"

Ava nodded.

"What is it?"

"It's . . ." How could she put it into words? They carried death and life, destruction and creation, scarcity and abundance within themselves, all the time. Soon, Margot would bleed too, venturing out of girlhood into new fertile territory. And soon, Ava would fade into the land of hot flashes and regret, of vaginal dryness and unmitigated grief. But that couldn't be the only thing waiting for her.

There was also magic, wisdom, communion. *When rage and insight merge the world trembles and a new landscape will arise,* Erin had written in an email that Ava periodically reread, like a hymn or a secret prayer.

Ava hugged Margot tight enough to feel Margot's heart beating steadily through her T-shirt, tight enough to whisper into her sweet-smelling hair, "You're growing up so fast."

Too fast.

Margot's eyes searched hers. "I know."

Be careful. Be careful.

"I wish I could keep you with me forever," Ava said, knowing it was impossible to encase Margot in glass, trapping her in a never-ending childhood as if in a fairy tale. Tears swam into her eyes, mourning all the risks that would come rushing at Margot, all the dangers and trials from which Ava couldn't rescue her. A conversation she'd had with Erin a while back still haunted her. Ava had admitted how worried she was about Margot approaching adolescence, especially because girls were so much more vulnerable than boys to social media, to body image, to the mixed messaging of these highly curated images and so on. Statistically, girls became more depressed, suicidal. Erin confessed that as a teenager she took laxatives to lose weight; she'd never felt good about her body. She added, "The things girls suffer . . . cutting, starving, bulimia, substance abuse, or sex with the wrong people . . . and this was *before* the internet."

Were these dangers inescapable? And wasn't it Ava's job, as her mother, to protect Margot from the avalanche of risks, or at least lessen their allure and impact?

But wasn't it also true that to be a mother was to fight to save, while also knowing that she could never save her children?

Inevitably, they would suffer and she would suffer seeing them suffer.

The starkness of it all made her chest constrict.

Margot hugged her tightly. "Mom, I'm fine. Don't worry."

Ava squeezed her eyes shut for a moment, breathing hard. And then, impulsively, she told Margot about the rituals, as a salve, a way to protect her. Perhaps the burden of keeping this secret was too much for Margot to carry, but she seemed ready to know.

She crouched down on the packed-earth floor, and Margot sat down, crossed-legged, while Ava explained that people once worshipped the Great Goddess at a time when the world hadn't always been dominated and controlled by men.

"We have so much power because we can create life and just as easily take it away. This has always scared men. It still scares them."

Margot nodded slowly.

"Because we carry the cycle of life within us, and that's powerful. For example, you're verging on the springtime of your life while I'm sliding into the early fall of mine."

"That sounds kind of sad."

"It's not, really. It's just the nature of things. We can't fight it. But we can acknowledge and celebrate it by participating in these rituals. That's what I've been learning about during my nights away when the sitter comes."

"Can I come with you to Greece?"

"How do you know about Greece?"

A smile crept into Margot's eyes. "I looked at your phone and saw some texts about it, between you and Isabel."

She was afraid to say yes, even though the word tingled on the tip of her tongue. "Let me think about it."

They caught a cab back to the hotel, Sam's and Margot's cheeks hot to the touch from sunburn. Sam spewed aggressive shooting sounds from the Nerf gun he'd won playing a dart-throwing game at a street carnival that they'd stumbled upon on their way back from the shrine. The driver drove recklessly through the narrow streets, the radio blaring Balkan folk music, a woman singing of a lover who had abandoned her. Or this is what Ava guessed as she listened to the tremulous voice and stared at the back of the driver's sunburnt, creased neck. They passed Spanish-style villas interspersed with broken-down construction sites, unfinished houses with rusted scaffolding, a few goats meandering on the side of the road munching sea grass.

The Fiat lurched forward and back when the driver came to a sudden stop, deciding against running a light. Ava's stomach clenched and unclenched, and she gripped Margot's and Sam's hands in hers, their sweaty palms reassuring.

On the hotel room balcony, overlooking the flat gray sea, she called Erin. She had tried calling a few other times, missing her, and when Erin phoned back last week, Ava was hiking in the woods. From two stories up, she watched the kids dive into the pool and Kasper cannonball in after them, making a disruptive splash that rippled outward. She saw the American family eating a late lunch under an umbrella at one of the tables next to the pool. The woman asked for ketchup, gesturing to her club sandwich. The husband spooned soup into his mouth.

"Hey," Erin answered, out of breath. "I was just doing yoga."

Ava leaned her forearms against the balcony railing. "How are you?"

Erin sighed, vaulting into a tirade about Nolan. "He's more of a child than my child. Last night he overturned a coffee table when we were fighting about going back to couples therapy. He was trying to scare me. With an overturned table. Pathetic." Erin breathed heavily into the phone. Ava wondered if she was in down dog or boat pose, Ava's least favorite.

"Are you okay?"

"I don't know what okay means anymore."

"I know," Ava said dryly, thinking of Richard and missing his erudite wisdom, his ability to see her life from a bird's-eye view, making everything feel less magnified and urgent for that sanctified hour. Ava lowered her voice. "Listen." She gripped the balcony railing, her knuckles whitening. "My old professor, Nikitas, is in Bulgaria. I bumped into her and we reconnected. Seeing her again was . . . intense."

"Was she the one who was really hard on you in college?"

"Yeah," Ava said. "I'm thinking about going with her and some other women to Eleusis, in Greece, to reenact these ancient religious practices."

"Okay," Erin replied tentatively. "What does Kasper think about all this?"

"He doesn't know," Ava whispered, flooded with a general sense of unease about the whole situation she was describing. "I mean, he can't know. It's a secret. That's part of how this works." Somehow explaining it out loud to Erin made the endeavor sound highly questionable, suspect, weird. As if they would run around naked bathed in body glitter, braying at the moon, as some kind of comical neo-pagan, new-agey performance of spirituality. A false, laughable substitute for what once was. But then she recalled the beginning of Burkert's book: he scolded the reader for harboring stereotypes about the mysteries, for imagining them as wild blood-fueled orgies, when in truth, this ancient religion left little evidence of what had actually occurred. So perhaps she was falling into the trap Burkert described, projecting fiendish ideas where there were none.

"I wish you could come."

Erin laughed. "Maybe it would help me sort out this mess with Nolan."

Ava watched Margot and Sam shivering in thick white towels. Kasper glanced up, signaling for her to come down.

She nodded and held up a finger. "One minute," she mouthed.

Ava turned around, pressing her back into the railing, cupping the phone to her mouth. "I miss you."

"I miss you too," Erin said. "Just be careful, okay?"

It was their last night in Sozopol, and everyone felt celebratory. Ava wore a long, fluttering silk dress and dangling earrings, her wet hair twisted up into a bun. Kasper kissed her on the neck and said she looked beautiful, and she half believed it, watching the red sun sink into the dark sea.

Margot and Sam observed them, pleased by such displays of affection. They ate dinner next to the pool, the kids still in their swimsuits, wrapped in gaping terry cloth towels while feasting on mussels and fries. Ava sipped a martini, the gin lightening her head, making her feel more forgiving than she really was.

While the waiter cleared the plates, Kasper read an email and from the look on his face, a new problem had arisen. Over dessert, he paced the length of the swimming pool, his ice cream melting in the delicate silver bowl while he informed the other producers that Olga demanded a meeting first thing tomorrow morning with all the department heads. She was flying in from Moscow especially for it.

Sam asked if he could finish Kasper's ice cream, adding in a bitter voice too old for his years, "It'll go to waste otherwise."

.   .   .

That night they had fumbling rushed sex, the sliding glass door open to the balcony, the gauzy curtains billowing in the sea-scented wind. They worried the kids would hear them from the adjoining room and traipse in, claiming bad dreams. But Kasper's body, tight and coiled with yearning, found hers under the thin sheets and she half wanted the kids to walk in and interrupt them, while at the same time, she wanted him; they hadn't had sex in weeks. She desired this contact; she also resented that her body served as a receptacle for his tension, absorbing and obliterating it, allowing him, in clichéd fashion, to coast into sleep afterward, utterly relaxed, while she raged over the injustice of not feeling wholly satisfied, listening to the furious crash of the waves that always sounded more angry at night.

Deciding not to lie here steeped in irritation, she switched on the little lamp next to the bed and resumed reading Burkert. Even though she was exhausted, she read greedily, turning each page as fast as she could process the sentences. The last passage would spin through her mind for days: *Who can tell what the experience is like without having undergone days and days of fasting, purifications, exhaustion, apprehension, and excitement? . . . Wanderings astray in the beginning, tiresome walkings in circles, some frightening paths in darkness that lead nowhere; then immediately before the end all the terrible things, panic and shivering and sweat, and amazement. And then some wonderful light comes to greet you, with sounds and dances and solemn, sacred words and holy views; and there the initiate, perfect by now, set free and loose from all bondage, walks about, crowned with a wreath, celebrating the festival together with other sacred and pure people, and he looks down on the uninitiated, unpurified crowd in this world in mud and fog beneath his feet.*

29

A week later, they were on their way to Eleusis, riding in a hot, dusty school bus Nikitas had wrangled. Nikitas drove, talking loudly over the din to Tonkova, who sat diagonally across from her. Their two German shepherds slept in the aisle, a portable water bowl next to them. A little bit of water splotched out of the bowl with every bump and turn.

Ava listened to Nikitas discuss logistics: they would arrive late in Athens and check into the bed and breakfast where Loukia would be waiting with a key to the rooms. She spoke of Loukia affectionately, and Ava decided they knew her well and had done this journey before. Tonkova said they needed to rise early, before the sun grew too hot, as the walk could become rigorous in the heat. Ava hoped Margot could make the fourteen-mile trek to Eleusis, that she wouldn't complain or stop, or suddenly decide against it.

Thinking about how best to prepare her, Ava held Margot's hand, watching Margot stare out at the verdant rolling hills. Sometimes a town appeared, nestled in the mountains, a collection of run-down houses and wending cobblestoned streets. A church always. Periodically Margot asked when they would cross the border and officially be in Greece. Ava kept saying a few more hours, feeling the sweat accumulate beneath her thighs, moist against the green vinyl seat.

The forests grew more primeval, the mountains craggier, the houses bright white with deep blue shutters, the town buildings made of misshapen stones with colorful doors painted green or red. They passed a white brick church with a wrought iron cross set against the stunningly blue sky. Kids played soccer in an open field. Centuries-old stone bridges arched over streams and rivers.

The sound of rushing water filtered in through the open windows. Ava squeezed Margot's hand, taking in the lush open greenery. She had seized this opportunity with a certain ferocity, still in disbelief that she had pulled it off.

They had left early that morning, the sky purplish, yawning awake, the birds beginning their morning song, Sam with the coverlet pulled up to his chin. Bending over, she kissed his damp forehead and he twitched slightly, as if her kiss was a disturbance, a pesky fly temporarily alighting on his face.

Overhearing Isabel talk to Sophie about boiling ginger and lemon for indigestion, a budding release spread through Ava as she traveled farther and farther away from Kasper, trying to ignore the slight pang of worry about leaving Sam. But it had been arranged that Sam would stay with Luca. Isabel had hired a babysitter, one of the camp counselors they trusted and liked, who would take Sam and Luca from camp to home every afternoon, feed them dinner, put them to sleep. Repeat that for the next three days.

She replayed telling Kasper about going to Greece, how distracted he had been, tangled up with all his troubles to finish the film on time, make their shooting days along with night shoots starting. She explained that they would visit a famous archaeological site that she was writing about, and while she talked a certain wildness stirred in her eyes, the color high in her cheeks, a tremor running through her body, causing her hands to shake slightly as she moved around the apartment, picking up random objects—a book, a pen, sunglasses—before putting them back down. It was unbelievable that he didn't detect anything amiss, that he didn't find her behavior odd. That he let her go so easily. She also made the trip sound casual and spontaneous. "We'll only be gone from Monday and back on Wednesday evening," she added and Kasper nodded, distracted by something on his phone. When he looked up he asked, "When are you coming back?"

Between her feet, she braced her backpack carrying a water canteen, a blanket, Burkert's book, a sweatshirt, and her phone, but no food, because they were fasting in preparation for the rituals. In another compartment of the backpack, she had folded up the white linen pants and blouse that Nikitas had given her to wear.

Isabel had packed the herbal mixture to add to the wine, and Yael the celebratory cakes that she had carefully wrapped into a large wicker basket.

Sophie's embarrassed laugh floated over the seat when Isabel listed natural fertility remedies to try. "Folate, zinc. Bee pollen and maca."

"Maca?"

"That increases sperm count, for Bill to take."

Yesterday, Ava had bumped into Sophie in the city center, where Sophie had just come from Zhenski Pazar, roughly translated as "the women's market," an open-air bazaar that sold braids of garlic, leeks, and other hard-to-find vegetables, as well as Middle Eastern spices and embroidered linens. Weighed down by netted bags filled with produce, Sophie admitted that all these ingredients were needed for cooking certain dishes that Bill had requested, which was difficult in their cramped apartment rental. She was flustered and sweating, and kept apologizing that she hadn't been in touch. She was trying to write her dissertation, although here she was shopping for groceries.

Perhaps it was reckless to invite Sophie when Ava barely knew what to tell her. No one could fully explain what might occur: not the ancient texts, or Burkert or Nikitas. But she had gleaned traces of information from reading and researching, from intuiting and imagining. She prepared herself to move between extremes of terror and happiness, darkness and light, a kind of waking dream in which one dies only to be reborn, protected by the empathetic ancient stones and blazing torches inflaming the night, by the secrets they pledged to keep.

Ava's phone vibrated. Two missed calls from Kasper. She thought about calling him back and then didn't.

"Royal jelly," Isabel added.

Margot turned toward Ava. "What's royal jelly?"

"It's made from bees."

"Will it help her get pregnant?" she whispered.

"I think so."

"Is that what your period is for, getting pregnant?"

Ava considered how little she had actually explained to Margot:

the ovaries releasing unfertilized eggs traveling down the fallopian tubes, the shedding of cells and uterine lining in the form of blood each month. She had told her some of those things, but it seemed Margot had forgotten or wasn't really sure about the biological mechanics.

"I mean, eventually, yes."

Margot's eyes widened. "I could have a baby now?"

"If you got your period, I guess you could."

"I think I'll wait until I'm twenty."

"I think you'll wait longer than that. I didn't have you until I was thirty-two."

"That's old."

"Not really," Ava said, smiling at how buoyant and distant thirty-two sounded, how energized and rounded with promise.

She pulled out her phone to make sure there wasn't any kind of emergency with Sam. A broken arm. A high fever. A bad fall.

There wasn't.

Kasper had only texted that Olga was making his life hell. *Call me* he added with a crying emoji. She didn't want to call and hear about Olga's erratic tyrannical behavior. A few days ago, she'd seen her in the flesh at the production offices. She was there to drop off the car keys for Kasper when Olga, trailed by two assistants, stormed through the place. Her blond hair carried an odd strawberry tint to it and she wore a powder-blue silk tunic over matching MC Hammer pants and chunky Alexander McQueen sneakers, reminiscent of a recalcitrant pastel-hued genie released from a bottle. Because of her baggy clothing and all the work she'd had done on her face, it was hard to determine her age, but Ava guessed she hovered around sixty. She spoke harshly to one of her assistants in Russian, and Ava could have sworn she saw her jab him in the ribs with her finger while conferring with someone on the phone, her Hermès enameled bangles clanging against her heavy gold watch. People avoided her, skittering to the side, dashing into open offices to remove themselves from her path.

Ava had flattened herself against the wall, waiting for Olga to pass; in that moment, Olga's gaze rested on Ava's face, her small black eyes as sharp as glass. Before continuing her tirade into the phone, she gave Ava a fleeting sarcastic smile, as if she found the whole situation here oddly amusing, like a cat pawing a mouse, tossing it around before devouring it whole. Her expensive perfume lingered in the air, the cedar and amber top notes rich and intoxicating, and Ava inhaled her power and mystery, wondering how she commanded these Russian men, untouched by feminism and bursting with Eastern European machismo, while they scurried around, trying to please her, fear springing into their eyes at the mention of her name.

The bus bumped along and the general din of womanly chatter surrounded them, a soft wall of sound. Yael and the woman from yoga sat together a few seats back. Yael clapped her hands and laughed energetically, exclaiming something in Bulgarian. The other women talked or read or listened to music, their eyelids shimmering with sweat. Some wore their thick hair twisted up into a clip or plaited down their backs. Tonkova cooled herself with a paper fan, her collarbone speckled with sun spots, speckled with life. Every once in a while she smoked a cigarette and passed it to Nikitas, who inhaled deeply before passing it back.

Margot flipped her hair over her shoulder, the thick, soft strands lashing Ava across the face. It felt oddly soothing, the sensation of her daughter's hair on her skin.

"I don't want to wait that long to have a baby. I don't want to be an old mom."

"Hmmm," Ava said, thinking that Margot deserved to know what lay ahead, that it was right to bring her, despite also experiencing occasional stabs of anxiety over her decision. But Margot shouldn't stumble into the mess of womanhood the way Ava and her friends had, afraid of it, looking for others to define it, nearly every sexual encounter rife with misunderstanding and overlaid by a patina of humiliation, squelching the possibility of pleasure, which was so easily won by their male counterparts.

And then motherhood arrived, swallowing them whole for the last decades with ceaseless demands, endless tasks, a sharp undercurrent of fear and self-loathing running beneath all she did, especially when she fell short. Was she a *good enough* mother? Maybe over the years, she'd lost her temper too often, her patience dwindling every time they left their clothing on the floor, forgoing the hamper, and the rushed mornings and forgotten homework, the spills and stains, the sleepless nights and squandered hours, along with all those lost years, her youth incinerated by motherhood and its attendant anxieties. And despite how much she thought she'd sacrificed for them, Sam and Margot might still look back at her in anger, insistent on blaming her for their mediocre childhoods. For the store-bought birthday cakes and Halloween costumes ordered in a rush from Amazon. For the extinction of the natural world. For not saving all their baby teeth. For the abundance of microplastics in the water supply, in the food, swishing through their blood, disrupting their endocrine systems. For the times she got there late to pick them up from school or had to arrange for aftercare or a sitter. For the times she left the house to walk around the block in hope of restoring her sanity, dreading the moment she would have to come back.

And now the next stage loomed, a stage that veteran parents referred to as being filled with "curveballs." They spoke of this period as stoically as embattled warriors, and Ava shivered at what a "curveball" might look like: getting a call in the middle of the night from a seventeen-year-old Margot announcing that she had a flat tire on a dark highway, or the precarious moment Sam discovers a line of cocaine in the bathroom of a club, the possibility of escaping from himself seductive, too hard to pass up.

How will I lose them? Let me pick the ways, she thought grimly.

So when would she be in the clear as a mother, as a person?

Never.

But before Margot ventured into the world, Ava wanted her to understand why a woman might hurl a plate at the wall, why she might feel an inexorable urge to go over the edge. Before having a child, Margot should know that those first weeks alone with a newborn were terrifying, numinous, and undergirded with the crushing responsibility to keep the tiny human alive. And Margot should know that her future partner might leave sporadically and then act as though they hadn't, that they might tell her she was crazy, hysterical, too much, or not enough. How, in a marriage, everything could seem okay until it wasn't.

And she should know about that wild rushing desire to leave forever, to never look back.

The day deepened, the light slowly draining from the sky. They cheered when they crossed over into northern Greece, the coastline coming into view, the wind chiming through the sailboat masts in the harbors, the smudged lights of the seaside towns blinking back at them, the seagulls' plaintive cries echoing off the Aegean. The first stars appeared in the sky and the mood on the bus hushed into a milky calm. Most of the women had fallen asleep. Tonkova took over driving and sped down the one-lane highway while smoking cigarette after cigarette. Isabel listened to music, her eyes fluttering closed, while Sophie tried to read by the light of her iPhone before it died. Every so often Ava would turn around and Isabel would smile at her sleepily, as though they were greeting each other in a dream. And then Ava would turn back to Margot and watch her sleep with her cheek pressed against her balled-up sweatshirt. Giving in to her own tiredness, Ava rested her head against Margot's warm side, allowing sleep to take her too.

Soon, they would arrive in Athens.

30

Athens, 415 BC

In the blue dawn, I hear the herald's call and my chest constricts, my hands shaking as I don the specified pale linen garments. He cries out, "Those who dare to endure the great suffering of Demeter must experience the mysteries firsthand; nothing can prepare you for the great awe and terror, for the manifold revelations you will behold."

The morning heat thickens, promising fatigue. We start along the Sacred Way, linking arms, and we feel as sturdy as temple columns. Lysimache and her attendants walk before us, her voice as sweet as the Thracian Orpheus leading us onward. The reed pipes, the frenzied beating of frame drums and bronze cymbals punctuate the air and already I smell the distinct scent of meaty sacrificial smoke wafting from courtyards, nearby altars, and crossroads shrines. Priests, priestesses, magistrates, and ephebes jostle among us. Singing choral girls infuse the atmosphere with fragments from *The Homeric Hymn to Demeter* and so sweetly do they lament Demeter's painful search that their voices prick my eyes with tears. Sensing my distress, Xanthe pulls me along and whispers that the sound of bronze has purifying powers, as if we are already steeped in the mysteries, as if we are already healed.

Glancing around at the buzzing crowd, I glimpse my stepmother with her grim countenance, but she pretends not to see me, as she has always done. And I spot the balding head of Theandros, my husband's brother. He cranes his neck as though he's missing something, although he is right here among us. He has always grasped after more, unhappy with his lot, and I wonder if he will endure the fright of what's to come, or if he will, as many of those walking among us, decide at the last minute to stay back where the path is safe and known.

Beads of sweat pepper Eirene's upper lip, her hand moist in mine. Xanthe presses a compress of peppermint oil against the back of our necks to cool us. From a distance, the sanctuary gleams on the southeastern slope of the hill overlooking the Bay of Salamis, its high walls fortifying the Telesterion, which stands within the sanctuary. We gaze upon the north gate, which marks the threshold between the sanctuary and the Sacred Way, knowing we will pass through it.

The road stretches and shimmers before us, Lysimache's singing the only solace as this arduous path is akin to Demeter's relentless toils; she would not stop to eat or drink. She did not rest until she found her daughter.

My head lightens. Eirene stumbles but I catch her. Xanthe steadies us, her palm spreading over the small of my back. We push forward, toward the sea, where we bathe and purify ourselves.

By the time we reach the shore the crowd has thinned. Theandros split off from the procession a while back. I imagine him slumped on the side of the road, beset by heatstroke. He was always delicate, fainting at the sight of blood, even during the solemnity of a ritual slaughter, to the point where my husband grew embarrassed of him, told him to stay home—otherwise he might offend the gods, bringing misfortune upon us.

My stepmother turns her back to me as she bends over to splash water on her face and withered thighs, over her bony shoulders. She tries to impress others by bathing so vigorously, as if this will rinse away a lifetime of resentment.

The bracing water cools my tired feet and licks the backs of my knees. We have left our sandals on the black pebbled beach. Piglets gambol along the shoreline, squealing with delight, the high-pitched cries intermingling with the gulls above who occasionally swoop down, skimming the water's surface before angling up again. The little pigs are unblemished, perfect, ready for sacrifice, as Demeter prefers the pig. Soon, when we are done washing ourselves, we will each bathe a piglet and carry it into the sanctuary. I hope this will please Demeter. I pray she will appear and fill us with her presence.

Eirene tosses back her head in relief, water flecking her white neck. Xanthe sinks down into the sea, her garments rising up around her, saying she doesn't care, the fabric will dry soon enough once we're back on land. Of course, I waver in the cool water, torn between total submersion and my unsatisfying half crouch. Lysimache floats on her back, her eyes closed, the sun hitting her tan spotted face, her gray hair appearing almost black when wet. Through her now translucent garments I observe her well-proportioned breasts and still-thick pubic hair, her elegant clavicle and delicate knees, and I think: *She is still attractive, still beautiful, even at this advanced age. The gods must love her.*

Watching her float effortlessly in the water, I envy her freedom, yearning for a share of it.

31

They walked the Sacred Way, just as the ancients had, which was then the only paved road in all of Greece that wasn't a goat path, Nikitas said. They left after lunch to arrive at dusk, when the sanctuary would be lit up, lending the ruins a certain magic that perhaps could not be found in raw unfiltered daylight. The two German shepherds trotted behind them, herding stragglers. Tonkova harnessed a rope around a goat's neck, pulling it along with the procession, smacking its hind legs with a thin reed every now and then. This morning the goat had appeared in the hotel courtyard, bedecked in ribbons and bells, coins hanging from its neck, gilt speckled across its brow, its eyes glinting with celebration. Margot petted it affectionately, the back of her hand running along its snout, and Sophie said it reminded her of a goat she used to feed on her grandfather's farm. It paused periodically to munch on some weeds before Tonkova lost her patience and stuck it again with the switch, commanding the goat to keep moving.

Tapered cypress trees and poplars lined the white sandy road, the salty scent of the Aegean wafting through olive groves that lent a sporadic patch of shade before they met the blistering sun again. Ava skimmed her palm along the ancient upright stones, known as herms, marking crossroads and boundaries. The stones also provided divine protection to travelers and merchants as any journey, no matter how short, could prove dangerous in the ancient world.

Despite the fact that they were nearly alone on this road, aside from a few tourist groups who temporarily stepped out of their black gleaming tour buses, squinting into the sun with bewilderment, Ava thought she detected a faint buzzing in her ear of impending crowds. She looked back toward Athens, the Acropolis rising above the smoldering city, but she only saw a few walking tour groups in the distance, in their sun hats and hiking shoes and nylon backpacks, similar to the way her own group looked.

She tried to breathe deeply, her head lightening in the heat, thinking she was hallucinating, that all the research was getting to her, making her feel things that weren't here. She sensed the buzzing tension of crowds, the music and laughter. She caught a whiff of meaty smoke, the scent of a pig roasting on a spit. She reached for Margot's hand, and Margot grabbed her hand back. Slowing, Ava paused in the shade, resting against an olive tree, its sturdy trunk reassuring. Isabel poured some cool water from her canteen onto her bandana and then sprinkled it with peppermint oil from a little vial. She pressed the cool compress onto Ava's forehead and told her to keep it there. Then she walked on to join the others.

Ava closed her eyes, and still holding Margot's hand, she felt a sharp current of fear run from Margot's hand into hers, perhaps harkening back to when such virginal youth meant an early marriage. She felt the intimate terror of being married off as a child to bear a child. Maybe this was why ancient women were granted temporary bursts of freedom to participate in these religious rites, as a release, a consolation prize for the mean smallness of their real lives. And despite their secret experiences of divine potency, to only know power in the absence of men wasn't real power.

Ava opened her eyes. "Are you okay?"

Margot shook her head.

"What's wrong?"

"I don't know where we're going. I mean, how much longer is this walk?"

"Do you wish I hadn't taken you?"

"I wanted to come."

"And you still want to?"

Margot nodded, balling up her hair, cooling the back of her neck with the peppermint compress. "Everything is changing. Sometimes I wish I could be little again, when things were simpler. Remember when you used to pick me up from preschool and take me for a snack? We would get lemonade. You let me pick out a sugar cookie. I was so happy with it all."

"I remember," Ava said, hesitating. "But don't forget about how you couldn't do anything for yourself or make any decisions on your own. I had to buckle you into your car seat and put you to bed by six, even if you were wide awake. You used to hate wearing shoes and you would tear off your bib during dinner. You never wanted to leave the park but I always had to pick you up, kicking and screaming, and take you home. You didn't have any power. You would hate that now."

"But it was nice, not having to think about anything."

"I know," Ava said. "But now you have to think. You have to find your way in the world, without me always there to catch you." Saying this, Ava felt a similar sadness, fearing that she had explained this too harshly to cover the painful fact that Margot would never need her as she once had.

When they arrived at the sea, they set down the ceramic wine amphoras mixed in advance with Isabel's herbs. Ava helped Yael with her woven basket filled with the small cakes and meat pies that they were saving for after the rites, when they would break the fast. On the beach, Ava glimpsed a pair of abandoned leather sandals, worn and braided, and she felt the urge to slip into them.

Nikitas motioned for them to wade into the water as part of the preliminary purifications, and they felt great relief at the refreshment after the arduous walk. Isabel sank immediately into the sea, her hair swirling on the water's surface. Tearing off her clothes in a rush, Margot ran into the water, complaining of the heat, how sticky and sweaty her skin felt. She sprinted so unselfconsciously, without thinking of her body or how it looked, reminding Ava of Margot's younger self, when she was five or six, a body unmarked by shame and denial, free of the projections of beauty or disparagement, a body content with itself.

The goat blinked at Ava from the shore.

Ava slowly waded into the ocean, lowering herself into the water.

Margot splashed her, forcefully creating a little wave toward Ava, the cold water seeping through her shirt and washing over her stomach, making her cringe.

"C'mon. Don't be so afraid."

"I'm not afraid," Ava yelled back, staring down at her soaked linen shirt, the pants appearing blurry underwater.

Isabel swam toward them, taking their hands in hers. "Seawater," she said, pulling them along, "is good for you. It's clearing."

Once back on the beach, they wrung out their clothes, the sun warming their skin, their hair dripping a confetti of dots onto the pebbled shore. Ava slipped her feet into the abandoned sandals, feeling the life in them.

32

We arrive at Eleusis at dusk, my feet coated in sand as I forgot my sandals on the black pebbled beach, but it doesn't matter. We are in the realm of the gods now. In the shadow of the towering sanctuary, we cross the river Cephisus, and while we pass over the bridge of jests, the currents rushing beneath us, the uninitiated pelt us with wheat and acorns. They hurl insults, ridiculing us for our efforts, the jeering crowd positioned on either side of the bridge with the intent to strip away the last filament of our pride so that we may stand before the gods ready and open. But maybe we do look foolish, each one of us holding our woolen sack with a piglet inside it, trying to fight its way out, snorting and kicking and yanking at the fabric.

In the deafening cacophony of whirling tambourines, thumping drums, and ribald jokes, I look over at Xanthe and she smiles, her green eyes calm and clear. Lysimache jerks her head forward, urging us to move faster, but the thronging marchers are slow and indecisive; some of them hang back or turn around, moving against the crowd. Some release doves into the air that they had intended to sacrifice. An older man with a sweating face elbows his way back, pulling along a goat, muttering grievances. Perhaps he has changed his mind, fearing the night inauspicious.

Ethereal colors infuse the sky—light gold, lapis, streaks of inflamed coral—which only make the sanctuary appear more beautiful, the grand limestone walls rising up before us. We move together, Eirene, Xanthe, and I, following Lysimache, who has traveled over these stone steps and earthen paths many times.

Before entering the sanctuary, outside the walls, people dance, make small sacrifices. At various altars and around the Kallichoron Well, maidens recite their choral songs in honor of Demeter and Persephone. Wine, smoke, and laughter hang in the air. A thermal wind rustles through the cypress trees, and sprouting from crevices and chasms wildflowers grow.

I clutch my piglet close, feeling its beating heart through the cloth. We are about to enter and pass through the first gate into the sanctuary. I don't see anyone I know anymore from my normal life; only Lysimache, Eirene, and Xanthe. My stepmother disappeared at some point when we were crossing the bridge. Perhaps someone shoved her off. And Theandros never even made it to the sea.

When the light drains from the sky, we file into the sanctuary. The Telesterion sits squarely in the middle of the peaceful shaded courtyard, an imposing temple flanked by columns as wide as barrels with ivory figures of Demeter and Persephone sculpted onto the pediment, along with carved pomegranates and bundles of wheat, miniature pigs, goats, and snakes. As we walk into the courtyard, out of the corner of my eye I catch the unsettling sight of a cave nestled into the rock, illuminated by flickering torchlight. Caves are passages into the underworld, where the pale restless shades wander under Hades's watchful eye. Within the cave, my vision blurred by the failing light, I think I see the goddess Demeter, sitting on her rock of sorrow, lamenting Persephone's disappearance. I am about to call out and share in her lamenting, but then Xanthe tugs on my arm and motions for me to follow her to the side of the Telesterion, where the pits, chambers dug deep into the earth, await, spiraling downward where we must throw our still-alive piglets.

She throws hers from her sack into the pit, knowing it will die and rot away to further purify us and ensure fertility. This is why Demeter demands the pig and not some other animal. Later in the year, during the Thesmophoria, the pigs' bones will be dug up and displayed on altars, both the soil and our souls bettered by the sacrifice. The pigs scream, as human as any scream, my chest heaving at the sound of pain. I hold my piglet close, its soft head tucked under my chin, and I invoke Demeter once again. "Goddess of the earth, goddess of the grain, giver of life," I whisper, "I give this to You so that you may give Eirene safe passage in marriage, so that we may endure this separation, come to me now and again and deliver me from oppressive anxieties, reassure me that spring will return after winter, and the earth will bloom again, and that my daughter will return to me no longer a daughter but a mother herself, that the cycle will prevail, the generations streaming down from my body to her body to another body, oh Holy Goddess Who has suffered great sorrow and great joy, bestow this upon me."

At the sound of the gong I throw my piglet into the dark pit and turn away from its plaintive cries and scrambling, its grunts and barking. Another gong slices through the distressing sounds. It is Lysimache, summoning us to begin our wanderings, the doors of the Telesterion thrown open to the night. I glance around wildly. Eirene is gone. Then I hear her cries echoing from the cave, crying out for me to help her, to find her. Demeter's black rage, her unfathomable sorrow, rushes into me. Someone hands me a torch and we begin our wanderings through the dark, my chest constricting with pain for the daughter I am about to lose, for the child I have already lost, for all the ways, if I choose to name them, I could lose my children.

The other thing that was lost: a distant history that strikes a blow to all of us. King Cecrops, the first king of Athens, called for a vote to assign our city a deity. The women voted for Athena, and we offered the olive tree, her symbol, because it never dies, perennially bearing fruit. The men voted for Poseidon, god of the seas, and they offered warships to protect the city from invaders and to use these same ships to conquer others. Because there were more women than men in the city at that time, we won and Athena became the city's deity. But to punish us, as men are often poor losers, the men took away our vote. Our power. We were no longer called Athenians and our children no longer carried our names.

The industrial town of Elefsina, once called Eleusis, smoldered in the distance, the oil refineries emitting gusts of smoke, the high-rise apartment buildings curved around the bay. Skeletal remains of old factories baked in the summer heat. Farther still, the Penteli Mountains rose up over the sea, tinted a fiery red in the setting sun. They were nearly at the sanctuary, most of the Sacred Way behind them, beneath which, Nikitas pointed out, many people had been buried, in particular children, along with vessels to catch the tears of their grieving relatives. "And over there," Nikitas continued in her imperious voice, "is the bridge of jests. The initiates crossed it while townspeople hurled insults and vulgarities at them, I suppose to disabuse them of their own importance as they prepared to make contact with the divine."

Dusk had fallen, the sky hazed in a purplish pink. They were dusty and thirsty, having walked all afternoon by the time they arrived at the sanctuary. Ava was beyond hunger, her body light and adrenaline fueled, her focus sharpened to the hypnotic sounds of double flutes and frame drums that some of the women played as they approached the ruins, red poppies and wildflowers sprouting from cracks in the crumbling stones. Stopping before the entrance, Isabel repeatedly poured water from her canteen into Ava's cupped palms, and the goat slurped from it. Nikitas filled a foldable bowl with water for the dogs, who drank eagerly for a few minutes, the repetitive sound of their lapping tongues soothing. Margot sat down on a nearby rock and stretched out her long legs. Yael and Sophie and the other women put down the amphoras of wine and water, along with baskets of food that they would enjoy after the rituals.

A modern sadness infused this ancient place, and for a brief moment, Ava caught her breath, struck by how little was left, while a certain religious gravity still hung in the air, a tangible heaviness from centuries of sacrifices and prayers, from all that accumulated faith.

It was quiet and peaceful, almost preternaturally so, the wind, rocks, and the setting sun their only companions. Ava wondered why there weren't any other tourists, such as the ones they'd seen hours ago along the Sacred Way. Tonkova joked that they were too fainthearted to make it here. But then one of the younger women said that Nikitas was an old friend of Eleni Drakos, who had been the chief archaeologist and curator of this site for the last thirty years. As a favor to Nikitas, she had granted them after-hours access.

Sitting down next to Margot, Nikitas tilted her head back to drink from her water bottle. "Eleni and I go way back." She smiled warmly, the olive trees casting prismatic shadows across her face. She told everyone to take a short rest. They would enter the sanctuary when night fell.

Ava glanced up at the traces of summer light still lingering in the sky. She sat down on the other side of Margot, feeling the urge to put a hand on her knee or around her shoulders, but she anticipated how Margot might recoil from such public affection. Instead she sat beside her on a tree stump. It was enough just to be near her.

She imagined hearing her phone ring even though it was dead, and her mind traveled back to this morning, when she'd briefly spoken to Kasper. He reassured her that everything was fine. Sam was happy staying with Luca because the babysitter played video games with them. Then he said the director stormed off set yesterday after watching the dailies and Marc had to finish shooting his scenes. Olga was making his life hell, complaining about the size of the sets, that they weren't impressive enough, threatening to seize creative control of the film, and Kasper imagined himself trapped in a fiery cage, constantly trying to appease her although appeasement only escalated the depth of her wrath. Ava had listened and nodded, adding encouragements at the appropriate times, conveying understanding and warmth while realizing that perhaps she was, like Olga, also fashioning Kasper into her sacrificial lamb, readying to slaughter him at the opportune time, once this movie was over. After years of silently surrendering herself to his career, his advancement, his well-being, it would be so easy to attack him in a blinding flash of rage and tear him apart. A blunt overcorrection, but a tempting one.

She recalled how, a few months after Kasper had left for Bulgaria, she had told Richard she fantasized about leaving her family to join a monastery, somewhere high in the mountains shrouded in fog, where she could think in silence without so many competing demands, impossible expectations, the material, maternal concerns fraying her sanity. Without this urgent familial need pressing down on her. Even after she tended to everyone's bids for emotional sustenance and to the little physical emergencies—the ingrown toenails, yeast infections, canker sores, and seasonal allergies that waxed and waned—the need was still there, insatiable, asking for more, demanding that she make it better, fill it up.

She had been particularly fragile that spring morning, having lost sleep over a comment Margot's therapist had made the day before about how Kasper had left so abruptly, without a transitional object, without scheduled times to talk to the kids, without any psychological preparation, *without without without* pounding through her, the therapist's grave tone implying a grave outcome unless Ava repaired the situation, figured out how to fill the void, become both mother and father. She explained to Richard that she didn't want to say anything to Kasper about this, especially since he was gone. And it wasn't just geographic distance keeping her silent. She worried that she wanted too much from him, or that she was, in essence, *too much* for him. For anyone. As always, she folded her desires into herself because it was better to dazzle everyone with her self-reliance, with an armor of perfection, instead of feeling that old pain. She was unable to sleep that night, her phone pinging with wildfire notifications about a blaze in the next canyon, the wind kicking up, rattling the blinds, shaking the trees. As usual, she packed a duffel bag with the kids' birth certificates, passports, her computer, a few valuables, prepared to snatch things quickly if ordered to evacuate. They awoke to the sound of air tankers flying overhead dumping seawater onto the mountains, but they were still okay. The morning unfurled roughly with Margot's refusal to take off all that blush (filched from Ava's drawer) that she had doused on her face before school. And then there was Sam's scowling resentment when Kasper FaceTimed while they were driving on the PCH, ash swirling in the air like malevolent snow, dusting the windshield, the sky competing shades of apocalyptic orange. Seeing Kasper's name pop up, she'd thrown the phone forcefully against the dashboard. It bounced off and landed under the passenger seat, near an old muddy tennis ball and a bag of half-eaten pretzels.

"Life is the sum of what we pay attention to," Richard had said crisply after she'd finished describing the hellish night that had bled into a hellish morning. "So you can choose to leave and no longer pay attention to all this. And you don't have to wait until the kids are in college; you're not going to screw them up if you get a divorce and carve out some time and space for yourself. It would be inflating your own importance to believe that, for instance, getting a divorce or not getting a divorce has that much influence over your kids' life trajectory." His statement dangled enticingly in the air while Ava also suspected that Richard had transformed into a bald evil wizard, whispering dark suggestions of another life into her ear, making her think she didn't really love Kasper, or that love and history weren't enough if she felt invisible, exhausted, fed up.

Now, contemplating her marriage as night fell, Ava realized that they were the performers and the audience all at once; she would both observe the rituals as well as enact them. At Nikitas's sharp cry, overlaid by the crashing cymbals, they filed into the sanctuary, one by one, solemn and silent. Up ahead, Nikitas and Tonkova carried fiery torches above their heads, lighting the way. Ava thought she smelled incense, sacrificial smoke, burning wood. She struggled to carry the ceramic amphora mixed with the wine and herbs while Isabel held its other handle. Margot walked before her and she felt the urge to touch her hair, slide her fingers through the silky strands. The bright slim crescent moon shone down on the Kallichoron Well, a circular construction of stones, and a small cave carved into rock loomed to the right, where most likely Demeter wept for Persephone. As they made their way upward and in, Ava knew they were heading toward the main courtyard of the sanctuary, where the Telesterion had once stood, a beautiful columned temple that would have towered above them. With her free hand, Ava absently stroked the backs of Tonkova's German shepherds, who trotted alongside them, ears upright, alert to the small animals darting through the trees, to the footsteps echoing throughout this ancient place. Tonkova and Nikitas sang from *The Homeric Hymn to Demeter*, the words shivering in the air, beginning from the beginning: *I begin my song of the holy goddess, fair-haired Demeter, and of her slim-ankled daughter whom Hades snatched away . . . She was playing with the deep-bosomed daughters of Ocean, away from Demeter of the golden weapon and glorious fruit . . .*

They climbed a bit higher, up to a flat plateau that overlooked the Bay of Salamis, where the Telesterion would have been. Ava felt a pang in her chest, wanting to throw herself onto the ground, to weep into these moss-covered stones for all that had been destroyed and lost. In the clearing, overgrown with weeds and poppies and wildflowers, the temple remnants appeared: a vast rectangular stone platform demarcated on all four sides by eight shallow steps where the initiates would have sat to watch the performance of the myth. Marble stumps of broken columns lay in the grass, columns that would have supported the Telesterion's ceiling. The dogs shambled around the ruins. The goat, tied to a nearby olive tree, bleated in the wind. Tonkova and Nikita held little ceramic cups to the amphora's lip, while Isabel and Ava tilted the wine vessel downward to begin pouring the wine. Yael and Sophie took the filled cups and passed them out.

Ava searched for Margot in the crowd, and saw her with another girl about her age who looked Bulgarian or Greek because of her long braids and embroidered dress. The girl was talking to Margot, explaining something, probably about what would happen next. Margot looked relaxed, a small smile spreading over her face, and Ava refocused on balancing the amphora, the container growing lighter and lighter as the wine emptied out of it. She began passing out more cups of wine, her fingertips fleetingly touching other women's fingertips, a jolt of electric knowledge coursing through her, sensing, in that span of seconds, a particular woman's struggle: a critical mother, an absent father, broken relationships, thwarted creativity, abuse, sexual assault, a painful miscarriage from decades ago, or how a woman had yearned for a child that never came. Handing an older Greek woman a cup, she sensed an ancient history of sacrifice, subordination, regret.

"Efcharistó," the woman said, her dark eyes swimming with emotion, with a buried past. *Thank you.*

Ava motioned to Margot and the woman's daughter, who stood on the far end of the temple platform. "How old is she?"

"I kóri mou einai dekatrión kai arravoniasméni gai gámo. Óti i kóri tis prépei na katálavei ti periménei."

Ava smiled, only getting that her daughter (kóri meant "maiden") was also thirteen, dekatrión.

"Like my daughter, my kóri," Ava said, and the woman nodded, her expression serious.

Tonkova overheard and Ava asked her what the woman had said. They watched the woman walk toward her daughter, bringing an extra cup for her.

"She said her daughter is thirteen and betrothed for marriage. That her daughter must understand what awaits."

"She's too young!"

"They're promised for marriage young in rural Bulgaria and Greece, an old tribal custom, rare these days but more common in the countryside. Not in the city. Not anymore."

Ava nodded, a sharp nervousness spreading through her body.

Nikitas clapped her hands together and announced, "Before we begin, we drink the kykeon!"

Would everyone drink? Should she drink? What about Margot? She searched for her and found her still with the Greek woman and her daughter. Gripped by panic, she momentarily felt the urge to turn back, to grab Margot and run, but then Isabel raised her cup and Ava raised hers and they repeated the following lines, lines that she felt she had known all her life, or in another life: "I fasted, I drank the kykeon, I approached the frontier of death. I set foot on the threshold of Persephone. I journeyed through all the elements and came back. I saw at midnight the sun, sparkling in white light, I came close to the gods of the upper and nether world and adored them from near at hand." The ancient words became her words, blending into all words. When the wine hit her tongue, she tasted honeyed wheat with traces of cloves and mint. Isabel drank more, her lambent eyes finding Ava's, her mouth berry stained. Ava watched Isabel's pupils dilate, black overtaking the green, while her own cheeks flushed with heat, the wine warming her insides, making her limbs watery, fluid and light.

"Raging with grief and despair," Nikitas yelled over the din, "we reenact Demeter searching for her lost Persephone as we wander through the interior of this temple." She swept a hand over the flat expanse of patchy grass. "Imagine the onlookers watching the performance from the surrounding seats." She paused to drink.

Ava drank more, her temples throbbing. The cypress trees grew into columns, the grass beneath her feet a marble floor, the temple enclosing her, enclosing all of them, as she was handed a torch and then another one. Holding the flaming torches aloft, she began searching for her lost daughter, her lost son, and for the lost pieces of herself that she had misplaced along the way. Nikitas's voice rang through the vast candlelit interior: "We ask Demeter, goddess of the grain, goddess who encompasses all life and death, for forgiveness so that life will prevail. We ask for a future to give to our children and our children's children." Nikitas wrapped her dark cashmere shawl over her head and imperiously swept the thick tail of it over her shoulder before peering out at them with keen intensity, the flaming heat of the surrounding torches fracturing her features. Ava covered her head with a threadbare blanket from the Sofia apartment; it still smelled of the peppermint tea Sam had accidentally spilled on it a few nights ago, and she missed Sam and missed the ordinariness of the messy apartment and missed the smell of Kasper's clean T-shirts when she held them to her face before folding them away.

Everyone gathered in the center of the temple, and Ava took in the Corinthian columns supporting the sumptuous ceiling, at the decorative frieze bordering the room that displayed rosettes and crossed torches, bundles of wheat and pomegranates. Nikitas and Tonkova reclined on the stone seats, awaiting the performance. The women parted, scattering to all four corners of the temple and then Margot and the Greek girl ran into the center stage, and began pantomiming picking flowers, dancing and laughing in their innocence, throwing petals into the wind, their hair loose, their feet bare. And then there was a great terrible rumbling of drums, the cymbals clashing together triumphantly, signaling that Hades had emerged from the underworld and taken Persephone away. Ava watched, an odd numb tingling spreading over her body, as she listened to Margot's distant cries. The stage was empty, the girls gone, swallowed up by a chasm in the earth. A sob escaped her, breaking open her chest, and she let out a ritual cry inciting the next part of the hymn: "Then a grief more terrible and oppressive came upon her heart and in anger at Zeus, shrouded in clouds, Demeter deserted the gatherings of the gods and went far from Olympus to the cities and farms of men and for a long time disguised her appearance."

"Margot!" Ava yelled into the flickering darkness. "Where are you?" The visceral fear sent her hurtling and Ava became Demeter as all the surrounding women did and they began their wanderings throughout the temple. Multiple layers of grief subsumed her and she knew that this temple, this sanctum, was no longer a metaphor for the underworld but the underworld itself, dissolving consciousness and boundaries, dipping them beneath the surface of the present.

She found herself under a black dark wave, at the most bottom fifth layer of the ocean, beneath the abyss, in the hadal zone, where it was so frigid and cold, where no life seemed to exist, the pressure immense. She knew she had to stay down here for the dark wave to pass, before she returned to air and life. Perhaps this was where her son lived, not in the heavens, but thousands of meters beneath the earth, trapped in these cracks and canyons.

Where are you? she cried under the black wave, sensing its heaviness rolling above her, sensing the other women's sorrow forming whirlpools, riptides, currents.

She couldn't swim back up yet, the wave refusing to pass over until she returned to the moment of rupture, of final separation. Twenty-seven weeks pregnant, she lay on the examining table. The nurse had already tried to find a heartbeat, until the doctor walked in, impatiently taking the Doppler from the nurse.

"You should have come earlier," the doctor announced. *Earlier than what?* Ava wanted to ask but didn't, cowed by the doctor's tense jaw and brusque manner. Ava remembered staring at her navy silk dress dotted with daisies beneath her white lab coat, but by that time the doctor was frantically fumbling with the Doppler and dresses and patterns and fabric and the material world ceased to matter.

She remembered the ghostly swish of her blood rushing through the Doppler and nothing else. It sounded as if someone was whistling through the skeletal shells of bombed-out buildings, sheet metal rattling in the wind. The doctor swiftly moved on to a sonogram. The screen with the image of the baby was behind Ava's right shoulder. Ava remembered thinking that she didn't have to ask what was wrong. She already knew from the doctor's face, a face stripped down to its bare elements as if blinded by the sun.

After a pause, the doctor looked down at Ava's jellied abdomen and said, "I'm so sorry."

Ava heard herself ask, "Is he gone?" the question dying in her throat.

The doctor nodded. Then she left the room, saying she'd be right back, but before the door closed she heard the doctor curse under her breath, "Jesus fucking Christ."

Ava sat there, her legs dangling off the examining table, the thin white paper crinkling under her clammy thighs, unwilling to accept that this was real and happening, but she knew it was real and she knew that she would have to call Kasper soon, the phone warm in her palm. She would tell him what had happened and then it would be real for him too and the more people who knew, the more real this would become and the less real everything that preceded it would be.

She cried into a rock in the middle of the sanctuary, maybe the same one Demeter had wept over, marked by the kind of rupture all mothers fear, the kind you can't stop, reliving the sensation of birthing someone who was already gone, the singular moment filled with dread and levity, relief and agony, the hospital room lightening all around her, as if, once freed from her body—a body that had betrayed both Ava and her son, her body that she now hated—he could begin his ascent, rapidly becoming more spirit than matter.

And the beautiful nurse who helped her through the delivery, her orb-like eyes the color of heaven, who became Ava's mother for the length of her shift. Her name was Michelle and Ava clung to her, inhaling the bleached scent of her scrubs, listening to her steady voice explain that Ava's breasts would soon fill with milk, harden into rocks, she must press them with ice packs. Michelle held both of Ava's forearms, her eyes widening, checking to make sure Ava understood. Chin crumpled into her chest, Ava nodded while gulping down snot and tears, rendered mute by the mixture of guilt, grief, and fury crashing around inside her with such force and velocity, such vengeance.

"My mother," Michelle whispered into the gauzy light splintering through the blinds, "lost her first child. Full term. A boy. I was born a year later."

All Ava could say as tears streamed down her face: "Thank you. Thank you. Thank you."

After the delivery, Michelle brought him to her and she held him, allowing herself to kiss the top of his head, his smattering of dark hair brushing against her chapped lips, his body so light, less than five pounds, but there was enough of him to hold. Swaddled in a hospital blanket, he was taken away; they must have known that if she saw any more of him, his foot, his hand, his perfectly formed shoulders, she would never give him back.

At home, at the end of every sleepless night, she had tracked dawn's first light, as if he might be in the burgeoning day, in the first birdsong, in the smudged horizon the color of a bruise.

Ava pressed her breasts against the rock, tunneling back to hugging herself under the showerhead, the water pressure causing her breasts to leak milk, the milk running down her distended stomach, down her thighs and feet, spiraling into the drain.

After a number of days sequestered at home, she finally ventured out, squinting into the too bright sunlight, on a walk with her mother, who didn't know what else to do with her. Her mother suggested they stop for coffee, and standing in line, a man ogled Ava's engorged breasts bursting beneath her T-shirt. He couldn't see the ice packs she had shoved into her nursing bra. He couldn't tell that she had just lost her child. He only saw what he wanted to see: a tall young woman with enormous breasts. As she cupped the hot coffee, her milk started to flow, wetting the bra, despite the ice packs, despite the rage thrumming through her, despite the burning tears hidden by her large black sunglasses, and the straw hat, and the bandana around her neck that she used to constantly dry her face.

She didn't ever want to leave the house again after that, even though her mother insisted exercise was good for her, while Kasper chimed in about the importance of getting outside, offering in an overly casual tone every few days, "How about we get some air?"

Ava had watched in stunned amazement that Kasper could eat, go to a restaurant, talk normally on the phone, and drive a car, but she couldn't venture down the street without tearing up at the sight of a pregnant woman, a pram, a pacifier abandoned on the sidewalk, a baby in a sling. She avoided parks, playgrounds, farmer's markets, grocery stores, libraries, coffee shops, malls, the beach; she avoided any place where mothers and children might go, which ended up being every place. Her bedroom the only refuge, insulated from external triggers, but not excluding the most powerful one: her erratic and unpredictable mind, which behaved like a trip wire. One wrong move and losing him crashed over her again and again, and she was trapped beneath a tidal wave, the ocean bracingly cold and black, not knowing when it would pass. If it would pass.

Her mother came to visit on an overcast Tuesday afternoon, perched at the foot of Ava's bed, and repeated that she simply couldn't imagine it, such an awful thing had never happened to her, promptly washing her hands of such messy grief. Ava remembered staring at her mother's hands, the way they rested in her lap, inert, incapable, and in a searing flash, Ava saw that her mother refused to mother her, an impervious bystander to the accident that was now Ava's life.

The only thing her mother had admitted that day was that when she was seventeen, she had gotten an abortion in Mexico City because in 1960 abortion was illegal in the United States. Ava thought the story would continue as some kind of consolation, or comparison to what Ava had endured. That perhaps her mother might still mourn the loss, even though she hadn't wanted a child then. Or that it had been painful and terrifying. But her mother then said that shortly thereafter she went to a beach club and met the scion of a wealthy Mexican family, who wooed her to dinner at his family's estate. After dinner, he showed her their private zoo, where every type of animal roamed. Ava didn't understand what this story had to do with her story, and she hated her mother for telling it.

Afterward, they tried to find out what happened with science, thinking science would get to the bottom of it, but the highly trained pathologists and maternal-fetal medicine specialists didn't know. They ran multiple tests. The autopsy results came back inconclusive, and all the usual reasons, such as a cord accident, chromosomal or genetic abnormalities, an undetected infection, or a lack of amniotic fluid, hadn't happened. The doctors kept saying that finding nothing was better than something, because if they found something then there would be an issue to treat, a complication the next time around. And Ava thought, *If there's a next time,* because no one knew that. No one knew anything.

Instead of listening to the doctors with their non-theories, she took matters into her own hands. She burned sticks of white sage to clear out evil spirits, wielding the smoking sage as a wand, crossing every doorway with it, every threshold, every window, every opening where evil might have slithered in and spirited him away. Unable to sleep at night, she awaited a sign from him, because some mothers, she had read on blogs dedicated to God's "little angels," still communicated with their dead children: lights flickering on and off at the time of death, even years later. Dreams and visions in which the child is grown up, reassuring the mother that he is okay, that he loves her. A sense that the lines of communication remained open, lit up by a mother's love, a portal into healing. She never felt his presence, which she took as another failure on her part. Maybe he was too far away by now, whisked into some far corner of the universe, a collection of scattered stars and dust.

The other idea was that nothing follows after death but a great yawning darkness and this was why she never sensed him or saw him or felt his small hand in hers.

The last haunting thought, the one that had sunk its teeth into her, that wouldn't let go: had she been a better mother, with keener instincts, armed with a better sense of her body's invisible machinations, she could have rescued him in time. A recurring fantasy: bringing him home premature but alive, thanks to her female intuition.

You should have come earlier.

"It's not your fault," the Greek woman said, parting the oceanic darkness. "You came as quickly as you could. You're a good mother. I *know* you are."

Opening her eyes, the coffered ceiling swayed above her and the torches blazed, illuminating the edges of the temple.

The woman took hold of Ava's shoulders, her grip firm and insistent. "He's waiting for you on the other side, in golden fields. He knows that you love him. That you will love him forever."

Ava nodded, tears streaming down her face, before she realized that she was surrounded by all the other women, by their stories of grief. Isabel whispered that she had suffered another miscarriage a few months ago, the blood awakening her in the middle of the night while Marc slept peacefully. "I hear you," the women murmured, forming concentric circles around one another, their bodies warm and pressing. Sophie shouted out that she too had lost a child, and Ava remembered this now. She felt the pressure of the Greek woman's chest against her back, and in distorted dreamlike imagery, Ava saw what had happened to her: a stillbirth in the middle of a tangled forest, too young to be alone, the light of the moon shining down on her, revealing that her child was dead, unmoving. She'd bundled his small form into a muslin cloth, still afraid she might hurt or disturb him in some way. Then there was the long walk home over an uneven path, the glittering eyes of animals peering through the underbrush. The women of the household awaited, her mother-in-law among them, as if they already knew what she carried.

Ava turned toward her, flinging her arms around the woman and her daughter, and around Margot, who had reappeared. Ava kissed the woman's face, tasting the salty sting of their intermingled tears. Pitch-blackness flooded the room, so dark she could almost hold it in her hands before a great blazing light blinded Ava, thousands of torches flooding her field of vision, so bright she could barely see, but she felt Margot's arms around her, hugging her tightly, and Ava held her close, inhaling Margot's milky rose scent, her hair and her skin, a chorus of singing and clapping rising up around them, infused with the unbridled joy of witnessing mother and daughter together again.

Eleusis, August 2019

The pale purple dawn greeted them, the dewy air hitting her face. They had fallen asleep inside the temple beside a low-burning bonfire, their warm bodies overlapping. When Ava opened her eyes, she expected to see the coffered ceiling, the staggered Corinthian columns, the thousands of torches swaying in the temple darkness. But instead she took in the broadening sky, birds alighting from branch to branch, olive trees and cypresses and ancient ruins, the grass moist, a slight chill in the air. Isabel said it was nautical dawn, just before the sky lightens, the stars and moon fading. Ava cupped Margot's cheek. Looking down at her sleeping daughter, she was relieved they'd made it through, her sweat dried and stale, her stomach sharp with hunger. When she removed her hand from Margot's cheek, Margot began to stir, her eyes slowly opening.

Famished, they prepared to eat. Tonkova and Nikitas relit the bonfire using leaves and branches, Ava helped Yael arrange the cakes and meat pies on a ceramic platter, the food mouthwatering. She thought she might pass out from hunger, the ground tilting upward at an alarming angle. But soon they would eat and rejoice and bathe in a flood of relief. Tonkova winked at Ava and whispered, "The hard part is over. Go sit."

The other women sat in a lopsided circle around the fire, and Margot and Ava joined them. The goat was still tied to the olive tree, straining on the rope. The German shepherds were coiled in a furry heap near the fire, as if they were one breathing animal, their liquid eyes opening slowly to the movements around them. Isabel placed sprigs of peony and rosemary along the edges of the platter. Margot leaned against Ava, and she felt their closeness.

Nikitas stoked the fire, stabbing its blue embers and recited from the hymn: "Baubo understood Demeter's grief and made plenty of jokes and jests that made the holy Lady smile with kindly heart, and ever afterward she continues to delight in her spirit."

The goat bleated and Ava stared into its black squinty eyes. Sensing her gaze, it bleated louder, its hoof pawing dirt, lurching toward Ava. Margot calmed the goat, stroking its head, feeding it mounds of weeds.

Nikitas and Tonkova began to dance in an exaggerated, comical way, inhabiting the spirit of old bawdy Baubo, the goddess of mirth, the one who finally makes Demeter laugh, shattering the spell of her grief and rejoicing in Persephone's return from the underworld. The woman from yoga shook a tambourine and another girl hunched over a drum, creating steady alternating beats with the flat of her hand.

Tonkova and Nikitas stamped on the ground and lifted up their robes, flashing their furry gray vulvas, and Ava smiled at how shocked she had been as a college student, when Nikitas stood before her, fresh out of the shower, unapologetically naked.

"If a man ever follows us, to pry open these mysteries," Tonkova bellowed, her eyes shining, "I'll cut off his penis . . . a little man with his little penis. It's so small, it'll get lost in here." And then she produced a miniature terra-cotta penis from her vagina, pinching it between her forefinger and thumb, exhibiting it as a prize. Seized by the shift in mood, everyone burst out laughing.

Looking around at the cackling women, Margot half smiled. Ava wondered what Margot thought of all this; did she understand their dark humor, their mockery of the age-old glorification of the phallus? Probably not. Maybe she wouldn't have to contend with the self-aggrandizing myth of male sexual power, or the term "penis envy," so outdated by now it teetered on erasure. She might even consider it okay and kind of cool to have a vagina, as it was currently no longer considered a regretful source of lack and shame, especially since a certain female celebrity now sold, on her wildly popular digital platform, candles that smelled like her vagina, as well as jade vaginal eggs and moon juice "sex dust." The candles had sold out in a number of minutes. Still, Ava reflected, all this trendy vagina veneration had gotten women nowhere politically.

Nikitas stomped on the ground, raising up her robe and then pulling it down in mock modesty while the girl banged harder on the frame drum.

Isabel glanced over at Ava, and when their eyes met, they started laughing too.

Yael stood up and joked about the number of times she had faked an orgasm to please a man. She squeezed her breasts together and threw back her head in mock surrender. "Yes, yes, that was great, you were *great*," and they all laughed knowingly. "How fragile they are that we must praise them after every ejaculation," Yael added, her curls haloing her flushed face.

Sophie shouted out, "And when my husband can't get an erection, I have to smother and soothe him with kisses. Suddenly I'm his mother, not his lover!"

Margot gave Ava a look, her eyes widening, and Ava smiled. She would explain later, knowing that erection and orgasm and ejaculation were all possibly new words. Or maybe she knew them. It was time to find out.

Nikitas let the goat loose and straddled him, riding him toward the fire. Everyone screamed gleefully, clapping and dancing, some of the women twirling, their skirts skimming the bonfire's flames.

The goat began gamboling about, snorting and grunting. Tonkova clapped, riling the goat up even more. They exchanged jokes of increasing vulgarity, employing silly puns rife with innuendo.

Ava danced with the other women, jesting about the wayward wiry hairs sprouting from their chins and areolas, about their crinkly stomachs and loosening flesh, about their ringed necks and crow's-feet, about the absurd indignities of aging. Remembering the arrogance of their own youth, they laughed uproariously about how young women today didn't know what was coming for them, anticipating that it would all be equal and great, believing they were no longer beholden to the body or to the expectations of their gender and that, with their wonderfully progressive ideas, they would elide history, skating over centuries of religious, economic, and cultural punishment for being female. *Oh no*, Ava internally cackled, tears of hysterical laughter forming in the corners of her eyes. *When it's their turn, they'll see how it is.*

The commotion halted at the sound of Tonkova's and Nikitas's harsh succession of claps. The drumroll grew louder, building thunderously. Tonkova motioned to the goat, who blinked into the fire. Suddenly she pulled the goat's neck, jerking it in front of the altar. From an amphora, Nikitas poured water over the goat's rigid back. Then she poured more water over their outstretched hands, all of them anticipating its coolness and purity.

After Nikitas sprinkled the goat's head with the last drops of water, it nodded slightly, as if offering consent. Nikitas instructed them to reach into the woven basket next to the altar and gather handfuls of barley to throw onto the goat and altar. Solemn quiet marshaled around them. Margot flashed Ava a look of alarm and Ava mouthed, *It's okay*. The surrounding forest calmed, as if the birds in the trees and the animals rummaging through the undergrowth knew to stop their continuous activity, as if the forest grew a mind and breathed stillness through its branches, environs, and mossy passageways.

They hoisted the goat over the altar. He struggled and squirmed but they held him fast.

Margot blinked back tears, burrowing her head into Ava's chest. Ava held her, shielding her from the ensuing violence, knowing that Margot didn't yet understand the ancient belief of sacrificing something alive, shedding its blood, in exchange for more life. A protection to make sure life continues, cycles forward, keeps going.

Nikitas bludgeoned his head with an axe before opening up the artery on the side of its neck, the blood flowing over her hands. The basin under the altar collected the excess blood and they cried out in shrill tones. Ava didn't know who started shrieking but it didn't matter, the origin of it throbbed in the back of her throat, awaiting release, awaiting this moment of life screaming over death.

Margot opened her eyes and screamed too, her scream as piercing as those of the women, who had experienced so much more.

Tonkova expertly extracted the animal's still-beating heart, spearing a stick through it and roasting it on the fire before disemboweling the goat and tasting its entrails. She called the dogs over and cupped the entrails in her hands and they devoured them.

They put the goat on a spit over the bonfire, throwing wine over the flames, the fire heightening. While the goat roasted, they passed out little round grain cakes and more kykeon, which made Ava's head heavy and dense, the images of the rotating goat and the laughing supplicants more brilliant, saturated in color.

35

Eleusis, 415 BC

On the Sacred Way, images flicker before my eyes in the hot sun. We head toward home, my city glittering in the distance, our throats parched and throbbing with soreness from our singing and crying. Eirene whisked away into the underworld, my tears strewn over the mirthless rock, the shades of the dead parading before me, my beloved nurse and grandmother among them, while I searched and searched, roaming the dark sanctuary as if a heavy black cloth covered my face even though my eyes were wide open, struggling to see through the unending dark. I called out Eirene's name, I called out for my dead son, the first child I lost, the only one. Blinding light, a thousand torches, dancing flames and shifting bodies. The temple flooded with a numinous light, my heart in my throat, a sob shooting down my spine when I beheld mighty Demeter cloaked in cerulean blue, her hair as golden as wheat, with her daughter Persephone beside her, their arms inter-linked, their gazes penetrating, terrifying, impossible to look at, threatening immolation.

This is what I saw. What I think I saw. I cannot speak for anyone else and we will never speak of it, especially not in the mundane daylight. We will keep these secrets bound up in our chests, as tightly as our most prized possessions, as guarded as our inner-most thoughts, never to be shared or revealed, as that will infuriate the goddess. She might relinquish her promise of fecundity. She might rage across the fertile plains and turn crops barren, cattle diseased, just as she did in times of old if we dare betray her mysteries.

Eirene and Xanthe trail behind me while I walk ahead, following

Lysimache and her attendants. Approaching home, I have the feeling that a child or a slave is sick, that they will rush at me the moment I enter the courtyard with all sorts of questions, news, gossip, and pressing needs that must be met. Dreading it, I yearn to return to the ecstatic night, the revelry and singing, the shared sisterhood of rage bleeding into grief. These flickering memories sustain me as the thud of daily life returns: my dirty feet and smoky hair, my tight dry skin in need of a bath, the work that awaits at the loom. The wedding garment for Eirene's future husband that she must finish, that she resists finishing, her nimble fingers turning to lead the moment she resumes.

We stop for a moment in the shade of an olive grove to drink from a nearby stream, dipping our ceramic bowls into the rushing water. The water tastes clean and good and temporarily dispels my headache. Her gaze opaque, glazed, and distant, Eirene looks as if she's seen another world, perhaps the future. Or the past, when we were called Athenians, when the family line passed from mother to daughter. The mother line. Watching her stare off into the trees, I wonder if my husband will ever return, if I want him to return. I don't need him anymore; I've had my children, they are healthy and strong. But do I still wish to look upon his face? Chart his irregular moods and whims? Absorb his criticisms or delight in the temporary elation of his praise? On the off chance that he comes to me for pleasure in the dead of night, will I still welcome his body, however deformed it is by war and age?

Or maybe I've had enough of these material concerns. I could live in a temple as a priestess, or with Lysimache, the world with its urgencies a faint echo in my ear.

I could carve out another kind of life, one that is filled with enough silence for the gods to speak through me.

36

Sofia, August 2019

They returned to Sofia just before sunrise, the bus depositing them in the parking lot at the edge of the city where they had met three days prior. Isabel then drove Ava and Margot home, racing through the sleepy city streets, cutting off cabs and buses, almost running over a cat. Ava expected recriminations for her lateness, as she'd promised to return last night, but she'd called to explain the change of plan, her voice hurried, not giving Kasper time to question her as they filed onto the bus in Athens. He rushed one last question at her, about getting a sitter to cover tonight because he would still be away on shoots. Of course, Ava had said. Get a sitter.

Margot wondered if Papa would be there when they got home. Ava squinted at the digital clock on the dashboard. "It's only six a.m. Maybe not."

"I miss him," Margot said plaintively.

Ava stared out at the blur of Eastern bloc apartment buildings, the lush oak trees along the boulevard, electricity from the tramline sporadically sparking above them. "I can't remember exactly when he gets home from night shoots."

"I miss him."

Ava twisted around in her seat. "You'll see him soon enough," she said, trying to keep the irritation out of her voice. They were all tired, her head still heavy from the kykeon, from the ordeal of grief, from the celebratory dancing that followed, the goat slowly rotating on a spit cycling through her mind, as if this had all happened on a parallel plane of existence, and maybe it had. Shuffling histories and stories like playing cards, she thought about the Greek woman and her daughter, wondering how real they were, and how much her intense research had morphed these women into other women from antiquity. Margot had said very little about the rituals, except that she had participated in a play, acting out the part of Persephone along with the Greek girl, that they became mysteriously interchangeable. And at the end of the third act they were reunited with their mothers, the blazing torches, the clapping and singing enveloping them. "And what did you do while you were in the 'underworld,'" Ava had asked nervously once they were back on the bus, ensconced in their seats, everyone asleep around them.

Margot shrugged and gave Ava a secret smile. "Aren't we supposed to keep the mysteries a secret? I'm not asking what you saw."

"You're right," Ava said. "You're entitled to your own mysteries. That's part of growing up."

Before they got out of the car, they all hugged, their breath intermingling, their hair still smelling of campfire, their skin coated in a fine sheen of dust and dried sweat. Isabel squeezed Ava's hand and said in her relaxed Brazilian accent, "Don't worry. Everything will be okay."

In front of the apartment building, Ava fumbled with the keys, dropping them a few times on the pavement, her head pounding. Margot stood impatiently beside her, saying she wanted to sleep, shivering in her thin white sweater. An older man in tattered clothes, chewing tobacco, started yelling at them in Bulgarian, spit jettisoning from his mouth. Early morning workers passed by, their expressions bored and tired. Turning the key again, Ava pushed the door open with her shoulder, throwing all her weight into it, and finally it opened and they hurried into the dark vestibule. She slammed the door shut, the man's angry shouts still audible through the thick metal slab.

The moment they came into the apartment she knew Kasper was home, the sitter gone. The coffee machine emitted its throaty brewing and orange slices gleamed on the cutting board. Watching the coffee percolate, she prepared her face to appear serene, relaxed, as if she had nothing to hide.

The bathroom door opened into the hallway and Kasper came out frowning at his phone. When he noticed her standing there, he jumped slightly, as if she were a wild animal who'd wandered inside.

"Jesus. You scared me."

"It's just me."

He glanced at Ava strangely, sensing an air of lawlessness, something pried loose. Margot rushed down the hallway and barreled into Kasper, throwing her arms around him. "Papa!"

He kissed the top of her head, his eyes locked on Ava's face. "I called you like ten times."

"Well, everything seems fine here."

A tense pause hung between them.

"Sam still asleep?" she asked.

"Yeah."

Margot released her grip around him and said she needed a shower.

He could probably tell Ava was treading water, trying to steer clear of the trip, which only increased his curiosity. "I actually called you a bunch more times over the last few days, but your phone was always off, or something. It kept going straight to voice mail."

"Was there a problem here, with Sam, or . . . ?"

He shook his head. "No. I don't know."

The bathroom door closed behind Margot and they listened to the shower running.

Kasper leaned against the opposite wall, crossing his arms over his chest. "So you had a good trip?"

"Yup," Ava said, feeling the center of herself harden.

"That's it?"

She threw up her hands. "What do you want me to say? We went to Eleusis to visit the ancient site. It was amazing. Very informative for my book."

"You fell off the radar. It's not like you. And Margot was with you. I wanted you to check in. I wanted more check-ins."

"Is this about Nikitas? Are you jealous that we had this time together?"

Kasper stared down at his bare feet against the scuffed hardwood floor. "No."

"Then what is it?" she demanded, emboldened by the double standard he was creating with all these questions, these underhanded complaints about her lack of attentiveness, her lack of care for him. That she had simply left, forgetting the fact that he had done the same to them. Not for three days but for three months, prompting her to come all this way to see if they still had a marriage.

"I guess I was worried that you might not come back." He let out a half-hearted laugh.

"Well, here I am." Was she, though? That pulsing wildness still ran through her, flecks of goat meat wedged between her teeth, her hair smelling of forest and smoke.

"When I was trying to get hold of you, Marc teased that you and Isabel had joined an all-female cult, taking Margot with you. That you would disappear into Greece. We'd have to get the Bulgarian police involved," he joked, but beneath the jokiness was fear, suspicion. She heard it: that tightening in his voice, the way he scanned her face, trying to decipher her unreadable expression.

"Maybe we did." She cracked a smile, waiting for him to smile too, to laugh it off, but he didn't.

Walking into the kitchen, he poured fresh coffee into two mugs. Ava bit her lip, willing herself not to escalate things. The number of times she couldn't get hold of him, allowing him to evaporate into his work, to forget them. As if it were some kind of male birthright to be unquestionably unavailable, to vanish from the domestic scene. And now that she had done the same? And if she told him what had really happened, would he understand? Would any man? Was it possible, or even necessary, for him to meet her in those depths?

But most men, she reckoned, tended to ruin things they didn't understand, just as they had centuries ago with the destruction of the mystery religions. A shiver of rage passed through her as she recalled how every ancient temple dedicated to Demeter and Persephone, and to all the other goddesses across the Mediterranean world, had been abandoned and destroyed or turned into churches a few hundred years after Christ's birth. Alaric the Goth had destroyed the entire sanctuary at Eleusis in AD 395, leaving just the foundations of the temple, broken columns, heaps of stones.

Ava sipped her coffee, aware of Kasper's discerning eyes on her, wondering what he imagined had happened at Eleusis, and how unnerved he was by her new demeanor, the way she didn't care to comfort or soothe him but just sat here drinking coffee, satisfied with her own thoughts.

Out of habit, she started to prepare breakfast, pulling out the egg carton from the fridge, cracking each one against the side of the bowl. As she cooked, a strange unsteadiness spread through her like a web. She started beating the eggs, hoping the frenetic whirling of the fork against the ceramic bowl would channel all this pent-up energy, smoothing out the jagged feelings. The door to the bathroom opened and Margot, flushed from the shower, a towel wrapped around her, said she was going to take a nap.

Putting the bowl aside, Ava sliced up the rest of the orange.

Kasper suddenly stood up and took the knife from her. "I got this," he said softly.

She held on to the knife. "You should really get some sleep. You look exhausted."

He hugged her, holding her close, his strong arms wrapping around her, the blade flattened between them. A sob almost escaped her from his tight embrace, from the pressure to contain all she had experienced.

Centuries' worth.

He kissed her deeply on the mouth, as if trying to root out what she held so tightly within her, and whispered that she tasted of wine, and something sweet, like a Turkish delight, and Ava wondered if traces of the honeyed kykeon remained on her lips, the substance that had made the Corinthian columns elongate and tower above them, the cavernous temple an ocean of grief, the hymns falling so naturally from her lips as if she'd recited the words every day of her life.

His phone vibrated in his pocket and he pulled away, swearing at the number, and after answering, he barked into the phone, explaining that they were not over budget, Olga's claims were spurious. "She doesn't know how to read a fucking cost report!"

Ava walked away from his ranting, refusing to allow the urgency of his concerns to disturb her. Surveying the mismatched socks drying on the rack and the scattered Hot Wheels cars, she vowed to protect the mysteries and hold them close. She went into the bedroom and lay down on the unmade bed, closing her eyes as if that would make the experience last a little longer, and soften the force of ordinary life shoving into her, demanding attention.

She listened to Kasper performing his habitual pacing, filling every room with his aggravation while she fended off the pressure of her impending future: leaving Sofia and returning home. It made her cringe to consider the heaps of mail, the dying rosemary bushes in the front yard, ordering school supplies for the kids, and preparing for her own teaching semester. She recalled the tidy manila grade books, the way she marked students absent with a little x next to their name, her fingertips dusted in chalk after class, her black jeans always smudged white with it.

But now, sitting here with a throbbing headache and a dry mouth, teaching all those classes and grading all those papers, caring for the children and tending to her husband, attending faculty and committee meetings and laboring over academic articles no one ever read or cared about seemed incomprehensible. Her old life among the magenta bougainvillea and evacuation warnings, the skinny coyotes that prowled the backyard thirsty for water, the detritus of housework and homework and schoolwork, recycling cans filled with unrecyclable material, mounds of hardened dog shit stuck to yellowed grass, and a husband who drifted in and out of her life no longer seemed tenable.

But she wasn't leaving Sofia yet.

One last ritual remained. Next Thursday. On the full moon.

It would be celebratory, Nikitas had explained on the bus ride home, honoring Dionysus, Bacchus as the Romans called him, the god of wine and madness.

From the kitchen, she overhead Kasper now talking to his mother in Swedish, the sweet rise and fall of the sentences melodic. From what Ava gathered, he explained that he couldn't come visit her after all, given the hectic production schedule. "Jag ar ledsen," he said, *I'm sorry,* his voice growing softer and guilt laden, a voice he only used with his mother.

Ava pictured Greta with her windblown gray hair, the color of steel, and a heavy cashmere shawl wrapped around her as she stood before wide windows overlooking the North Sea. Greta had never liked her, and at the same time, Ava empathized with her mother-in-law: she'd lost her only son to a foreign woman and a foreign country. Her grandchildren didn't speak her language. And now, she only had Kasper's telephone calls to look forward to, along with the occasional visit, a pittance compared to when she'd cradled Kasper in her arms, when he was all hers. What if Sam moved far away, leading a life that didn't include her? Would she endure the separation as gracefully as Greta?

But then she was reminded of sons who had failed to leave their mothers—Oedipus, Attis, Pentheus. Their stories never ended well.

37

Athens, 415 BC

A t first light, we begin with the ritual bath, marking the day
we have dreaded for years. Late-summer sun shrouds the
morning in deep amber, the light seeping through the cracks in the
limestone walls, filling the room with a dim golden hue.

In the tub, Eirene draws her knees into her chest while I pour
warm water over her head and birdlike shoulders from the very
vase she once tried to smash. She bows her head, burrowing her
face into the gap between her knees, her body trembling, and I
know that while she struggles to imagine an uncertain future,
appearing stoic, her tears run down her legs before getting washed
away with the rest of the water. Xanthe helps me bathe her, sighing
heavily, and in her release of breath we sense the weight of what
is to come and what came before: the fearful anticipation all
new brides have undergone for generations and will continue to
undergo. Through my touch, I communicate to Eirene that she too
will wash her own daughter's body in preparation for marriage, the
pit in her stomach tightening at the thought of that final moment,
just as the sun sets, when her daughter is torn away from her.

As I pour the last of the water over her domed back, our severing
is only hours away. Tonight, after the celebratory feasting is done
and she is gone, I will blow out the oil lamp and watch the darkness
rush before my eyes, my chest heavy with the knowledge that she is
no longer mine.

Eirene stands shivering in the fresh air as Xanthe dries her
body, massaging Eirene's skin with rose oil and almond blossom.
I comb olive oil through her hair before threading it through with
filaments of silvery string, achieving the desired appearance of

fresh morning dew. Eirene steps carefully into her dress. A decent dress, if one is lucky, sports purple along the border, but this dress has outer braidings of gold, the linen dyed a deep regal purple of no casual tint.

Next we bring out the jewelry box. Of course, she has already chosen, but we act as though this is the first time she's laid eyes on the offerings. First she picks my lapis amulet, and my chest swells with pride as I fasten it around her neck. Xanthe lifts up her hair as I squint to find the clasp, my fingers suddenly thick and clumsy, as though I have never clasped a chain around her neck. She then points to a necklace in which the gems, embedded in gold, compete in their brilliance: rose quartz, amethyst, a sizable emerald, and a sapphire of pure deep blue. Her collarbone rises and falls, exhibiting the wealth she will take with her, that her husband is lucky to have, for we were careful that she bring a proper dowry, that she not arrive on her mother-in-law's doorstep with nothing. Aside from jewelry, linens, and household ceramics, she brings with her twenty acres of pine forest to combine with her husband's land upon his inheritance. Finally, I manage to clasp the necklace around her neck and she turns to face me, her eyes ablaze with foreboding, her lower lip dry and bitten. I try to smile but my eyes are sad. I hold her firmly by the shoulders and tell her that she is an apparition of light and beauty, as golden and fertile as Aphrodite, as strong and competent as Hera.

"I am your mother," I say. "Even after you leave this house."

"I know," she says and we silently dismiss the oft-repeated phrase that I am only her "temporary mother" and that she is only "a guest in my house." Relatives have parroted these cruel words since her birth as all girls are destined to spend far more of their years with their mothers-in-law than with their actual mothers.

I embrace her, and Xanthe embraces us, the three of us huddled together, murmuring our secret wishes and I catch my breath, pained by the absence of my own mother in this tableau. A yawning void that shadows my heart, a void Xanthe shares with me.

We must be our own mothers.

We must be our own mothers, I repeat to myself as I stand in the darkened hallway next to my husband's brother, Theandros. He is here to give Eirene away, even though I am really the one who is giving her away. My husband has not returned from his military campaign, and last night I dreamed he was dead at sea, his swollen body bobbing in the rough surf off the coast of Syracuse.

Eirene stands poised before me. I could reach out and touch the length of her saffron veil, woven so thickly I wonder how she sees through it. Stiff with fear, she's as rigid as a wooden doll. The household breathes behind us: relatives and slaves, my other sons and daughters. Xanthe's arm skims my elbow, and in a quick moment I squeeze her hand in mine, comforted by the thought that once his death is confirmed, I will be a widow, free to buy Xanthe's freedom with my dowry, free to do what we like. My eldest son, when he comes of age, will inherit my dowry and support me with it if I am still alive. Perhaps I will have the pleasure of greeting his new bride with the same cold judgment with which I was greeted, with which Eirene will soon be greeted.

The wedding procession echoes down the street, coming closer and closer. I bristle at the sound of hostile male yelling, victorious shouts and bawdy jokes splitting through the summer night. Theandros passes me a guarded glance, as if he thinks I will leap, panther-like, from the hall and bar the door. Eirene stands as still as death, and for a second I fear she might faint and collapse into my arms. But Theandros girds her upright. Someone pounds on the door and we hear Photius, the bridegroom, laughing, the crowd surging behind him. The door opens to a night aflame with torches and jesting as revelers stream into our courtyard. The olive trees have never looked more beautiful, their delicate branches silhouetted against an indigo sky. Photius is stout with a well-molded nose and small black eyes that have always reminded me of shiny beetles. I can see he's grown fatter over the past months. Perhaps his mother has been feeding him too much. But, I remind myself, he has no physical defects. And as the only remaining son, after having lost a brother in the siege of Melos last year, without him the family line will perish. So they are eager to accept Eirene into their household, hotly awaiting that she bear them sons.

He seizes Eirene's forearm, wrenching her from me. Eirene resists, and I both fear and desire that she will shove him away, kicking and screaming the way she's done at home with me for years. But at the last crushing moment, she capitulates. Her head bows, her body softening as she allows him to drag her off. He grins, his face sheened in sweat, delighting in the performance of capturing her, echoing centuries past when brides were taken in raids or as prisoners of war. Rage flares in my chest as I watch her become subordinate, her shoulders hunched, her gaze demurely downcast.

Theandros announces, "With those here as my witness, I now give you this maiden for the purpose of plowing legitimate children."

Photius guides her through our courtyard. The crowd showers them with dried fruits, coins, and nuts. Carrying two torches, I trail behind her. Crowned in her golden diadem, her saffron veil fluttering in the wind, Eirene allows herself to be led, her face obscured by the heavy cloth lest she protest or whimper or cry, designed so that no one witnesses her sorrow. It is said that a girl should be raised seeing, hearing, and saying as little as possible, and at this idea a small smile escapes me, for once Eirene settles in and assumes her wifely position in her new oikos, they will never hear the end of her opinions, as docile as she appears now.

The mule cart awaits the wedding couple. I was told it would be a chariot instead of this crude cart, built from applewood, intended for single use. But when she reaches her new home, Eirene will burn the axle as a sign that there's no going back.

One of the young men hoists Eirene onto the cart and Photius scrambles up there, his inelegant form inspiring a string of jokes about his fatness, that Eirene will be crushed beneath his weight, that the marriage bed will surely break, that their offspring will inherit her beauty and his . . . No one can think of a redeeming feature, and the crowd roars with laughter.

Eirene and Photius are now together up on the cart, visible from balconies and from the street below as people gawk from their doorways, admiring the couple. I run next to the cart on Eirene's side holding up two torches, as is the custom, but why I must run

like this is beyond me. She is gone. It's as if there's an untrammeled hope she will jump off and return to me. My chest tight, my
face awash in perspiration, it's torturous to run like this. Eirene's
expression beneath the veil is stony. An unfeeling blankness
pervades her eyes. She has become his property, a golden youthful
decoration for Photius, who has fallen silent, sitting up there
with his bride, shy and unsure, and I realize he too feels nervous.
He doesn't know her from a stranger, and they both stare silently
ahead as the raucous procession swings through the street.

The pressing tide of bodies pushes us forward, the groom's
house finally coming into view, the courtyard gates flung open,
welcoming wedding guests and revelers. We spill into the groom's
courtyard, where his mother awaits Eirene's entrance at the
threshold of the house. She stands regal and tall, a formidable
woman, holding two torches. She will lead Eirene inside, to the
hearth where Eirene will be yoked with her new oikos and severed
from mine.

I stand back and allow for Photius to help Eirene down from the
high cart. Then, along with everyone else, I begin to throw figs and
coins and nuts, showering them with blessings of fertility. Xanthe
stands next to me; she has found me in the crowd and holds my
torches while I pelt the dried figs at Eirene and Photius as they
walk toward the threshold, his mother's face solemn, a certain
coldness in her eyes, as she too knows that this is the beginning of
the end of her control, further weakened when Eirene bears a son.
I can see they both feel intimidated by each other's presence, but
then his mother uncharacteristically lowers her head, gesturing for
Eirene to come into the house. A wave of relief washes over me as
she leads the couple inside.

My knees weaken and my head lightens, filled with the knowledge that I will no longer see my daughter. Xanthe holds me up,
disallowing me from collapse in this courtyard surrounded by
naysayers and onlookers. The last wedding ritual, the one I feel
spreading through my bones, is the consummation. Xanthe's
hand encircles my arm, steadying me. A few guests rush inside to
station themselves on either side of the bedroom door, guarding
the hallway to keep people out of the bedroom chamber while also
ensuring that the bride or groom does not escape.

All around us, people begin to sing the epithalamium, the wedding song recited forcefully to mask the cries of the bride, while beneath the din, I hear Eirene crying out for me.

My voice breaking in the back of my throat, we will sing until dawn, until we can barely sing one more note, until our voices are nearly gone, but we will sing and sing.

38

Sofia, August 2019

K asper reiterated that the dinner would only last a few hours, promising not to go out for drinks afterward with the crew, but she didn't know if she could sit there with a stiff smile on her face while they talked shop in that agitated, performative, distinctly male way.

Only a few days had passed since Eleusis, but it had imprinted a new internal authority within her, disallowing her from falling back into her old accommodating ways of remaining silent, biting her tongue, swallowing down all the rage. She knew too much now, imagining herself as the woman in the Astra Tablet, the tablet dedicated by an ancient Athenian woman named Astra to the Temple at Eleusis. She remembered seeing it at the National History Museum, the tablet showing Astra traveling from darkness into light, from the underworld to the upper pediment in which her initiation is complete.

Standing before the full-length mirror, Kasper explained that Olga had recently flown back to Moscow, "which was reason alone to celebrate." But soon enough, the movie would wrap, they'd shoot a few scenes on green screen in London, and he'd return home to oversee postproduction in L.A. He buttoned up his shirt, adding that he could now finally do his job instead of sitting in meetings with Olga all day, dealing with her outlandish demands.

Sitting at the foot of the bed, Ava heard the sound of his voice without listening to him, his nattering akin to the rising crescendo of cicadas that had permeated the sanctuary. She wondered if he would die with such material concerns still dusted on his lips, without having ever seen or felt the mysteries, the way birth and death drummed within them, within their children, without having known the pulse of the transcendent, even for a flickering second.

Ava asked him to zip up the back of her linen dress. "The babysitter is here . . . I have to . . . ," she said, turning around, her voice catching in her throat, catching on the invasion of the mundane, on how quickly the experience at Eleusis could fade, swallowed up by normal life. How difficult it was to preserve the impressions and sensations, traveling from darkness into light, the feeling that her son existed in the air and the particles, in the swirling atoms and molecules, that he lived in her, in Margot and Sam. And then the great relief of finding her daughter again while knowing that finding her was preparation for letting her go. Which was why Astra had fashioned the tablet as a record of her experience, a reminder of what she understood but couldn't reveal. But when she gazed upon it, she knew what she was looking at.

The restaurant was all steel and glass, hard surfaces and asymmetrical rooms, mirrors in odd corners elongating people's reflections, the recessed spotlights in the ceiling sharp and buzzing. Everyone was already seated at a large round table in the center of the room. Kasper sat down between Marc and Rafe, inserting himself into their conversation. The waiter, a young, energetic Bulgarian man, performed some dance moves before taking their order, swiveling his hips, his bright white sneakers squeaking across the marble floor, saying that it was his job to make this a perfect night, he wanted everyone to feel happy, to have an extraordinary time! He blew exaggerated kisses into the air before promising to return with more drinks.

The men dove back into their loud, hostile talking, regaling one another with stories about crew members whom Ava had never met, laughing uproariously at inside jokes, slamming fists down to punctuate a point, their pale sweating faces reddening from the strong vodka cocktails that littered the table. Techno music thumped from little black speakers positioned in high corners.

Kasper's voice boomed, rising above the others, louder than she remembered it.

Isabel asked Rafe if he had another job lined up after this one wrapped. Leaning in closer, she repeated the question, but he didn't hear her or pretended not to.

Ava combed through the ends of her hair with her fingers, feeling increasingly agitated.

Rafe raised his shot glass announcing a toast to Olga, bitch in chief.

"Yeah, man!" Marc shouted. "She'd ruin this movie if she could."

"Believe me, I know." Kasper shook his head, casting a conspiratorial glance around the table.

They started to make fun of Olga, mocking her baggy parachute pants and bad teeth along with her general unattractiveness. Marc said she was probably fucking the line producer, fixing the budget to her benefit.

Kasper leaned back into his chair. "I don't know, Marc. Seems like you kind of want to fuck her."

"No way, man. Her pussy is made out of sandpaper."

Rafe shouted, "I bet she's got piranhas swimming up in there waiting for a feeding frenzy!"

Kasper held up a hand. "Hold on, wait. Rafe, you're the only single guy here. You're the one to do it."

Everyone laughed, the music pumping louder, the waiter setting down various foam concoctions. Blood pounded in Ava's ears, her muscles tightening with adrenaline. The periphery of her vision blurred slightly, distorting these men into people she didn't recognize.

Distorting Kasper.

She stood up, her voice shaking. "I can't sit here anymore, listening to this." Gripping the back of her chair, she caught Kasper's eye, and she saw the fear in it, knowing she might hurl the chair at him.

At all of them.

Instead, she left.

The cool damp air provided immediate relief, the bustling streets and cloudy purpling sky a salve. She started walking back to the apartment, clenching her hands into fists, wanting Olga to take her revenge on these men, tear holes through them. To triumph.

Saturday night energy pulsed through the city streets, a heavy bass thrumming from bars, and from smaller dark alcoves the sound of an acoustic guitar, followed by clapping. The lit-up churches were dramatic against the twilight, with their spires and crosses and golden domes, and the migrating clouds promised rain, the air heavy with moisture. Scooters buzzed past her and children ran ahead on the sidewalk. Taxis dropped off fashionable young couples who breezed past old women clutching bulging canvas bags, their wizened faces staring plaintively into the fading light.

She told herself to calm down, to understand that this was Kasper's dinner. His summer. His year. But did the movie, which had clearly turned into some cult male fantasy where they perpetually existed in an action film, have to consume Kasper to this degree? It was as if the men had all fallen into a collective trance, acting in ways she didn't recognize—or maybe she recognized it all too well.

While she tried to rationalize her anger, that ancient rage churned, threatening to burst forth with even greater force; she didn't know how much longer she could contain it. Glancing up from the cigarette-strewn pavement, she caught sight of Nikolay plodding down the block across the street. He was carrying two paper grocery bags against his chest, his forehead creased with worry, his bearing devoid of all arrogance. He looked like any other middle-aged Bulgarian man in his acid-washed jeans and tight T-shirt, the sleeves rolled up over his biceps, the faded blue-green tattoos marking his weathered skin. He seemed lost in a fog. Ava felt sorry for him in that moment, remembering he'd said that driving the van for a week barely afforded him a meal at McDonald's. "Cheaper to cook simple things," he had emphasized, "like borscht and shopska salad." Ava imagined him unlocking the door to his cramped apartment and setting down the groceries under the fluorescent kitchen lights, the stove ticking as he waited for the flame to catch hold.

She watched him round the corner, disappearing behind a dilapidated office building. When she was almost at her favorite church square, where she had first caught sight of Nikitas, her phone pinged with a text.

Kasper: *Where are you?*

Ava: *Getting some air.*

Kasper: *Are you okay?*

Ava: *You have to ask me that?*

Kasper: *We were just joking, letting off steam.*

Ava: *It's degrading, the way you mock Olga.*

Kasper: *So you're running off to cry into Nikitas's lap? She'll tell you what you want to hear: all men are pigs, women should rule the world, let's get out the long knives and kill them all.*

Ava: *Fuck you. You don't understand anything.*

Sitting down on a bench in the square, she rested her forearms on her thighs, her stomach in knots. Trying to take deep breaths, she told herself everyone had gotten caught up in the moment, Kasper wasn't really like this, and neither was she, jarred by the thick rage thrashing through her, afraid of it, not wanting to feel it. Glaring at the skateboarders clattering against the flagstones, she rubbed her eyes, frayed and exhausted. Given her state of mind, maybe she wasn't viewing the situation clearly. The men were drunk, performing for each other with their sexist humor. That wasn't the Kasper she knew. But he hadn't really been himself for a long time. And neither had she. In the past, she used to endure those types of dinners, not minding her invisibility, her secondary status, letting her mind drift to other things while playing the prop, the wife, the appendage for the evening because it was only an evening, the annoyance and boredom temporary. But something about tonight felt different, worse. The scene reverberated with an old shared wound of a woman belittled and mocked, her power a threat.

Back at the apartment, she was relieved that Kasper wasn't home yet. After paying the sitter and taking a long hot shower, she read Burkert's book in bed, finding the chapter on the Dionysian rites, which he described as rife with chaos, unbridled emotion, and excess, but she kept losing her place, the sentences merging together, her eyes stinging with dryness.

Finally, she heard the front door unlock and waited for Kasper to come into the bedroom. She listened to him shuffling through some papers in the living room followed by the distinct sound of emails zooming off into cyberspace. Then he snapped his laptop shut and went into the bathroom, avoiding her at all costs, and she felt as taut and ready as a coiled serpent, waiting to strike.

Ten minutes later, he stood on the threshold of the bedroom, already changed into boxers and a T-shirt, as though he didn't trust her without clothes on.

"Can I come in?"

She sat up in bed and nodded, trying to calibrate her rising anger, to not fully unleash it, not yet. Unless he tried to gaslight her, tell her she'd misinterpreted the jokes, that they didn't act the way they had acted, it was all in her head.

Kasper perched on the edge of the bed. He stared up at the slow-moving ceiling fan. "I was a jerk."

"You were all jerks."

"You're right." He passed a hand through his hair. "I didn't realize how angry you were. I mean, how angry you *are*. Clearly, you have a lot to get off your chest."

"And clearly, you're annoyed by my relationship with Nikitas. You think she's brainwashed me or something."

"I don't think that."

"Then what do you think?"

His hand moved toward her thigh and then stopped midway across the sheets. "You've been distant. Further away since Nikitas. What's going on?"

"I thought that by coming here, things would get better. But being here makes it clear to me how far apart we are. And then I reconnected with Nikitas. If it wasn't for her, I would have flown home a long time ago." Her mind tunneled back to magical Eleusis, standing on a continuum with the other women as they stretched into the past and leaned into the future. Kasper could never understand what had transpired: the acute sense of existing outside of time and the deep loss that had flooded her, flooded all the women. Her son was strewn in the stars and planets, undulating throughout the ocean depths. He was stardust and light, circulating through the air they breathed. And when her own life ended, she imagined that she would somehow thread through the next generations, just as the past generations threaded through her. The infinite cycle would keep rolling onward, living and dying and living again.

He didn't understand this. He never would, as he had never made life and then lost it.

She balanced on her elbow. "Listen . . . you've been checked out for a long time, disappearing into work while I'm left to pick up the pieces, searching for you in the emotional fog and not finding anyone there. It's not a partnership, it's not a marriage. It's something else. Something I don't want." *It makes me want to kill you off,* she almost added.

He stood up, gesturing theatrically. "I don't want this either. Look, when I was in film school I didn't realize that making movies would mean spending months away from my family. I didn't even think about having a family at twenty-two!"

"And you still don't think about it, despite having one." She let the sentence hang there for a moment. "You left us. I had to come all the way here to see if we still had a marriage."

He looked stunned, afraid to ask what she had concluded.

One of the kids coughed in the next room.

"And the way you acted tonight, I really didn't recognize you."

He swallowed hard. "I got caught up in the group energy. But that's no excuse."

His phone vibrated on the nightstand. "I'm not going to get that." They waited for the vibrating to stop, which was then followed by a pinging cascade of incoming texts.

She pressed her back into the wrought iron headboard. "How are things going to change? For instance, when the next movie comes along, are you going to throw yourself into it, just as before, hurling yourself onto a funeral pyre while I become your temporary widow again to watch our marriage burn to the ground?"

"That's dark."

"Well," Ava said, gesturing into the darkness. "Yeah."

39

T he night after the epaulia, the nuptial gifting ceremony, I can't sleep, my blood coursing with energetic rage. The day's events cycle through my mind: in the harsh noonday sun, Eirene received many gifts as a consolation prize for her lost virginity, and it struck me how much we keep losing, how much the men keep taking.

My husband's brother, Theandros, stood close behind me during the ceremony, his breath sweeping hotly across my neck, murmuring that my husband most likely didn't survive, he was due back moons ago, and he has heard from others that I am still fertile, blood more often than not staining my woolen pads with every waxing moon. I shuddered under his covetous gaze. His wife died last year from an infection in the womb, leaving him with only one son, who is sickly, a hemophiliac, an unlikely heir. At the slightest bruise, he collapses, and Theandros has always blamed his wife for the boy's weakness. Believing himself to be comely, he flirted with me, and his crowded small teeth made my stomach churn as I asked myself why he wants me when he could pluck any girl, as young as Eirene, to plow, but I am a proven thing. I have produced healthy sons, and this is something he wants.

Under the beating sun, my cheeks burned, sensing that my long-sought freedom as a widow might be ripped away in an instant. If my husband is dead, his brother will marry me. I have no recourse, as such things are prearranged among the men of the house, and I nearly choked on my own rage, realizing this plan had already unfolded in Theandros's mind multiple times before this moment, and here I am, jolted by it, as startled as a clipped-wing dove trying to fly. I only bat around my cage, thinking I will take flight, when all I do is blindly repeat the same patterns out of habit, out of fear. I resisted inhaling his breath, stale with wine, as he discussed his plans for us.

Relatives approached from either side presenting carved boxes, pots and pans, sieves, soaps and oils, wedding vases inlaid with ivory and gold. I watched Eirene closely. She sat as though on a throne arrayed in all her finery, her head bent, her eyes downcast, as she's been trained to appear since birth: chaste, silent, obedient. But as I approached with my gift, a red clay tablet picturing, with symbolic imagery that only the initiated understand, our participation in the Eleusinian mysteries, she cast me a hooded glance. I wondered how last night went, searching for the answer in her eyes. Was it painful? Or laced with bits of unexpected pleasure? Did it take him very long to ejaculate?

Wordlessly, I communicated my love when our fingers fleetingly touched as I handed her the gift, but I feared, because of her stoic countenance, that she hated me for not telling her enough, or for telling her too much.

Lying here, I finally fall asleep, desperate not to ponder Theandros's motives and my uncertain freedom. As though a curtain parts, Dionysus appears before me, lifelike and real, as though I could reach out and touch his smooth skin, full voluptuous lips, that loose mane of curls. He is the foreign god from Thrace, who shares my origins, son of mortal Semele and Zeus. Slender and youthful, beardless and effeminate, he is the god of women, wine, and madness. He passes over thresholds and visits us in liminal states, especially when our status is changeable, questionable. Every woman who surrenders to the god must risk abandoning herself to madness so that she may temporarily break free from her looms and shuttles, from the crush of domestic life, from her powerlessness, from the fact that she is a woman.

To purify our grievous affliction, the ancient wrath we carry within us, if the god chooses, we must submit to his rites to become well again. We swarm the god, his frenzied votaries, abandoning ourselves, or who we thought we were, in exchange for raving blessedness. We watch as the forest transforms into a paradise; milk, honey, and wine surge from the ground. We offer our breasts to baby fawns and nurse them. We become hunters of men and wild animals, an inversion of maternity, and we tear any man apart who infringes on our rituals, eating his raw flesh, letting it hang from our hair and wedge beneath our fingernails, the gristle in our teeth.

I wake up in a sweat, heart throbbing, blood in my mouth from having bitten my tongue. Dream images swim before me even though I am awake, my eyes wild and open: the maenads, myself among them, roam through the forest draped in leopard skins, serpents lovingly coiled around our arms, licking our cheeks while Dionysus dances in a delirious whirl.

Sitting up in bed, I swallow down the blood in my mouth, hungry for recourse, for balancing the scales that will never be balanced.

40

O n the long wooden table, Nikitas arranged a line of giant fennel stalks that they would make into thyrsus staffs. Sorting through garlands of ivy with Margot, Ava felt jittery, an electricity coursing through her. After their fight, Kasper moved deftly around her, as though he were afraid, terrified even, of what she might do.

Isabel hummed to the low-playing sertanejo music, her hair in a loose bun with a chopstick speared through it. Luca and Sam were building a new Lego set in the other room. "It'll keep them busy for hours," she said, winking at Ava and Margot. Nikitas told them that the maenads, the lusty followers of Dionysus, carried these staffs through the forest. The sharpened point was disguised by leaves and pine cones, and if the tip injured someone, it incited madness.

Isabel offered Nikitas and Tonkova more chilled white wine, while Ava refilled Yael's and Sophie's glasses. Nikitas instructed each person to take a pine cone and secure it to the tip of the fennel stalk.

Twining ivy around her stalk, Isabel said, "After you left the restaurant last night, everyone was quiet, wondering what happened. Kasper looked pretty upset."

"The way they were acting . . ." Ava wound some slippery white string around the staff and then tucked more ivy leaves into the string.

"I know," Isabel said, taking a generous sip of wine.

"So then what happened?" Yael asked.

Margot's eyes glinted with interest.

Ava chose her words carefully. "We had an argument afterward. I didn't hold back." She speared her thyrsus tip with a pine cone and wrapped some wire around the center of the pine cone and then around the staff's neck to secure it.

"Good," Isabel said, bringing out a shallow basket filled with dried pennyroyal and explaining to Margot and Sophie that they would make it into an oil to add to the kykeon. Margot helped her set down six mason jars and a long skinny indigo bottle containing the carrier oil, and Isabel created a workstation for Margot and Sophie on the dining room table in the adjoining room, which was out of earshot of their conversation, perhaps purposefully so, Ava thought.

Margot began plucking the lavender thistles from a bundle of stems, one by one. "It doesn't have to be so exact," Isabel instructed. "Just get the thistles off as best as you can so we can fill the jars, about a handful in each jar."

Isabel then returned to the kitchen, joining Tonkova and Nikitas, who were working on more staffs, and she started to help them. "Sometimes you must make a decision and say: *This is what I'm doing. Deal with it.*" Isabel's hands worked quickly, winding sisal twine around the bottom handle of a staff, tucking tendrils of ivy under and over the string as decoration. Ava knew Isabel wanted to say this to Marc; she wanted to move back to Brazil and stop following him from country to country.

"Kasper said he doesn't want to leave for months at a time anymore." Ava lowered her voice in case Margot might overhear her, as Margot seemed to possess ultrasonic hearing whenever Ava discussed their marriage, or any other sensitive topic. "He agreed that it's clearly bad for the kids. And he promised to *do more* once he's home. But I don't think he understands that washing some extra dishes or helping with the kids' homework won't solve anything real between us."

Nikitas flashed Ava a devilish smile. "Heterosexuality is a failed project." She poured herself more wine. "Men can either fuck, be emotionally available, listen, make money, or take care of the children but never all five at once. Whereas women easily perform all five functions simultaneously."

Asa Seresin's term "heteropessimism" floated into Ava's mind, and she recalled what Kasper had said the other day about their differing parenting styles: he always did what was easiest for him, while Ava made things unnecessarily difficult for herself because of her attachment to her own motherly guilt. He suggested that she try swimming downstream once in a while. When he said this, she pictured him as an aquatic microorganism floating serenely along a river, naturally ensuring its own survival by leaving all the rest up to her.

She considered Claire and her semi-victorious experience of delegating 50 percent of the household chores and family needs to her husband. But Claire was still angry because, inevitably, he eventually forgot about her lists and spreadsheets. When she confronted him on his negligence, he asked for her forgiveness, like an embarrassed guilty son. She didn't want a guilty son. She wanted a real partner. Plus, it took a lot of effort and time to make the lists in the first place, to assign and monitor all the minutiae. The lists were a hopeless trap, Ava concluded, infantilizing men when they forgot the lists as well as when they diligently heeded them. Either way, such a dynamic only increased the vittles of wifely rage.

Claire said her flaring anger was akin to watching a covered pot of water boiling on the stove. When the water got too hot, the lid lifted and the bubbling water spilled over, extinguishing the flame. And then she relit the burner, set the lid over the pot, only to watch it happen all over again. An endless cycle of superficial improvements followed by intensifying flare-ups, which wasn't a real partnership but rather a Sisyphean hell of rinse, repeat, rinse again.

But all this rage begged the question: Did they really have the moral high ground here? Ava felt both justified and entirely unjustified in her anger, imbued with misgivings because, in addition to the cultural expectations of femininity, of motherhood, of womanhood, wasn't she also responsible for creating the circumstances of her own subjugation, persecuting herself with her own guilt, with her fear of failing as a mother, of not being "good enough" when the margin for error proved quite generous? Forgiving even, if one read the literature on it. But it also didn't seem correct to place the focal point of her rage entirely on the culture, on the prevailing winds of patriarchy, on history. Nevertheless, rage was still rage.

But then, what *would* be the remedy? The secret ingredient to balance the scales? Communal living? The all-female island off the coast of Estonia where men had slowly disappeared from daily life since the nineteenth century? Should she join Nikitas and her cohort of second-wave anti-porn anti-sex anti-male feminists? Even though she liked men and sex, and sometimes porn? Or they could move to Sweden, where mothers and fathers received an equal amount of paid leave after the birth of a child, one year each, followed by subsidized universal daycare and socialized medicine, free schooling and university and lots of bicycling through forests. Lingonberries in summer, saffron-infused sweet rolls in winter. The white nights and the aurora borealis. But the Swedish women, Ava knew through Kasper, were still pissed off, stomping around all the time about their adherence to systems created by men. Kasper's sisters had argued over dinner once, during one of Ava's few visits to Stockholm with Kasper, that this Swedish "equality" was on male terms, the whole society built from a male perspective. They didn't feel liberated. They felt terminally unsatisfied and told Ava, over the noisy restaurant, that the only options were revolution or withdrawal.

Still, how could she justify her anger toward Kasper when the problems of this dying world were boundless, leaping past patriarchy and hurtling into multiple crises that appeared irrevocable? Who had the energetic discipline to keep track of, and then haggle over, which one of them had last emptied the dishwasher, picked up the dog shit in the backyard, or monitored the kids' screen time while the world burned?

For now, she had the mysteries. Something he couldn't touch. Something that belonged to her and the other women, a reminder that this sacred history stretched forward and back, tenting over them like a canopy of protection. They hadn't been stranded in the wreckage of midlife. They could still make something of it, something of themselves.

Tonkova assessed her staff before adding more ivy to the top, obscuring the sharp tip. "As women, we're tasked with the emotional labor and intuitive understanding of everyone's needs while subordinating our own desires over and over again. Creating this simmering rage beneath the façade of the 'nurturing mother.' No one can get enough of that sweet good mother."

"Yes," Nikitas said, adding that the Dionysian rites demanded that Greek women abandon hearth and home for a night to roam wild in the forest. Inverting their normal maternal domestic roles, they surrendered to an explosion of rage, sexuality, violence. "An unleashing," she stated. "What woman doesn't dream of going over the edge? Without guilt and regret, without apologizing for it? We've been pushing down all that rage, as we've been taught to do, since birth."

Ava silently considered the piece Nikitas skidded over, the theory that such bright provisional explosions of female rage actually maintained the longevity of male dominance. Women letting off steam temporarily, in the confines of their rituals, allowed men to more easily regain control once the women were back at their looms, tending to their children, cooking and weaving and nursing the sick, and nursing the memory of the forest at night when they were unbridled and free, without anything actually changing in their real lives.

The thyrsus staffs completed, they joined Margot and Sophie, who were almost done sorting through seeds and herbs, while Isabel ground the seeds down into a moist mixture combined with oil, the air smelling sweetly of peppermint and lavender, wine and salt. The conversation slid back into the everyday. Sophie admitted that she'd told Bill she didn't want a baby after all. When he asked why, she blurted out that she already had one. "A cantankerous seventy-year-old baby who demands to be fed gourmet meals three times a day."

Tonkova shook her head. "He needs to learn how to make his own lunch."

"If not, you might try slipping some poison into the tomato gratin or whatever it is you cook for him," Nikitas said, snorting.

They laughed gently, bent over the table, working.

Isabel poured more olive oil into each mason jar, submerging the pennyroyal. Squinting as she poured the last bit of oil over the herbs, Isabel commented, "I heard Nikolay got fired."

"Why? What happened?" Ava asked.

"He sexually harassed Kiki Vega." Kiki Vega was one of the lead actresses, who played a journalist from the eighties outfitted in power suits with comically bulky shoulder pads. "He invited her to an orgy in the woods."

Nikitas laughed darkly. "Oh, he shouldn't go into the woods at night."

"Because of the wolves?" Margot asked nervously. "We once heard wolves at that restaurant in the forest, remember? Is that why Nikolay shouldn't go there?"

"Because of many things," Ava said, giving Margot a look implying that she'd explain later, in private. She sealed her jar with wax paper before securing a lid over it. "I heard Rafe grabbed Sonia's ass at a crew party last night." Sonia played the Macedonian princess from antiquity. "So he might get fired too."

"He'll just get a warning," Isabel said, holding up a jar for inspection. "A slap on the wrist, something like that, because he's a white guy from London. Not some local Bulgarian, who's poor and expendable."

Ava knew this was the truth about Hollywood, about everywhere.

They started to clean up, gathering the loose seeds and herbs and funneling them into extra jars that Isabel kept in the upper cabinets.

Sweeping some errant seeds into her cupped palm off the table's edge, Yael loudly joked that she wouldn't mind getting her ass grabbed once in a while. "It's been a long time since I've gotten so much as a whistle out of a construction worker."

They laughed again, and Ava saw Margot staring at Yael, clearly trying to puzzle out the various implications of the conversation: it was bad to grab a woman's ass, some women wanted it to happen, others found the attention disgusting, and so on.

Ava thought back to when she was in her early twenties riding the subway in Manhattan. It was an overheated train car packed with commuters in winter coats, briefcases and purses pressing into her back, and all of a sudden, she felt someone squeeze her ass. But she couldn't move, paralyzed by the crush of bodies against her on all sides. Feeling a stinging shame, she felt as if it were her fault for standing so still, gripping the leather strap up above. As if her body were an invitation. When the train halted and everyone dispersed, shuffling on and off, she glanced around, sure she would catch sight of him, whoever he was, but all she saw were ashen faces, tired and overworked, unassuming in their ordinariness when she had expected some leering flamboyant character to jump out of the crowd.

Nikitas and Tonkova stood behind the table laden with thyrsus staffs, admiring their handiwork. Nikitas picked one up and demonstrated how once the pine cone fell off, the tip was as sharp as the end point of a knife. The thyrsus balanced in the middle of her palm for a span of seconds. "It's quite decorative and attractive but it can do great harm."

That night, chaotic dreams paraded through her sleep. Ava endured a painful wound on her cheek, and when she removed the bandages to change the dressing, she was aghast at the sight of it in the mirror: a lopsided circle, purple mixed with deep crimson and tinged with yellowing edges, but the necessary ugliness implied that it was healing. She put a new dressing over it, but it hurt to smile, to function normally, while Kasper reassured her that she was fine. Fighting back tears, Ava knew he was right to say the wound would heal and she would get better again, but the sensation felt overwhelming. She couldn't think beyond the pain. And while she tried and failed to put on a brave face, as people had often urged her to do, she knew the wound was from her mother, a handed-down, mangled thing, a by-product of her mother's devotion to herself. After leaving her marriage, Cynthia had forged a path that didn't include Ava or anyone else. Some would say this was ruthlessly heroic in a feminist sense. But she had inflicted wounds in the process. Was it possible to put oneself first as a mother and still be a good mother? To be selfish on purpose?

This question collapsed into the distinct sensation of a spotted leopard's belly pressing into her face, its hoary fur a suffocating comfort. Warm milk sputtered from its nipples, coating her face with a filmy protective layer. She opened her mouth and milk flooded under her tongue, but it tasted metallic, like blood. Bolting upright in bed, blinking into the surrounding darkness, she gently ran her fingertips over her cheek, reassured by its smoothness. Still tasting that metallic liquid, she spit into her palm, peering down at it in the dark, trying to discern if there was blood on her hands.

41

T heandros makes himself a nuisance with his entreaties and innuendos, acting as though my husband is dead when the sea only yields its eternal tides, bringing no news of the victors or the vanquished. I go about my weaving, filled with misgivings. I resist telling Xanthe about Dionysus appearing in my dream, insisting that I participate in his upcoming rites.

Rinsing a pot, slick with olive oil, watching water slide over it, I think about the daughters of Minyas who refused to take part in the dances of Dionysus as they were too busy at their looms, vying for Athena's praise, and hoping their husbands would commend their wifely diligence, how fast their fingers worked to produce beautiful garments. Suddenly, ivy and vine tendrils coiled around their looms and serpents lurked in the baskets where they had collected tufts of wool. From the roof dripped wine and milk. Fearful, knowing Dionysus was among them, they drew lots, and when the lot of Leukippe came out, she vowed to make a sacrifice to the god.

But it was too late. She had initially failed to heed his call, as she had been overly devoted to the loom, to her domestic duties. Such misplaced devotion induced the wrath of Dionysus, infecting her with it. Without warning, she fell into a delirious frenzy, unknowingly tearing her own son to pieces.

42

Sofia, August 2019

This afternoon, Margot was sent home from camp due to an upset stomach. She'd thrown up after eating the fish soup. Ava put a heating pad on her abdomen to lessen the cramping, but Margot pushed it away, saying it was too hot.

"Does it feel like a normal stomachache, or like something else?"

Margot shifted onto her side. "I don't know. It feels weird."

In the next room, Ava overhead Kasper playing a card game with Sam, something called war. Every time his phone buzzed and he didn't pick up she felt a little bit of hope.

"I'm leaving for the night. This time it's different, so I can't bring you. But I'll be home in the morning. Okay?"

Margot took a contemplative sip of chamomile tea. "I guess." She paused and Ava could tell she was debating whether or not to tell her something.

"What is it?"

"Well, today when I felt sick at camp?"

"Yeah?"

"After they called you and left a message, they called Nikolay."

Ava nodded, remembering that Nikolay's mobile number was still on file there, from when the kids had started camp.

"He said he was supposed to take me home and I should come with him."

"And then what happened?" Ava asked, keeping her voice level despite a rising panic.

"He came into the office and sat down next to me and started to rub my back while he was looking at his phone. Two seconds later, Yana walked in and said that you were on the way."

"And then?"

Margot stared into her tea. "He left."

Ava clenched Margot's free hand. "And you waited for me until I got there."

"Yeah," she said softly.

"Are you okay?"

"I'm okay," Margot said.

Ava dressed in the same white linen shirt and pants, but at the last minute, she stuffed a sweater in her backpack. Kasper was making meatballs for dinner, the oil and cardamom wafting in from the kitchen. He didn't ask Ava where she was going or when she'd be back, as though they had silently agreed not to talk about it.

Checking her backpack, which held the thyrsus staff wrapped in newspaper, she worried that maybe Margot had appendicitis. Or some other malady that would require immediate medical attention, and would Kasper know which hospital to go to in Sofia? Or what if she was about to get her period?

She came into the kitchen before she left, telling Kasper to keep an eye on Margot, maybe give her some Tylenol if needed. The meatballs simmered in the pan, grease flecking the tiled backsplash.

"Okay, I'll tell the sitter."

"What do you mean? I thought you were staying here with the kids."

Kasper shook the pan. "I'm meeting Jason for a drink later. He's in panic mode about the final action sequence. Wants to reshoot it, but we're out of time and money. Someone has to break it to him." He looked up from the stove and she tried to decipher what was behind his eyes.

"I didn't want to bother you about getting a sitter at the last minute because you have plans too. I contacted the same agency that you used in the past. I think they're sending that college girl, the one with the dog hotel."

"Okay," Ava said, sensing there was more to the story. "I mean, thanks for taking care of it."

Kasper nodded. "Have fun," he said before correcting himself. "I mean, fun probably isn't the right word, is it?"

She smiled tightly. "Not quite."

They strode up the same narrow path that they had taken on their first meeting, hiking up to the clearing, singing fragments from Homeric poetry: "Out of the land of Asia . . . speeding the service of the god, for Dionysus we come! Hard are the labors of god; hard, but his service is sweet. Sweet to serve, sweet to cry."

Her voice vibrated in her throat as she sang, fear still circulating through her over what Nikolay might have done to Margot if he had the chance, disappearing into Eastern Europe with his white van. Or maybe he wanted to help and was just trying to win back his job. But he could have so easily stolen her, violated her in some way. *Nothing happened,* Ava kept telling herself. *Margot is safe. And I'll keep teaching her.*

Nikitas and Tonkova carried winnowing baskets, and Isabel and Ava held the amphoras of wine. Some of the women wore fawn skins over jeans and wielded their thyrsi. Ava saw the Greek woman with the lapis amulet singing and laughing in the light of her torch, her loose hair cascading over her shoulders. Her daughter wasn't with her either. Ava also wore her hair loose, crowned with leaves and flowering bryony that Isabel had plucked from her garden.

Walking beside Isabel, she told her what had happened with Nikolay today. "He could have been trying to help. But you never know."

Isabel clucked her tongue. "He was fired already. There's no reason for him to fetch Margot. No reason other than the reason we both know."

Up ahead, Sophie and Yael linked arms.

When they arrived at the clearing, the same place as their first meeting in the woods, which seemed so long ago now, Tonkova climbed atop a rock and began playing her lyre. Nikitas started a bonfire, the branches and wooden planks overlapping in the shape of a triangular hut; once lit, the flames roared. They drank the kykeon from the same little ceramic cups, this time the ergot and spices stronger and more flavorful.

Ava's tongue numbed, her mind swimming with images that appeared as real as the towering pine trees and the ground beneath her feet. The tight red belt that she had always worn as a child snapped off, her stomach sighing with relief, the tiny pieces scattering into the dark forest.

The women started to clap and shout, chasing away any snakes that lived in the rock chasms and within the pits of the earth they began to dig up. Dirt wedged under her nails from digging, Ava struck the rocks with her thyrsus and joined the chorus singing, "O Iacchos! O Bromios!"

The pits, she understood, symbolized Persephone's passage into the underworld. They stamped and hissed into the pits. Snakes sprang up from the ground. Caspian whip snakes, copperheads, ring-necked snakes, and one as smooth and glossy as an intestine writhing on the ground, slipping through the undergrowth. Even some pit vipers encircled their ankles, sliding up their calves, but it felt as natural as blades of grass brushing their shins.

Some women encouraged the snakes to coil around their wrists, licking their cheeks. Others nestled baby foxes and fluffy squirrels to their breasts, singing to the animals, as if they intended to nurse them.

Ava had always been deathly afraid of snakes but now welcomed the warm slick tightness around her forearm, not caring that it was a viper. It nuzzled the top of its head into the crook of her arm. She saw that its scales were turning a light opalescent blue, as it prepared to shed its skin.

Isabel held a wolf pup to her neck, the wolf's nose rooting through her tangled hair, and Ava laughed. Was that really a wolf? And was this really a viper shimmering blue in the darkness, cinching her forearm?

Sophie dug into the earth, her eyes trained on the ground, urging honey to spring from the soil. Yael stroked the downy brow of a gazelle that had emerged from a copse of trees, staring at them with unblinking liquid eyes, and Ava faintly recalled that gazelles only lived in arid places such as the desert, but that fact melted away, useless and irrelevant.

The Greek woman squatted and scratched at the earth, rejoicing when water seeped from the soil. She tossed back her neck, her eyes rolling into her head, the milky whites visible, prayers falling from her lips: "Thrice blessed are those mortals who have seen these rites and enter into Hades: for them alone there is life, for all others misery."

Isabel signaled for Ava to come to Nikitas, arrayed on a tree stump, a fawn skin thrown over her lap, her face stark and unforgiving in the moonlight. Ava already knew what to do, having dreamed it, her body naturally folding over Nikitas's lap, her breasts pressed into her bony knees, her heart seeping into Nikitas's thighs.

She was vaguely aware of Isabel clashing bronze cymbals and spinning wildly, the front of her dress undone, her breasts exposed. And then Ava felt the cool night sweep over her bare back, and at the first stroke of the woven bark whip lashing her skin she cried out in pain. Yes, she was in the province of Dionysus now, the province of divine madness and the sympathy of souls breathing all around her, and she thrilled at the sensation of abandoning the vise grip of her identity, walking out of the house and slamming the front door, her keys tossed somewhere she'd never find them.

Undulating images swam before her, presenting a shadow of who she once was, of who they all once were. The younger version of Ava chastised her, disturbed by the little freedom Ava now had, such as the difficulty in arranging one night away, and even if she managed to be here in body, her mind always raced back to Margot and Sam, to whether they were safe, whether they were happy. But when she was with them, she felt unhappy to have lost the little freedom she'd eked out for herself. The younger Ava recoiled from the persistent claims of such a life: the burnt toast and sleepless nights and mind-numbing hours spent at playgrounds squinting into the sun, tracking the movements of the little bodies that were an extension of hers while bursting with their own dreams and rebellions.

Tears stung her eyes as she gazed into the fire, her cheek wet and pressed into Nikitas's thighs. Longing rushed into her; longing for her living children, for her dead one, and for the time when she had no children at all and only belonged to herself, before splitting into numerous tributaries that flowed to fulfill the needs of others, threatening to drain her own depths, leaving her as dried up as a riverbed scorched by the sun.

And once the children were all finished with what she had to give, once they left and happily went on their way, she would come face-to-face with terrifying menopause. If menopause were an animal it would be a mangled fox limping toward her, holding sterility in its mouth, dropping the carcass at her feet. She picked up this misconstrued gift while a crone crouched behind the bushes, beckoning Ava into sexless decades where she would fade into invisibility, lose all currency. The currency of having once been young and attractive.

A palpable sorrow engulfed her.

Nikitas did not console her but continued to strike Ava's back, her other hand holding down Ava's head, Nikitas's sturdy body radiating containment but not protection, as the experience could never be alleviated or softened. Ava muffled her cries and gathered up Nikitas's linen skirt in her mouth, sucking on the fabric, and wrapped her arms around Nikitas's knees.

Sophie's mortified expression passed before her. Ava wanted to call out to her, to tell her it was all right, but Sophie shook her head, shielding her eyes with her dirt-stained hands.

The whip came down harder.

Isabel danced more wildly, the cymbals clashing and the frame drums cresting to a panicked crescendo, and in the reddish golden glow Ava beheld Olga's radiant face, tiny flames licking her golden hair. Ava mouthed, *I thought you were in Moscow*, but no words came out. Olga smiled benevolently down at Ava before raising the winnowing basket, about to reveal what was inside when the gazelle leapt into the air, all four limbs outstretched and rigid, its young supple back domed into a perfect curve.

Everyone stopped their singing and dancing and digging.

Ava inhaled the hushed stillness, the unmoving forest, realizing that the gazelle was signaling a threat, warding off a potential predator with the performance of jumping so high. Then it bounded off, smoothly springing over boulders, and they were filled with the sense that someone was watching them from the trees up above.

Nikitas's hand froze on Ava's back.

Ava glanced up into the trees and caught a figure crouched in the branches. At first she thought it was one of the women, but his bulky build and large uncouth hands betrayed him.

"There!" Ava shouted, rising up from Nikitas's lap. "He's up there at the top of the fir tree!"

The women moved with speed and force, breaking loose like startled crows, through the woods and over the rushing streams, leaping from jagged rock to jagged rock, they flew toward him and climbed a great boulder that towered opposite the man's perch and showered him with stones and bayonets of fir while others hurled their thyrsus staffs at him.

They couldn't get to him. He shuddered just above their reach, the branch buckling under his weight.

Breathlessly they splintered branches from pines and with those wooden spears tried to lever up the tree by prying the roots loose.

But their efforts failed until Nikitas cried, "Women! Make a circle around the trunk and grip it with your hands."

Thousands of hands sprang from the darkness and shook the trunk with startling force. Blood sprouted from Ava's palms as she gripped the tree, shaking and tearing at it, panting and sweating. Torches crackled and encircled the tree and the faces of the others blurred before her until the women became one woman filled with fury, churning and unrequited, spilling over into now.

They ripped the fir tree from the earth, and the man cascaded down from his perch, falling into their eager arms. He was sobbing and screaming as he fell.

His body thudded to the ground.

They snatched off his blond wig.

Nikitas and Tonkova, along with Isabel and the Greek woman, hovered over him, their eyes shining.

Ava recognized him: Nikolay, weak and lecherous, ignorant and bumbling, who had committed the fatal error of trespassing. Who might have taken Margot away forever in his white van. Or maybe he meant no harm. She would never know. Dread overcame her as she prevaricated over Nikolay the symbol and Nikolay the individual, but the lines blurred, and she felt the edges of herself merge with the others, relishing this loss of self, the erasure of all distinctions.

She readied for the bloodshed that they had craved for a lifetime. For millennia.

Adrenaline pounded through her, the tension almost unbearable, her palms itching.

Ignoring his pleading cries, Ava and the others swarmed around him, clawing and hitting him, desperate to get a piece of him. Blood filled Ava's mouth and she didn't know if she'd bitten down on her own tongue, if it was his blood or all their blood mingled together, tasting of iron and salt. Bodies pressed around her on all sides, and in the dying throes of her consciousness, she sensed another figure crouching in the undergrowth. A man she recognized, a man she knew and loved, who had given her children.

Kasper.

The other women hadn't seen him yet, consumed with Nikolay, their prize. A mounting force in the back of Ava's throat threatened to cry out and expose Kasper to the others. She imagined setting upon him as they set upon Nikolay in a fit of savage hysteria. His eyes shone in the dark, finding hers. She gestured for him to flee, leave, get away as fast as he could.

He froze, unable to move, watching this brutality unfold. She screamed, "Go!" resisting the escalating hordes of female bodies urging her into violence, the urge so powerful that if Kasper hesitated one second longer, he would fall prey to her. To all of them.

Kasper ran, Nikolay's final shrieks masking the crunch of Kasper's sneakers over leaves and rocks.

Time passed. Minutes. Hours.

The forest stilled.

They sat on the cool rocks, the frenzy dwindling down like a sputtering flame. Some of them fell asleep, knees tucked into chests, shoulders hunched against the predawn chill. Others leaned into the trees and stared up at the voluminous sky, drinking in the heavens filled with distant galaxies, with gas clusters and dark matter. Against a tree trunk, Ava's heavy head lolled back, her eyes filling with tears. Tears that washed away the blood and the dirt, leaving clear tracks on her face, traces of experience.

With glowing torches held aloft, Tonkova and Nikitas led the way to the pure mountain stream where they would wash off, rinsing their hands clean, where they would return to themselves and sing into the dawning light.

Epilogue: Three Years Later

Joshua Tree, California, June 2022

I n the car on the way to the desert we listen to music, the lyrics simmering with female rage and joy, songs about jilted lovers and lost selves and menstrual blood finger-painted onto an ex-boyfriend's windshield in a fit of vengeful glee.

We drive past the slow-moving wind turbines and medical marijuana ads, our conversation akin to free association. I talk to Margot about the euphoria of falling in love and the disappointment that often follows such intensity and how hard it can be to distinguish between what you want versus what other people want you to want. While I'm talking and she's half listening, half checking her phone, I hope I'm a better mother than my mother, than my mother's mother. It's what I can give Margot, who may or may not experience as much rage or grief as I did. Or she might feel even more of it. And when Margot was stung by the sight of her own blood in her underwear for the first time, and in the future if she's left by a husband or a lover, destroyed by the loss of a child or wrecked by the birth of one, and years later, when she's confronted with another face in the mirror, a lined aging reflection she doesn't recognize as her own, I'll know about it. I won't turn away, say it's too much to deal with or act as if I've forgotten all the fury and heartache and everything in between.

Glancing up from her phone, she wonders if having a baby really hurts. I notice she's been watching a makeup video about how to apply a dab of bronzer beneath your lower lip to create the illusion of a fuller pout. It sounds like a good tip.

"Yeah. It really hurts. But it's worth it. I mean, it was worth it for me."

She nods thoughtfully, mulling this over.

When the celebratory ballad "All the Good Girls Go to Hell" comes on, Margot retorts, "What does being *good* as a girl even mean, really?" She sighs, looking down at her now-dead phone, dispirited by its black screen.

Plugging it into the charger, I explain that for centuries, no, for millennia, girls were taught to be submissive, obedient, chaste, maternal, selfless. All sweetness and light. In a word, *good*. "That's what good used to mean. In the past."

"So that's not the goal anymore?" Her kohl-rimmed eyes flash with challenge.

"It's up to you. How you want to be."

She skips to her favorite song.

The one about burning it all down and not giving a shit.

I start to dance, shimmying my shoulders and swiveling my hips in the seat, while accelerating along the aptly named Old Woman Springs Road. Margot yells at me to stop dancing, it's embarrassing.

I turn up the volume.

"Stop!" she yells again.

"Fine!" I shout back, keeping my eyes on the road lined with still-alive Joshua trees that have stood here for hundreds of years.

As evening approaches, the air thins, the sky a deep blue. The cabin is surrounded by cacti blooming swollen magenta orbs. Every so often a red-tailed hawk glides overhead, hovering in perfect suspension before swerving into the smudged horizon.

Cupping a mug of green tea after the long drive, I take another sip, astounded by the peace out here, which contains a certain layered density, alive with the sounds of rock wrens and mourning doves, songbirds and crickets, insects scrabbling over rocks. Sitting here on the porch, we see immense boulders rise up in the distance, boulders that look like a face or a knee, and I press my manuscript to my chest. I came here for a week to sit with the book, to check for errors, typos, for inconsistencies in the story. But any story about the mysteries will naturally have inconsistencies. Pieces left out, unsaid, protected by silence and the night.

A twinge of worry propels me to stand up from the deck chair, scanning the flat, parched landscape for Margot. She went on a walk, taking her phone with her, to talk to a boy. I don't know who this boy is but I suspect he's the one with the goth eyeliner and chipped blue nail polish whom Margot likes to watch skateboarding in the park, performing gravity-defying flips without a helmet. Last week I saw them sitting cross-legged on the hood of his parents' Volkswagen in the CVS parking lot. They were facing each other, talking about something, and then he reached out to fasten a loose strand of hair behind her ear.

When she stalked off with her phone, I called after her to be careful, to not cross two-lane highways without looking both ways, and she threw up her hands in defiance. I wonder if we're both remembering her impulsive sprint across the road three years ago when all she wanted was freedom and all I wanted was to keep it from her.

Freedom is even more fragile now after weathering lockdowns, school closures, and a deep fear of breathing close to other people. I wrote this book in our damp, cobwebbed garage while Kasper was also home, barred from travel, from even going to the office. During the period of homeschooling, I forced Kasper to take the afternoon shift with the kids while I took the morning, making sure Sam hadn't turned off his camera during math class. Making sure Margot wasn't scrolling through Instagram wishing her thighs were thinner, her eyes bigger, her face another face. While I wrote, I overheard yelling, frustration, tears and I felt satisfied to see him struggle as a parent, to experience what it feels like when you can't escape the domestic scene when that's all you want. Work is no longer used as a shield against family life because the way they define work, the office, the boundaries between home and not home are gone now, blurred into oblivion. And I know that he saw me with blood on my face in the middle of a Bulgarian forest and he still wants me. That my rage and heat didn't scare him away, that I'm not too much for him. He holds this secret too and it blooms between us.

When we pulled out of the driveway, Sam and Kasper stood on the front steps of the house waving, and my eyes watered, observing Sam, so absurdly tall, impossibly taller than last week. These days, his eyes flicker with disapproval because of the bulky sweater and these work boots I prefer to wear now. He says it's an ugly sweater so why do I wear it all the time? Once, I held him tightly while he giggled into my chest, and I delighted in his round softness, his light brown hair a wispy mess. Once, he made me little clay bowls swirling with kaleidoscope colors for my desk. Once, he asked me to tell him stories about when he was little, as if it were so long ago. His voice edges with sarcasm now, his elbows sharpening against my maternal fussing, erasing away a time I still cling to.

Margot perches on a boulder, the light falling around her, the sky shedding colors. Trying to determine her expression, my eyes tired from reading, it comes as it always does in these odd transitional moments. His eyes swimming with fear, his naked body bathed in bracing moonlight. The night feels real again, even here in the middle of an empty desert: our braying laugher, his head on a spike, the swollen goading moon, the whip striking my bare back, Nikitas's warm hand on my neck.

The question persists: How much of me thinks it was a collective hallucination brought on by the kykeon? That he was attacked by a bear? Or was it all a shared ancient dream of unleashed rage we willed into being?

A bee buzzes into my ear. I swat it away and go inside. Slowly, I prepare dinner, slicing an avocado, sprinkling it with sea salt and a squirt of lemon, boiling water for pasta. The knife slices deftly through the avocado, nicking my thumb, the tiny cut stinging from the lemon juice. Twining the bottom of my T-shirt around my thumb to stop the bleeding, I glance through the kitchen window and I don't see Margot anymore. I text her and check my phone for any missed calls, my mind automatically catapulting forward to times when I won't know where she's gone. In a jolt of anticipatory anxiety, I picture myself lying awake at three a.m., staring at the ceiling, my heart in my throat, waiting for a phone call, a text, for the front door to unlock.

Waiting for Margot to come home.

Let her go, let her go.

Outside, I yell her name. Cacti cast their elongated shadows onto the never-ending flatness. Wildflowers miraculously sprout from dirt. A scorpion scuttles across the path.

"Margot!" I yell again, half-delirious with rage that she doesn't care to respond, to check her phone, to hear me. I imagine she's sitting on the other side of that boulder tracing a design in the sand with a twig. I imagine she faintly hears my panicked calling, but she shrugs it off as an annoying interruption. The rage ebbs into fear when I scream her name again, worried I might not find her this time. She's too far away. It's too late. She can't hear me from whatever underworld has swallowed her up.

I kneel down, staring into the dirt, which is really just crushed-up rocks, sediment, sand. My dead son could be in this earth, and I scoop some up, clench it in my fists, fighting the urge to fill my mouth with it, to feel all the minerals and organic matter struggle down my throat as if I could rewind time and grow him up again. As if I could have him back.

Rising to stand, I become light-headed and my vision blurs, taking in the desolate setting sun, streaking gold and pink across the sky, the clouds lit up from within, as if on fire. I dig my fingernails into my palms before loosening my hands, letting go of the clenched earth, knowing it's not just my body and mind but everything that shimmers with an inevitable temporality: marriage and dogs, the polluted oceans and overpopulated continents, eroding hillsides and budding magnolia trees. Crimson-throated hummingbirds and pianos. In a thousand years, these boulder formations will dissolve into sediment before washing into the ocean. Mothers will lose their children to time, memory, to someone else's embrace. Every mother is a grieving mother, mourning the past and the future, mourning her children—here or no longer here—and the forsaken planet, damaged and sick from all the humans she made for it.

But I'm still here, trying to protect her, to stave off the inevitable. To save her when I know I can't.

I close my eyes, darkness rushing in, and I scream her name again: "Margot!"

As if manifested by Demeter's ancient motherly will, Margot appears, at first a distant figure emerging from the shadows of the desert, but as she approaches the house, coming closer and closer, I'm both relieved and angry to see that her expression is accusatory, her arms crossed over her chest. She unleashes a torrent of recriminations once I'm within earshot: "Why were you yelling, I'm right here, you can't get so freaked out every time I make a phone call!"

Calmer now because she's here, alive and unharmed, I reach out to her, my anger cooling, as if to say, *We're both a little bit right and a little bit wrong. I'll always worry and we'll have this fight a million more times so let's eat some dinner.*

Inside, I slide the pasta into the boiling water. Margot sets the table and we light the candles one by one. "How about some music?" she says before putting on that song, which has become my favorite song too, the one about burning it all down and starting over. She begins to dance, gesturing that I join her without the usual resistance or cool irony, and at first I'm self-conscious, afraid she'll change her mind, but then we're both dancing and laughing, the infectious music coursing through us, vibrating throughout the low-ceilinged room, the woman's vocals lurching and cresting, igniting a shared rebellion.

The water boils over, we turn up the music, we keep dancing.

ACKNOWLEDGMENTS

I would like to thank my wonderful agent, Alice Tasman, who read a much earlier version and loved it from the start. Thank you to Deborah Garrison, my brilliant editor, who carried the torch for this book in so many ways; I am thrilled to be working with you again. I am so grateful to Lexy Bloom, who suggested the insertion of the ancient sections, which was invaluable advice. I extend my gratitude to the team at Pantheon who worked on this book: Zuleima Ugalde, Maggie Hinders, Kathleen Fridella, Amy Ryan, Kelly Blair, Josefine Kals, Michiko Clark, Julianne Clancy, and Sarah Pannenberg, and special thanks to Denise Oswald and Lisa Lucas for their support.

Thank you to Deborah Netburn, the one who makes magic possible against the ordinary humdrum of life. I am grateful to Meghan Davis Mercer for our ongoing conversations about motherhood, marriage, female rage, grief, and creativity. Thank you to Sara Sandström, who encourages and inspires me with her art and wisdom. I am grateful to Jessica Piazza, Heather Turgeon, Catherine Elsworth, Cecily Gallup, and Beth Rosenblatt for their friendship and support. Thank you to Adam Christian and John Volturo for your encouragement and humor. Anna Mattos and Carl Hampe, thank you for our Bulgarian summer, which served as the genesis of this book.

I am grateful to my parents, my family, and my children, Lucia and Levi. I am indebted to Stephen Kenneally's wisdom as we delved into the mysteries during the writing of this book.

And most of all, thank you, Philip, for encouraging me to write and write more, for always being my first reader, for weathering life's storms together, and coming out on the other side.

SELECTED SOURCES

I am greatly indebted to the following sources for the research and writing of this book:

Blundell, Sue. *Women in Ancient Greece.*
Bolen, Jean Shinoda. *Goddesses in Older Women.*
Burkert, Walter. *Ancient Mystery Cults.*
———. *Greek Religion.*
Campbell, Joseph. *Goddesses: Mysteries of the Feminine Divine.*
Demand, Nancy. *Birth, Death, and Motherhood in Classical Greece.*
Edmonds III, Radcliffe G. *Drawing Down the Moon: Magic in the Ancient Greco-Roman World.*
Eisler, Riane. *The Chalice and the Blade.*
Lefkowitz, Mary, and Maureen Fant. *Women's Life in Greece and Rome: A Source Book in Translation.*
Marchiano, Lisa. *Motherhood: Facing and Finding Yourself.*
Matyszak, Philip. *24 Hours in Ancient Athens: A Day in the Life of the People Who Lived There.*
McClure, Laura K. *Women in Classical Antiquity.*
Meyer, Marvin W. *The Ancient Mysteries: A Sourcebook.*
Murareski, Brian. *The Immortality Key: The Secret History of the Religion with No Name.*
Petersen, Lauren Hackworth, and Patricia Salzman-Mitchell, eds. *Mothering and Motherhood in Ancient Greece and Rome.*
Pomeroy, Sarah. *Goddesses, Whores, Wives, and Slaves: Women in Classical Antiquity.*
Raja, Rubina, and Jörg Rüpke, eds. *A Companion to the Archaeology of Religion in the Ancient World.*
Sofroniew, Alexandra. *Household Gods: Private Devotion in Ancient Greece and Rome.*
Stone, Merlin. *When God Was a Woman.*
Wasson, R. Gordon, Albert Hofmann, and Carl A. P. Ruck. *The Road to Eleusis: Unveiling the Secret of the Mysteries.*

Alexis Landau is a graduate of Vassar College and received an MFA from Emerson College and a PhD in English literature and creative writing from the University of Southern California. She is the author of *The Empire of the Senses* and *Those Who Are Saved*. She lives with her husband and two children in Los Angeles.

A NOTE ON THE TYPE

This book was set in Charter, designed at Bitstream by Matthew Carter in 1987. Charter is a revival of eighteenth-century Roman type forms with narrow proportions and a large x-height. The square serifs were intended to maintain crisp letterforms on the low-resolution personal printers of the 1980s. However, the typeface has remained popular because of its eloquent modern design.

Typeset by Scribe, Philadelphia, Pennsylvania

Printed and bound by Berryville Graphics, Berryville, Virginia

Designed by Maggie Hinders